Classic Lite
Christian Homeschoolers
Volume 3: Classic Tales

A Christmas Carol

Charles Dickens

ROBINSON CRUSOE
Daniel Dafoe

JULIUS CAESAR

WILLIAM SHAKESPEARE

Edited by
Scott Clifton

Online Dual Enrollment College Credit Classes... With a Christian Worldview!

Conservative, Christian Worldview • Fun • Flexible
Great for Co-ops! • Support • Tests • Grades • Reports

Are you interested in helping your homeschooler earn college credits in high school...but concerned about leftist, gender-confused content, and potential brainwashing attempts by professors? If so, I've got great news!

My Christian high school English + History homeschool co-op (I've taught the classes since 2002) has partnered with a Christian university and awards college credits for the online classes— all with a Christian worldview! Here are the four class sets available (30 credits total; they can be taken in any order, and a student usually takes one class set per year):

- **Set 1 (6 Credits): American Government + English** (American Literature, Grammar, Vocabulary, Composition)

- **Set 2 (6 Credits): Civics + Economics + English** (Classic Literature, Grammar, Vocabulary, Composition)

- **Set 3 (9 Credits): World History I + World History II + English** (World Literature, Composition) – 9 Credits

- **Set 4 (9 Credits): U. S. History I + U. S. History II + English** (British Literature, Composition) – 9 Credits

My goal: to support Christian homeschooling parents like you as you pass on your Christian values and worldview to your children.

The classes also emphasize the government's *proper* function: limited, and focused on protecting life, liberty, and property—just what the Bible teaches! (You can download excerpts from my *American Government for Chris-tian Homeschoolers*, *Economics for Christian Homeschoolers*, and *Civics for Christian Homeschoolers* books at **www.homeschoolpartners.net/books**.)

My wife Julie and I have six homeschool graduates of our own, and I'm passionate about arming Christian young persons to stand up to the world's anti-Christian mindset. I also really enjoy working with high schoolers; we have a lot of fun and great discussions in class, and I'm always glad to help students with questions or writing tips and so on. You can get more details, including an informative video, here: **www.homeschoolpartners.net/online**.

How to Use This Book to Make Homeschooling High School Literature Easy and Fun!

The four volumes of *Classic Literature for Christian Homeschoolers* are designed to make it easy for parents to help their homeschooled high schoolers enjoy great classic literature, presented from a Christian world-view. Here's all you need to do:

(1) **Purchase *Classic Literature for Christian Homeschoolers*.** The set contains these four volumes (all four volumes are available at **www.homeschoolpartners.net/books**):

- *Volume 1: Classic Mysteries*
- *Volume 2: Science Fiction Classics*
- *Volume 3: Classic Tales*
- *Volume 4: Short Story Classics*

(2) **Use the 30-week, 4-days-per-week reading schedule to map out your student's reading for the year.** The reading plan is on the next page of this book.

   Parents, if your student is not in my class, you could use "Day 4" or your own "Day 5" to administer and score the scheduled quizzes and to go over the review questions for that week's read-ings.

   These quizzes and answer keys are available here:

www.homeschoolpartners.net/classiclitkeys

(3) **Consider these other literature sets:**

- *American Literature for Christian Homeschoolers (High School)*
- *British Literature for Christian Homeschoolers (High School)*
- *World Literature for Christian Homeschoolers (High School)*
- *Middle Literature for Christian Homeschoolers – 7th Grade*
- *Middle Literature for Christian Homeschoolers – 8th Grade*

Classic Literature for Christian Homeschoolers
30-Week Reading Plan/Quiz Plan
(Gray boxes indicate material found in this volume.)

Quiz Note: If your student is <u>not</u> in my high school class, You might use Day 4 to both review for <u>and</u> take quizzes!

Week	Day 1	Day 2	Day 3	Day 4
1	A Scandal in Bohemia	My Mysterious Foe	The Thinking Machine	The Celebrated Jumping Frog of Calaveras County
2	The Problem of Cell 13	Marjorie Daw	The Speckled Band	The Cop and the Anthem
3	Take Quiz 1 (open notes—covers Weeks 1-2 readings).	The Red-headed League	The Man on the Train	A Literary Nightmare
4	Take Quiz 2 (open notes—covers Week 3 readings).	*Dr. Jekyll and Mr. Hyde*, Ch. 1-2	*Dr. Jekyll and Mr. Hyde*, Ch. 3-4	*Dr. Jekyll and Mr. Hyde*, Ch. 5
5	*Dr. Jekyll and Mr. Hyde*, Ch. 6-7	*Dr. Jekyll and Mr. Hyde*, Ch. 8	*Dr. Jekyll and Mr. Hyde*, Ch. 9	*Dr. Jekyll and Mr. Hyde*, Ch. 10
6	Take Quiz 3 (open notes, Weeks 6-7).	The Shed Chamber	The Mouse	The Copper Beeches
7	About Barbers	The Doomdorf Mystery	Bernice Bobs Her Hair	The Final Problem
8	*War of the Worlds*, Book 1, Ch. 1-5	*War of the Worlds*, Book 1, Ch. 6-10	*War of the Worlds*, Book 1, Ch. 11-13	Review for Quiz 4 (covers Weeks 6-7 readings).
9	*War of the Worlds*, Book 1, Ch. 14-15	*War of the Worlds*, Book 1, Ch. 16-17	*War of the Worlds*, Book 2, Ch. 1-2	None!
10	*War of the Worlds*, Book 2, Ch. 3-5	*War of the Worlds*, Book 2, Ch. 6-7	*War of the Worlds*, Book 2, Ch. 8-10	None!

Week	Day 1	Day 2	Day 3	Day 4
11	An Act of God	How the Widow Won the Deacon	To Build a Fire	Review for Quiz 5 (covers Weeks 8-10 readings).
12	The Nice People	Private History of a Campaign That Failed	The Empty House	None!
13	*A Christmas Carol*, Stave I	None!	*A Christmas Carol*, Stave II	Review for Quiz 6 (covers Weeks 11-12 readings).
14	*A Christmas Carol*, Stave III	None!	*A Christmas Carol*, Staves IV & V	None!
15	Papa Panov's Special Christmas	A Defender of the Faith	The Blue Carbuncle	Aunt Cyrilla's Christmas Basket
16	*Robinson Crusoe*, Chapters 1-2	*Robinson Crusoe*, Chapter 3	*Robinson Crusoe*, Chapter 4	*Robinson Crusoe*, Chapter 5
17	*Robinson Crusoe*, Chapters 6-7	*Robinson Crusoe*, Chapter 8	*Robinson Crusoe*, Chapter 9	*Robinson Crusoe*, Chapter 10
18	*Robinson Crusoe*, Chapters 11-12	*Robinson Crusoe*, Chapters 13-14	*Robinson Crusoe*, Chapter 15	Review for Quiz 7 (covers Weeks 16-17 readings).
19	*Robinson Crusoe*, Chapters 16-17	*Robinson Crusoe*, Chapter 18	*Robinson Crusoe*, Chapter 19	*Robinson Crusoe*, Chapter 20
20	*The Invisible Man*, Chapters I-V	*The Invisible Man*, Chapters VI-X	*The Invisible Man*, Chapters XI-XV	Review for Quiz 8 (covers Weeks 18-19 readings).
21	*The Invisible Man*, Chapters XVI-XIX	*The Invisible Man*, Chapters XX-XXIII	*The Invisible Man*, Chapters XXIV-XXVII	*The Invisible Man*, Chapter XXVIII-Epilogue
22	Dr. Heidegger's Experiment	The Boom in the Calaveras *Clarion*	The Last Leaf . . . . . How I Killed a Bear	Review for Quiz 9 (covers Weeks 20-21 readings).

Week	Day 1	Day 2	Day 3	Day 4
23	*Julius Caesar*, Act I, Scene I	*Julius Caesar*, Act I, Scenes II-III	*Julius Caesar*, Act II, Scene I	Review for Quiz 10 (covers Week 22 readings).
24	*Julius Caesar*, Act II, Scene II	*Julius Caesar*, Act II, Scenes III-IV	*Julius Caesar*, Act III, Scene I	*Julius Caesar*, Act III, Scene II
25	*Julius Caesar*, Act III, Scene III – Act IV, Scene II	*Julius Caesar*, Act IV, Scene III	*Julius Caesar*, Act V, Scenes I-II	*Julius Caesar*, Act V, Scenes III-V
26	Take Quiz 11 (open notes, Weeks 23-25).	The Flaming Phantom	Journalism in Tennessee	The Ransom of Red Chief
27	*The Hound of the Baskervilles*, Chapters 1-2	*The Hound of the Baskervilles*, Chapters 3-4	*The Hound of the Baskervilles*, Chapters 5-6	Review for Quiz 12 (covers Week 26 readings).
28	*The Hound of the Baskervilles*, Chapter 7	*The Hound of the Baskervilles*, Chapter 8	*The Hound of the Baskervilles*, Chapter 9	*The Hound of the Baskervilles*, Chapter 10
29	*The Hound of the Baskervilles*, Chapters 11-12	*The Hound of the Baskervilles*, Chapter 13	*The Hound of the Baskervilles*, Chapter 14	*The Hound of the Baskervilles*, Chapter 15
30	Three Questions . . . . . A White Heron	For Better or Worse	Naboth's Vineyard	Review for Quiz 13 (covers Week 27-29 readings).

Table of Contents

A Christmas Carol

By Charles Dickens

Robinson Crusoe

By Daniel Defoe

Julius Caesar

By William Shakespeare

A

Christmas

Carol

By Charles Dickens

INTRODUCTION

Author Charles Dickens's *A Christmas Carol* left impressions in many ways: swelling the number of Christmas feasts and festivities and greetings of "Merry Christmas!" (especially in England); introducing to the world the character and name of "Scrooge" and his catchphrase "Bah! Humbug!"; even inspiring more modern works like *It's a Wonderful Life* and *How the Grinch Stole Christmas*.

If you think you know the story of *A Christmas Carol*, but haven't yet read every word of it, you are in for a treat! The greatness of the work and its well-deserved standing of influence and belovedness ring clear through a careful and joyful reading—much more than if the reader has only a vague familiarity with the plot and characters. Dickens's expressiveness with words and ingenious plotting—in addition to his contrasting humor and tragedy, disgrace and redemption—also make *A Christmas Carol* essential reading for anyone who loves the richness, precision, and excitement of the English language.

Charles Dickens (1812-1870) wrote *A Christmas Carol* in six weeks near the end of 1843, needing money for his growing family, his wife then expecting their fifth child. The book was an immediate hit with both the public and literary critics, and hundreds of millions have cherished the story ever since. And although Dickens did not give *A Christmas Carol* an explicitly Christian message, Christians can appreciate in his work Dickens's reverence of Jesus Christ and the valiant, heartfelt attempts by characters to do works of charity in the name of the Savior of the world.

May we Christians be encouraged to imitate Jesus, who "went about doing good" (Acts 10:38), and if you are not a Christian, I pray you would seek to do the work of God—which begins, first, by "believ-[ing] on him whom he hath sent" (John 6:29).

Stave One: Marley's Ghost

arley was dead: to begin with. There is no doubt whatever about that. The register of his burial was signed by the clergyman, the clerk, the undertaker, and the chief mourner. Scrooge signed it: and Scrooge's name was good upon 'Change,[1] for anything he chose to put his hand to. Old Marley was as dead as a door-nail.

Mind! I don't mean to say that I know, of my own knowledge, what there is particularly dead about a door-nail. I might have been inclined, myself, to regard a coffin-nail as the deadest piece of ironmongery in the trade. But the wisdom of our ancestors is in the simile; and my unhallowed hands shall not disturb it, or the Country's done for. You will therefore permit me to repeat, emphatically, that Marley was as dead as a door-nail.

Scrooge knew he was dead? Of course he did. How could it be otherwise? Scrooge and he were partners for I don't know how many years. Scrooge was his sole executor, his sole administrator, his sole assign, his sole residuary legatee,[2] his sole friend, and sole mourner. And even Scrooge was not so dreadfully cut up by the sad event, but that he was an excellent man of business on the very day of the funeral, and solemnised it with an undoubted bargain.

The mention of Marley's funeral brings me back to the point I started from. There is no doubt that Marley was dead. This must be distinctly understood, or nothing wonderful can come of the story I am going to relate. If we were not perfectly convinced that Hamlet's Father died before the play began, there would be nothing more remarkable in his taking a stroll at night, in an easterly wind, upon his own ramparts, than there would be in any other middle-aged gentleman rashly turning out after dark in a breezy spot—say Saint Paul's Churchyard for instance—literally to astonish his son's weak mind.

Scrooge never painted out Old Marley's name. There it stood, years afterwards, above the warehouse door: Scrooge and Marley. The firm was known as Scrooge and Marley. Sometimes people new to the business called Scrooge Scrooge, and sometimes Marley, but he answered to both names. It was all the same to him.

Oh! But he was a tight-fisted hand at the grindstone, Scrooge! a squeezing, wrenching, grasping, scraping, clutching, covetous, old sinner! Hard

---

[1] 'Change: The Exchange, or the British equivalent of Wall Street. To say that "Scrooge's name was good upon 'Change" is to say that he was trustworthy in financial transactions.

[2] assign, residuary legatee: heir, or the person to whom property is granted upon one's death, after all debts have been paid

and sharp as flint, from which no steel had ever struck out generous fire; secret, and self-contained, and solitary as an oyster. The cold within him froze his old features, nipped his pointed nose, shrivelled his cheek, stiffened his gait; made his eyes red, his thin lips blue; and spoke out shrewdly in his grating voice. A frosty rime was on his head, and on his eyebrows, and his wiry chin. He carried his own low temperature always about with him; he iced his office in the dog-days; and didn't thaw it one degree at Christmas.

External heat and cold had little influence on Scrooge. No warmth could warm, no wintry weather chill him. No wind that blew was bitterer than he, no falling snow was more intent upon its purpose, no pelting rain less open to entreaty. Foul weather didn't know where to have him. The heaviest rain, and snow, and hail, and sleet, could boast of the advantage over him in only one respect. They often "came down"[3] handsomely, and Scrooge never did.

Nobody ever stopped him in the street to say, with gladsome looks, "My dear Scrooge, how are you? When will you come to see me?" No beggars implored him to bestow a trifle, no children asked him what it was o'clock, no man or woman ever once in all his life inquired the way to such and such a place, of Scrooge. Even the blind men's dogs appeared to know him; and when they saw him coming on, would tug their owners into doorways and up courts; and then would wag their tails as though they said, "No eye at all is better than an evil eye, dark master!"

But what did Scrooge care! It was the very thing he liked. To edge his way along the crowded paths of life, warning all human sympathy to keep its distance, was what the knowing ones call "nuts" to Scrooge.

Once upon a time—of all the good days in the year, on Christmas Eve—old Scrooge sat busy in his counting-house. It was cold, bleak, biting weather: foggy withal: and he could hear the people in the court outside, go wheezing up and down, beating their hands upon their breasts, and stamping their feet upon the pavement stones to warm them. The city clocks had only just gone three, but it was quite dark already—it had not been light all day—and candles were flaring in the windows of the neighbouring offices, like ruddy smears upon the palpable[4] brown air. The fog came pouring in at every chink and keyhole, and was so dense without, that although the court was of the narrowest, the houses opposite were mere phantoms. To see the dingy cloud come drooping down, obscuring everything, one might have thought that Nature lived hard by, and was brewing on a large scale.

The door of Scrooge's counting-house was open that he might keep his eye upon his clerk, who in a dismal little cell beyond, a sort of tank, was

---

[3] came down: acted charitably with one's money
[4] almost able to be physically felt

copying letters. Scrooge had a very small fire, but the clerk's fire was so very much smaller that it looked like one coal. But he couldn't replenish it, for Scrooge kept the coal-box in his own room; and so surely as the clerk came in with the shovel, the master predicted that it would be necessary for them to part. Wherefore the clerk put on his white comforter, and tried to warm himself at the candle; in which effort, not being a man of a strong imagination, he failed.

"A merry Christmas, uncle! God save you!" cried a cheerful voice. It was the voice of Scrooge's nephew, who came upon him so quickly that this was the first intimation he had of his approach.

"Bah!" said Scrooge, "Humbug!"[5]

He had so heated himself with rapid walking in the fog and frost, this nephew of Scrooge's, that he was all in a glow; his face was ruddy and handsome; his eyes sparkled, and his breath smoked again.

"Christmas a humbug, uncle!" said Scrooge's nephew. "You don't mean that, I am sure?"

"I do," said Scrooge. "Merry Christmas! What right have you to be merry? What reason have you to be merry? You're poor enough."

"Come, then," returned the nephew gaily. "What right have you to be dismal? What reason have you to be morose?[6] You're rich enough."

Scrooge having no better answer ready on the spur of the moment, said, "Bah!" again; and followed it up with "Humbug."

"Don't be cross, uncle!" said the nephew.

"What else can I be," returned the uncle, "when I live in such a world of fools as this? Merry Christmas! Out upon merry Christmas! What's Christmas time to you but a time for paying bills without money; a time for finding yourself a year older, but not an hour richer; a time for balancing your books and having every item in 'em through a round dozen of months presented dead against you? If I could work my will," said Scrooge indignantly, "every idiot who goes about with 'Merry Christmas' on his lips, should be boiled with his own pudding, and buried with a stake of holly through his heart. He should!"[7]

"Uncle!" pleaded the nephew.

"Nephew!" returned the uncle sternly, "keep Christmas in your own way, and let me keep it in mine."

"Keep it!" repeated Scrooge's nephew. "But you don't keep it."

---

[5] This means, in a nutshell, "Phooey!" or "Baloney!" It's Scrooge's way of saying he believes Christmas, or the goodness surrounding it, is fake or insincere.

[6] gloomy, depressed

[7] In England, mainly before the seventeenth century, suicide was officially a felony, and it was considered a supremely shameful act. A person who committed suicide (or murder) was often buried with a stake through his heart. You read that right.

"Let me leave it alone, then," said Scrooge. "Much good may it do you! Much good it has ever done you!"

"There are many things from which I might have derived good, by which I have not profited, I dare say," returned the nephew. "Christmas among the rest. But I am sure I have always thought of Christmas time, when it has come round—apart from the veneration[8] due to its sacred name and origin, if anything belonging to it can be apart from that—as a good time; a kind, forgiving, charitable, pleasant time; the only time I know of, in the long calendar of the year, when men and women seem by one consent to open their shut-up hearts freely, and to think of people below them as if they really were fellow-passengers to the grave, and not another race of creatures bound on other journeys. And therefore, uncle, though it has never put a scrap of gold or silver in my pocket, I believe that it *has* done me good, and *will* do me good; and I say, God bless it!"

The clerk in the Tank involuntarily applauded. Becoming immediately sensible of the impropriety, he poked the fire, and extinguished the last frail spark for ever.

"Let me hear another sound from *you*," said Scrooge, "and you'll keep your Christmas by losing your situation![9] You're quite a powerful speaker, sir," he added, turning to his nephew. "I wonder you don't go into Parliament."

"Don't be angry, uncle. Come! Dine with us to-morrow."

Scrooge said that he would see him—yes, indeed he did. He went the whole length of the expression, and said that he would see him in that extremity first.[10]

"But why?" cried Scrooge's nephew. "Why?"

"Why did you get married?" said Scrooge.

"Because I fell in love."

"Because you fell in love!" growled Scrooge, as if that were the only one thing in the world more ridiculous than a merry Christmas. "Good afternoon!"

"Nay, uncle, but you never came to see me before that happened. Why give it as a reason for not coming now?"

"Good afternoon," said Scrooge.

"I want nothing from you; I ask nothing of you; why cannot we be friends?"

"Good afternoon," said Scrooge.

---

[8] reverence, respect
[9] situation: job, position
[10] That is, Scrooge tells Fred he will see Fred, uh, somewhere else, before he sees him at his house for a Christmas dinner.

"I am sorry, with all my heart, to find you so resolute. We have never had any quarrel, to which I have been a party. But I have made the trial in homage to Christmas, and I'll keep my Christmas humour to the last. So A Merry Christmas, uncle!"

"Good afternoon!" said Scrooge.

"And A Happy New Year!"

"Good afternoon!" said Scrooge.

His nephew left the room without an angry word, notwithstanding. He stopped at the outer door to bestow the greetings of the season on the clerk, who, cold as he was, was warmer than Scrooge; for he returned them cordially.

"There's another fellow," muttered Scrooge; who overheard him: "my clerk, with fifteen shillings a week,[11] and a wife and family, talking about a merry Christmas. I'll retire to Bedlam."[12]

This lunatic, in letting Scrooge's nephew out, had let two other people in. They were portly gentlemen, pleasant to behold, and now stood, with their hats off, in Scrooge's office. They had books and papers in their hands, and bowed to him.

"Scrooge and Marley's, I believe," said one of the gentlemen, referring to his list. "Have I the pleasure of addressing Mr. Scrooge, or Mr. Marley?"

"Mr. Marley has been dead these seven years," Scrooge replied. "He died seven years ago, this very night."

"We have no doubt his liberality is well represented by his surviving partner," said the gentleman, presenting his credentials.

It certainly was; for they had been two kindred spirits. At the ominous word "liberality," Scrooge frowned, and shook his head, and handed the credentials back.

"At this festive season of the year, Mr. Scrooge," said the gentleman, taking up a pen, "it is more than usually desirable that we should make some slight provision for the Poor and destitute, who suffer greatly at the present time. Many thousands are in want of common necessaries; hundreds of thousands are in want of common comforts, sir."

"Are there no prisons?" asked Scrooge.

"Plenty of prisons," said the gentleman, laying down the pen again.

"And the Union workhouses?"[13] demanded Scrooge. "Are they still in operation?"

---

[11] This is not a rich salary by any means, but it does not mean Cratchit was poverty-striken. Stretching his salary to feed a family with six children, however, would take some doing.

[12] "Bedlam" is another name for The Hospital of St. Mary's of Bethlehem—a well-known asylum for mentally deranged persons.

[13] Union workhouses: local workhouses for the poor and needy

"They are. Still," returned the gentleman, "I wish I could say they were not."

"The Treadmill and the Poor Law[14] are in full vigour, then?" said Scrooge.

"Both very busy, sir."

"Oh! I was afraid, from what you said at first, that something had occurred to stop them in their useful course," said Scrooge. "I'm very glad to hear it."

"Under the impression that they scarcely furnish Christian cheer of mind or body to the multitude," returned the gentleman, "a few of us are endeavouring to raise a fund to buy the Poor some meat and drink, and means of warmth. We choose this time, because it is a time, of all others, when Want is keenly felt, and Abundance rejoices. What shall I put you down for?"

"Nothing!" Scrooge replied.

"You wish to be anonymous?"

"I wish to be left alone," said Scrooge. "Since you ask me what I wish, gentlemen, that is my answer. I don't make merry myself at Christmas and I can't afford to make idle people merry. I help to support the establishments I have mentioned—they cost enough; and those who are badly off must go there."

"Many can't go there; and many would rather die."

"If they would rather die," said Scrooge, "they had better do it, and decrease the surplus population. Besides—excuse me—I don't know that."

"But you might know it," observed the gentleman.

"It's not my business," Scrooge returned. "It's enough for a man to understand his own business, and not to interfere with other people's. Mine occupies me constantly. Good afternoon, gentlemen!"

Seeing clearly that it would be useless to pursue their point, the gentlemen withdrew. Scrooge resumed his labours with an improved opinion of himself, and in a more facetious[15] temper than was usual with him.

Meanwhile the fog and darkness thickened so, that people ran about with flaring links, proffering their services to go before horses in carriages, and conduct them on their way. The ancient tower of a church, whose gruff old bell was always peeping slily down at Scrooge out of a Gothic window in the wall, became invisible, and struck the hours and quarters in the clouds, with tremulous vibrations afterwards as if its teeth were chattering in its frozen head up there. The cold became intense. In the main street, at the corner of the court, some labourers were repairing the gas-pipes, and had

---

[14] The Treadmill was a punishment for criminals, who were forced to walk on an actual treadmill; the Poor Law refers to England's attempts via government programs to deal with the poor, in ways that were sometimes inhumane and ineffective.
[15] light-hearted, playful

lighted a great fire in a brazier,[16] round which a party of ragged men and boys were gathered: warming their hands and winking their eyes before the blaze in rapture. The water-plug[17] being left in solitude, its overflowings sullenly congealed, and turned to misanthropic ice. The brightness of the shops where holly sprigs and berries crackled in the lamp heat of the windows, made pale faces ruddy as they passed. Poulterers' and grocers' trades became a splendid joke: a glorious pageant, with which it was next to impossible to believe that such dull principles as bargain and sale had anything to do. The Lord Mayor, in the stronghold of the mighty Mansion House, gave orders to his fifty cooks and butlers to keep Christmas as a Lord Mayor's household should; and even the little tailor, whom he had fined five shillings on the previous Monday for being drunk and bloodthirsty in the streets, stirred up to-morrow's pudding in his garret, while his lean wife and the baby sallied out to buy the beef.

Foggier yet, and colder. Piercing, searching, biting cold. If the good Saint Dunstan[18] had but nipped the Evil Spirit's nose with a touch of such weather as that, instead of using his familiar weapons, then indeed he would have roared to lusty purpose. The owner of one scant young nose, gnawed and mumbled by the hungry cold as bones are gnawed by dogs, stooped down at Scrooge's keyhole to regale him with a Christmas carol: but at the first sound of

> *God bless ye merry, gentlemen!*
> *May nothing you dismay!*

Scrooge seized the ruler with such energy of action, that the singer fled in terror, leaving the keyhole to the fog and even more congenial[19] frost.

At length the hour of shutting up the counting-house arrived. With an ill-will Scrooge dismounted from his stool, and tacitly[20] admitted the fact to the expectant clerk in the Tank, who instantly snuffed his candle out, and put on his hat.

"You'll want all day to-morrow, I suppose?" said Scrooge.

"If quite convenient, sir."

"It's not convenient," said Scrooge, "and it's not fair. If I was to stop half-a-crown[21] for it, you'd think yourself ill-used, I'll be bound?"

The clerk smiled faintly.

---

[16] open fire

[17] fire hydrant

[18] "Saint" Dunstan was the patron saint of goldsmiths. Legend has it that the devil appeared to him in the form of a pretty woman, and Dunstan used his metal tongs to pinch "her" nose.

[19] friendly, pleasant

[20] quietly, barely speaking

[21] one sixth of Cratchit's weekly salary

"And yet," said Scrooge, "you don't think *me* ill-used, when I pay a day's wages for no work."

The clerk observed that it was only once a year.

"A poor excuse for picking a man's pocket every twenty-fifth of December!" said Scrooge, buttoning his great-coat to the chin. "But I suppose you must have the whole day. Be here all the earlier next morning."

The clerk promised that he would; and Scrooge walked out with a growl. The office was closed in a twinkling, and the clerk, with the long ends of his white comforter dangling below his waist (for he boasted no great-coat), went down a slide on Cornhill, at the end of a lane of boys, twenty times, in honour of its being Christmas Eve, and then ran home to Camden Town as hard as he could pelt, to play at blindman's-buff.

Scrooge took his melancholy dinner in his usual melancholy tavern; and having read all the newspapers, and beguiled[22] the rest of the evening with his banker's-book, went home to bed. He lived in chambers which had once belonged to his deceased partner. They were a gloomy suite of rooms, in a lowering pile of building up a yard, where it had so little business to be, that one could scarcely help fancying it must have run there when it was a young house, playing at hide-and-seek with other houses, and forgotten the way out again. It was old enough now, and dreary enough, for nobody lived in it but Scrooge, the other rooms being all let out as offices. The yard was so dark that even Scrooge, who knew its every stone, was fain to grope with his hands. The fog and frost so hung about the black old gateway of the house, that it seemed as if the Genius of the Weather sat in mournful meditation on the threshold.

Now, it is a fact, that there was nothing at all particular about the knocker on the door, except that it was very large. It is also a fact, that Scrooge had seen it, night and morning, during his whole residence in that place; also that Scrooge had as little of what is called fancy[23] about him as any man in the city of London, even including—which is a bold word—the corporation, aldermen, and livery. Let it also be borne in mind that Scrooge had not bestowed one thought on Marley, since his last mention of his seven years' dead partner that afternoon. And then let any man explain to me, if he can, how it happened that Scrooge, having his key in the lock of the door, saw in the knocker, without its undergoing any intermediate process of change—not a knocker, but Marley's face.

Marley's face. It was not in impenetrable shadow as the other objects in the yard were, but had a dismal light about it, like a bad lobster in a dark cellar. It was not angry or ferocious, but looked at Scrooge as Marley used

[22] charmed, fascinated
[23] superstition, imagination

to look: with ghostly spectacles turned up on its ghostly forehead. The hair was curiously stirred, as if by breath or hot air; and, though the eyes were wide open, they were perfectly motionless. That, and its livid colour, made it horrible; but its horror seemed to be in spite of the face and beyond its control, rather than a part of its own expression.

As Scrooge looked fixedly at this phenomenon, it was a knocker again.

To say that he was not startled, or that his blood was not conscious of a terrible sensation to which it had been a stranger from infancy, would be untrue. But he put his hand upon the key he had relinquished, turned it sturdily, walked in, and lighted his candle.

He *did* pause, with a moment's irresolution, before he shut the door; and he *did* look cautiously behind it first, as if he half expected to be terrified with the sight of Marley's pigtail sticking out into the hall. But there was nothing on the back of the door, except the screws and nuts that held the knocker on, so he said "Pooh, pooh!" and closed it with a bang.

The sound resounded through the house like thunder. Every room above, and every cask in the wine-merchant's cellars below, appeared to have a separate peal of echoes of its own. Scrooge was not a man to be frightened by echoes. He fastened the door, and walked across the hall, and up the stairs; slowly too: trimming his candle as he went.

You may talk vaguely about driving a coach-and-six up a good old flight of stairs, or through a bad young Act of Parliament; but I mean to say you might have got a hearse up that staircase, and taken it broad-wise, with the splinter-bar towards the wall and the door towards the balustrades: and done it easy. There was plenty of width for that, and room to spare; which is perhaps the reason why Scrooge thought he saw a locomotive hearse going on before him in the gloom. Half-a-dozen gas-lamps out of the street wouldn't have lighted the entry too well, so you may suppose that it was pretty dark with Scrooge's dip.

Up Scrooge went, not caring a button for that. Darkness is cheap, and Scrooge liked it. But before he shut his heavy door, he walked through his rooms to see that all was right. He had just enough recollection of the face to desire to do that.

Sitting-room, bedroom, lumber-room. All as they should be. Nobody under the table, nobody under the sofa; a small fire in the grate; spoon and basin ready; and the little saucepan of gruel (Scrooge had a cold in his head) upon the hob.[24] Nobody under the bed; nobody in the closet; nobody in his dressing-gown, which was hanging up in a suspicious attitude against the wall. Lumber-room as usual. Old fire-guard, old shoes, two fish-baskets, washing-stand on three legs, and a poker.

---

[24] stove

Quite satisfied, he closed his door, and locked himself in; double-locked himself in, which was not his custom. Thus secured against surprise, he took off his cravat;[25] put on his dressing-gown and slippers, and his nightcap; and sat down before the fire to take his gruel.

It was a very low fire indeed; nothing on such a bitter night. He was obliged to sit close to it, and brood over it, before he could extract the least sensation of warmth from such a handful of fuel. The fireplace was an old one, built by some Dutch merchant long ago, and paved all round with quaint Dutch tiles, designed to illustrate the Scriptures. There were Cains and Abels, Pharaoh's daughters; Queens of Sheba, Angelic messengers descending through the air on clouds like feather-beds, Abrahams, Belshazzars, Apostles putting off to sea in butter-boats, hundreds of figures to attract his thoughts; and yet that face of Marley, seven years dead, came like the ancient Prophet's rod, and swallowed up the whole.[26] If each smooth tile had been a blank at first, with power to shape some picture on its surface from the disjointed fragments of his thoughts, there would have been a copy of old Marley's head on every one.

"Humbug!" said Scrooge; and walked across the room.

After several turns, he sat down again. As he threw his head back in the chair, his glance happened to rest upon a bell, a disused bell, that hung in the room, and communicated for some purpose now forgotten with a chamber in the highest story of the building. It was with great astonishment, and with a strange, inexplicable dread, that as he looked, he saw this bell begin to swing. It swung so softly in the outset that it scarcely made a sound; but soon it rang out loudly, and so did every bell in the house.

This might have lasted half a minute, or a minute, but it seemed an hour. The bells ceased as they had begun, together. They were succeeded by a clanking noise, deep down below; as if some person were dragging a heavy chain over the casks in the wine-merchant's cellar. Scrooge then remembered to have heard that ghosts in haunted houses were described as dragging chains.

The cellar-door flew open with a booming sound, and then he heard the noise much louder, on the floors below; then coming up the stairs; then coming straight towards his door.

"It's humbug still!" said Scrooge. "I won't believe it."

His colour changed though, when, without a pause, it came on through the heavy door, and passed into the room before his eyes. Upon its coming in, the dying flame leaped up, as though it cried, "I know him; Marley's Ghost!" and fell again.

---

[25] tie
[26] See Exodus 7:7-12.

The same face: the very same. Marley in his pigtail, usual waist-coat, tights and boots; the tassels on the latter bristling, like his pigtail, and his coat-skirts, and the hair upon his head. The chain he drew was clasped about his middle. It was long, and wound about him like a tail; and it was made (for Scrooge observed it closely) of cash-boxes, keys, padlocks, ledgers, deeds, and heavy purses wrought in steel. His body was transparent; so that Scrooge, observing him, and looking through his waistcoat, could see the two buttons on his coat behind.

Scrooge had often heard it said that Marley had no bowels,[27] but he had never believed it until now.

No, nor did he believe it even now. Though he looked the phantom through and through, and saw it standing before him; though he felt the chilling influence of its death-cold eyes; and marked the very texture of the folded kerchief bound about its head and chin, which wrapper he had not observed before; he was still incredulous, and fought against his senses.

"How now!" said Scrooge, caustic and cold as ever. "What do you want with me?"

"Much!"—Marley's voice, no doubt about it.

"Who are you?"

"Ask me who I *was*."

"Who *were* you then?" said Scrooge, raising his voice. "You're particular, for a shade." He was going to say "*to* a shade," but substituted this, as more appropriate.

"In life I was your partner, Jacob Marley."

"Can you—can you sit down?" asked Scrooge, looking doubtfully at him.

"I can."

"Do it, then."

Scrooge asked the question, because he didn't know whether a ghost so transparent might find himself in a condition to take a chair; and felt that in the event of its being impossible, it might involve the necessity of an embarrassing explanation. But the ghost sat down on the opposite side of the fireplace, as if he were quite used to it.

"You don't believe in me," observed the Ghost.

"I don't," said Scrooge.

"What evidence would you have of my reality beyond that of your senses?"

"I don't know," said Scrooge.

"Why do you doubt your senses?"

---

[27] "Bowels" mean in this instance "the source of human compassion or sympathy." 1 John 3:17 says, for example, "But whoso hath this world's good, and seeth his brother have need, and shutteth up his **bowels** of compassion from him, how dwelleth the love of God in him?"

"Because," said Scrooge, "a little thing affects them. A slight disorder of the stomach makes them cheats. You may be an undigested bit of beef, a blot of mustard, a crumb of cheese, a fragment of an underdone potato. There's more of gravy than of grave about you, whatever you are!"

Scrooge was not much in the habit of cracking jokes, nor did he feel, in his heart, by any means waggish then. The truth is, that he tried to be smart, as a means of distracting his own attention, and keeping down his terror; for the spectre's voice disturbed the very marrow in his bones.

To sit, staring at those fixed glazed eyes, in silence for a moment, would play, Scrooge felt, the very deuce with him. There was something very awful, too, in the spectre's being provided with an infernal atmosphere of its own. Scrooge could not feel it himself, but this was clearly the case; for though the Ghost sat perfectly motionless, its hair, and skirts, and tassels, were still agitated as by the hot vapour from an oven.

"You see this toothpick?" said Scrooge, returning quickly to the charge, for the reason just assigned; and wishing, though it were only for a second, to divert the vision's stony gaze from himself.

"I do," replied the Ghost.

"You are not looking at it," said Scrooge.

"But I see it," said the Ghost, "notwithstanding."

"Well!" returned Scrooge, "I have but to swallow this, and be for the rest of my days persecuted by a legion of goblins, all of my own creation. Humbug, I tell you! humbug!"

At this the spirit raised a frightful cry, and shook its chain with such a dismal and appalling noise, that Scrooge held on tight to his chair, to save himself from falling in a swoon. But how much greater was his horror, when the phantom taking off the bandage round its head, as if it were too warm to wear indoors, its lower jaw dropped down upon its breast!

Scrooge fell upon his knees, and clasped his hands before his face.

"Mercy!" he said. "Dreadful apparition, why do you trouble me?"

"Man of the worldly mind!" replied the Ghost, "do you believe in me or not?"

"I do," said Scrooge. "I must. But why do spirits walk the earth, and why do they come to me?"

"It is required of every man," the Ghost returned, "that the spirit within him should walk abroad among his fellowmen, and travel far and wide; and if that spirit goes not forth in life, it is condemned to do so after death. It is doomed to wander through the world—oh, woe is me!—and witness what it cannot share, but might have shared on earth, and turned to happiness!"

Again the spectre raised a cry, and shook its chain and wrung its shadowy hands.

"You are fettered,"[28] said Scrooge, trembling. "Tell me why?"

I wear the chain I forged in life," replied the Ghost. "I made it link by link, and yard by yard; I girded it on of my own free will, and of my own free will I wore it. Is its pattern strange to *you?*"

Scrooge trembled more and more.

"Or would you know," pursued the Ghost, "the weight and length of the strong coil you bear yourself? It was full as heavy and as long as this, seven Christmas Eves ago. You have laboured on it, since. It is a ponderous chain!"

Scrooge glanced about him on the floor, in the expectation of finding himself surrounded by some fifty or sixty fathoms of iron cable: but he could see nothing.

"Jacob," he said, imploringly. "Old Jacob Marley, tell me more. Speak comfort to me, Jacob!"

"I have none to give," the Ghost replied. "It comes from other regions, Ebenezer Scrooge,[29] and is conveyed by other ministers, to other kinds of men. Nor can I tell you what I would. A very little more is all permitted to me. I cannot rest, I cannot stay, I cannot linger anywhere. My spirit never walked beyond our counting-house—mark me!—in life my spirit never roved beyond the narrow limits of our money-changing hole; and weary journeys lie before me!"

It was a habit with Scrooge, whenever he became thoughtful, to put his hands in his breeches pockets. Pondering on what the Ghost had said, he did so now, but without lifting up his eyes, or getting off his knees.

"You must have been very slow about it, Jacob," Scrooge observed, in a business-like manner, though with humility and deference.

"Slow!" the Ghost repeated.

"Seven years dead," mused Scrooge. "And travelling all the time!"

---

[28] chained

[29] This is the first time Scrooge's first name is given. The name "Ebenezer" (which means "stone of help") is used in the book of 1 Samuel (4:1, 5:1, and 7:12), and it refers to the stone that Samuel erected to commemorate when God helped the Israelites defeat the Philistines. Probably Dickens named Scrooge "Ebenezer" to indicate his hard, stony heart.

"The whole time," said the Ghost. "No rest, no peace. Incessant torture of remorse."

"You travel fast?" said Scrooge.

"On the wings of the wind,"[30] replied the Ghost.

"You might have got over a great quantity of ground in seven years," said Scrooge.

The Ghost, on hearing this, set up another cry, and clanked its chain so hideously in the dead silence of the night, that the Ward would have been justified in indicting it for a nuisance.

"Oh! captive, bound, and double-ironed," cried the phantom, "not to know, that ages of incessant labour by immortal creatures, for this earth must pass into eternity before the good of which it is susceptible is all developed. Not to know that any Christian spirit working kindly in its little sphere, whatever it may be, will find its mortal life too short for its vast means of usefulness. Not to know that no space of regret can make amends for one life's opportunity misused! Yet such was I! Oh! such was I!"

"But you were always a good man of business, Jacob," faltered Scrooge, who now began to apply this to himself.

"Business!" cried the Ghost, wringing its hands again. "Mankind was my business. The common welfare was my business; charity, mercy, forbearance, and benevolence, were, all, my business. The dealings of my trade were but a drop of water in the comprehensive ocean of my business!"

It held up its chain at arm's length, as if that were the cause of all its unavailing grief, and flung it heavily upon the ground again.

"At this time of the rolling year," the spectre said, "I suffer most. Why did I walk through crowds of fellow-beings with my eyes turned down, and never raise them to that blessed Star which led the Wise Men to a poor abode! Were there no poor homes to which its light would have conducted *me!*"

Scrooge was very much dismayed to hear the spectre going on at this rate, and began to quake exceedingly.[31]

"Hear me!" cried the Ghost. "My time is nearly gone."

"I will," said Scrooge. "But don't be hard upon me! Don't be flowery, Jacob! Pray!"

"How it is that I appear before you in a shape that you can see, I may not tell. I have sat invisible beside you many and many a day."

It was not an agreeable idea. Scrooge shivered, and wiped the perspiration from his brow.

---

[30] See Psalm 18:1-10.
[31] See Hebrews 12:17-21.

"That is no light part of my penance," pursued the Ghost. "I am here to-night to warn you, that you have yet a chance and hope of escaping my fate. A chance and hope of my procuring, Ebenezer."

"You were always a good friend to me," said Scrooge. "Thank'ee!"

"You will be haunted," resumed the Ghost, "by Three Spirits."

Scrooge's countenance fell almost as low as the Ghost's had done.

"Is that the chance and hope you mentioned, Jacob?" he demanded, in a faltering voice.

"It is."

"I—I think I'd rather not," said Scrooge.

"Without their visits," said the Ghost, "you cannot hope to shun the path I tread. Expect the first to-morrow, when the bell tolls One."

"Couldn't I take 'em all at once, and have it over, Jacob?" hinted Scrooge.

"Expect the second on the next night at the same hour. The third upon the next night when the last stroke of Twelve has ceased to vibrate. Look to see me no more; and look that, for your own sake, you remember what has passed between us!"

When it had said these words, the spectre took its wrapper from the table, and bound it round its head, as before. Scrooge knew this, by the smart sound its teeth made, when the jaws were brought together by the bandage. He ventured to raise his eyes again, and found his supernatural visitor confronting him in an erect attitude, with its chain wound over and about its arm.

The apparition walked backward from him; and at every step it took, the window raised itself a little, so that when the spectre reached it, it was wide open.

It beckoned Scrooge to approach, which he did. When they were within two paces of each other, Marley's Ghost held up its hand, warning him to come no nearer. Scrooge stopped.

Not so much in obedience, as in surprise and fear: for on the raising of the hand, he became sensible of confused noises in the air; incoherent sounds of lamentation and regret; wailings inexpressibly sorrowful and self-accusatory. The spectre, after listening for a moment, joined in the mournful dirge; and floated out upon the bleak, dark night.

Scrooge followed to the window: desperate in his curiosity. He looked out.

The air was filled with phantoms, wandering hither and thither in restless haste, and moaning as they went. Every one of them wore chains like Marley's Ghost; some few (they might be guilty governments) were linked together; none were free. Many had been personally known to Scrooge in their lives. He had been quite familiar with one old ghost, in a white waistcoat, with a monstrous iron safe attached to its ankle, who cried piteously at being unable to assist a wretched woman with an infant, whom it saw below, upon a door-step. The misery with them all was, clearly, that they sought to interfere, for good, in human matters, and had lost the power for ever.

Whether these creatures faded into mist, or mist enshrouded them, he could not tell. But they and their spirit voices faded together; and the night became as it had been when he walked home.

Scrooge closed the window, and examined the door by which the Ghost had entered. It was double-locked, as he had locked it with his own hands, and the bolts were undisturbed. He tried to say "Humbug!" but stopped at the first syllable. And being, from the emotion he had undergone, or the fatigues of the day, or his glimpse of the Invisible World, or the dull conversation of the Ghost, or the lateness of the hour, much in need of repose; went straight to bed, without undressing, and fell asleep upon the instant.

Questions for Review:

1. Look up the term "stave." Why do you think Dickens called his chapters "staves" instead of chapters?

2. Why does Dickens emphasize the fact of Marley's death in the story's opening? How does Scrooge feel about his death?

3. List examples that show Scrooge's miserable nature. How does Dickens still create a sense of pity for Scrooge in the reader's mind?

4. How are the weather, Scrooge's apartment, and Scrooge's office similar? Why do you think Dickens chose to do this?

5. Explain Scrooge's encounter with Marley. How does this already work a slight change in his (Scrooge's) temperament?

Stave Two:

The First of the Three Spirits

When Scrooge awoke, it was so dark, that looking out of bed, he could scarcely distinguish the transparent window from the opaque walls of his chamber. He was endeavouring to pierce the darkness with his ferret eyes, when the chimes of a neighbouring church struck the four quarters. So he listened for the hour.

To his great astonishment the heavy bell went on from six to seven, and from seven to eight, and regularly up to twelve; then stopped. Twelve! It was past two when he went to bed. The clock was wrong. An icicle must have got into the works. Twelve!

He touched the spring of his repeater, to correct this most preposterous clock. Its rapid little pulse beat twelve: and stopped.

"Why, it isn't possible," said Scrooge, "that I can have slept through a whole day and far into another night. It isn't possible that anything has happened to the sun, and this is twelve at noon!"

The idea being an alarming one, he scrambled out of bed, and groped his way to the window. He was obliged to rub the frost off with the sleeve of his dressing-gown before he could see anything; and could see very little then. All he could make out was, that it was still very foggy and extremely cold, and that there was no noise of people running to and fro, and making a great stir, as there unquestionably would have been if night had beaten off bright day, and taken possession of the world. This was a great relief, because "three days after sight of this First of Exchange pay to Mr. Ebenezer Scrooge or his order," and so forth, would have become a mere United States' security[32] if there were no days to count by.

Scrooge went to bed again, and thought, and thought, and thought it over and over and over, and could make nothing of it. The more he thought, the more perplexed he was; and the more he endeavoured not to think, the more he thought.

Marley's Ghost bothered him exceedingly. Every time he resolved within himself, after mature inquiry, that it was all a dream, his mind flew back again, like a strong spring released, to its first position, and presented the same problem to be worked all through, "Was it a dream or not?"

Scrooge lay in this state until the chime had gone three quarters more, when he remembered, on a sudden, that the Ghost had warned him of a visitation when the bell tolled one. He resolved to lie awake until the hour was passed; and, considering that he could no more go to sleep than go to Heaven, this was perhaps the wisest resolution in his power.

The quarter was so long, that he was more than once convinced he must have sunk into a doze unconsciously, and missed the clock. At length it broke upon his listening ear.

"Ding, dong!"

"A quarter past," said Scrooge, counting.

---

[32] United States' security: This is Dickens's way of mocking the U. S. economy in the 1840s, which was in the middle of a depression. A "United States security" debt would be paid at only a fraction of its original value.

"Ding, dong!"

"Half-past!" said Scrooge.

"Ding, dong!"

"A quarter to it," said Scrooge.

"Ding, dong!"

"The hour itself," said Scrooge, triumphantly, "and nothing else!"

He spoke before the hour bell sounded, which it now did with a deep, dull, hollow, melancholy One. Light flashed up in the room upon the instant, and the curtains of his bed were drawn.

The curtains of his bed were drawn aside, I tell you, by a hand. Not the curtains at his feet, nor the curtains at his back, but those to which his face was addressed. The curtains of his bed were drawn aside; and Scrooge, starting up into a half-recumbent[33] attitude, found himself face to face with the unearthly visitor who drew them: as close to it as I am now to you, and I am standing in the spirit at your elbow.

It was a strange figure—like a child: yet not so like a child as like an old man, viewed through some supernatural medium, which gave him the appearance of having receded from the view, and being diminished to a child's proportions. Its hair, which hung about its neck and down its back, was white as if with age; and yet the face had not a wrinkle in it, and the tenderest bloom was on the skin. The arms were very long and muscular; the hands the same, as if its hold were of uncommon strength. Its legs and feet, most delicately formed, were, like those upper members, bare. It wore a tunic of the purest white; and round its waist was bound a lustrous belt, the sheen of which was beautiful. It held a branch of fresh green holly in its hand; and, in singular contradiction of that wintry emblem, had its dress trimmed with summer flowers. But the strangest thing about it was, that from the crown of its head there sprung a bright clear jet of light, by which all this was visible; and which was doubtless the occasion of its using, in its duller moments, a great extinguisher for a cap, which it now held under its arm.

Even this, though, when Scrooge looked at it with increasing steadiness, was *not* its strangest quality. For as its belt sparkled and glittered now in one part and now in another, and what was light one instant, at another time was dark, so the figure itself fluctuated in its distinctness: being now a thing with one arm, now with one leg, now with twenty legs, now a pair of legs without a head, now a head without a body: of which dissolving parts, no outline would be visible in the dense gloom wherein they melted away. And in the very wonder of this, it would be itself again; distinct and clear as ever.

"Are you the Spirit, sir, whose coming was foretold to me?" asked Scrooge.

---

[33] half lying down, half sitting up

"I am!"

The voice was soft and gentle. Singularly low, as if instead of being so close beside him, it were at a distance.

"Who, and what are you?" Scrooge demanded.

"I am the Ghost of Christmas Past."

"Long Past?" inquired Scrooge: observant of its dwarfish stature.

"No. Your past."

Perhaps, Scrooge could not have told anybody why, if anybody could have asked him; but he had a special desire to see the Spirit in his cap; and begged him to be covered.

"What!" exclaimed the Ghost, "would you so soon put out, with worldly hands, the light I give? Is it not enough that you are one of those whose passions made this cap, and force me through whole trains of years to wear it low upon my brow!"

Scrooge reverently disclaimed all intention to offend or any knowledge of having wilfully "bonneted" the Spirit at any period of his life. He then made bold to inquire what business brought him there.

"Your welfare!" said the Ghost.

Scrooge expressed himself much obliged, but could not help thinking that a night of unbroken rest would have been more conducive to that end. The Spirit must have heard him thinking, for it said immediately:

"Your reclamation, then. Take heed!"

It put out its strong hand as it spoke, and clasped him gently by the arm. "Rise! and walk with me!"

It would have been in vain for Scrooge to plead that the weather and the hour were not adapted to pedestrian purposes; that bed was warm, and the thermometer a long way below freezing; that he was clad but lightly in his slippers, dressing-gown, and nightcap; and that he had a cold upon him at that time. The grasp, though gentle as a woman's hand, was not to be resisted. He rose: but finding that the Spirit made towards the window, clasped his robe in supplication.

"I am a mortal," Scrooge remonstrated, "and liable to fall."

"Bear but a touch of my hand *there*," said the Spirit, laying it upon his heart, "and you shall be upheld in more than this!"

As the words were spoken, they passed through the wall, and stood upon an open country road, with fields on either hand. The city had entirely vanished. Not a vestige of it was to be seen. The darkness and the mist had vanished with it, for it was a clear, cold, winter day, with snow upon the ground.

"Good Heaven!" said Scrooge, clasping his hands together, as he looked about him. "I was bred in this place. I was a boy here!"

The Spirit gazed upon him mildly. Its gentle touch, though it had been light and instantaneous, appeared still present to the old man's sense of feeling. He was conscious of a thousand odours floating in the air, each one connected with a thousand thoughts, and hopes, and joys, and cares long, long, forgotten!

"Your lip is trembling," said the Ghost. "And what is that upon your cheek?"

Scrooge muttered, with an unusual catching in his voice, that it was a pimple; and begged the Ghost to lead him where he would.

"You recollect the way?" inquired the Spirit.

"Remember it!" cried Scrooge with fervour; "I could walk it blind-fold."

"Strange to have forgotten it for so many years!" observed the Ghost. "Let us go on."

They walked along the road, Scrooge recognising every gate, and post, and tree; until a little market-town appeared in the distance, with its bridge, its church, and winding river. Some shaggy ponies now were seen trotting towards them with boys upon their backs, who called to other boys in country gigs and carts, driven by farmers. All these boys were in great spirits, and shouted to each other, until the broad fields were so full of merry music, that the crisp air laughed to hear it!

"These are but shadows of the things that have been," said the Ghost. "They have no consciousness of us."

The jocund[34] travellers came on; and as they came, Scrooge knew and named them every one. Why was he rejoiced beyond all bounds to see them! Why did his cold eye glisten, and his heart leap up as they went past! Why was he filled with gladness when he heard them give each other Merry Christmas, as they parted at cross-roads and bye-ways, for their several homes! What was merry Christmas to Scrooge? Out upon merry Christmas! What good had it ever done to him?

"The school is not quite deserted," said the Ghost. "A solitary child, neglected by his friends, is left there still."

Scrooge said he knew it. And he sobbed.

They left the high-road, by a well-remembered lane, and soon approached a mansion of dull red brick, with a little weathercock-surmounted cupola,[35] on the roof, and a bell hanging in it. It was a large house, but one of broken fortunes; for the spacious offices were little used, their walls were damp and mossy, their windows broken, and their gates decayed. Fowls clucked and strutted in the stables; and the coach-houses and sheds were over-run with grass. Nor was it more retentive of its ancient state, within;

[34] merry, jolly
[35] dome-shaped roof

for entering the dreary hall, and glancing through the open doors of many rooms, they found them poorly furnished, cold, and vast. There was an earthy savour in the air, a chilly bareness in the place, which associated it-self somehow with too much getting up by candle-light, and not too much to eat.

They went, the Ghost and Scrooge, across the hall, to a door at the back of the house. It opened before them, and disclosed a long, bare, melancholy room, made barer still by lines of plain deal forms[36] and desks. At one of these a lonely boy was reading near a feeble fire; and Scrooge sat down upon a form, and wept to see his poor forgotten self as he used to be.

Not a latent echo in the house, not a squeak and scuffle from the mice behind the panelling, not a drip from the half-thawed water-spout in the dull yard behind, not a sigh among the leafless boughs of one despondent poplar, not the idle swinging of an empty storehouse door, no, not a clicking in the fire, but fell upon the heart of Scrooge with a softening influence, and gave a freer passage to his tears.

The Spirit touched him on the arm, and pointed to his younger self, intent upon his reading. Suddenly a man, in foreign garments: wonderfully real and distinct to look at: stood outside the window, with an axe stuck in his belt, and leading by the bridle an ass laden with wood.

"Why, it's Ali Baba!" Scrooge exclaimed in ecstasy. "It's dear old honest Ali Baba! Yes, yes, I know! One Christmas time, when yonder solitary child was left here all alone, he *did* come, for the first time, just like that. Poor boy! And Valentine," said Scrooge, "and his wild brother, Orson; there they go! And what's his name, who was put down in his drawers, asleep, at the Gate of Damascus; don't you see him! And the Sultan's Groom turned upside down by the Genii; there he is upon his head! Serve him right. I'm glad of it. What business had *he* to be married to the Princess!"[37]

To hear Scrooge expending all the earnestness of his nature on such subjects, in a most extraordinary voice between laughing and crying; and to see his heightened and excited face; would have been a surprise to his business friends in the city, indeed.

"There's the Parrot!" cried Scrooge. "Green body and yellow tail, with a thing like a lettuce growing out of the top of his head; there he is! Poor Robin Crusoe, he called him, when he came home again after sailing round the island. 'Poor Robin Crusoe, where have you been, Robin Crusoe?' The man thought he was dreaming, but he wasn't. It was the Parrot, you know. There goes Friday, running for his life to the little creek! Halloa! Hoop! Halloo!"

---

[36] plain deal forms: unpainted (plain) school benches
[37] These names and occurrences that Scrooge recalls are from ancient tales, including *One Thousand and One Nights (Arabian Nights)*.

Then, with a rapidity of transition very foreign to his usual character, he said, in pity for his former self, "Poor boy!" and cried again.

"I wish," Scrooge muttered, putting his hand in his pocket, and looking about him, after drying his eyes with his cuff: "but it's too late now."

"What is the matter?" asked the Spirit.

"Nothing," said Scrooge. "Nothing. There was a boy singing a Christmas Carol at my door last night. I should like to have given him something: that's all."

The Ghost smiled thoughtfully, and waved its hand: saying as it did so, "Let us see another Christmas!"

Scrooge's former self grew larger at the words, and the room became a little darker and more dirty. The panels shrunk, the windows cracked; fragments of plaster fell out of the ceiling, and the naked laths were shown instead; but how all this was brought about, Scrooge knew no more than you do. He only knew that it was quite correct; that everything had happened so; that there he was, alone again, when all the other boys had gone home for the jolly holidays.

He was not reading now, but walking up and down despairingly. Scrooge looked at the Ghost, and with a mournful shaking of his head, glanced anxiously towards the door.

It opened; and a little girl, much younger than the boy, came darting in, and putting her arms about his neck, and often kissing him, addressed him as her "Dear, dear brother."

"I have come to bring you home, dear brother!" said the child, clapping her tiny hands, and bending down to laugh. "To bring you home, home, home!"

"Home, little Fan?" returned the boy.

"Yes!" said the child, brimful of glee. "Home, for good and all. Home, for ever and ever. Father is so much kinder than he used to be, that home's like Heaven! He spoke so gently to me one dear night when I was going to bed, that I was not afraid to ask him once more if you might come home; and he said Yes, you should; and sent me in a coach to bring you. And you're to be a man!" said the child, opening her eyes, "and are never to come back here; but first, we're to be together all the Christmas long, and have the merriest time in all the world."

"You are quite a woman, little Fan!" exclaimed the boy.

She clapped her hands and laughed, and tried to touch his head; but being too little, laughed again, and stood on tiptoe to embrace him. Then she began to drag him, in her childish eagerness, towards the door; and he, nothing loth to go, accompanied her.

A terrible voice in the hall cried, "Bring down Master Scrooge's box, there!" and in the hall appeared the schoolmaster himself, who glared on

Master Scrooge with a ferocious condescension, and threw him into a dreadful state of mind by shaking hands with him. He then conveyed him and his sister into the veriest old well of a shivering best-parlour that ever was seen, where the maps upon the wall, and the celestial and terrestrial globes in the windows, were waxy with cold. Here he produced a decanter of curiously light wine, and a block of curiously heavy cake, and administered instalments of those dainties to the young people: at the same time, sending out a meagre servant to offer a glass of "something" to the postboy, who answered that he thanked the gentleman, but if it was the same tap as he had tasted before, he had rather not. Master Scrooge's trunk being by this time tied on to the top of the chaise, the children bade the schoolmaster good-bye right willingly; and getting into it, drove gaily down the garden-sweep: the quick wheels dashing the hoar-frost and snow from off the dark leaves of the evergreens like spray.

"Always a delicate creature, whom a breath might have withered," said the Ghost. "But she had a large heart!"

"So she had," cried Scrooge. "You're right. I will not gainsay[38] it, Spirit. God forbid!"

"She died a woman," said the Ghost, "and had, as I think, children."

"One child," Scrooge returned.

"True," said the Ghost. "Your nephew!"

Scrooge seemed uneasy in his mind; and answered briefly, "Yes."

Although they had but that moment left the school behind them, they were now in the busy thoroughfares of a city, where shadowy passengers passed and repassed; where shadowy carts and coaches battled for the way, and all the strife and tumult of a real city were. It was made plain enough, by the dressing of the shops, that here too it was Christmas time again; but it was evening, and the streets were lighted up.

The Ghost stopped at a certain warehouse door, and asked Scrooge if he knew it.

"Know it!" said Scrooge. "Was I apprenticed here!"

They went in. At sight of an old gentleman in a Welsh wig, sitting behind such a high desk, that if he had been two inches taller he must have knocked his head against the ceiling, Scrooge cried in great excitement:

"Why, it's old Fezziwig! Bless his heart; it's Fezziwig alive again!"

Old Fezziwig laid down his pen, and looked up at the clock, which pointed to the hour of seven. He rubbed his hands; adjusted his capacious[39] waistcoat; laughed all over himself, from his shoes to his organ of benevolence;[40] and called out in a comfortable, oily, rich, fat, jovial voice:

---

[38] contradict, argue

[39] large, roomy

[40] organ of benevolence: forehead

"Yo ho, there! Ebenezer! Dick!"

Scrooge's former self, now grown a young man, came briskly in, accompanied by his fellow-'prentice.

"Dick Wilkins, to be sure!" said Scrooge to the Ghost. "Bless me, yes. There he is. He was very much attached to me, was Dick. Poor Dick! Dear, dear!"

"Yo ho, my boys!" said Fezziwig. "No more work to-night. Christmas Eve, Dick. Christmas, Ebenezer! Let's have the shutters up," cried old Fezziwig, with a sharp clap of his hands, "before a man can say Jack Robinson!"

You wouldn't believe how those two fellows went at it! They charged into the street with the shutters—one, two, three—had 'em up in their places—four, five, six—barred 'em and pinned 'em—seven, eight, nine—and came back before you could have got to twelve, panting like race-horses.

"Hilli-ho!" cried old Fezziwig, skipping down from the high desk, with wonderful agility. "Clear away, my lads, and let's have lots of room here! Hilli-ho, Dick! Chirrup, Ebenezer!"

Clear away! There was nothing they wouldn't have cleared away, or couldn't have cleared away, with old Fezziwig looking on. It was done in a minute. Every movable was packed off, as if it were dismissed from public life for evermore; the floor was swept and watered, the lamps were trimmed, fuel was heaped upon the fire; and the warehouse was as snug, and warm, and dry, and bright a ball-room, as you would desire to see upon a winter's night.

In came a fiddler with a music-book, and went up to the lofty desk, and made an orchestra of it, and tuned like fifty stomachaches. In came Mrs. Fezziwig, one vast substantial smile. In came the three Miss Fezziwigs, beaming and lovable. In came the six young followers whose hearts they broke. In came all the young men and women employed in the business. In came the housemaid, with her cousin, the baker. In came the cook, with her brother's particular friend, the milkman. In came the boy from over the way, who was suspected of not having board enough from his master; trying to hide himself behind the girl from next door but one, who was proved to have had her ears pulled by her mistress. In they all came, one after another; some shyly, some boldly, some gracefully, some awkwardly, some pushing, some pulling; in they all came, anyhow and everyhow. Away they all went, twenty couple at once; hands half round and back again the other way; down the middle and up again; round and round in various stages of affectionate grouping; old top couple always turning up in the wrong place; new top couple starting off again, as soon as they got there; all top couples at last, and not a bottom one to help them! When this result was brought about, old Fezziwig, clapping his hands to stop the dance, cried out, "Well done!" and the fiddler plunged his hot face into a pot of porter, especially provided for that purpose. But scorning rest, upon his reappearance, he instantly began again, though there were no dancers yet, as if the other fiddler had been carried home, exhausted, on a shutter, and he were a brand-new man resolved to beat him out of sight, or perish.

There were more dances, and there were forfeits,[41] and more dances, and there was cake, and there was negus,[42] and there was a great piece of Cold Roast, and there was a great piece of Cold Boiled, and there were mince-pies, and plenty of beer. But the great effect of the evening came after the Roast and Boiled, when the fiddler (an artful dog, mind! The sort of man who knew his business better than you or I could have told it him!) struck up "Sir Roger de Coverley." Then old Fezziwig stood out to dance with Mrs. Fezziwig. Top couple, too; with a good stiff piece of work cut out for them; three or four and twenty pair of partners; people who were not to be trifled with; people who *would* dance, and had no notion of walking.

But if they had been twice as many—ah, four times—old Fezziwig would have been a match for them, and so would Mrs. Fezziwig. As to *her*, she was worthy to be his partner in every sense of the term. If that's not high praise, tell me higher, and I'll use it. A positive light appeared to issue from Fezziwig's calves. They shone in every part of the dance like moons. You couldn't have predicted, at any given time, what would have become of them next. And when old Fezziwig and Mrs. Fezziwig had gone all through the dance; advance and retire, both hands to your partner, bow and curtsey, corkscrew, thread-the-needle, and back again to your place; Fezziwig "cut"—cut so deftly, that he appeared to wink with his legs, and came upon his feet again without a stagger.

When the clock struck eleven, this domestic ball broke up. Mr. and Mrs. Fezziwig took their stations, one on either side of the door, and shaking

---

[41] games in which something is forfeited if a player misses a question (sometimes a small amount of money, sometimes...a kiss!)

[42] a drink made from wine, sugar, lemon, and hot water

hands with every person individually as he or she went out, wished him or her a Merry Christmas. When everybody had retired but the two 'prentices, they did the same to them; and thus the cheerful voices died away, and the lads were left to their beds; which were under a counter in the back-shop.

During the whole of this time, Scrooge had acted like a man out of his wits. His heart and soul were in the scene, and with his former self. He corroborated everything, remembered everything, enjoyed everything, and underwent the strangest agitation. It was not until now, when the bright faces of his former self and Dick were turned from them, that he remembered the Ghost, and became conscious that it was looking full upon him, while the light upon its head burnt very clear.

"A small matter," said the Ghost, "to make these silly folks so full of gratitude."

"Small!" echoed Scrooge.

The Spirit signed to him to listen to the two apprentices, who were pouring out their hearts in praise of Fezziwig: and when he had done so, said,

"Why! Is it not? He has spent but a few pounds of your mortal money: three or four perhaps. Is that so much that he deserves this praise?"

It isn't that," said Scrooge, heated by the remark, and speaking unconsciously like his former, not his latter, self. "It isn't that, Spirit. He has the power to render us happy or unhappy; to make our service light or burdensome; a pleasure or a toil. Say that his power lies in words and looks; in things so slight and insignificant that it is impossible to add and count 'em up: what then? The happiness he gives, is quite as great as if it cost a fortune."

He felt the Spirit's glance, and stopped.

"What is the matter?" asked the Ghost.

"Nothing particular," said Scrooge.

"Something, I think?" the Ghost insisted.

"No," said Scrooge, "No. I should like to be able to say a word or two to my clerk just now. That's all."

His former self turned down the lamps as he gave utterance to the wish; and Scrooge and the Ghost again stood side by side in the open air.

"My time grows short," observed the Spirit. "Quick!"

This was not addressed to Scrooge, or to any one whom he could see, but it produced an immediate effect. For again Scrooge saw himself. He was older now; a man in the prime of life. His face had not the harsh and rigid lines of later years; but it had begun to wear the signs of care and avarice.[43] There was an eager, greedy, restless motion in the eye, which showed the

---

[43] greed

passion that had taken root, and where the shadow of the growing tree would fall.

He was not alone, but sat by the side of a fair young girl in a mourning-dress: in whose eyes there were tears, which sparkled in the light that shone out of the Ghost of Christmas Past.

"It matters little," she said, softly. "To you, very little. Another idol has displaced me; and if it can cheer and comfort you in time to come, as I would have tried to do, I have no just cause to grieve."

"What Idol has displaced you?" he rejoined.

"A golden one."

"This is the even-handed dealing of the world!" he said. "There is nothing on which it is so hard as poverty; and there is nothing it professes to condemn with such severity as the pursuit of wealth!"

"You fear the world too much," she answered, gently. "All your other hopes have merged into the hope of being beyond the chance of its sordid reproach. I have seen your nobler aspirations fall off one by one, until the master-passion, Gain, engrosses you. Have I not?"

"What then?" he retorted. "Even if I have grown so much wiser, what then? I am not changed towards you."

She shook her head.

"Am I?"

"Our contract is an old one. It was made when we were both poor and content to be so, until, in good season, we could improve our worldly fortune by our patient industry. You *are* changed. When it was made, you were another man."

"I was a boy," he said impatiently.

"Your own feeling tells you that you were not what you are," she returned. "I am. That which promised happiness when we were one in heart, is fraught with misery now that we are two. How often and how keenly I have thought of this, I will not say. It is enough that I *have* thought of it, and can release you."

"Have I ever sought release?"

"In words. No. Never."

"In what, then?"

"In a changed nature; in an altered spirit; in another atmosphere of life; another Hope as its great end. In everything that made my love of any worth or value in your sight. If this had never been between us," said the girl, looking mildly, but with steadiness, upon him; "tell me, would you seek me out and try to win me now? Ah, no!"

He seemed to yield to the justice of this supposition, in spite of himself. But he said with a struggle, "You think not."

"I would gladly think otherwise if I could," she answered, "Heaven knows! When *I* have learned a Truth like this, I know how strong and irresistible it must be. But if you were free to-day, to-morrow, yesterday, can even I believe that you would choose a dowerless girl[44]—you who, in your very confidence with her, weigh everything by Gain: or, choosing her, if for a moment you were false enough to your one guiding principle to do so, do I not know that your repentance and regret would surely follow? I do; and I release you. With a full heart, for the love of him you once were."

He was about to speak; but with her head turned from him, she resumed.

"You may—the memory of what is past half makes me hope you will—have pain in this. A very, very brief time, and you will dismiss the recollection of it, gladly, as an unprofitable dream, from which it happened well that you awoke. May you be happy in the life you have chosen!"

She left him, and they parted.

"Spirit!" said Scrooge, "show me no more! Conduct me home. Why do you delight to torture me?"

"One shadow more!" exclaimed the Ghost.

"No more!" cried Scrooge. "No more. I don't wish to see it. Show me no more!"

But the relentless Ghost pinioned him in both his arms, and forced him to observe what happened next.

They were in another scene and place; a room, not very large or handsome, but full of comfort. Near to the winter fire sat a beautiful young girl, so like that last that Scrooge believed it was the same, until he saw *her*, now a comely matron, sitting opposite her daughter. The noise in this room was perfectly tumultuous, for there were more children there, than Scrooge in his agitated state of mind could count; and, unlike the celebrated herd in the poem,[45] they were not forty children conducting themselves like one, but every child was conducting itself like forty. The consequences were uproarious beyond belief; but no one seemed to care; on the contrary, the mother and daughter laughed heartily, and enjoyed it very much; and the latter, soon beginning to mingle in the sports, got pillaged by the young brigands most ruthlessly. What would I not have given to be one of them! Though I never could have been so rude, no, no! I wouldn't for the wealth of all the world have crushed that braided hair, and torn it down; and for the precious little shoe, I wouldn't have plucked it off, God bless my soul! to save my life. As to measuring her waist in sport, as they did, bold young brood, I couldn't have done it; I should have expected my arm to have grown round

---

[44] dowerless girl: a young woman without any money or property that might entice a man to marry her (meaning the marriage was for love only)
[45] This is a reference to William Wordsworth's 1802 poem "Written in March," which reads, in part, "The cattle are grazing, Their heads never raising; There are forty feeding like one!"

it for a punishment, and never come straight again. And yet I should have dearly liked, I own, to have touched her lips; to have questioned her, that she might have opened them; to have looked upon the lashes of her down-cast eyes, and never raised a blush; to have let loose waves of hair, an inch of which would be a keepsake beyond price: in short, I should have liked, I do confess, to have had the lightest licence of a child, and yet to have been man enough to know its value.

But now a knocking at the door was heard, and such a rush immediately ensued that she with laughing face and plundered dress was borne towards it the centre of a flushed and boisterous group, just in time to greet the father, who came home attended by a man laden with Christmas toys and presents. Then the shouting and the struggling, and the onslaught that was made on the defenceless porter! The scaling him with chairs for ladders to dive into his pockets, despoil him of brown-paper parcels, hold on tight by his cravat, hug him round his neck, pommel his back, and kick his legs in irrepressible affection! The shouts of wonder and delight with which the development of every package was received! The terrible announcement that the baby had been taken in the act of putting a doll's frying-pan into his mouth, and was more than suspected of having swallowed a fictitious turkey, glued on a wooden platter! The immense relief of finding this a false alarm! The joy, and gratitude, and ecstasy! They are all indescribable alike. It is enough that by degrees the children and their emotions got out of the parlour, and by one stair at a time, up to the top of the house; where they went to bed, and so subsided.

And now Scrooge looked on more attentively than ever, when the master of the house, having his daughter leaning fondly on him, sat down with her and her mother at his own fireside; and when he thought that such another creature, quite as graceful and as full of promise, might have called him father, and been a spring-time in the haggard winter of his life, his sight grew very dim indeed.

"Belle," said the husband, turning to his wife with a smile, "I saw an old friend of yours this afternoon."

"Who was it?"

"Guess!"

"How can I? Tut, don't I know?" she added in the same breath, laughing as he laughed. "Mr. Scrooge."

"Mr. Scrooge it was. I passed his office window; and as it was not shut up, and he had a candle inside, I could scarcely help seeing him. His partner lies upon the point of death, I hear; and there he sat alone. Quite alone in the world, I do believe."

"Spirit!" said Scrooge in a broken voice, "remove me from this place."

"I told you these were shadows of the things that have been," said the Ghost. "That they are what they are, do not blame me!"

"Remove me!" Scrooge exclaimed, "I cannot bear it!"

He turned upon the Ghost, and seeing that it looked upon him with a face, in which in some strange way there were fragments of all the faces it had shown him, wrestled with it.

"Leave me! Take me back. Haunt me no longer!"

In the struggle, if that can be called a struggle in which the Ghost with no visible resistance on its own part was undisturbed by any effort of its adversary, Scrooge observed that its light was burning high and bright; and dimly connecting that with its influence over him, he seized the extinguisher-cap, and by a sudden action pressed it down upon its head.

The Spirit dropped beneath it, so that the extinguisher covered its whole form; but though Scrooge pressed it down with all his force, he could not hide the light: which streamed from under it, in an unbroken flood upon the ground.

He was conscious of being exhausted, and overcome by an irresistible drowsiness; and, further, of being in his own bedroom. He gave the cap a parting squeeze, in which his hand relaxed; and had barely time to reel to bed, before he sank into a heavy sleep.

Questions for Review:

1. Describe the Ghost of Christmas Past.

2. Briefly sum up what Scrooge sees in his own past.

3. At this stave's opening, what does Scrooge beg the Ghost of Christmas Past to do with his (the Ghost's) hat—an act that is reprised at end of the stave? What might this action by Scrooge represent?

4. Do you believe that this revelation of Scrooge's past is enough to justify his present life? Why or why not?

5. Give some evidence that Scrooge's heart is softening.

Stave Three:

The Second of the Three Spirits

Awaking in the middle of a prodigiously tough snore, and sitting up in bed to get his thoughts together, Scrooge had no occasion to be told that the bell was again upon the stroke of One. He felt that he was restored to consciousness in the right nick of time, for the especial purpose of holding a conference with the second messenger despatched to him through Jacob Marley's intervention. But finding that he turned uncomfortably cold when he began to wonder which of his curtains this new spectre would draw back, he put them every one aside with his own hands; and lying down again, established a sharp look-out all round the bed. For he wished to challenge the Spirit on the moment of its appearance, and did not wish to be taken by surprise, and made nervous.

Gentlemen of the free-and-easy sort, who plume themselves[46] on being acquainted with a move or two, and being usually equal to the time-of-day, express the wide range of their capacity for adventure by observing that they are good for anything from pitch-and-toss to man-slaughter; between which opposite extremes, no doubt, there lies a tolerably wide and comprehensive range of subjects. Without venturing for Scrooge quite as hardily as this, I don't mind calling on you to believe that he was ready for a good broad field of strange appearances, and that nothing between a baby and rhinoceros would have astonished him very much.

Now, being prepared for almost anything, he was not by any means prepared for nothing; and, consequently, when the Bell struck One, and no shape appeared, he was taken with a violent fit of trembling. Five minutes, ten minutes, a quarter of an hour went by, yet nothing came. All this time, he lay upon his bed, the very core and centre of a blaze of ruddy light, which streamed upon it when the clock proclaimed the hour; and which, being only light, was more alarming than a dozen ghosts, as he was powerless to make out what it meant, or would be at; and was sometimes apprehensive

---

[46] plume themselves: pride themselves

that he might be at that very moment an interesting case of spontaneous combustion, without having the consolation of knowing it. At last, however, he began to think—as you or I would have thought at first; for it is always the person not in the predicament who knows what ought to have been done in it, and would unquestionably have done it too—at last, I say, he began to think that the source and secret of this ghostly light might be in the adjoining room, from whence, on further tracing it, it seemed to shine. This idea taking full possession of his mind, he got up softly and shuffled in his slippers to the door.

The moment Scrooge's hand was on the lock, a strange voice called him by his name, and bade him enter. He obeyed.

It was his own room. There was no doubt about that. But it had undergone a surprising transformation. The walls and ceiling were so hung with living green, that it looked a perfect grove; from every part of which, bright gleaming berries glistened. The crisp leaves of holly, mistletoe, and ivy reflected back the light, as if so many little mirrors had been scattered there; and such a mighty blaze went roaring up the chimney, as that dull petrification of a hearth had never known in Scrooge's time, or Marley's, or for many and many a winter season gone. Heaped up on the floor, to form a kind of throne, were turkeys, geese, game, poultry, brawn, great joints of meat, sucking-pigs, long wreaths of sausages, mince-pies, plum-puddings, barrels of oysters, red-hot chestnuts, cherry-cheeked apples, juicy oranges, luscious pears, immense twelfth-cakes, and seething bowls of punch, that made the chamber dim with their delicious steam. In easy state upon this couch, there sat a jolly Giant, glorious to see; who bore a glowing torch, in shape not unlike Plenty's horn, and held it up, high up, to shed its light on Scrooge, as he came peeping round the door.

"Come in!" exclaimed the Ghost. "Come in! and know me better, man!"

Scrooge entered timidly, and hung his head before this Spirit. He was not the dogged Scrooge he had been; and though the Spirit's eyes were clear and kind, he did not like to meet them.

"I am the Ghost of Christmas Present," said the Spirit. "Look upon me!"

Scrooge reverently did so. It was clothed in one simple green robe, or mantle, bordered with white fur. This garment hung so loosely on the figure, that its capacious breast was bare, as if disdaining to be warded or concealed by any artifice. Its feet, observable beneath the ample folds of the garment, were also bare; and on its head it wore no other covering than a holly wreath, set here and there with shining icicles. Its dark brown curls were long and free; free as its genial face, its sparkling eye, its open hand, its cheery voice, its unconstrained demeanour, and its joyful air. Girded round its middle was an antique scabbard; but no sword was in it, and the ancient sheath was eaten up with rust.

"You have never seen the like of me before!" exclaimed the Spirit.

"Never," Scrooge made answer to it.

"Have never walked forth with the younger members of my family; meaning (for I am very young) my elder brothers born in these later years?" pursued the Phantom.

"I don't think I have," said Scrooge. "I am afraid I have not. Have you had many brothers, Spirit?"

"More than eighteen hundred," said the Ghost.

"A tremendous family to provide for!" muttered Scrooge.

The Ghost of Christmas Present rose.

"Spirit," said Scrooge submissively, "conduct me where you will. I went forth last night on compulsion, and I learnt a lesson which is working now. To-night, if you have aught[47] to teach me, let me profit by it."

"Touch my robe!"

Scrooge did as he was told, and held it fast.

Holly, mistletoe, red berries, ivy, turkeys, geese, game, poultry, brawn, meat, pigs, sausages, oysters, pies, puddings, fruit, and punch, all vanished instantly. So did the room, the fire, the ruddy glow, the hour of night, and they stood in the city streets on Christmas morning, where (for the weather was severe) the people made a rough, but brisk and not unpleasant kind of music, in scraping the snow from the pavement in front of their dwellings, and from the tops of their houses, whence it was mad delight to the boys to see it come plumping down into the road below, and splitting into artificial little snow-storms.

The house fronts looked black enough, and the windows blacker, contrasting with the smooth white sheet of snow upon the roofs, and with the dirtier snow upon the ground; which last deposit had been ploughed up in deep furrows by the heavy wheels of carts and waggons; furrows that crossed and re-crossed each other hundreds of times where the great streets branched off; and made intricate channels, hard to trace in the thick yellow mud and icy water. The sky was gloomy, and the shortest streets were choked up with a dingy mist, half thawed, half frozen, whose heavier particles descended in a shower of sooty atoms, as if all the chimneys in Great Britain had, by one consent, caught fire, and were blazing away to their dear hearts' content. There was nothing very cheerful in the climate or the town, and yet was there an air of cheerfulness abroad that the clearest summer air and brightest summer sun might have endeavoured to diffuse in vain.

For, the people who were shovelling away on the house-tops were jovial and full of glee; calling out to one another from the parapets, and now and then exchanging a facetious snowball—better-natured missile far than

---

[47] anything

many a wordy jest—laughing heartily if it went right and not less heartily if it went wrong. The poulterers' shops were still half open, and the fruiterers' were radiant in their glory. There were great, round, pot-bellied baskets of chestnuts, shaped like the waistcoats of jolly old gentlemen, lolling at the doors, and tumbling out into the street in their apoplectic opulence. There were ruddy, brown-faced, broad-girthed Spanish Onions, shining in the fatness of their growth like Spanish Friars, and winking from their shelves in wanton slyness at the girls as they went by, and glanced demurely at the hung-up mistletoe. There were pears and apples, clustered high in blooming pyra-

mids; there were bunches of grapes, made, in the shopkeepers' benevolence to dangle from conspicuous hooks, that people's mouths might water gratis[48] as they passed; there were piles of filberts,[49] mossy and brown, recalling, in their fragrance, ancient walks among the woods, and pleasant shufflings ankle deep through withered leaves; there were Norfolk Biffins,[50] squat and swarthy, setting off the yellow of the oranges and lemons, and, in the great compactness of their juicy persons, urgently entreating and beseeching to be carried home in paper bags and eaten after dinner. The very gold and silver fish, set forth among these choice fruits in a bowl, though members of a dull and stagnant-blooded race, appeared to know that there was something going on; and, to a fish, went gasping round and round their little world in slow and passionless excitement.

The Grocers! oh, the Grocers! nearly closed, with perhaps two shutters down, or one; but through those gaps such glimpses! It was not alone that the scales descending on the counter made a merry sound, or that the twine and roller parted company so briskly, or that the canisters were rattled up and down like juggling tricks, or even that the blended scents of tea and

---

[48] free of charge
[49] hazelnuts
[50] red apples, baked and flattened

coffee were so grateful to the nose, or even that the raisins were so plentiful and rare, the almonds so extremely white, the sticks of cinnamon so long and straight, the other spices so delicious, the candied fruits so caked and spotted with molten sugar as to make the coldest lookers-on feel faint and subsequently bilious. Nor was it that the figs were moist and pulpy, or that the French plums blushed in modest tartness from their highly-decorated boxes, or that everything was good to eat and in its Christmas dress; but the customers were all so hurried and so eager in the hopeful promise of the day, that they tumbled up against each other at the door, crashing their wicker baskets wildly, and left their purchases upon the counter, and came running back to fetch them, and committed hundreds of the like mistakes, in the best humour possible; while the Grocer and his people were so frank and fresh that the polished hearts with which they fastened their aprons behind might have been their own, worn outside for general inspection, and for Christmas daws[51] to peck at if they chose.

But soon the steeples called good people all, to church and chapel, and away they came, flocking through the streets in their best clothes, and with their gayest faces. And at the same time there emerged from scores of bye-streets, lanes, and nameless turnings, innumerable people, carrying their dinners to the bakers' shops. The sight of these poor revellers appeared to interest the Spirit very much, for he stood with Scrooge beside him in a baker's doorway, and taking off the covers as their bearers passed, sprinkled incense on their dinners from his torch. And it was a very uncommon kind of torch, for once or twice when there were angry words between some dinner-carriers who had jostled each other, he shed a few drops of water on them from it, and their good humour was restored directly. For they said, it was a shame to quarrel upon Christmas Day. And so it was! God love it, so it was!

In time the bells ceased, and the bakers were shut up; and yet there was a genial shadowing forth of all these dinners and the progress of their cooking, in the thawed blotch of wet above each baker's oven; where the pavement smoked as if its stones were cooking too.

"Is there a peculiar flavour in what you sprinkle from your torch?" asked Scrooge.

"There is. My own."

"Would it apply to any kind of dinner on this day?" asked Scrooge.

"To any kindly given. To a poor one most."

"Why to a poor one most?" asked Scrooge.

"Because it needs it most."

---

[51] jackdaws (crow-like birds)

"Spirit," said Scrooge, after a moment's thought, "I wonder you, of all the beings in the many worlds about us, should desire to cramp these people's opportunities of innocent enjoyment."

"I!" cried the Spirit.

"You would deprive them of their means of dining every seventh day, often the only day on which they can be said to dine at all," said Scrooge. "Wouldn't you?"

"I!" cried the Spirit.

"You seek to close these places on the Seventh Day?" said Scrooge. "And it comes to the same thing."

"*I* seek!" exclaimed the Spirit.

"Forgive me if I am wrong. It has been done in your name, or at least in that of your family," said Scrooge.[52]

"There are some upon this earth of yours," returned the Spirit, "who lay claim to know us, and who do their deeds of passion, pride, ill-will, hatred, envy, bigotry, and selfishness in our name, who are as strange to us and all our kith and kin, as if they had never lived. Remember that, and charge their doings on themselves, not us."

Scrooge promised that he would; and they went on, invisible, as they had been before, into the suburbs of the town. It was a remarkable quality of the Ghost (which Scrooge had observed at the baker's), that notwithstanding his gigantic size, he could accommodate himself to any place with ease; and that he stood beneath a low roof quite as gracefully and like a supernatural creature, as it was possible he could have done in any lofty hall.

And perhaps it was the pleasure the good Spirit had in showing off this power of his, or else it was his own kind, generous, hearty nature, and his sympathy with all poor men, that led him straight to Scrooge's clerk's; for there he went, and took Scrooge with him, holding to his robe; and on the threshold of the door the Spirit smiled, and stopped to bless Bob Cratchit's dwelling with the sprinkling of his torch. Think of that! Bob had but fifteen "Bob" a-week himself; he pocketed on Saturdays but fifteen copies of his Christian name; and yet the Ghost of Christmas Present blessed his four-roomed house!

Then up rose Mrs. Cratchit, Cratchit's wife, dressed out but poorly in a twice-turned gown, but brave in ribbons, which are cheap and make a goodly show for sixpence; and she laid the cloth, assisted by Belinda Cratchit, second of her daughters, also brave in ribbons; while Master Peter Cratchit plunged a fork into the saucepan of potatoes, and getting the corners of his monstrous shirt collar (Bob's private property, conferred upon his son and

---

[52] In England there were many attempts, some with a certain measure of success, to force all citizens to observe the Israelites' practice of abstaining from work or recreation on "the Sabbath." This practice is called *Sabbatarianism*.

heir in honour of the day) into his mouth, rejoiced to find himself so gallantly attired, and yearned to show his linen in the fashionable Parks. And now two smaller Cratchits, boy and girl, came tearing in, screaming that outside the baker's they had smelt the goose, and known it for their own; and basking in luxurious thoughts of sage and onion, these young Cratchits danced about the table, and exalted Master Peter Cratchit to the skies, while he (not proud, although his collars nearly choked him) blew the fire, until the slow potatoes bubbling up, knocked loudly at the saucepan-lid to be let out and peeled.

"What has ever got your precious father then?" said Mrs. Cratchit. "And your brother, Tiny Tim! And Martha warn't as late last Christmas Day by half-an-hour?"

"Here's Martha, mother!" said a girl, appearing as she spoke.

"Here's Martha, mother!" cried the two young Cratchits. "Hurrah! There's *such* a goose, Martha!"

"Why, bless your heart alive, my dear, how late you are!" said Mrs. Cratchit, kissing her a dozen times, and taking off her shawl and bonnet for her with officious zeal.

"We'd a deal of work to finish up last night," replied the girl, "and had to clear away this morning, mother!"

"Well! Never mind so long as you are home," said Mrs. Cratchit. "Sit ye down before the fire, my dear, and have a warm, Lord bless ye!"

"No, no! There's father coming," cried the two young Cratchits, who were everywhere at once. "Hide, Martha, hide!"

So Martha hid herself, and in came little Bob, the father, with at least three feet of comforter exclusive of the fringe, hanging down before him; and his threadbare clothes darned up and brushed, to look seasonable; and Tiny Tim upon his shoulder. Alas for Tiny Tim, he bore a little crutch, and had his limbs supported by an iron frame![53]

"Why, where's our Martha?" cried Bob Cratchit, looking round.

"Not coming," said Mrs. Cratchit.

"Not coming!" said Bob, with a sudden declension in his high spirits; for he had been Tim's blood horse all the way from church, and had come home rampant. "Not coming upon Christmas Day!"

Martha didn't like to see him disappointed, if it were only in joke; so she came out prematurely from behind the closet door, and ran into his arms, while the two young Cratchits hustled Tiny Tim, and bore him off into the wash-house, that he might hear the pudding singing in the copper.[54]

---

[53] Various commentators on *A Christmas Carol* have speculated Tiny Tim's condition as being anything from a kidney disease to spinal tuberculosis.

[54] copper: a large pot in which a family would boil (wash) clothes

"And how did little Tim behave?" asked Mrs. Cratchit, when she had rallied Bob on his credulity,[55] and Bob had hugged his daughter to his heart's content.

"As good as gold," said Bob, "and better. Somehow he gets thoughtful, sitting by himself so much, and thinks the strangest things you ever heard. He told me, coming home, that he hoped the people saw him in the church, because he was a cripple, and it might be pleasant to them to remember upon Christmas Day, who made lame beggars walk, and blind men see."

Bob's voice was tremulous[56] when he told them this, and trembled more when he said that Tiny Tim was growing strong and hearty.

His active little crutch was heard upon the floor, and back came Tiny Tim before another word was spoken, escorted by his brother and sister to his stool before the fire; and while Bob, turning up his cuffs—as if, poor fellow, they were capable of being made more shabby—compounded some hot mixture in a jug with gin and lemons, and stirred it round and round and put it on the hob to simmer; Master Peter, and the two ubiquitous[57] young Cratchits went to fetch the goose, with which they soon returned in high procession.

Such a bustle ensued that you might have thought a goose the rarest of all birds; a feathered phenomenon, to which a black swan was a matter of course—and in truth it was something very like it in that house. Mrs. Cratchit made the gravy (ready beforehand in a little sauce-pan) hissing hot; Master Peter mashed the potatoes with incredible vigour; Miss Belinda sweetened up the apple-sauce; Martha dusted the hot plates; Bob took Tiny Tim beside him in a tiny corner at the table; the two young Cratchits set chairs for everybody, not forgetting themselves, and mounting guard upon their posts, crammed spoons into their mouths, lest they should shriek for goose before their turn came to be helped. At last the dishes were set on, and grace was said. It was succeeded by a breathless pause, as Mrs. Cratchit, looking slowly all along the carving-knife, prepared to plunge it in the breast; but when she did, and when the long expected gush of stuffing issued forth, one murmur of delight arose all round the board, and even Tiny Tim, excited by the two young Cratchits, beat on the table with the handle of his knife, and feebly cried Hurrah!

There never was such a goose. Bob said he didn't believe there ever was such a goose cooked. Its tenderness and flavour, size and cheapness, were the themes of universal admiration. Eked out by apple-sauce and mashed potatoes, it was a sufficient dinner for the whole family; indeed, as Mrs. Cratchit said with great delight (surveying one small atom of a bone upon

---

[55] gullibility
[56] shaky, quivering
[57] appearing to be everywhere at once

the dish), they hadn't ate it all at last! Yet every one had had enough, and the youngest Cratchits in particular, were steeped in sage and onion to the eyebrows! But now, the plates being changed by Miss Belinda, Mrs. Cratchit left the room alone—too nervous to bear witnesses—to take the pudding up and bring it in.

Suppose it should not be done enough! Suppose it should break in turning out! Suppose somebody should have got over the wall of the back-yard, and stolen it, while they were merry with the goose—a supposition at which the two young Cratchits became livid! All sorts of horrors were supposed.

Hallo! A great deal of steam! The pudding was out of the copper. A smell like a washing-day! That was the cloth. A smell like an eating-house and a pastrycook's next door to each other, with a laundress's next door to that! That was the pudding! In half a minute Mrs. Cratchit entered—flushed, but smiling proudly—with the pudding, like a speckled cannon-ball, so hard and firm, blazing in half of half-a-quartern of ignited brandy, and bedight with Christmas holly stuck into the top.

Oh, a wonderful pudding! Bob Cratchit said, and calmly too, that he regarded it as the greatest success achieved by Mrs. Cratchit since their marriage. Mrs. Cratchit said that now the weight was off her mind, she would confess she had had her doubts about the quantity of flour. Everybody had something to say about it, but nobody said or thought it was at all a small pudding for a large family. It would have been flat heresy to do so. Any Cratchit would have blushed to hint at such a thing.

At last the dinner was all done, the cloth was cleared, the hearth swept, and the fire made up. The compound in the jug being tasted, and considered perfect, apples and oranges were put upon the table, and a shovel-full of chestnuts on the fire. Then all the Cratchit family drew round the hearth, in what Bob Cratchit called a circle, meaning half a one; and at Bob Cratchit's elbow stood the family display of glass. Two tumblers, and a custard-cup without a handle.

These held the hot stuff from the jug, however, as well as golden goblets would have done; and Bob served it out with beaming looks, while the chestnuts on the fire sputtered and cracked noisily. Then Bob proposed:

"A Merry Christmas to us all, my dears. God bless us!"

Which all the family re-echoed.

"God bless us every one!" said Tiny Tim, the last of all.

He sat very close to his father's side upon his little stool. Bob held his withered little hand in his, as if he loved the child, and wished to keep him by his side, and dreaded that he might be taken from him.

"Spirit," said Scrooge, with an interest he had never felt before, "tell me if Tiny Tim will live."

"I see a vacant seat," replied the Ghost, "in the poor chimney-corner, and a crutch without an owner, carefully preserved. If these shadows remain unaltered by the Future, the child will die."

"No, no," said Scrooge. "Oh, no, kind Spirit! say he will be spared."

"If these shadows remain unaltered by the Future, none other of my race," returned the Ghost, "will find him here. What then? If he be like to die, he had better do it, and decrease the surplus population."

Scrooge hung his head to hear his own words quoted by the Spirit, and was overcome with penitence and grief.

"Man," said the Ghost, "if man you be in heart, not adamant,[58] forbear that wicked cant[59] until you have discovered What the surplus is, and Where it is. Will you decide what men shall live, what men shall die? It may be, that in the sight of Heaven, you are more worthless and less fit to live than millions like this poor man's child. To hear the Insect on the leaf pronouncing on the too much life among his hungry brothers in the dust!"

Scrooge bent before the Ghost's rebuke, and trembling cast his eyes upon the ground. But he raised them speedily, on hearing his own name.

"Mr. Scrooge!" said Bob; "I'll give you Mr. Scrooge, the Founder of the Feast!"

"The Founder of the Feast indeed!" cried Mrs. Cratchit, reddening. "I wish I had him here. I'd give him a piece of my mind to feast upon, and I hope he'd have a good appetite for it."

"My dear," said Bob, "the children! Christmas Day."

"It should be Christmas Day, I am sure," said she, "on which one drinks the health of such an odious, stingy, hard, unfeeling man as Mr. Scrooge. You know he is, Robert! Nobody knows it better than you do, poor fellow!"

"My dear," was Bob's mild answer, "Christmas Day."

"I'll drink his health for your sake and the Day's," said Mrs. Cratchit, "not for his. Long life to him! A merry Christmas and a happy new year! He'll be very merry and very happy, I have no doubt!"

The children drank the toast after her. It was the first of their proceedings which had no heartiness. Tiny Tim drank it last of all, but he didn't care twopence for it. Scrooge was the Ogre of the family. The mention of his name cast a dark shadow on the party, which was not dispelled for full five minutes.

After it had passed away, they were ten times merrier than before, from the mere relief of Scrooge the Baleful being done with. Bob Cratchit told them how he had a situation in his eye for Master Peter, which would bring in, if obtained, full five-and-sixpence weekly. The two young Cratchits

[58] stubborn
[59] forbear that wicked cant: refrain from saying that terrible thing

laughed tremendously at the idea of Peter's being a man of business; and Peter himself looked thoughtfully at the fire from between his collars, as if he were deliberating what particular investments he should favour when he came into the receipt of that bewildering income. Martha, who was a poor apprentice at a milliner's, then told them what kind of work she had to do, and how many hours she worked at a stretch, and how she meant to lie abed to-morrow morning for a good long rest; to-morrow being a holiday she passed at home. Also how she had seen a countess and a lord some days before, and how the lord "was much about as tall as Peter;" at which Peter pulled up his collars so high that you couldn't have seen his head if you had been there. All this time the chestnuts and the jug went round and round; and by-and-bye they had a song, about a lost child travelling in the snow, from Tiny Tim, who had a plaintive[60] little voice, and sang it very well indeed.

There was nothing of high mark in this. They were not a handsome family; they were not well dressed; their shoes were far from being water-proof; their clothes were scanty; and Peter might have known, and very likely did, the inside of a pawnbroker's. But, they were happy, grateful, pleased with one another, and contented with the time; and when they faded, and looked happier yet in the bright sprinklings of the Spirit's torch at parting, Scrooge had his eye upon them, and especially on Tiny Tim, until the last.

By this time it was getting dark, and snowing pretty heavily; and as Scrooge and the Spirit went along the streets, the brightness of the roaring fires in kitchens, parlours, and all sorts of rooms, was wonderful. Here, the flickering of the blaze showed preparations for a cosy dinner, with hot plates baking through and through before the fire, and deep red curtains, ready to be drawn to shut out cold and darkness. There all the children of the house were running out into the snow to meet their married sisters, brothers, cousins, uncles, aunts, and be the first to greet them. Here, again, were shadows on the window-blind of guests assembling; and there a group of handsome girls, all hooded and fur-booted, and all chattering at once, tripped lightly off to some near neighbour's house; where, woe upon the single man who saw them enter—artful witches, well they knew it—in a glow!

But, if you had judged from the numbers of people on their way to friendly gatherings, you might have thought that no one was at home to give them welcome when they got there, instead of every house expecting company, and piling up its fires half-chimney high. Blessings on it, how the Ghost exulted! How it bared its breadth of breast, and opened its capacious palm, and floated on, outpouring, with a generous hand, its bright and harmless mirth on everything within its reach! The very lamplighter, who ran on

---

[60] melancholy, wistful

before, dotting the dusky street with specks of light, and who was dressed to spend the evening somewhere, laughed out loudly as the Spirit passed, though little kenned[61] the lamplighter that he had any company but Christmas!

And now, without a word of warning from the Ghost, they stood upon a bleak and desert moor, where monstrous masses of rude stone were cast about, as though it were the burial-place of giants; and water spread itself wheresoever it listed,[62] or would have done so, but for the frost that held it prisoner; and nothing grew but moss and furze,[63] and coarse rank grass. Down in the west the setting sun had left a streak of fiery red, which glared upon the desolation for an instant, like a sullen eye, and frowning lower, lower, lower yet, was lost in the thick gloom of darkest night.

"What place is this?" asked Scrooge.

"A place where Miners live, who labour in the bowels of the earth," returned the Spirit. "But they know me. See!"

A light shone from the window of a hut, and swiftly they advanced towards it. Passing through the wall of mud and stone, they found a cheerful company assembled round a glowing fire. An old, old man and woman, with their children and their children's children, and another generation beyond that, all decked out gaily in their holiday attire. The old man, in a voice that seldom rose above the howling of the wind upon the barren waste, was singing them a Christmas song—it had been a very old song when he was a boy—and from time to time they all joined in the chorus. So surely as they raised their voices, the old man got quite blithe[64] and loud; and so surely as they stopped, his vigour sank again.

The Spirit did not tarry here, but bade Scrooge hold his robe, and passing on above the moor, sped—whither? Not to sea? To sea. To Scrooge's horror, looking back, he saw the last of the land, a frightful range of rocks, behind them; and his ears were deafened by the thundering of water, as it rolled and roared, and raged among the dreadful caverns it had worn, and fiercely tried to undermine the earth.

Built upon a dismal reef of sunken rocks, some league or so from shore, on which the waters chafed and dashed, the wild year through, there stood a solitary lighthouse. Great heaps of sea-weed clung to its base, and storm-birds—born of the wind one might suppose, as sea-weed of the water—rose and fell about it, like the waves they skimmed.

But even here, two men who watched the light had made a fire, that through the loophole in the thick stone wall shed out a ray of brightness on

---

[61] perceived, realized
[62] See John 3:8.
[63] an evergreen shrub
[64] lighthearted

the awful sea. Joining their horny hands over the rough table at which they sat, they wished each other Merry Christmas in their can of grog;[65] and one of them: the elder, too, with his face all damaged and scarred with hard weather, as the figure-head of an old ship might be: struck up a sturdy song that was like a Gale in itself.

Again the Ghost sped on, above the black and heaving sea—on, on—until, being far away, as he told Scrooge, from any shore, they lighted on a ship. They stood beside the helmsman at the wheel, the look-out in the bow, the officers who had the watch; dark, ghostly figures in their several stations; but every man among them hummed a Christmas tune, or had a Christmas thought, or spoke below his breath to his companion of some bygone Christmas Day, with homeward hopes belonging to it. And every man on board, waking or sleeping, good or bad, had had a kinder word for another on that day than on any day in the year; and had shared to some extent in its festivities; and had remembered those he cared for at a distance, and had known that they delighted to remember him.

It was a great surprise to Scrooge, while listening to the moaning of the wind, and thinking what a solemn thing it was to move on through the lonely darkness over an unknown abyss, whose depths were secrets as profound as Death: it was a great surprise to Scrooge, while thus engaged, to hear a hearty laugh. It was a much greater surprise to Scrooge to recognise it as his own nephew's and to find himself in a bright, dry, gleaming room, with the Spirit standing smiling by his side, and looking at that same nephew with approving affability!

"Ha, ha!" laughed Scrooge's nephew. "Ha, ha, ha!"

If you should happen, by any unlikely chance, to know a man more blest in a laugh than Scrooge's nephew, all I can say is, I should like to know him too. Introduce him to me, and I'll cultivate his acquaintance.

It is a fair, even-handed, noble adjustment of things, that while there is infection in disease and sorrow, there is nothing in the world so irresistibly contagious as laughter and good-humour. When Scrooge's nephew laughed in this way: holding his sides, rolling his head, and twisting his face into the most extravagant contortions: Scrooge's niece, by marriage, laughed as heartily as he. And their assembled friends being not a bit behindhand, roared out lustily.

"Ha, ha! Ha, ha, ha, ha!"

"He said that Christmas was a humbug, as I live!" cried Scrooge's nephew. "He believed it too!"

"More shame for him, Fred!" said Scrooge's niece, indignantly. Bless those women; they never do anything by halves. They are always in earnest.

---

[65] rum and water

She was very pretty: exceedingly pretty. With a dimpled, surprised-looking, capital face; a ripe little mouth, that seemed made to be kissed—as no doubt it was; all kinds of good little dots about her chin, that melted into one another when she laughed; and the sunniest pair of eyes you ever saw in any little creature's head. Altogether she was what you would have called provoking, you know; but satisfactory, too. Oh, perfectly satisfactory.

"He's a comical old fellow," said Scrooge's nephew, "that's the truth: and not so pleasant as he might be. However, his offences carry their own punishment, and I have nothing to say against him."

"I'm sure he is very rich, Fred," hinted Scrooge's niece. "At least you always tell *me* so."

"What of that, my dear!" said Scrooge's nephew. "His wealth is of no use to him. He don't do any good with it. He don't make himself comfortable with it. He hasn't the satisfaction of thinking—ha, ha, ha!—that he is ever going to benefit US with it."

"I have no patience with him," observed Scrooge's niece. Scrooge's niece's sisters, and all the other ladies, expressed the same opinion.

"Oh, I have!" said Scrooge's nephew. "I am sorry for him; I couldn't be angry with him if I tried. Who suffers by his ill whims! Himself, always. Here, he takes it into his head to dislike us, and he won't come and dine with us. What's the consequence? He don't lose much of a dinner."

"Indeed, I think he loses a very good dinner," interrupted Scrooge's niece. Everybody else said the same, and they must be allowed to have been competent judges, because they had just had dinner; and, with the dessert upon the table, were clustered round the fire, by lamplight.

"Well! I'm very glad to hear it," said Scrooge's nephew, "because I haven't great faith in these young housekeepers. What do *you* say, Topper?"

Topper had clearly got his eye upon one of Scrooge's niece's sisters, for he answered that a bachelor was a wretched outcast, who had no right to express an opinion on the subject. Whereat Scrooge's niece's sister—the plump one with the lace tucker: not the one with the roses—blushed.

"Do go on, Fred," said Scrooge's niece, clapping her hands. "He never finishes what he begins to say! He is such a ridiculous fellow!"

Scrooge's nephew revelled in another laugh, and as it was impossible to keep the infection off; though the plump sister tried hard to do it with aromatic vinegar; his example was unanimously followed.

"I was only going to say," said Scrooge's nephew, "that the consequence of his taking a dislike to us, and not making merry with us, is, as I think, that he loses some pleasant moments, which could do him no harm. I am sure he loses pleasanter companions than he can find in his own thoughts, either in his mouldy old office, or his dusty chambers. I mean to give him the same chance every year, whether he likes it or not, for I pity him. He may rail at Christmas till he dies, but he can't help thinking better of it—I defy him—if he finds me going there, in good temper, year after year, and saying Uncle Scrooge, how are you? If it only puts him in the vein to leave his poor clerk fifty pounds, *that's* something; and I think I shook him yesterday."

It was their turn to laugh now at the notion of his shaking Scrooge. But being thoroughly good-natured, and not much caring what they laughed at, so that they laughed at any rate, he encouraged them in their merriment, and passed the bottle joyously.

After tea, they had some music. For they were a musical family, and knew what they were about, when they sung a Glee or Catch, I can assure you: especially Topper, who could growl away in the bass like a good one, and never swell the large veins in his forehead, or get red in the face over it. Scrooge's niece played well upon the harp; and played among other tunes a simple little air (a mere nothing: you might learn to whistle it in two minutes), which had been familiar to the child who fetched Scrooge from the boarding-school, as he had been reminded by the Ghost of Christmas Past. When this strain of music sounded, all the things that Ghost had shown him, came upon his mind; he softened more and more; and thought that if he could have listened to it often, years ago, he might have cultivated the kindnesses of life for his own happiness with his own hands, without resorting to the sexton's spade that buried Jacob Marley.

But they didn't devote the whole evening to music. After a while they played at forfeits; for it is good to be children sometimes, and never better than at Christmas, when its mighty Founder was a child himself. Stop! There was first a game at blind-man's buff. Of course there was. And I no more believe Topper was really blind than I believe he had eyes in his boots. My opinion is, that it was a done thing between him and Scrooge's nephew; and that the Ghost of Christmas Present knew it. The way he went after that plump sister in the lace tucker, was an outrage on the credulity of human nature. Knocking down the fire-irons, tumbling over the chairs, bumping against the piano, smothering himself among the curtains, wherever she went, there went he! He always knew where the plump sister was. He wouldn't catch anybody else. If you had fallen up against him (as some of them did), on purpose, he would have made a feint of endeavouring to seize you, which would have been an affront to your understanding, and would instantly have sidled off in the direction of the plump sister. She often cried out that it wasn't fair; and it really was not. But when at last, he caught her; when, in spite of all her silken rustlings, and her rapid flutterings past him, he got her into a corner whence there was no escape; then his conduct was the most execrable. For his pretending not to know her; his pretending that it was necessary to touch her head-dress, and further to assure himself of her identity by pressing a certain ring upon her finger, and a certain chain about her neck; was vile, monstrous! No doubt she told him her opinion of it, when, another blind-man being in office, they were so very confidential together, behind the curtains.

Scrooge's niece was not one of the blind-man's buff party, but was made comfortable with a large chair and a footstool, in a snug corner, where the Ghost and Scrooge were close behind her. But she joined in the forfeits, and loved her love to admiration with all the letters of the alphabet. Likewise at the game of How, When, and Where, she was very great, and to the secret joy of Scrooge's nephew, beat her sisters hollow:[66] though they were sharp girls too, as Topper could have told you. There might have been twenty people there, young and old, but they all played, and so did Scrooge; for wholly forgetting in the interest he had in what was going on, that his voice made no sound in their ears, he sometimes came out with his guess quite loud, and very often guessed quite right, too; for the sharpest needle, best Whitechapel, warranted not to cut in the eye, was not sharper than Scrooge; blunt as he took it in his head to be.

The Ghost was greatly pleased to find him in this mood, and looked upon him with such favour, that he begged like a boy to be allowed to stay until the guests departed. But this the Spirit said could not be done.

"Here is a new game," said Scrooge. "One half hour, Spirit, only one!"

It was a Game called Yes and No,[67] where Scrooge's nephew had to think of something, and the rest must find out what; he only answering to their questions yes or no, as the case was. The brisk fire of questioning to which he was exposed, elicited from him that he was thinking of an animal, a live animal, rather a disagreeable animal, a savage animal, an animal that growled and grunted sometimes, and talked sometimes, and lived in London, and walked about the streets, and wasn't made a show of, and wasn't led by anybody, and didn't live in a menagerie,[68] and was never killed in a market, and was not a horse, or an ass, or a cow, or a bull, or a tiger, or a dog, or a pig, or a cat, or a bear. At every fresh question that was put to him, this nephew burst into a fresh roar of laughter; and was so inexpressibly tickled, that he was obliged to get up off the sofa and stamp. At last the plump sister, falling into a similar state, cried out:

"I have found it out! I know what it is, Fred! I know what it is!"

"What is it?" cried Fred.

"It's your Uncle Scro-o-o-o-oge!"

Which it certainly was. Admiration was the universal sentiment, though some objected that the reply to "Is it a bear?" ought to have been "Yes;"

---

[66] beat her sisters hollow: defeated them soundly

[67] "Yes and No" is similar to the game in our day we call "Twenty Questions."

[68] zoo

inasmuch as an answer in the negative was sufficient to have diverted their thoughts from Mr. Scrooge, supposing they had ever had any tendency that way.

"He has given us plenty of merriment, I am sure," said Fred, "and it would be ungrateful not to drink his health. Here is a glass of mulled wine ready to our hand at the moment; and I say, 'Uncle Scrooge!' "

"Well! Uncle Scrooge!" they cried.

"A Merry Christmas and a Happy New Year to the old man, whatever he is!" said Scrooge's nephew. "He wouldn't take it from me, but may he have it, nevertheless. Uncle Scrooge!"

Uncle Scrooge had imperceptibly become so gay and light of heart, that he would have pledged the unconscious company in return, and thanked them in an inaudible speech, if the Ghost had given him time. But the whole scene passed off in the breath of the last word spoken by his nephew; and he and the Spirit were again upon their travels.

Much they saw, and far they went, and many homes they visited, but always with a happy end. The Spirit stood beside sick beds, and they were cheerful; on foreign lands, and they were close at home; by struggling men, and they were patient in their greater hope; by poverty, and it was rich. In almshouse, hospital, and jail, in misery's every refuge, where vain man in his little brief authority had not made fast the door, and barred the Spirit out, he left his blessing, and taught Scrooge his precepts.[69]

It was a long night, if it were only a night; but Scrooge had his doubts of this, because the Christmas Holidays appeared to be condensed into the space of time they passed together. It was strange, too, that while Scrooge remained unaltered in his outward form, the Ghost grew older, clearly older. Scrooge had observed this change, but never spoke of it, until they left a children's Twelfth Night party, when, looking at the Spirit as they stood together in an open place, he noticed that its hair was grey.

"Are spirits' lives so short?" asked Scrooge.

"My life upon this globe, is very brief," replied the Ghost. "It ends to-night."

"To-night!" cried Scrooge.

"To-night at midnight. Hark! The time is drawing near."

The chimes were ringing the three quarters past eleven at that moment.

"Forgive me if I am not justified in what I ask," said Scrooge, looking intently at the Spirit's robe, "but I see something strange, and not belonging to yourself, protruding from your skirts. Is it a foot or a claw?"

"It might be a claw, for the flesh there is upon it," was the Spirit's sorrowful reply. "Look here."

---

[69] teachings, principles

From the foldings of its robe, it brought two children; wretched, abject, frightful, hideous, miserable. They knelt down at its feet, and clung upon the outside of its garment.

"Oh, Man! look here. Look, look, down here!" exclaimed the Ghost.

They were a boy and girl. Yellow, meagre, ragged, scowling, wolfish; but prostrate, too, in their humility. Where graceful youth should have filled their features out, and touched them with its freshest tints, a stale and shrivelled hand, like that of age, had pinched, and twisted them, and pulled them into shreds. Where angels might have sat enthroned, devils lurked, and glared out menacing. No change, no degradation, no perversion of humanity, in any grade, through all the mysteries of wonderful creation, has monsters half so horrible and dread.

Scrooge started back, appalled. Having them shown to him in this way, he tried to say they were fine children, but the words choked themselves, rather than be parties to a lie of such enormous magnitude.

"Spirit! are they yours?" Scrooge could say no more.

"They are Man's," said the Spirit, looking down upon them. "And they cling to me, appealing from their fathers. This boy is Ignorance. This girl is Want. Beware them both, and all of their degree, but most of all beware this boy, for on his brow I see that written which is Doom, unless the writing be erased. Deny it!" cried the Spirit, stretching out its hand towards the city. "Slander those who tell it ye! Admit it for your factious[70] purposes, and make it worse. And bide the end!"

"Have they no refuge or resource?" cried Scrooge.

"Are there no prisons?" said the Spirit, turning on him for the last time with his own words. "Are there no workhouses?"

The bell struck twelve.

Scrooge looked about him for the Ghost, and saw it not. As the last stroke ceased to vibrate, he remembered the prediction of old Jacob Marley, and lifting up his eyes, beheld a solemn Phantom, draped and hooded, coming, like a mist along the ground, towards him.

---

[70] divisive

Questions for Review:

1. Describe the appearance of the Ghost of Christmas Present and the room he shows Scrooge. What is the significance of these?

2. Based on the conversation between Scrooge and the Ghost of Christmas Present, what do you think Dickens believed about the practice of Sabbatarianism? Why?

3. What does the Ghost of Christmas Present tell Scrooge about Tiny Tim? What shameful words does the Ghost bring back to Scrooge?

4. Why does the Ghost of Christmas Present show Scrooge various scenes around the world?

5. Describe the boy and girl who are revealed under the robe of the Ghost of Christmas Present. How does their presence affect Scrooge? How does the Ghost of Christmas Present use his own words against him?

6. Give some more evidence that Scrooge is softening even more.

Stave Four: The Last of the Spirits

The Phantom slowly, gravely, silently, approached. When it came near him, Scrooge bent down upon his knee; for in the very air through which this Spirit moved it seemed to scatter gloom and mystery.

It was shrouded in a deep black garment, which concealed its head, its face, its form, and left nothing of it visible save one outstretched hand. But for this it would have been difficult to detach its figure from the night, and separate it from the darkness by which it was surrounded.

He felt that it was tall and stately when it came beside him, and that its mysterious presence filled him with a solemn dread. He knew no more, for the Spirit neither spoke nor moved.

"I am in the presence of the Ghost of Christmas Yet To Come?" said Scrooge.

The Spirit answered not, but pointed onward with its hand.

"You are about to show me shadows of the things that have not happened, but will happen in the time before us," Scrooge pursued. "Is that so, Spirit?"

The upper portion of the garment was contracted for an instant in its folds, as if the Spirit had inclined its head. That was the only answer he received.

Although well used to ghostly company by this time, Scrooge feared the silent shape so much that his legs trembled beneath him, and he found that he could hardly stand when he prepared to follow it. The Spirit paused a moment, as observing his condition, and giving him time to recover.

But Scrooge was all the worse for this. It thrilled him with a vague uncertain horror, to know that behind the dusky shroud, there were ghostly eyes intently fixed upon him, while he, though he stretched his own to the utmost, could see nothing but a spectral hand and one great heap of black.

"Ghost of the Future!" he exclaimed, "I fear you more than any spectre I have seen. But as I know your purpose is to do me good, and as I hope to live to be another man from what I was, I am prepared to bear you company, and do it with a thankful heart. Will you not speak to me?"

It gave him no reply. The hand was pointed straight before them.

"Lead on!" said Scrooge. "Lead on! The night is waning fast, and it is precious time to me, I know. Lead on, Spirit!"

The Phantom moved away as it had come towards him. Scrooge followed in the shadow of its dress, which bore him up, he thought, and carried him along.

They scarcely seemed to enter the city; for the city rather seemed to spring up about them, and encompass them of its own act. But there they were, in the heart of it; on 'Change, amongst the merchants; who hurried up and down, and chinked the money in their pockets, and conversed in groups, and looked at their watches, and trifled thoughtfully with their great gold seals; and so forth, as Scrooge had seen them often.

The Spirit stopped beside one little knot of business men. Observing that the hand was pointed to them, Scrooge advanced to listen to their talk.

"No," said a great fat man with a monstrous chin, "I don't know much about it, either way. I only know he's dead."

"When did he die?" inquired another.

"Last night, I believe."

"Why, what was the matter with him?" asked a third, taking a vast quantity of snuff out of a very large snuff-box. "I thought he'd never die."

"Heaven knows," said the first, with a yawn.

"What has he done with his money?" asked a red-faced gentleman with a pendulous excrescence[71] on the end of his nose, that shook like the gills of a turkey-cock.

"I haven't heard," said the man with the large chin, yawning again. "Left it to his company, perhaps. He hasn't left it to *me*. That's all I know."

This pleasantry was received with a general laugh.

---

[71] pendulous excrescence: hanging growth

"It's likely to be a very cheap funeral," said the same speaker; "for upon my life I don't know of anybody to go to it. Suppose we make up a party and volunteer?"

"I don't mind going if a lunch is provided," observed the gentleman with the excrescence on his nose. "But I must be fed, if I make one."

Another laugh.

"Well, I am the most disinterested among you, after all," said the first speaker, "for I never wear black gloves, and I never eat lunch. But I'll offer to go, if anybody else will. When I come to think of it, I'm not at all sure that I wasn't his most particular friend; for we used to stop and speak whenever we met. Bye, bye!"

Speakers and listeners strolled away, and mixed with other groups. Scrooge knew the men, and looked towards the Spirit for an explanation.

The Phantom glided on into a street. Its finger pointed to two persons meeting. Scrooge listened again, thinking that the explanation might lie here.

He knew these men, also, perfectly. They were men of business: very wealthy, and of great importance. He had made a point always of standing well in their esteem: in a business point of view, that is; strictly in a business point of view.

"How are you?" said one.

"How are you?" returned the other.

"Well!" said the first. "Old Scratch[72] has got his own at last, hey?"

"So I am told," returned the second. "Cold, isn't it?"

"Seasonable for Christmas time. You're not a skater, I suppose?"

"No. No. Something else to think of. Good morning!"

Not another word. That was their meeting, their conversation, and their parting.

Scrooge was at first inclined to be surprised that the Spirit should attach importance to conversations apparently so trivial; but feeling assured that they must have some hidden purpose, he set himself to consider what it was likely to be. They could scarcely be supposed to have any bearing on the death of Jacob, his old partner, for that was Past, and this Ghost's province was the Future. Nor could he think of any one immediately connected with himself, to whom he could apply them. But nothing doubting that to whomsoever they applied they had some latent[73] moral for his own improvement, he resolved to treasure up every word he heard, and everything he saw; and especially to observe the shadow of himself when it appeared. For he had

---

[72] that is, the devil
[73] concealed, not yet revealed

an expectation that the conduct of his future self would give him the clue he missed, and would render the solution of these riddles easy.

He looked about in that very place for his own image; but another man stood in his accustomed corner, and though the clock pointed to his usual time of day for being there, he saw no likeness of himself among the multitudes that poured in through the Porch. It gave him little surprise, however; for he had been revolving in his mind a change of life, and thought and hoped he saw his new-born resolutions carried out in this.

Quiet and dark, beside him stood the Phantom, with its outstretched hand. When he roused himself from his thoughtful quest, he fancied from the turn of the hand, and its situation in reference to himself, that the Unseen Eyes were looking at him keenly. It made him shudder, and feel very cold.

They left the busy scene, and went into an obscure part of the town, where Scrooge had never penetrated before, although he recognised its situation, and its bad repute. The ways were foul and narrow; the shops and houses wretched; the people half-naked, drunken, slipshod, ugly. Alleys and archways, like so many cesspools, disgorged their offences of smell, and dirt, and life, upon the straggling streets; and the whole quarter reeked with crime, with filth, and misery.

Far in this den of infamous resort, there was a low-browed, beetling shop, below a pent-house roof, where iron, old rags, bottles, bones, and greasy offal,[74] were bought. Upon the floor within, were piled up heaps of rusty keys, nails, chains, hinges, files, scales, weights, and refuse iron of all kinds. Secrets that few would like to scrutinise were bred and hidden in mountains of unseemly rags, masses of corrupted fat, and sepulchres of bones. Sitting in among the wares he dealt in, by a charcoal stove, made of old bricks, was a grey-haired rascal, nearly seventy years of age; who had screened himself from the cold air without, by a frousy[75] curtaining of miscellaneous tatters, hung upon a line; and smoked his pipe in all the luxury of calm retirement.

Scrooge and the Phantom came into the presence of this man, just as a woman with a heavy bundle slunk into the shop. But she had scarcely entered, when another woman, similarly laden, came in too; and she was closely followed by a man in faded black, who was no less startled by the sight of them, than they had been upon the recognition of each other. After a short period of blank astonishment, in which the old man with the pipe had joined them, they all three burst into a laugh.

"Let the charwoman[76] alone to be the first!" cried she who had entered first. "Let the laundress alone to be the second; and let the undertaker's man

---

[74] garbage, or possibly waste from a butchered animal
[75] dirty, neglected
[76] maid

alone to be the third. Look here, old Joe, here's a chance! If we haven't all three met here without meaning it!"

"You couldn't have met in a better place," said old Joe, removing his pipe from his mouth. "Come into the parlour. You were made free of it long ago, you know; and the other two an't strangers. Stop till I shut the door of the shop. Ah! How it skreeks! There an't such a rusty bit of metal in the place as its own hinges, I believe; and I'm sure there's no such old bones here, as mine. Ha, ha! We're all suitable to our calling, we're well matched. Come into the parlour. Come into the parlour."

The parlour was the space behind the screen of rags. The old man raked the fire together with an old stair-rod, and having trimmed his smoky lamp (for it was night), with the stem of his pipe, put it in his mouth again.

While he did this, the woman who had already spoken threw her bundle on the floor, and sat down in a flaunting manner on a stool; crossing her elbows on her knees, and looking with a bold defiance at the other two.

"What odds then! What odds, Mrs. Dilber?" said the woman. "Every person has a right to take care of themselves. *He* always did."

"That's true, indeed!" said the laundress. "No man more so."

"Why then, don't stand staring as if you was afraid, woman; who's the wiser? We're not going to pick holes in each other's coats, I suppose?"

"No, indeed!" said Mrs. Dilber and the man together. "We should hope not."

"Very well, then!" cried the woman. "That's enough. Who's the worse for the loss of a few things like these? Not a dead man, I suppose."

"No, indeed," said Mrs. Dilber, laughing.

"If he wanted to keep 'em after he was dead, a wicked old screw," pursued the woman, "why wasn't he natural in his lifetime? If he had been, he'd have had somebody to look after him when he was struck with Death, instead of lying gasping out his last there, alone by himself."

"It's the truest word that ever was spoke," said Mrs. Dilber. "It's a judgment on him."

"I wish it was a little heavier judgment," replied the woman; "and it should have been, you may depend upon it, if I could have laid my hands on anything else. Open that bundle, old Joe, and let me know the value of it. Speak out plain. I'm not afraid to be the first, nor afraid for them to see it. We know pretty well that we were helping ourselves, before we met here, I believe. It's no sin. Open the bundle, Joe."

But the gallantry of her friends would not allow of this; and the man in faded black, mounting the breach first, produced *his* plunder. It was not extensive. A seal or two, a pencil-case, a pair of sleeve-buttons, and a brooch of no great value, were all. They were severally examined and appraised by old Joe, who chalked the sums he was disposed to give for each, upon the wall, and added them up into a total when he found there was nothing more to come.

"That's your account," said Joe, "and I wouldn't give another sixpence, if I was to be boiled for not doing it. Who's next?"

Mrs. Dilber was next. Sheets and towels, a little wearing apparel, two old-fashioned silver teaspoons, a pair of sugar-tongs, and a few boots. Her account was stated on the wall in the same manner.

"I always give too much to ladies. It's a weakness of mine, and that's the way I ruin myself," said old Joe. "That's your account. If you asked me for another penny, and made it an open question, I'd repent of being so liberal and knock off half-a-crown."

"And now undo *my* bundle, Joe," said the first woman.

Joe went down on his knees for the greater convenience of opening it, and having unfastened a great many knots, dragged out a large and heavy roll of some dark stuff.

"What do you call this?" said Joe. "Bed-curtains!"

"Ah!" returned the woman, laughing and leaning forward on her crossed arms. "Bed-curtains!"

"You don't mean to say you took 'em down, rings and all, with him lying there?" said Joe.

"Yes I do," replied the woman. "Why not?"

"You were born to make your fortune," said Joe, "and you'll certainly do it."

"I certainly shan't hold my hand, when I can get anything in it by reaching it out, for the sake of such a man as He was, I promise you, Joe," returned the woman coolly. "Don't drop that oil upon the blankets, now."

"His blankets?" asked Joe.

"Whose else's do you think?" replied the woman. "He isn't likely to take cold without 'em, I dare say."

"I hope he didn't die of anything catching? Eh?" said old Joe, stopping in his work, and looking up.

"Don't you be afraid of that," returned the woman. "I an't so fond of his company that I'd loiter about him for such things, if he did. Ah! you may look through that shirt till your eyes ache; but you won't find a hole in it, nor a threadbare place. It's the best he had, and a fine one too. They'd have wasted it, if it hadn't been for me."

"What do you call wasting of it?" asked old Joe.

"Putting it on him to be buried in, to be sure," replied the woman with a laugh. "Somebody was fool enough to do it, but I took it off again. If calico an't good enough for such a purpose, it isn't good enough for anything. It's quite as becoming to the body. He can't look uglier than he did in that one."

Scrooge listened to this dialogue in horror. As they sat grouped about their spoil, in the scanty light afforded by the old man's lamp, he viewed them with a detestation and disgust, which could hardly have been greater, though they had been obscene demons, marketing the corpse itself.

"Ha, ha!" laughed the same woman, when old Joe, producing a flannel bag with money in it, told out their several gains upon the ground. "This is the end of it, you see! He frightened every one away from him when he was alive, to profit us when he was dead! Ha, ha, ha!"

"Spirit!" said Scrooge, shuddering from head to foot. "I see, I see. The case of this unhappy man might be my own. My life tends that way, now. Merciful Heaven, what is this!"

He recoiled in terror, for the scene had changed, and now he almost touched a bed: a bare, uncurtained bed: on which, beneath a ragged sheet, there lay a something covered up, which, though it was dumb, announced itself in awful language.

The room was very dark, too dark to be observed with any accuracy, though Scrooge glanced round it in obedience to a secret impulse, anxious to know what kind of room it was. A pale light, rising in the outer air, fell straight upon the bed; and on it, plundered and bereft, unwatched, unwept, uncared for, was the body of this man.

Scrooge glanced towards the Phantom. Its steady hand was pointed to the head. The cover was so carelessly adjusted that the slightest raising of it, the motion of a finger upon Scrooge's part, would have disclosed the face. He thought of it, felt how easy it would be to do, and longed to do it; but had no more power to withdraw the veil than to dismiss the spectre at his side.

Oh cold, cold, rigid, dreadful Death, set up thine altar here, and dress it with such terrors as thou hast at thy command: for this is thy dominion! But of the loved, revered, and honoured head, thou canst not turn one hair to thy dread purposes, or make one feature odious. It is not that the hand is heavy and will fall down when released; it is not that the heart and pulse are still; but that the hand was open, generous, and true; the heart brave, warm, and tender; and the pulse a man's. Strike, Shadow, strike! And see his good deeds springing from the wound, to sow the world with life immortal!

No voice pronounced these words in Scrooge's ears, and yet he heard them when he looked upon the bed. He thought, if this man could be raised up now, what would be his foremost thoughts? Avarice, hard-dealing, griping cares? They have brought him to a rich end, truly!

He lay, in the dark empty house, with not a man, a woman, or a child, to say that he was kind to me in this or that, and for the memory of one kind word I will be kind to him. A cat was tearing at the door, and there was a sound of gnawing rats beneath the hearth-stone. What *they* wanted in the room of death, and why they were so restless and disturbed, Scrooge did not dare to think.

"Spirit!" he said, "this is a fearful place. In leaving it, I shall not leave its lesson, trust me. Let us go!"

Still the Ghost pointed with an unmoved finger to the head.

"I understand you," Scrooge returned, "and I would do it, if I could. But I have not the power, Spirit. I have not the power."

Again it seemed to look upon him.

"If there is any person in the town, who feels emotion caused by this man's death," said Scrooge quite agonised, "show that person to me, Spirit, I beseech you!"

The Phantom spread its dark robe before him for a moment, like a wing; and withdrawing it, revealed a room by daylight, where a mother and her children were.

She was expecting some one, and with anxious eagerness; for she walked up and down the room; started at every sound; looked out from the window; glanced at the clock; tried, but in vain, to work with her needle; and could hardly bear the voices of the children in their play.

At length the long-expected knock was heard. She hurried to the door, and met her husband; a man whose face was careworn and depressed, though he was young. There was a remarkable expression in it now; a kind of serious delight of which he felt ashamed, and which he struggled to re-press.

He sat down to the dinner that had been hoarding for him by the fire; and when she asked him faintly what news (which was not until after a long silence), he appeared embarrassed how to answer.

"Is it good?" she said, "or bad?"—to help him.

"Bad," he answered.

"We are quite ruined?"

"No. There is hope yet, Caroline."

"If *he* relents," she said, amazed, "there is! Nothing is past hope, if such a miracle has happened."

"He is past relenting," said her husband. "He is dead."

She was a mild and patient creature if her face spoke truth; but she was thankful in her soul to hear it, and she said so, with clasped hands. She prayed forgiveness the next moment, and was sorry; but the first was the emotion of her heart.

"What the half-drunken woman whom I told you of last night, said to me, when I tried to see him and obtain a week's delay; and what I thought was a mere excuse to avoid me; turns out to have been quite true. He was not only very ill, but dying, then."

"To whom will our debt be transferred?"

"I don't know. But before that time we shall be ready with the money; and even though we were not, it would be a bad fortune indeed to find so merciless a creditor in his successor. We may sleep to-night with light hearts, Caroline!"

Yes. Soften it as they would, their hearts were lighter. The children's faces, hushed and clustered round to hear what they so little understood, were brighter; and it was a happier house for this man's death! The only emotion that the Ghost could show him, caused by the event, was one of pleasure.

"Let me see some tenderness connected with a death," said Scrooge; "or that dark chamber, Spirit, which we left just now, will be for ever present to me."

The Ghost conducted him through several streets familiar to his feet; and as they went along, Scrooge looked here and there to find himself, but nowhere was he to be seen. They entered poor Bob Cratchit's house; the dwelling he had visited before; and found the mother and the children seated round the fire.

Quiet. Very quiet. The noisy little Cratchits were as still as statues in one corner, and sat looking up at Peter, who had a book before him. The mother and her daughters were engaged in sewing. But surely they were very quiet!

"'And He took a child, and set him in the midst of them.'"[77]

Where had Scrooge heard those words? He had not dreamed them. The boy must have read them out, as he and the Spirit crossed the threshold. Why did he not go on?

The mother laid her work upon the table, and put her hand up to her face.

"The colour hurts my eyes," she said.

The colour? Ah, poor Tiny Tim!

"They're better now again," said Cratchit's wife. "It makes them weak by candle-light; and I wouldn't show weak eyes to your father when he comes home, for the world. It must be near his time."

"Past it rather," Peter answered, shutting up his book. "But I think he has walked a little slower than he used, these few last evenings, mother."

They were very quiet again. At last she said, and in a steady, cheerful voice, that only faltered once:

"I have known him walk with—I have known him walk with Tiny Tim upon his shoulder, very fast indeed."

"And so have I," cried Peter. "Often."

"And so have I," exclaimed another. So had all.

---

[77] See Mark 9:33-37.

"But he was very light to carry," she resumed, intent upon her work, "and his father loved him so, that it was no trouble: no trouble. And there is your father at the door!"

She hurried out to meet him; and little Bob in his comforter—he had need of it, poor fellow—came in. His tea was ready for him on the hob, and they all tried who should help him to it most. Then the two young Cratchits got upon his knees and laid, each child a little cheek, against his face, as if they said, "Don't mind it, father. Don't be grieved!"

Bob was very cheerful with them, and spoke pleasantly to all the family. He looked at the work upon the table, and praised the industry and speed of Mrs. Cratchit and the girls. They would be done long before Sunday, he said.

"Sunday! You went to-day, then, Robert?" said his wife.

"Yes, my dear," returned Bob. "I wish you could have gone. It would have done you good to see how green a place it is. But you'll see it often. I promised him that I would walk there on a Sunday. My little, little child!" cried Bob. "My little child!"

He broke down all at once. He couldn't help it. If he could have helped it, he and his child would have been farther apart perhaps than they were.

He left the room, and went up-stairs into the room above, which was lighted cheerfully, and hung with Christmas. There was a chair set close beside the child, and there were signs of some one having been there, lately. Poor Bob sat down in it, and when he had thought a little and composed himself, he kissed the little face. He was reconciled to what had happened, and went down again quite happy.

They drew about the fire, and talked; the girls and mother working still. Bob told them of the extraordinary kindness of Mr. Scrooge's nephew, whom he had scarcely seen but once, and who, meeting him in the street that day, and seeing that he looked a little—"just a little down you know," said Bob, inquired what had happened to distress him. "On which," said Bob, "for he is the pleasantest-spoken gentleman you ever heard, I told him. 'I am heartily sorry for it, Mr. Cratchit,' he said, 'and heartily sorry for your good wife.' By the bye, how he ever knew *that*, I don't know."

"Knew what, my dear?"

"Why, that you were a good wife," replied Bob.

"Everybody knows that!" said Peter.

"Very well observed, my boy!" cried Bob. "I hope they do. 'Heartily sorry,' he said, 'for your good wife. If I can be of service to you in any way,' he said, giving me his card, 'that's where I live. Pray come to me.' Now, it wasn't," cried Bob, "for the sake of anything he might be able to do for us, so much as for his kind way, that this was quite delightful. It really seemed as if he had known our Tiny Tim, and felt with us."

"I'm sure he's a good soul!" said Mrs. Cratchit.

"You would be surer of it, my dear," returned Bob, "if you saw and spoke to him. I shouldn't be at all surprised—mark what I say!—if he got Peter a better situation."

"Only hear that, Peter," said Mrs. Cratchit.

"And then," cried one of the girls, "Peter will be keeping company with some one, and setting up for himself."

"Get along with you!" retorted Peter, grinning.

"It's just as likely as not," said Bob, "one of these days; though there's plenty of time for that, my dear. But however and whenever we part from one another, I am sure we shall none of us forget poor Tiny Tim—shall we—or this first parting that there was among us?"

"Never, father!" cried they all.

"And I know," said Bob, "I know, my dears, that when we recollect how patient and how mild he was; although he was a little, little child; we shall not quarrel easily among ourselves, and forget poor Tiny Tim in doing it."

"No, never, father!" they all cried again.

"I am very happy," said little Bob, "I am very happy!"

Mrs. Cratchit kissed him, his daughters kissed him, the two young Cratchits kissed him, and Peter and himself shook hands. Spirit of Tiny Tim, thy childish essence was from God!

"Spectre," said Scrooge, "something informs me that our parting moment is at hand. I know it, but I know not how. Tell me what man that was whom we saw lying dead?"

The Ghost of Christmas Yet To Come conveyed him, as before—though at a different time, he thought: indeed, there seemed no order in these latter visions, save that they were in the Future—into the resorts of business men, but showed him not himself. Indeed, the Spirit did not stay for anything, but went straight on, as to the end just now desired, until besought by Scrooge to tarry for a moment.

"This court," said Scrooge, "through which we hurry now, is where my place of occupation is, and has been for a length of time. I see the house. Let me behold what I shall be, in days to come!"

The Spirit stopped; the hand was pointed elsewhere.

"The house is yonder," Scrooge exclaimed. "Why do you point away?"

The inexorable[78] finger underwent no change.

Scrooge hastened to the window of his office, and looked in. It was an office still, but not his. The furniture was not the same, and the figure in the chair was not himself. The Phantom pointed as before.

---

[78] unchangeable, relentless

He joined it once again, and wondering why and whither he had gone, accompanied it until they reached an iron gate. He paused to look round before entering.

A churchyard. Here, then; the wretched man whose name he had now to learn, lay underneath the ground. It was a worthy place. Walled in by houses; overrun by grass and weeds, the growth of vegetation's death, not life; choked up with too much burying; fat with repleted appetite. A worthy place!

The Spirit stood among the graves, and pointed down to One. He advanced towards it trembling. The Phantom was exactly as it had been, but he dreaded that he saw new meaning in its solemn shape.

"Before I draw nearer to that stone to which you point," said Scrooge, "answer me one question. Are these the shadows of the things that Will be, or are they shadows of things that May be, only?"

Still the Ghost pointed down-ward to the grave by which it stood.

"Men's courses will foreshadow certain ends, to which, if persevered in, they must lead," said Scrooge. "But if the courses be departed from, the ends will change. Say it is thus with what you show me!"

The Spirit was immovable as ever.

Scrooge crept towards it, trembling as he went; and following the finger, read upon the stone of the neglected grave his own name, EBENEZER SCROOGE.

"Am *I* that man who lay upon the bed?" he cried, upon his knees.

The finger pointed from the grave to him, and back again.

"No, Spirit! Oh no, no!"

The finger still was there.

"Spirit!" he cried, tight clutch-ing at its robe, "hear me! I am not the man I was. I will not be the man I must have been but for this intercourse. Why show me this, if I am past all hope!"

For the first time the hand appeared to shake.

"Good Spirit," he pursued, as down upon the ground he fell before it: "Your nature intercedes for me, and pities me. Assure me that I yet may change these shadows you have shown me, by an altered life!"

The kind hand trembled.

"I will honour Christmas in my heart, and try to keep it all the year. I will live in the Past, the Present, and the Future. The Spirits of all Three shall strive within me. I will not shut out the lessons that they teach. Oh, tell me I may sponge away the writing on this stone!"

In his agony, he caught the spectral hand. It sought to free itself, but he was strong in his entreaty, and detained it. The Spirit, stronger yet, repulsed him.

Holding up his hands in a last prayer to have his fate reversed, he saw an alteration in the Phantom's hood and dress. It shrunk, collapsed, and dwindled down into a bedpost.

Questions for Review:

1. How is the Ghost of Things Yet to Come different in appearance and behavior than the previous two ghosts?

2. How does the men's reaction toward their dead colleague mirror Scrooge's behavior at a previous point in *A Christmas Carol*?

3. What does Scrooge ask the Ghost of Things Yet to Come to show him? What does the ghost show him?

Stave Five: The End of It

Yes! and the bedpost was his own. The bed was his own, the room was his own. Best and happiest of all, the Time before him was his own, to make amends in!

"I will live in the Past, the Present, and the Future!" Scrooge repeated, as he scrambled out of bed. "The Spirits of all Three shall strive within me. Oh Jacob Marley! Heaven, and the Christmas Time be praised for this! I say it on my knees, old Jacob; on my knees!"

He was so fluttered and so glowing with his good intentions, that his broken voice would scarcely answer to his call. He had been sobbing violently in his conflict with the Spirit, and his face was wet with tears.

"They are not torn down," cried Scrooge, folding one of his bed-curtains in his arms, "they are not torn down, rings and all. They are here—I am here—the shadows of the things that would have been, may be dispelled. They will be. I know they will!"

His hands were busy with his garments all this time; turning them inside out, putting them on upside down, tearing them, mislaying them, making them parties to every kind of extravagance.

"I don't know what to do!" cried Scrooge, laughing and crying in the same breath; and making a perfect Laocoön of himself with his stockings.[79] "I am as light as a feather, I am as happy as an angel, I am as merry as a schoolboy. I am as giddy as a drunken man. A merry Christmas to everybody! A happy New Year to all the world. Hallo here! Whoop! Hallo!"

He had frisked into the sitting-room, and was now standing there: perfectly winded.

"There's the saucepan that the gruel was in!" cried Scrooge, starting off again, and going round the fireplace. "There's the door, by which the Ghost of Jacob Marley entered! There's the corner where the Ghost of Christmas Present, sat! There's the window where I saw the wandering Spirits! It's all right, it's all true, it all happened. Ha ha ha!"

Really, for a man who had been out of practice for so many years, it was a splendid laugh, a most illustrious laugh. The father of a long, long line of brilliant laughs!

"I don't know what day of the month it is!" said Scrooge. "I don't know how long I've been among the Spirits. I don't know anything. I'm quite a baby. Never mind. I don't care. I'd rather be a baby. Hallo! Whoop! Hallo here!"

He was checked in his transports by the churches ringing out the lustiest peals he had ever heard. Clash, clang, hammer; ding, dong, bell. Bell, dong, ding; hammer, clang, clash! Oh, glorious, glorious!

Running to the window, he opened it, and put out his head. No fog, no mist; clear, bright, jovial, stirring, cold; cold, piping for the blood to dance to; Golden sunlight; Heavenly sky; sweet fresh air; merry bells. Oh, glorious! Glorious!

"What's to-day!" cried Scrooge, calling downward to a boy in Sunday clothes, who perhaps had loitered in to look about him.

"Eh?" returned the boy, with all his might of wonder.

"What's to-day, my fine fellow?" said Scrooge.

"To-day!" replied the boy. "Why, Christmas Day."

"It's Christmas Day!" said Scrooge to himself. "I haven't missed it. The Spirits have done it all in one night. They can do anything they like. Of course they can. Of course they can. Hallo, my fine fellow!"

"Hallo!" returned the boy.

"Do you know the Poulterer's, in the next street but one, at the corner?" Scrooge inquired.

"I should hope I did," replied the lad.

---

[79] In Greek mythology, Laocoön was killed by Poseidon, who sent two snakes against him. Here Dickens is comparing Scrooge's two stockings to the pair of snakes.

"An intelligent boy!" said Scrooge. "A remarkable boy! Do you know whether they've sold the prize Turkey that was hanging up there? —Not the little prize Turkey: the big one?"

"What, the one as big as me?" returned the boy.

"What a delightful boy!" said Scrooge. "It's a pleasure to talk to him. Yes, my buck!"

"It's hanging there now," replied the boy.

"Is it?" said Scrooge. "Go and buy it."

"Walk-er!"[80] exclaimed the boy.

"No, no," said Scrooge, "I am in earnest. Go and buy it, and tell 'em to bring it here, that I may give them the direction where to take it. Come back with the man, and I'll give you a shilling. Come back with him in less than five minutes and I'll give you half-a-crown!"

The boy was off like a shot. He must have had a steady hand at a trigger who could have got a shot off half so fast.

"I'll send it to Bob Cratchit's!" whispered Scrooge, rubbing his hands, and splitting with a laugh. "He sha'n't know who sends it. It's twice the size of Tiny Tim. Joe Miller never made such a joke as sending it to Bob's will be!"[81]

The hand in which he wrote the address was not a steady one, but write it he did, somehow, and went down-stairs to open the street door, ready for the coming of the poulterer's man. As he stood there, waiting his arrival, the knocker caught his eye.

"I shall love it, as long as I live!" cried Scrooge, patting it with his hand. "I scarcely ever looked at it before. What an honest expression it has in its face! It's a wonderful knocker!—Here's the Turkey! Hallo! Whoop! How are you! Merry Christmas!"

It *was* a Turkey! He never could have stood upon his legs, that bird. He would have snapped 'em short off in a minute, like sticks of sealing-wax.

"Why, it's impossible to carry that to Camden Town," said Scrooge. "You must have a cab."

The chuckle with which he said this, and the chuckle with which he paid for the Turkey, and the chuckle with which he paid for the cab, and the chuckle with which he recompensed the boy, were only to be exceeded by the chuckle with which he sat down breathless in his chair again, and chuckled till he cried.

Shaving was not an easy task, for his hand continued to shake very much; and shaving requires attention, even when you don't dance while you are at

---

[80] a sarcastic or mocking expression similar to today's phrase, "Yeah, *right!*"
[81] Joe Miller: a joke that is not very funny

it. But if he had cut the end of his nose off, he would have put a piece of sticking-plaister over it, and been quite satisfied.

He dressed himself "all in his best," and at last got out into the streets. The people were by this time pouring forth, as he had seen them with the Ghost of Christmas Present; and walking with his hands behind him, Scrooge regarded every one with a delighted smile. He looked so irresistibly pleasant, in a word, that three or four good-humoured fellows said, "Good morning, sir! A merry Christmas to you!" And Scrooge said often afterwards, that of all the blithe sounds he had ever heard, those were the blithest in his ears.

He had not gone far, when coming on towards him he beheld the portly gentleman, who had walked into his counting-house the day before, and said, "Scrooge and Marley's, I believe?" It sent a pang across his heart to think how this old gentleman would look upon him when they met; but he knew what path lay straight before him, and he took it.

"My dear sir," said Scrooge, quickening his pace, and taking the old gentleman by both his hands. "How do you do? I hope you succeeded yesterday. It was very kind of you. A merry Christmas to you, sir!"

"Mr. Scrooge?"

"Yes," said Scrooge. "That is my name, and I fear it may not be pleasant to you. Allow me to ask your pardon. And will you have the goodness"—here Scrooge whispered in his ear.

"Lord bless me!" cried the gentleman, as if his breath were taken away. "My dear Mr. Scrooge, are you serious?"

"If you please," said Scrooge. "Not a farthing less. A great many back-payments are included in it, I assure you. Will you do me that favour?"

My dear sir," said the other, shaking hands with him. "I don't know what to say to such munifi—"[82]

"Don't say anything, please," retorted Scrooge. "Come and see me. Will you come and see me?"

"I will!" cried the old gentleman. And it was clear he meant to do it.

"Thank'ee," said Scrooge. "I am much obliged to you. I thank you fifty times. Bless you!"

He went to church, and walked about the streets, and watched the people hurrying to and fro, and patted children on the head, and questioned beggars, and looked down into the kitchens of houses, and up to the windows, and found that everything could yield him pleasure. He had never dreamed that any walk—that anything—could give him so much happiness. In the afternoon he turned his steps towards his nephew's house.

---

[82] The gentleman is doubtless starting to say "munificence," or generosity.

He passed the door a dozen times, before he had the courage to go up and knock. But he made a dash, and did it:

"Is your master at home, my dear?" said Scrooge to the girl. Nice girl! Very.

"Yes, sir."

"Where is he, my love?" said Scrooge.

"He's in the dining-room, sir, along with mistress. I'll show you up-stairs, if you please."

"Thank'ee. He knows me," said Scrooge, with his hand already on the dining-room lock. "I'll go in here, my dear."

He turned it gently, and sidled his face in, round the door. They were looking at the table (which was spread out in great array); for these young housekeepers are always nervous on such points, and like to see that every-thing is right.

"Fred!" said Scrooge.

Dear heart alive, how his niece by marriage started! Scrooge had for-gotten, for the moment, about her sitting in the corner with the foot-stool, or he wouldn't have done it, on any account.

"Why bless my soul!" cried Fred, "who's that?"

"It's I. Your uncle Scrooge. I have come to dinner. Will you let me in, Fred?"

Let him in! It is a mercy he didn't shake his arm off. He was at home in five minutes. Nothing could be heartier. His niece looked just the same. So did Topper when *he* came. So did the plump sister when *she* came. So did every one when *they* came. Wonderful party, wonderful games, wonderful unanimity, wonderful happiness!

But he was early at the office next morning. Oh, he was early there. If he could only be there first, and catch Bob Cratchit coming late! That was the thing he had set his heart upon.

And he did it; yes, he did! The clock struck nine. No Bob. A quarter past. No Bob. He was full eighteen minutes and a half behind his time. Scrooge sat with his door wide open, that he might see him come into the Tank.

His hat was off, before he opened the door; his comforter too. He was on his stool in a jiffy; driving away with his pen, as if he were trying to overtake nine o'clock.

"Hallo!" growled Scrooge, in his accustomed voice, as near as he could feign it. "What do you mean by coming here at this time of day?"

"I am very sorry, sir," said Bob. "I *am* behind my time."

"You are?" repeated Scrooge. "Yes. I think you are. Step this way, sir, if you please."

"It's only once a year, sir," pleaded Bob, appearing from the Tank. "It shall not be repeated. I was making rather merry yesterday, sir."

"Now, I'll tell you what, my friend," said Scrooge, "I am not going to stand this sort of thing any longer. And therefore," he continued, leaping from his stool, and giving Bob such a dig in the waistcoat that he staggered back into the Tank again; "and therefore I am about to raise your salary!"

Bob trembled, and got a little nearer to the ruler. He had a momentary idea of knocking Scrooge down with it, holding him, and calling to the people in the court for help and a strait-waistcoat.[83]

"A merry Christmas, Bob!" said Scrooge, with an earnestness that could not be mistaken, as he clapped him on the back. "A merrier Christmas, Bob, my good fellow, than I have given you, for many a year! I'll raise your salary, and endeavour to assist your struggling family, and we will discuss your affairs this very afternoon, over a Christmas bowl of smoking bishop, Bob! Make up the

fires, and buy another coal-scuttle before you dot another i, Bob Cratchit!"

Scrooge was better than his word. He did it all, and infinitely more; and to Tiny Tim, who did not die, he was a second father. He became as good a friend, as good a master, and as good a man, as the good old city knew, or any other good old city, town, or borough, in the good old world. Some people laughed to see the alteration in him, but he let them laugh, and little heeded them; for he was wise enough to know that nothing ever happened on this globe, for good, at which some people did not have their fill of laughter in the outset; and knowing that such as these would be blind anyway, he thought it quite as well that they should wrinkle up their eyes in grins, as have the malady[84] in less attractive forms. His own heart laughed: and that was quite enough for him.

---

[83] strait-waistcoat: a straitjacket to wrap around an insane person
[84] sickness, trouble

He had no further intercourse with Spirits, but lived upon the Total Abstinence Principle,[85] ever afterwards; and it was always said of him, that he knew how to keep Christmas well, if any man alive possessed the knowledge. May that be truly said of us, and all of us! And so, as Tiny Tim observed, God bless Us, Every One!

Questions for Review:

1. Describe Scrooge's Christmas Day.

2. What happens the next day at Scrooge's office? How is the tale resolved?

---

[85] Total Abstinence Principle: the complete avoidance of all alcoholic beverages (or "spirits"). Dickens is making a little joke here by using the word "Spirits," which can refer to alcohol.

ROBINSON CRUSOE

By Daniel Defoe

Introduction

The virtues of *Robinson Crusoe* are exhausting to list. It is considered by many as the first novel written in the English language, and it is believed to be one of the first examples—maybe *the* first example—of realistic fiction. (It is so realistic that a great number of readers initially believed author Daniel Defoe had really been shipwrecked and simply recorded his real-life events.) The book has, for the last 300 years, been ranked with the world's greatest pieces of literature, inspiring many other important masterpieces such as *Gulliver's Travels*, *Treasure Island*, *Swiss Family Robinson*, and *Gilligan's Island*.

Well, maybe not that last one.

First published in 1719 by Defoe, an English author, *Robinson Crusoe* is a classic, in the very best case of the word. That is, it's one of the "classics" that you don't have to dread plowing through, like a pile of pickled beets on a dinner plate, because someone thought it would be "good for you." When I was in school, for example, and an English teacher announced, "Class, for the next few weeks we'll be reading a *classic!*" she got the same reaction she would have heard if she had said, for example, "Class, for the next few weeks we'll be eating shards of broken glass!" Happily, *Robinson Crusoe* doesn't fall into *that* category of "classic." It entertains, provides suspense, and piles on the action until its satisfying conclusion.

American author Edgar Allan Poe famously praised Defoe's novel this way:

> Not one person in ten—nay, not one person in five hundred, has, during the perusal [careful reading] of *Robinson Crusoe*, the most remote conception that any particle of genius, or even of common talent, has been employed in its creation! Men do not look upon it in the light of a literary performance. Defoe has none of their thoughts—Robinson all.

Even more importantly, *Robinson Crusoe* teaches great moral lessons and greatly emphasizes the Christian virtues of honesty, self-control, justice, and trust in God. It is one of the most profoundly Christian classic novels ever written, with the gospel message vividly and touchingly proclaimed and evident in the lives of characters.

Thanks be to God, who offers salvation through Jesus Christ, the only mediator between God and man, who gave himself a penalty for sin for all mankind (1 Timothy 2:5-6)!

THE
LIFE,
And Strange Surprizing
ADVENTURES
OF
ROBINSON CRUSOE,
Of YORK, Mariner:

Who lived eight and twenty Years all alone in
an un-inhabited Island on the Coast of America,
near the Mouth of the Great River *Oroonoque*;
having been cast on Shore by Shipwreck, wherein all the Men perished but himself.

With an ACCOUNT how he was at last as
strangely deliver'd by Pyrates.

Written by Himself.

The Fifth Edition.

To which is added a Map of the World, in which is
Delineated the Voyages of *ROBINSON CRUSOE.*

LONDON: Printed for W. Taylor at the
Ship in *Pater-Noster-Row*. MDCCXX.

CHAPTER I:
START IN LIFE

I was born in the year 1632, in the city of York,[1] of a good family, though not of that country, my father being a foreigner of Bremen,[2] who settled first at Hull.[3] He got a good estate by merchandise, and leaving off his trade, lived afterwards at York, from whence he had married my mother, whose relations were named Robinson, a very good family in that country, and from whom I was called Robinson Kreutznaer;[4] but, by the usual corruption of words in England, we are now called—nay we call ourselves and write our name—Crusoe; and so my companions always called me.

I had two elder brothers, one of whom was lieutenant-colonel to an English regiment of foot in Flanders, formerly commanded by the famous Colonel Lockhart,[5] and was killed at the battle near Dunkirk against the Spaniards. What became of my second brother I never knew, any more than my father or mother knew what became of me.

Being the third son of the family and not bred to any trade, my head began to be filled very early with rambling thoughts. My father, who was very ancient, had given me a competent share of learning, as far as house-education and a country free school generally go, and designed me for the law; but I would be satisfied with nothing but going to sea; and my inclination to this led me so strongly against the will, nay, the commands of my father, and against all the entreaties and persuasions of my mother and other friends, that there seemed to be something fatal in that propensity[6] of nature, tending directly to the life of misery which was to befall me.

My father, a wise and grave man, gave me serious and excellent counsel against what he foresaw was my design. He called me one morning into his chamber, where he was confined by the gout,[7] and expostulated[8] very warmly with me upon this subject. He asked me what reasons, more than a

---

[1] in central England
[2] city in northwest Germany
[3] city in England
[4] Kreutznaer is German for either "cross-nearer" or "to journey."
[5] Sir William Lockhart (1612-1675)
[6] inclination, tendency
[7] a disease characterized by pain and inflammation (often in the big toe), and typically caused by eating too much meat or rich foods
[8] complained, objected

mere wandering inclination, I had for leaving father's house and my native country, where I might be well introduced, and had a prospect of raising my fortune by application and industry, with a life of ease and pleasure. He told me it was men of desperate fortunes on one hand, or of aspiring, superior fortunes on the other, who went abroad upon adventures, to rise by enterprise, and make themselves famous in undertakings of a nature out of the common road; that these things were all either too far above me or too far below me; that mine was the middle state, or what might be called the upper station of low life, which he had found, by long experience, was the best state in the world, the most suited to human happiness, not exposed to the miseries and hardships, the labour and sufferings of the mechanic part of mankind, and not embarrassed with the pride, luxury, ambition, and envy of the upper part of mankind. He told me I might judge of the happiness of this state by this one thing—viz.[9] that this was the state of life which all other people envied; that kings have frequently lamented the miserable consequence of being born to great things, and wished they had been placed in the middle of the two extremes, between the mean and the great; that the wise man gave his testimony to this, as the standard of felicity, when he prayed to have neither poverty nor riches.[10]

He bade me observe it, and I should always find that the calamities of life were shared among the upper and lower part of mankind, but that the middle station had the fewest disasters, and was not exposed to so many vicissitudes[11] as the higher or lower part of mankind; nay, they were not subjected to so many distempers and uneasinesses, either of body or mind, as those were who, by vicious living, luxury, and extravagances on the one hand, or by hard labour, want[12] of necessaries, and mean or insufficient diet on the other hand, bring distemper upon themselves by the natural consequences of their way of living; that the middle station of life was calculated for all kind of virtue and all kind of enjoyments; that peace and plenty were the handmaids of a middle fortune; that temperance, moderation, quietness, health, society, all agreeable diversions, and all desirable pleasures, were the blessings attending the middle station of life; that this way men went silently and smoothly through the world, and comfortably out of it, not embarrassed with the labours of the hands or of the head, not sold to a life of slavery for daily bread, nor harassed with perplexed circumstances, which rob the soul of peace and the body of rest, nor enraged with the passion of

---

[9] "viz.": Latin for "that is to say" or "namely"
[10] Proverbs 30:8-9: "Remove far from me vanity and lies: give me neither poverty nor riches; feed me with food convenient for me: Lest I be full, and deny thee, and say, Who is the LORD? or lest I be poor, and steal, and take the name of my God in vain."
[11] variations, drastic changes
[12] lack

envy, or the secret burning lust of ambition for great things; but, in easy circumstances, sliding gently through the world, and sensibly tasting the
sweets of living, without the bitter; feeling that they are happy, and learning
by every day's experience to know it more sensibly.

After this he pressed me earnestly, and in the most affectionate manner,
not to play the young man, nor to precipitate myself into miseries which
nature, and the station of life I was born in, seemed to have provided against;
that I was under no necessity of seeking my bread; that he would do well
for me, and endeavour to enter me fairly into the station of life which he
had just been recommending to me; and that if I was not very easy and happy in the world, it must be my mere fate or fault that must hinder it; and that
he should have nothing to answer for, having thus discharged his duty in
warning me against measures which he knew would be to my hurt; in a
word, that as he would do very kind things for me if I would stay and settle
at home as he directed, so he would not have so much hand in my misfortunes as to give me any encouragement to go away; and to close all, he told
me I had my elder brother for an example, to whom he had used the same
earnest persuasions to keep him from going into the Low Country wars,[13]
but could not prevail, his young desires prompting him to run into the army,
where he was killed; and though he said he would not cease to pray for me,
yet he would venture to say to me, that if I did take this foolish step, God
would not bless me, and I should have leisure hereafter to reflect upon having neglected his counsel when there might be none to assist in my recovery.

I observed in this last part of his discourse, which was truly prophetic,
though I suppose my father did not know it to be so himself—I say, I observed the tears run down his face very plentifully, especially when he
spoke of my brother who was killed: and that when he spoke of my having
leisure to repent, and none to assist me, he was so moved that he broke off
the discourse, and told me his heart was so full he could say no more to me.

I was sincerely affected with this discourse, and, indeed, who could be
otherwise? and I resolved not to think of going abroad any more, but to settle at home according to my father's desire. But alas! a few days wore it all
off; and, in short, to prevent any of my father's further importunities, in a
few weeks after I resolved to run quite away from him. However, I did not
act quite so hastily as the first heat of my resolution prompted; but I took
my mother at a time when I thought her a little more pleasant than ordinary,
and told her that my thoughts were so entirely bent upon seeing the world
that I should never settle to anything with resolution enough to go through
with it, and my father had better give me his consent than force me to go
without it; that I was now eighteen years old, which was too late to go ap-

---

[13] the Dutch War of Independence against Spain (1568-1648)

prentice to a trade or clerk to an attorney; that I was sure if I did I should never serve out my time, but I should certainly run away from my master before my time was out, and go to sea; and if she would speak to my father to let me go one voyage abroad, if I came home again, and did not like it, I would go no more; and I would promise, by a double diligence, to recover the time that I had lost.

This put my mother into a great passion; she told me she knew it would be to no purpose to speak to my father upon any such subject; that he knew too well what was my interest to give his consent to anything so much for my hurt; and that she wondered how I could think of any such thing after the discourse I had had with my father, and such kind and tender expressions as she knew my father had used to me; and that, in short, if I would ruin myself, there was no help for me; but I might depend I should never have their consent to it; that for her part she would not have so much hand in my destruction; and I should never have it to say that my mother was willing when my father was not.

Though my mother refused to move it to my father, yet I heard afterwards that she reported all the discourse to him, and that my father, after showing a great concern at it, said to her, with a sigh, "That boy might be happy if he would stay at home; but if he goes abroad, he will be the most miserable wretch that ever was born: I can give no consent to it."

It was not till almost a year after this that I broke loose, though, in the meantime, I continued obstinately deaf to all proposals of settling to business, and frequently expostulated with my father and mother about their being so positively determined against what they knew my inclinations prompted me to. But being one day at Hull, where I went casually, and without any purpose of making an elopement at that time; but, I say, being there, and one of my companions being about to sail to London in his father's ship, and prompting me to go with them with the common allurement of seafaring men, that it should cost me nothing for my passage, I consulted neither father nor mother any more, nor so much as sent them word of it; but leaving them to hear of it as they might, without asking God's blessing or my father's, without any consideration of circumstances or consequences, and in an ill hour, God knows, on the 1st of September 1651, I went on board a ship bound for London. Never any young adventurer's misfortunes, I believe, began sooner, or continued longer than mine. The ship was no sooner out of the Humber[14] than the wind began to blow and the sea to rise in a most frightful manner; and, as I had never been at sea before, I was most inexpressibly sick in body and terrified in mind. I began now seriously to reflect upon what I had done, and how justly I was overtaken by the judg-

---

[14] port on the east coast of Northern England

ment of Heaven for my wicked leaving my father's house, and abandoning my duty. All the good counsels of my parents, my father's tears and my mother's entreaties, came now fresh into my mind; and my conscience, which was not yet come to the pitch of hardness to which it has since, reproached me with the contempt of advice, and the breach of my duty to God and my father.

All this while the storm increased, and the sea went very high, though nothing like what I have seen many times since; no, nor what I saw a few days after; but it was enough to affect me then, who was but a young sailor, and had never known anything of the matter. I expected every wave would have swallowed us up, and that every time the ship fell down, as I thought it did, in the trough or hollow of the sea, we should never rise more; in this agony of mind, I made many vows and resolutions that if it would please God to spare my life in this one voyage, if ever I got once my foot upon dry land again, I would go directly home to my father, and never set it into a ship again while I lived; that I would take his advice, and never run myself into such miseries as these any more. Now I saw plainly the goodness of his observations about the middle station of life, how easy, how comfortably he had lived all his days, and never had been exposed to tempests at sea or troubles on shore; and I resolved that I would, like a true repenting prodigal, go home to my father.

These wise and sober thoughts continued all the while the storm lasted, and indeed some time after; but the next day the wind was abated,[15] and the sea calmer, and I began to be a little inured[16] to it; however, I was very grave for all that day, being also a little sea-sick still; but towards night the weather cleared up, the wind was quite over, and a charming fine evening followed; the sun went down perfectly clear, and rose so the next morning; and having little or no wind, and a smooth sea, the sun shining upon it, the sight was, as I thought, the most delightful that ever I saw.

I had slept well in the night, and was now no more sea-sick, but very cheerful, looking with wonder upon the sea that was so rough and terrible the day before, and could be so calm and so pleasant in so little a time after. And now, lest my good resolutions should continue, my companion, who had enticed me away, comes to me; "Well, Bob," says he, clapping me upon the shoulder, "how do you do after it? I warrant you were frighted, wer'n't you, last night, when it blew but a capful of wind?" "A capful d'you call it?" said I; "'twas a terrible storm." "A storm, you fool you," replies he; "do you call that a storm? why, it was nothing at all; give us but a good ship and sea-room, and we think nothing of such a squall of wind as that; but you're

---

[15] lessened, stopped
[16] accustomed, toughened

but a fresh-water sailor, Bob. Come, let us make a bowl of punch, and we'll forget all that; d'ye see what charming weather 'tis now?" To make short this sad part of my story, we went the way of all sailors; the punch was made and I was made half drunk with it: and in that one night's wickedness I drowned all my repentance, all my reflections upon my past conduct, all my resolutions for the future. In a word, as the sea was returned to its smoothness of surface and settled calmness by the abatement of that storm, so the hurry of my thoughts being over, my fears and apprehensions of being swallowed up by the sea being forgotten, and the current of my former desires returned, I entirely forgot the vows and promises that I made in my distress.[17] I found, indeed, some intervals of reflection; and the serious thoughts did, as it were, endeavour to return again sometimes; but I shook them off, and roused myself from them as it were from a distemper, and applying myself to drinking and company, soon mastered the return of those fits—for so I called them; and I had in five or six days got as complete a victory over conscience as any young fellow that resolved not to be troubled with it could desire. But I was to have another trial for it still; and Providence,[18] as in such cases generally it does, resolved to leave me entirely without excuse; for if I would not take this for a deliverance, the next was to be such a one as the worst and most hardened wretch among us would confess both the danger and the mercy of.

The sixth day of our being at sea we came into Yarmouth Roads; the wind having been contrary and the weather calm, we had made but little way since the storm. Here we were obliged to come to an anchor, and here we lay, the wind continuing contrary—viz. at south-west—for seven or eight days, during which time a great many ships from Newcastle came into the same Roads, as the common harbour where the ships might wait for a wind for the river.

We had not, however, rid here so long but we should have tided it up the river, but that the wind blew too fresh, and after we had lain four or five days, blew very hard. However, the Roads being reckoned as good as a harbour, the anchorage good, and our ground-tackle very strong, our men were unconcerned, and not in the least apprehensive of danger, but spent the time in rest and mirth,[19] after the manner of the sea; but the eighth day, in the morning, the wind increased, and we had all hands at work to strike our topmasts, and make everything snug and close, that the ship might ride as easy as possible. By noon the sea went very high indeed, and our ship rode forecastle in, shipped several seas, and we thought once or twice our anchor had

---

[17] "Better *is it* that thou shouldest not vow, than that thou shouldest vow and not pay" (Ecclesiastes 5:5).
[18] "Providence" is a way of saying "God."
[19] merriment, good humor

come home; upon which our master ordered out the sheet-anchor, so that we rode with two anchors ahead, and the cables veered out to the bitter end.

By this time it blew a terrible storm indeed; and now I began to see terror and amazement in the faces even of the seamen themselves. The master, though vigilant in the business of preserving the ship, yet as he went in and out of his cabin by me, I could hear him softly to himself say, several times, "Lord be merciful to us! we shall be all lost! we shall be all undone!" and the like. During these first hurries I was stupid, lying still in my cabin, which was in the steerage, and cannot describe my temper: I could ill resume the first penitence[20] which I had so apparently trampled upon and hardened my-self against: I thought the bitterness of death had been past, and that this would be nothing like the first; but when the master himself came by me, as I said just now, and said we should be all lost, I was dreadfully frighted. I got up out of my cabin and looked out; but such a dismal sight I never saw: the sea ran mountains high, and broke upon us every three or four min-utes; when I could look about, I could see nothing but distress round us; two ships that rode near us, we found, had cut their masts by the board, being deep laden; and our men cried out that a ship which rode about a mile ahead of us was foundered. Two more ships, being driven from their anchors, were run out of the Roads to sea, at all adventures, and that with not a mast standing. The light ships fared the best, as not so much labouring in the sea; but two or three of them drove, and came close by us, running away with only their spritsail out before the wind.

Towards evening the mate and boatswain[21] begged the master of our ship to let them cut away the foremast, which he was very unwilling to do; but the boatswain protesting to him that if he did not the ship would founder, he consented; and when they had cut away the fore-mast, the main-mast stood so loose, and shook the ship so much, they were obliged to cut that away also, and make a clear deck.

Any one may judge what a condition I must be in at all this, who was but a young sailor, and who had been in such a fright before at but a little. But if I can express at this distance the thoughts I had about me at that time, I was in tenfold more horror of mind upon account of my former convictions, and the having returned from them to the resolutions I had wickedly taken at first, than I was at death itself; and these, added to the terror of the storm, put me into such a condition that I can by no words describe it. But the worst was not come yet; the storm continued with such fury that the seamen themselves acknowledged they had never seen a worse. We had a good ship, but she was deep laden, and wallowed in the sea, so that the seamen every

[20] regret, repentance
[21] officer in charge of rigging, sails, and so on

now and then cried out she would founder. It was my advantage in one respect, that I did not know what they meant by *founder* till I inquired.[22] However, the storm was so violent that I saw, what is not often seen, the master, the boatswain, and some others more sensible than the rest, at their prayers, and expecting every moment when the ship would go to the bottom. In the middle of the night, and under all the rest of our distresses, one of the men that had been down to see cried out we had sprung a leak; another said there was four feet water in the hold. Then all hands were called to the pump. At that word, my heart, as I thought, died within me: and I fell backwards upon the side of my bed where I sat, into the cabin. However, the men roused me, and told me that I, that was able to do nothing before, was as well able to pump as another; at which I stirred up and went to the pump, and worked very heartily. While this was doing the master, seeing some light colliers,[23] who, not able to ride out the storm were obliged to slip and run away to sea, and would come near us, ordered to fire a gun as a signal of distress. I, who knew nothing what they meant, thought the ship had broken, or some dreadful thing happened. In a word, I was so surprised that I fell down in a swoon. As this was a time when everybody had his own life to think of, nobody minded me, or what was become of me; but another man stepped up to the pump, and thrusting me aside with his foot, let me lie, thinking I had been dead; and it was a great while before I came to myself.

We worked on; but the water increasing in the hold, it was apparent that the ship would founder; and though the storm began to abate a little, yet it was not possible she could swim till we might run into any port; so the master continued firing guns for help; and a light ship, who had rid it out just ahead of us, ventured a boat out to help us. It was with the utmost hazard the boat came near us; but it was impossible for us to get on board, or for the boat to lie near the ship's side, till at last the men rowing very heartily, and venturing their lives to save ours, our men cast them a rope over the stern with a buoy to it, and then veered it out a great length, which they, after much labour and hazard, took hold of, and we hauled them close under our stern, and got all into their boat. It was to no purpose for them or us, after we were in the boat, to think of reaching their own ship; so all agreed to let her drive, and only to pull her in towards shore as much as we could; and our master promised them, that if the boat was staved upon shore, he would make it good to their master: so partly rowing and partly driving, our boat went away to the northward, sloping towards the shore almost as far as Winterton Ness.[24]

---

[22] "Founder" means to fill with water and sink.
[23] small ships carrying coal
[24] on the North Norfolk coast of England

We were not much more than a quarter of an hour out of our ship till we saw her sink, and then I understood for the first time what was meant by a ship foundering in the sea. I must acknowledge I had hardly eyes to look up when the seamen told me she was sinking; for from the moment that they rather put me into the boat than that I might be said to go in, my heart was, as it were, dead within me, partly with fright, partly with horror of mind, and the thoughts of what was yet before me.

While we were in this condition—the men yet labouring at the oar to bring the boat near the shore—we could see (when, our boat mounting the waves, we were able to see the shore) a great many people running along the strand to assist us when we should come near; but we made but slow way towards the shore; nor were we able to reach the shore till, being past the lighthouse at Winterton, the shore falls off to the westward towards Cromer, and so the land broke off a little the violence of the wind. Here we got in, and though not without much difficulty, got all safe on shore, and walked afterwards on foot to Yarmouth, where, as unfortunate men, we were used with great humanity, as well by the magistrates of the town, who assigned us good quarters, as by particular merchants and owners of ships, and had money given us sufficient to carry us either to London or back to Hull as we thought fit.

Had I now had the sense to have gone back to Hull, and have gone home, I had been happy, and my father, as in our blessed Saviour's parable, had even killed the fatted calf for me;[25] for hearing the ship I went away in was cast away in Yarmouth Roads, it was a great while before he had any assurances that I was not drowned.

But my ill fate pushed me on now with an obstinacy that nothing could resist; and though I had several times loud calls from my reason and my more composed judgment to go home, yet I had no power to do it. I know not what to call this, nor will I urge that it is a secret overruling decree, that hurries us on to be the instruments of our own destruction, even though it be before us, and that we rush upon it with our eyes open. Certainly, nothing but some such decreed unavoidable misery, which it was impossible for me to escape, could have pushed me forward against the calm reasonings and persuasions of my most retired thoughts, and against two such visible instructions as I had met with in my first attempt.

My comrade, who had helped to harden me before, and who was the master's son, was now less forward than I. The first time he spoke to me after we were at Yarmouth, which was not till two or three days, for we were separated in the town to several quarters; I say, the first time he saw me, it appeared his tone was altered; and, looking very melancholy, and shaking

---

[25] See Luke 15:11-32.

his head, he asked me how I did, and telling his father who I was, and how I had come this voyage only for a trial, in order to go further abroad, his father, turning to me with a very grave and concerned tone, "Young man," says he, "you ought never to go to sea any more; you ought to take this for a plain and visible token that you are not to be a seafaring man." "Why, sir," said I, "will you go to sea no more?" "That is another case," said he; "it is my calling, and therefore my duty; but as you made this voyage on trial, you see what a taste Heaven has given you of what you are to expect if you persist. Perhaps this has all befallen us on your account, like Jonah in the ship of Tarshish. Pray," continues he, "what are you; and on what account did you go to sea?" Upon that I told him some of my story; at the end of which he burst out into a strange kind of passion: "What had I done," says he, "that such an unhappy wretch should come into my ship? I would not set my foot in the same ship with thee again for a thousand pounds." This indeed was, as I said, an excursion of his spirits, which were yet agitated by the sense of his loss, and was farther than he could have authority to go. However, he afterwards talked very gravely to me, exhorting me to go back to my father, and not tempt Providence to my ruin, telling me I might see a visible hand of Heaven against me. "And, young man," said he, "depend upon it, if you do not go back, wherever you go, you will meet with nothing but disasters and disappointments, till your father's words are fulfilled upon you."

We parted soon after; for I made him little answer, and I saw him no more; which way he went I knew not. As for me, having some money in my pocket, I travelled to London by land; and there, as well as on the road, had many struggles with myself what course of life I should take, and whether I should go home or to sea.

As to going home, shame opposed the best motions that offered to my thoughts, and it immediately occurred to me how I should be laughed at among the neighbours, and should be ashamed to see, not my father and mother only, but even everybody else; from whence I have since often observed, how incongruous[26] and irrational the common temper of mankind is, especially of youth, to that reason which ought to guide them in such cases—viz. that they are not ashamed to sin, and yet are ashamed to repent; not ashamed of the action for which they ought justly to be esteemed fools, but are ashamed of the returning, which only can make them be esteemed wise men.

In this state of life, however, I remained some time, uncertain what measures to take, and what course of life to lead. An irresistible reluctance continued to going home; and as I stayed away a while, the remembrance of the

---

[26] inconsistent, incompatible

distress I had been in wore off, and as that abated, the little motion I had in my desires to return wore off with it, till at last I quite laid aside the thoughts of it, and looked out for a voyage.

CHAPTER II: SLAVERY AND ESCAPE

That evil influence which carried me first away from my father's house—which hurried me into the wild and indigested notion of raising my fortune, and that impressed those conceits so forcibly upon me as to make me deaf to all good advice, and to the entreaties and even the commands of my father—I say, the same influence, whatever it was, presented the most unfortunate of all enterprises to my view; and I went on board a vessel bound to the coast of Africa; or, as our sailors vulgarly[27] called it, a voyage to Guinea.[28]

It was my great misfortune that in all these adventures I did not ship myself as a sailor; when, though I might indeed have worked a little harder than ordinary, yet at the same time I should have learnt the duty and office of a foremast man, and in time might have qualified myself for a mate or lieutenant, if not for a master. But as it was always my fate to choose for the worse, so I did here; for having money in my pocket and good clothes upon my back, I would always go on board in the habit of a gentleman; and so I neither had any business in the ship, nor learned to do any.

It was my lot first of all to fall into pretty good company in London, which does not always happen to such loose and misguided young fellows as I then was; the devil generally not omitting to lay some snare for them very early; but it was not so with me. I first got acquainted with the master of a ship who had been on the coast of Guinea; and who, having had very good success there, was resolved to go again. This captain taking a fancy to my conversation, which was not at all disagreeable at that time, hearing me say I had a mind to see the world, told me if I would go the voyage with

---

[27] commonly

[28] This indicates the ship was intent on bringing back African slaves from Guinea, which is on the northwest side of Africa.

him I should be at no expense; I should be his messmate[29] and his companion; and if I could carry anything with me, I should have all the advantage of it that the trade would admit; and perhaps I might meet with some encouragement.

I embraced the offer; and entering into a strict friendship with this captain, who was an honest, plain-dealing man, I went the voyage with him, and carried a small adventure with me, which, by the disinterested honesty of my friend the captain, I increased very considerably; for I carried about £40 in such toys and trifles as the captain directed me to buy. These £40 I had mustered together by the assistance of some of my relations whom I corresponded with; and who, I believe, got my father, or at least my mother, to contribute so much as that to my first adventure.

This was the only voyage which I may say was successful in all my adventures, which I owe to the integrity and honesty of my friend the captain; under whom also I got a competent knowledge of the mathematics and the rules of navigation, learned how to keep an account of the ship's course, take an observation, and, in short, to understand some things that were needful to be understood by a sailor; for, as he took delight to instruct me, I took delight to learn; and, in a word, this voyage made me both a sailor and a merchant; for I brought home five pounds nine ounces of gold-dust for my adventure, which yielded me in London, at my return, almost £300; and this filled me with those aspiring thoughts which have since so completed my ruin.

Yet even in this voyage I had my misfortunes too; particularly, that I was continually sick, being thrown into a violent calenture[30] by the excessive heat of the climate; our principal trading being upon the coast, from latitude of 15 degrees north even to the line itself.

I was now set up for a Guinea trader; and my friend, to my great misfortune, dying soon after his arrival, I resolved to go the same voyage again, and I embarked in the same vessel with one who was his mate in the former voyage, and had now got the command of the ship. This was the unhappiest voyage that ever man made; for though I did not carry quite £100 of my new-gained wealth, so that I had £200 left, which I had lodged with my friend's widow, who was very just to me, yet I fell into terrible misfortunes. The first was this: our ship making her course towards the Canary Islands,[31] or rather between those islands and the African shore, was surprised in the grey of the morning by a Turkish rover of Sallee,[32] who gave chase to us with all the sail she could make. We crowded also as much canvas as our

---

[29] one who eats meals with someone else on a ship
[30] stroke or fever, sometimes accompanied by hallucinations
[31] located off the northwest coast of Africa
[32] "rover of Sallee": pirate ship from the city of Sallee, located in the same area

yards would spread, or our masts carry, to get clear; but finding the pirate gained upon us, and would certainly come up with us in a few hours, we prepared to fight; our ship having twelve guns, and the rogue eighteen. About three in the afternoon he came up with us, and bringing to, by mistake, just athwart our quarter, instead of athwart our stern, as he intended, we brought eight of our guns to bear on that side, and poured in a broadside upon him, which made him sheer off again, after returning our fire, and pouring in also his small shot from near two hundred men which he had on board. However, we had not a man touched, all our men keeping close. He prepared to attack us again, and we to defend ourselves. But laying us on board the next time upon our other quarter, he entered sixty men upon our decks, who immediately fell to cutting and hacking the sails and rigging. We plied them with small shot, half-pikes, powder-chests, and such like, and cleared our deck of them twice. However, to cut short this melancholy part of our story, our ship being disabled, and three of our men killed, and eight wounded, we were obliged to yield, and were carried all prisoners into Sallee, a port belonging to the Moors.[33]

The usage I had there was not so dreadful as at first I apprehended; nor was I carried up the country to the emperor's court, as the rest of our men were, but was kept by the captain of the rover as his proper prize, and made his slave, being young and nimble, and fit for his business. At this surprising change of my circumstances, from a merchant to a miserable slave, I was perfectly overwhelmed; and now I looked back upon my father's prophetic discourse to me, that I should be miserable and have none to relieve me, which I thought was now so effectually brought to pass that I could not be worse; for now the hand of Heaven had overtaken me, and I was undone without redemption; but, alas! this was but a taste of the misery I was to go through, as will appear in the sequel of this story.

As my new patron, or master, had taken me home to his house, so I was in hopes that he would take me with him when he went to sea again, believing that it would some time or other be his fate to be taken by a Spanish or Portugal man-of-war;[34] and that then I should be set at liberty. But this hope of mine was soon taken away; for when he went to sea, he left me on shore to look after his little garden, and do the common drudgery[35] of slaves about his house; and when he came home again from his cruise, he ordered me to lie in the cabin to look after the ship.

Here I meditated nothing but my escape, and what method I might take to effect it, but found no way that had the least probability in it; nothing presented to make the supposition of it rational; for I had nobody to communi-

---

[33] Muslims or persons from the Middle East or Africa (or both)
[34] "man-of-war": armed naval vessel
[35] boring, tedious labor

cate it to that would embark with me—no fellow-slave, no Englishman, Irishman, or Scotchman there but myself; so that for two years, though I often pleased myself with the imagination, yet I never had the least encouraging prospect of putting it in practice.

After about two years, an odd circumstance presented itself, which put the old thought of making some attempt for my liberty again in my head. My patron lying at home longer than usual without fitting out his ship, which, as I heard, was for want of money, he used constantly, once or twice a week, sometimes oftener if the weather was fair, to take the ship's pinnace[36] and go out into the road a-fishing; and as he always took me and young Maresco with him to row the boat, we made him very merry, and I proved very dexterous[37] in catching fish; insomuch that sometimes he would send me with a Moor, one of his kinsmen, and the youth—the Maresco, as they called him—to catch a dish of fish for him.

It happened one time, that going a-fishing in a calm morning, a fog rose so thick that, though we were not half a league[38] from the shore, we lost sight of it; and rowing we knew not whither or which way, we laboured all day, and all the next night; and when the morning came we found we had pulled off to sea instead of pulling in for the shore; and that we were at least two leagues from the shore. However, we got well in again, though with a great deal of labour and some danger; for the wind began to blow pretty fresh in the morning; but we were all very hungry.

But our patron, warned by this disaster, resolved to take more care of himself for the future; and having lying by him the longboat of our English ship that he had taken, he resolved he would not go a-fishing any more without a compass and some provision; so he ordered the carpenter of his ship, who also was an English slave, to build a little state-room, or cabin, in the middle of the long-boat, like that of a barge, with a place to stand behind it to steer, and haul home the main-sheet; the room before for a hand or two to stand and work the sails. She sailed with what we call a shoulder-of-mutton sail; and the boom jibed over the top of the cabin, which lay very snug and low, and had in it room for him to lie, with a slave or two, and a table to eat on, with some small lockers to put in some bottles of such liquor as he thought fit to drink; and his bread, rice, and coffee.

We went frequently out with this boat a-fishing; and as I was most dexterous to catch fish for him, he never went without me. It happened that he had appointed to go out in this boat, either for pleasure or for fish, with two or three Moors of some distinction in that place, and for whom he had provided extraordinarily, and had, therefore, sent on board the boat overnight

---

[36] rowboat
[37] handy, expert
[38] A league is three miles, so this is about one-and-a-half miles.

a larger store of provisions than ordinary; and had ordered me to get ready three fusees[39] with powder and shot, which were on board his ship, for that they designed some sport of fowling as well as fishing.

I got all things ready as he had directed, and waited the next morning with the boat washed clean, her ancient[40] and pendants[41] out, and everything to accommodate his guests; when by-and-by my patron came on board alone, and told me his guests had put off going from some business that fell out, and ordered me, with the man and boy, as usual, to go out with the boat and catch them some fish, for that his friends were to sup at his house, and commanded that as soon as I got some fish I should bring it home to his house; all which I prepared to do.

This moment my former notions of deliverance darted into my thoughts, for now I found I was likely to have a little ship at my command; and my master being gone, I prepared to furnish myself, not for fishing business, but for a voyage; though I knew not, neither did I so much as consider, whither I should steer—anywhere to get out of that place was my desire.

My first contrivance was to make a pretence to speak to this Moor, to get something for our subsistence on board; for I told him we must not presume to eat of our patron's bread. He said that was true; so he brought a large basket of rusk or biscuit, and three jars of fresh water, into the boat. I knew where my patron's case of bottles stood, which it was evident, by the make, were taken out of some English prize, and I conveyed them into the boat while the Moor was on shore, as if they had been there before for our master. I conveyed also a great lump of beeswax into the boat, which weighed about half a hundred-weight, with a parcel of twine or thread, a hatchet, a saw, and a hammer, all of which were of great use to us afterwards, especially the wax, to make candles. Another trick I tried upon him, which he innocently came into also: his name was Ismael, which they call Muley, or Moely; so I called to him—"Moely," said I, "our patron's guns are on board the boat; can you not get a little powder and shot? It may be we may kill some alcamies (a fowl like our curlews) for ourselves, for I know he keeps the gunner's stores in the ship." "Yes," says he, "I'll bring some;" and accordingly he brought a great leather pouch, which held a pound and a half of powder, or rather more; and another with shot, that had five or six pounds, with some bullets, and put all into the boat. At the same time I had found some powder of my master's in the great cabin, with which I filled one of the large bottles in the case, which was almost empty, pouring what was in it into another; and thus furnished with everything needful, we sailed out of the port to fish. The castle, which is at the entrance of the port, knew who

---

[39] a musket (rifle)

[40] banner, sign

[41] hanging ropes used to attach hooks for tackles

we were, and took no notice of us; and we were not above a mile out of the port before we hauled in our sail and set us down to fish. The wind blew from the N.N.E., which was contrary to my desire, for had it blown southerly I had been sure to have made the coast of Spain, and at least reached to the bay of Cadiz; but my resolutions were, blow which way it would, I would be gone from that horrid place where I was, and leave the rest to fate.

After we had fished some time and caught nothing—for when I had fish on my hook I would not pull them up, that he might not see them—I said to the Moor, "This will not do; our master will not be thus served; we must stand farther off." He, thinking no harm, agreed, and being in the head of the boat, set the sails; and, as I had the helm, I ran the boat out near a league farther, and then brought her to, as if I would fish; when, giving the boy the helm, I stepped forward to where the Moor was, and making as if I stooped for something behind him, I took him by surprise with my arm under his waist, and tossed him clear overboard into the sea. He rose immediately, for he swam like a cork, and called to me, begged to be taken in, told me he would go all over the world with me. He swam so strong after the boat that he would have reached me very quickly, there being but little wind; upon which I stepped into the cabin, and fetching one of the fowling-pieces,[42] I presented it at him, and told him I had done him no hurt, and if he would be quiet I would do him none. "But," said I, "you swim well enough to reach to the shore, and the sea is calm; make the best of your way to shore, and I will do you no harm; but if you come near the boat I'll shoot you through the head, for I am resolved to have my liberty;" so he turned himself about, and swam for the shore, and I make no doubt but he reached it with ease, for he was an excellent swimmer.

I could have been content to have taken this Moor with me, and have drowned the boy, but there was no venturing to trust him. When he was gone, I turned to the boy, whom they called Xury, and said to him, "Xury, if you will be faithful to me, I'll make you a great man; but if you will not stroke your face to be true to me"—that is, swear by Mahomet[43] and his father's beard—"I must throw you into the sea too." The boy smiled in my face, and spoke so innocently that I could not distrust him, and swore to be faithful to me, and go all over the world with me.

While I was in view of the Moor that was swimming, I stood out directly to sea with the boat, rather stretching to windward, that they might think me gone towards the Straits' mouth (as indeed any one that had been in their wits must have been supposed to do): for who would have supposed we were sailed on to the south-ward, to the truly Barbarian coast, where whole

---

[42] a gun used to bring down birds
[43] Muhammed, the founder of Islam

nations of negroes were sure to surround us with their canoes and destroy us; where we could not go on shore but we should be devoured by savage beasts, or more merciless savages of human kind.

But as soon as it grew dusk in the evening, I changed my course, and steered directly south and by east, bending my course a little towards the east, that I might keep in with the shore; and having a fair, fresh gale of wind, and a smooth, quiet sea, I made such sail that I believe by the next day, at three o'clock in the afternoon, when I first made the land, I could not be less than one hundred and fifty miles south of Sallee; quite beyond the Emperor of Morocco's dominions, or indeed of any other king thereabouts, for we saw no people.

Yet such was the fright I had taken of the Moors, and the dreadful apprehensions I had of falling into their hands, that I would not stop, or go on shore, or come to an anchor; the wind continuing fair till I had sailed in that

manner five days; and then the wind shifting to the southward, I concluded also that if any of our vessels were in chase of me, they also would now give over; so I ventured to make to the coast, and came to an anchor in the mouth of a little river, I knew not what, nor where, neither what latitude, what country, what nation, or what river. I neither saw, nor desired to see any people; the principal thing I wanted was fresh water. We came into this creek in the evening, resolving to swim on shore as soon as it was dark,

and discover the country; but as soon as it was quite dark, we heard such dreadful noises of the barking, roaring, and howling of wild creatures, of we knew not what kinds, that the poor boy was ready to die with fear, and begged of me not to go on shore till day. "Well, Xury," said I, "then I won't; but it may be that we may see men by day, who will be as bad to us as those lions." "Then we give them the shoot gun," says Xury, laughing, "make them run wey." Such English Xury spoke by conversing among us slaves. However, I was glad to see the boy so cheerful, and I gave him a dram[44]

---

[44] a small amount of drink

(out of our patron's case of bottles) to cheer him up. After all, Xury's advice was good, and I took it; we dropped our little anchor, and lay still all night; I say still, for we slept none; for in two or three hours we saw vast great creatures (we knew not what to call them) of many sorts, come down to the sea-shore and run into the water, wallowing and washing themselves for the pleasure of cooling themselves; and they made such hideous howlings and yellings, that I never indeed heard the like.

Xury was dreadfully frighted, and indeed so was I too; but we were both more frighted when we heard one of these mighty creatures come swimming towards our boat; we could not see him, but we might hear him by his blowing to be a monstrous huge and furious beast. Xury said it was a lion, and it might be so for aught I know; but poor Xury cried to me to weigh the anchor and row away; "No," says I, "Xury; we can slip our cable, with the buoy to it, and go off to sea; they cannot follow us far." I had no sooner said so, but I perceived the creature (whatever it was) within two oars' length, which something surprised me; however, I immediately stepped to the cabin door, and taking up my gun, fired at him; upon which he immediately turned about and swam towards the shore again.

But it is impossible to describe the horrid noises, and hideous cries and howlings that were raised, as well upon the edge of the shore as higher within the country, upon the noise or report of the gun, a thing I have some reason to believe those creatures had never heard before: this convinced me that there was no going on shore for us in the night on that coast, and how to venture on shore in the day was another question too; for to have fallen into the hands of any of the savages had been as bad as to have fallen into the hands of the lions and tigers; at least we were equally apprehensive of the danger of it.

Be that as it would, we were obliged to go on shore somewhere or other for water, for we had not a pint left in the boat; when and where to get to it was the point. Xury said, if I would let him go on shore with one of the jars, he would find if there was any water, and bring some to me. I asked him why he would go? why I should not go, and he stay in the boat? The boy answered with so much affection as made me love him ever after. Says he, "If wild mans come, they eat me, you go wey." "Well, Xury," said I, "we will both go and if the wild mans come, we will kill them, they shall eat neither of us." So I gave Xury a piece of rusk bread to eat, and a dram out of our patron's case of bottles which I mentioned before; and we hauled the boat in as near the shore as we thought was proper, and so waded on shore, carrying nothing but our arms and two jars for water.

I did not care to go out of sight of the boat, fearing the coming of canoes with savages down the river; but the boy seeing a low place about a mile up the country, rambled to it, and by-and-by I saw him come running towards me. I thought he was pursued by some savage, or frighted with some wild beast, and I ran forward towards him to help him; but when I came nearer to him I saw something hanging over his shoulders, which was a creature that he had shot, like a hare, but different in colour, and longer legs; however, we were very glad of it, and it was very good meat; but the great joy that poor Xury came with, was to tell me he had found good water and seen no wild mans.

But we found afterwards that we need not take such pains for water, for a little higher up the creek where we were we found the water fresh when the tide was out, which flowed but a little way up; so we filled our jars, and feasted on the hare he had killed, and prepared to go on our way, having seen no footsteps of any human creature in that part of the country.

As I had been one voyage to this coast before, I knew very well that the islands of the Canaries, and the Cape de Verde Islands[45] also, lay not far off from the coast. But as I had no instruments to take an observation to know what latitude we were in, and not exactly knowing, or at least remembering, what latitude they were in, I knew not where to look for them, or when to stand off to sea towards them; otherwise I might now easily have found some of these islands. But my hope was, that if I stood along this coast till I came to that part where the English traded, I should find some of their vessels upon their usual design of trade, that would relieve and take us in.

By the best of my calculation, that place where I now was must be that country which, lying between the Emperor of Morocco's dominions and the negroes, lies waste and uninhabited, except by wild beasts; the negroes having abandoned it and gone farther south for fear of the Moors, and the Moors not thinking it worth inhabiting by reason of its barrenness; and indeed, both forsaking it because of the prodigious number of tigers, lions, leopards, and other furious creatures which harbour there; so that the Moors use it for their hunting only, where they go like an army, two or three thousand men at a time; and indeed for near a hundred miles together upon this coast we saw nothing but a waste, uninhabited country by day, and heard nothing but howlings and roaring of wild beasts by night.

Once or twice in the daytime I thought I saw the Pico of Teneriffe, being the high top of the Mountain Teneriffe in the Canaries, and had a great mind to venture out, in hopes of reaching thither; but having tried twice, I was forced in again by contrary winds, the sea also going too high for my little vessel; so, I resolved to pursue my first design, and keep along the shore.

Several times I was obliged to land for fresh water, after we had left

[45] about 350 miles off the coast of western Africa

this place; and once in partic-ular, being early in morning, we came to an an-chor under a little point of land, which was pretty high; and the tide be-ginning to flow, we lay still to go farther in. Xury, whose eyes were more about him than it seems mine were, calls softly to me, and tells me that we had best go farther off the shore; "For," says he, "look, yonder lies a dreadful monster on the side of that hillock, fast asleep." I looked where he pointed, and saw a dreadful

monster indeed, for it was a terrible, great lion that lay on the side of the shore, under the shade of a piece of the hill that hung as it were a little over him. "Xury," says I, "you shall on shore and kill him." Xury looked frighted and said, "Me kill! he eat me at one mouth!"—one mouthful he meant. However, I said no more to the boy, but bade him lie still, and I took our biggest gun, which was almost musket-bore, and loaded it with a good charge of powder, and with two slugs, and laid it down; then I loaded another gun with two bullets; and the third (for we had three pieces) I loaded with five smaller bullets. I took the best aim I could with the first piece to have shot him in the head, but he lay so with his leg raised a little above his nose, that the slugs hit his leg about the knee and broke the bone. He started up, growling at first, but finding his leg broken, fell down again; and then got upon three legs, and gave the most hideous roar that ever I heard. I was a little surprised that I had not hit him on the head; however, I took up the second piece immediately, and though he began to move off, fired again, and shot him in the head, and had the pleasure to see him drop and make but little noise, but lie struggling for life. Then Xury took heart, and would have me let him go on shore. "Well, go," said I: so the boy jumped into the water and taking a little gun in one hand, swam to shore with the other hand, and coming close to the creature, put the muzzle of the piece to his ear, and shot him in the head again, which despatched him quite.

This was game indeed to us, but this was no food; and I was very sorry to lose three charges of powder and shot upon a creature that was good for nothing to us. However, Xury said he would have some of him; so he comes on board, and asked me to give him the hatchet. "For what, Xury?" said I. "Me cut off his head," said he. However, Xury could not cut off his head, but he cut off a foot, and brought it with him, and it was a monstrous great one.

I bethought myself, however, that, perhaps the skin of him might, one way or other, be of some value to us; and I resolved to take off his skin if I could. So Xury and I went to work with him; but Xury was much the better workman at it, for I knew very ill how to do it. Indeed, it took us both up the whole day, but at last we got off the hide of him, and spreading it on the top of our cabin, the sun effectually dried it in two days' time, and it afterwards served me to lie upon.

Questions for Review:

1. Sum up Robinson Crusoe's background and current state in life. What do his parents advise? How does Robinson Crusoe react to this?

2. How does Robinson Crusoe's decision not bode well even from the start? Describe what he vows, and how the vow turns out.

3. How is Robinson Crusoe linked to both the prodigal son and Jonah?

4. How does Robinson Crusoe benefit by his trip to Africa? What happens on his next voyage?

5. Describe how Robinson Crusoe escapes. What is Xury like? What happens to them when they sail close to an island for water?

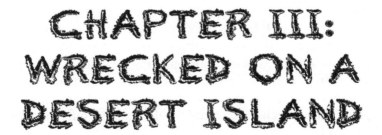

CHAPTER III: WRECKED ON A DESERT ISLAND

After this stop, we made on to the southward continually for ten or twelve days, living very sparingly on our provisions, which began to abate very much, and going no oftener to the shore than we were obliged to for fresh water. My design in this was to make the river Gambia or Senegal, that is to say anywhere about the Cape de Verde, where I was in hopes to meet with some European ship; and if I did not, I knew not what course I had to take, but to seek for the islands, or perish there among the negroes. I knew that all the ships from Europe, which sailed either to the coast of Guinea or to Brazil, or to the East Indies, made this cape, or those islands; and, in a word, I put the whole of my fortune upon this single point, either that I must meet with some ship or must perish.

When I had pursued this resolution about ten days longer, as I have said, I began to see that the land was inhabited; and in two or three places, as we sailed by, we saw people stand upon the shore to look at us; we could also perceive they were quite black and naked. I was once inclined to have gone on shore to them; but Xury was my better counsellor, and said to me, "No go, no go." However, I hauled in nearer the shore that I might talk to them, and I found they ran along the shore by me a good way. I observed they had no weapons in their hand, except one, who had a long slender stick, which Xury said was a lance, and that they could throw them a great way with good aim; so I kept at a distance, but talked with them by signs as well as I could; and particularly made signs for something to eat: they beckoned to me to stop my boat, and they would fetch me some meat. Upon this I lowered the top of my sail and lay by, and two of them ran up into the country, and in less than half-an-hour came back, and brought with them two pieces of dried flesh and some corn, such as is the produce of their country; but we neither knew what the one or the other was; however, we were willing to accept it, but how to come at it was our next dispute, for I would not venture on shore to them, and they were as much afraid of us; but they took a safe way for us all, for they brought it to the shore and laid it down, and went and stood a great way off till we fetched it on board, and then came close to us again.

We made signs of thanks to them, for we had nothing to make them amends; but an opportunity offered that very instant to oblige them wonderfully; for while we were lying by the shore came two mighty creatures, one pursuing the other (as we took it) with great fury from the mountains towards the sea; whether it was the male pursuing the female, or whether they were in sport or in rage, we could not tell, any more than we could tell whether it was usual or strange, but I believe it was the latter; because, in the first place, those ravenous creatures seldom appear but in the night; and, in the second place, we found the people terribly frighted, especially the women. The man that had the lance or dart did not fly from them, but the rest did; however, as the two creatures ran directly into the water, they did not offer to fall upon any of the negroes, but plunged themselves into the sea, and swam about, as if they had come for their diversion; at last one of them began to come nearer our boat than at first I expected; but I lay ready for him, for I had loaded my gun with all possible expedition, and bade Xury load both the others. As soon as he came fairly within my reach, I fired, and shot him directly in the head; immediately he sank down into the water, but rose instantly, and plunged up and down, as if he were struggling for life, and so indeed he was; he immediately made to the shore; but between the wound, which was his mortal hurt, and the strangling of the water, he died just before he reached the shore.

It is impossible to express the astonishment of these poor creatures at the noise and fire of my gun: some of them were even ready to die for fear, and fell down as dead with the very terror; but when they saw the creature dead, and sunk in the water, and that I made signs to them to come to the shore, they took heart and came, and began to search for the creature. I found him by his blood staining the water; and by the help of a rope, which I slung round him, and gave the negroes to haul, they dragged him on shore, and found that it was a most curious leopard, spotted, and fine to an admirable degree; and the negroes held up their hands with admiration, to think what it was I had killed him with.

The other creature, frighted with the flash of fire and the noise of the gun, swam on shore, and ran up directly to the mountains from whence they came; nor could I, at that distance, know what it was. I found quickly the negroes wished to eat the flesh of this creature, so I was willing to have them take it as a favour from me; which, when I made signs to them that they might take him, they were very thankful for. Immediately they fell to work with him; and though they had no knife, yet, with a sharpened piece of wood, they took off his skin as readily, and much more readily, than we could have done with a knife. They offered me some of the flesh, which I declined, pointing out that I would give it them; but made signs for the skin, which they gave me very freely, and brought me a great deal more of their provisions, which, though I did not understand, yet I accepted. I then made signs to them for some water, and held out one of my jars to them, turning it bottom upward, to show that it was empty, and that I wanted to have it filled. They called immediately to some of their friends, and there came two women, and brought a great vessel made of earth, and burnt, as I supposed, in the sun, this they set down to me, as before, and I sent Xury on shore with my jars, and filled them all three....

I was now furnished with roots and corn, such as it was, and water; and leaving my friendly negroes, I made forward for about eleven days more, without offering to go near the shore, till I saw the land run out a great length into the sea, at about the distance of four or five leagues before me; and the sea being very calm, I kept a large offing to make this point. At length, doubling the point, at about two leagues from the land, I saw plainly land on the other side, to seaward; then I concluded, as it was most certain indeed, that this was the Cape de Verde, and those the islands called, from thence, Cape de Verde Islands. However, they were at a great distance, and I could not well tell what I had best to do; for if I should be taken with a fresh of wind, I might neither reach one or other.

In this dilemma, as I was very pensive,[46] I stepped into the cabin and sat down, Xury having the helm; when, on a sudden, the boy cried out, "Master, master, a ship with a sail!" and the foolish boy was frighted out of his wits, thinking it must needs be some of his master's ships sent to pursue us, but I knew we were far enough out of their reach. I jumped out of the cabin, and immediately saw, not only the ship, but that it was a Portuguese ship; and, as I thought, was bound to the coast of Guinea, for negroes. But, when I observed the course she steered, I was soon convinced they were bound some other way, and did not design to come any nearer to the shore; upon which I stretched out to sea as much as I could, resolving to speak with them if possible.

With all the sail I could make, I found I should not be able to come in their way, but that they would be gone by before I could make any signal to them: but after I had crowded to the utmost, and began to despair, they, it seems, saw by the help of their glasses that it was some European boat, which they supposed must belong to some ship that was lost; so they shortened sail to let me come up. I was encouraged with this, and as I had my patron's ancient on board, I made a waft of it to them, for a signal of distress, and fired a gun, both which they saw; for they told me they saw the smoke, though they did not hear the gun. Upon these signals they very kindly brought to, and lay by for me; and in about three hours; time I came up with them.

They asked me what I was, in Portuguese, and in Spanish, and in French, but I understood none of them; but at last a Scotch sailor, who was on board, called to me: and I answered him, and told him I was an Englishman, that I had made my escape out of slavery from the Moors, at Sallee; they then bade me come on board, and very kindly took me in, and all my goods.

It was an inexpressible joy to me, which any one will believe, that I was thus delivered, as I esteemed it, from such a miserable and almost hopeless condition as I was in; and I immediately offered all I had to the captain of the ship, as a return for my deliverance; but he generously told me he would take nothing from me, but that all I had should be delivered safe to me when I came to the Brazils. "For," says he, "I have saved your life on no other terms than I would be glad to be saved myself: and it may, one time or other, be my lot to be taken up in the same condition. Besides," said he, "when I carry you to the Brazils, so great a way from your own country, if I should take from you what you have, you will be starved there, and then I only take away that life I have given. No, no," says he: "Seignior Inglese" (Mr. Englishman), "I will carry you thither in charity, and those things will help to

---

[46] thoughtful

buy your subsistence there, and your passage home again."

As he was charitable in this proposal, so he was just in the performance to a tittle;[47] for he ordered the seamen that none should touch anything that I had: then he took everything into his own possession, and gave me back an exact inventory of them, that I might have them, even to my three earthen jars.

As to my boat, it was a very good one; and that he saw, and told me he would buy it of me for his ship's use; and asked me what I would have for it? I told him he had been so generous to me in everything that I could not offer to make any price of the boat, but left it entirely to him: upon which he told me he would give me a note of hand to pay me eighty pieces of eight for it at Brazil; and when it came there, if any one offered to give more, he would make it up. He offered me also sixty pieces of eight more for my boy Xury, which I was loth[48] to take; not that I was unwilling to let the captain have him, but I was very loth to sell the poor boy's liberty, who had assisted me so faithfully in procuring my own. However, when I let him know my reason, he owned it to be just, and offered me this medium,[49] that he would give the boy an obligation to set him free in ten years, if he turned Christian: upon this, and Xury saying he was willing to go to him, I let the captain have him.

We had a very good voyage to the Brazils, and I arrived in the Bay de Todos los Santos,[50] or All Saints' Bay, in about twenty-two days after. And now I was once more delivered from the most miserable of all conditions of life; and what to do next with myself I was to consider.

The generous treatment the captain gave me I can never enough remember: he would take nothing of me for my passage, gave me twenty ducats[51] for the leopard's skin, and forty for the lion's skin, which I had in my boat, and caused everything I had in the ship to be punctually delivered to me; and what I was willing to sell he bought of me, such as the case of bottles, two of my guns, and a piece of the lump of bees-wax—for I had made candles of the rest: in a word, I made about two hundred and twenty pieces of eight of all my cargo; and with this stock I went on shore in the Brazils.

I had not been long here before I was recommended to the house of a good honest man like himself, who had an *ingenio*, as they call it (that is, a plantation and a sugar-house). I lived with him some time, and acquainted myself by that means with the manner of planting and making of sugar; and seeing how well the planters lived, and how they got rich suddenly, I re-

---

[47] "to a tittle": even to the tiniest amount
[48] "loathe" (unwilling, not inclined)
[49] compromise
[50] on the eastern coast of Brazil
[51] gold coins

solved, if I could get a licence to settle there, I would turn planter among them: resolving in the meantime to find out some way to get my money, which I had left in London, remitted to me. To this purpose, getting a kind of letter of naturalisation, I purchased as much land that was uncured as my money would reach, and formed a plan for my plantation and settlement; such a one as might be suitable to the stock which I proposed to myself to receive from England.

I had a neighbour, a Portuguese, of Lisbon, but born of English parents, whose name was Wells, and in much such circumstances as I was. I call him my neighbour, because his plantation lay next to mine, and we went on very sociably together. My stock was but low, as well as his; and we rather planted for food than anything else, for about two years. However, we began to increase, and our land began to come into order; so that the third year we planted some tobacco, and made each of us a large piece of ground ready for planting canes in the year to come. But we both wanted help; and now I found, more than before, I had done wrong in parting with my boy Xury.

But, alas! for me to do wrong that never did right, was no great wonder. I hail no remedy but to go on: I had got into an employment quite remote to my genius, and directly contrary to the life I delighted in, and for which I forsook my father's house, and broke through all his good advice. Nay, I was coming into the very middle station, or upper degree of low life, which my father advised me to before, and which, if I resolved to go on with, I might as well have stayed at home, and never have fatigued myself in the world as I had done; and I used often to say to myself, I could have done this as well in England, among my friends, as have gone five thousand miles off to do it among strangers and savages, in a wilderness, and at such a distance as never to hear from any part of the world that had the least knowledge of me.

In this manner I used to look upon my condition with the utmost regret. I had nobody to converse with, but now and then this neighbour; no work to be done, but by the labour of my hands; and I used to say, I lived just like a man cast away upon some desolate island, that had nobody there but himself. But how just has it been—and how should all men reflect, that when they compare their present conditions with others that are worse, Heaven may oblige them to make the exchange, and be convinced of their former felicity[52] by their experience—I say, how just has it been, that the truly solitary life I reflected on, in an island of mere desolation, should be my lot, who had so often unjustly compared it with the life which I then led, in which, had I continued, I had in all probability been exceeding prosperous and rich.

---

[52] blessedness, contentment

I was in some degree settled in my measures for carrying on the plantation before my kind friend, the captain of the ship that took me up at sea, went back—for the ship remained there, in providing his lading and preparing for his voyage, nearly three months—when telling him what little stock I had left behind me in London, he gave me this friendly and sincere advice:—"Seignior Inglese," says he (for so he always called me), "if you will give me letters, and a procuration in form to me, with orders to the person who has your money in London to send your effects to Lisbon, to such persons as I shall direct, and in such goods as are proper for this country, I will bring you the produce of them, God willing, at my return; but, since human affairs are all subject to changes and disasters, I would have you give orders but for one hundred pounds sterling, which, you say, is half your stock, and let the hazard be run for the first; so that, if it come safe, you may order the rest the same way, and, if it miscarry, you may have the other half to have recourse to for your supply."

This was so wholesome advice, and looked so friendly, that I could not but be convinced it was the best course I could take; so I accordingly prepared letters to the gentlewoman with whom I had left my money, and a procuration to the Portuguese captain, as he desired.

I wrote the English captain's widow a full account of all my adventures—my slavery, escape, and how I had met with the Portuguese captain at sea, the humanity of his behaviour, and what condition I was now in, with all other necessary directions for my supply; and when this honest captain came to Lisbon, he found means, by some of the English merchants there, to send over, not the order only, but a full account of my story to a merchant in London, who represented it effectually to her; whereupon she not only delivered the money, but out of her own pocket sent the Portugal captain a very handsome present for his humanity and charity to me.

The merchant in London, vesting this hundred pounds in English goods, such as the captain had written for, sent them directly to him at Lisbon, and he brought them all safe to me to the Brazils; among which, without my direction (for I was too young in my business to think of them), he had taken care to have all sorts of tools, ironwork, and utensils necessary for my plantation, and which were of great use to me.

When this cargo arrived I thought my fortune made, for I was surprised with the joy of it; and my stood steward, the captain, had laid out the five pounds, which my friend had sent him for a present for himself, to purchase and bring me over a servant, under bond for six years' service, and would not accept of any consideration, except a little tobacco, which I would have him accept, being of my own produce.

Neither was this all; for my goods being all English manufacture, such as cloths, stuffs, baize,[53] and things particularly valuable and desirable in the country, I found means to sell them to a very great advantage; so that I might say I had more than four times the value of my first cargo, and was now infinitely beyond my poor neighbour—I mean in the advancement of my plantation; for the first thing I did, I bought me a negro slave, and an European servant also—I mean another besides that which the captain brought me from Lisbon.

But as abused prosperity is oftentimes made the very means of our greatest adversity, so it was with me. I went on the next year with great success in my plantation: I raised fifty great rolls of tobacco on my own ground, more than I had disposed of for necessaries among my neighbours; and these fifty rolls, being each of above a hundredweight, were well cured, and laid by against the return of the fleet from Lisbon: and now increasing in business and wealth, my head began to be full of projects and undertakings beyond my reach; such as are, indeed, often the ruin of the best heads in business. Had I continued in the station I was now in, I had room for all the happy things to have yet befallen me for which my father so earnestly recommended a quiet, retired life, and of which he had so sensibly described the middle station of life to be full of; but other things attended me, and I was still to be the wilful agent of all my own miseries; and particularly, to increase my fault, and double the reflections upon myself, which in my future sorrows I should have leisure to make, all these miscarriages were procured by my apparent obstinate adhering to my foolish inclination of wandering abroad, and pursuing that inclination, in contradiction to the clearest views of doing myself good in a fair and plain pursuit of those prospects, and those measures of life, which nature and Providence concurred to present me with, and to make my duty.

As I had once done thus in my breaking away from my parents, so I could not be content now, but I must go and leave the happy view I had of being a rich and thriving man in my new plantation, only to pursue a rash and immoderate desire of rising faster than the nature of the thing admitted; and thus I cast myself down again into the deepest gulf of human misery that ever man fell into, or perhaps could be consistent with life and a state of health in the world.

To come, then, by the just degrees to the particulars of this part of my story. You may suppose, that having now lived almost four years in the Brazils, and beginning to thrive and prosper very well upon my plantation, I had not only learned the language, but had contracted acquaintance and friendship among my fellow-planters, as well as among the merchants at St. Salvador, which was our port; and that, in my discourses among them, I had

---

[53] thick, woolen cloth

frequently given them an account of my two voyages to the coast of Guinea: the manner of trading with the negroes there, and how easy it was to purchase upon the coast for trifles—such as beads, toys, knives, scissors, hatchets, bits of glass, and the like—not only gold-dust, Guinea grains, elephants' teeth, &c., but negroes, for the service of the Brazils, in great numbers.

They listened always very attentively to my discourses on these heads, but especially to that part which related to the buying of negroes, which was a trade at that time, not only not far entered into, but, as far as it was, had been carried on by assientos, or permission of the kings of Spain and Portugal, and engrossed in the public stock: so that few negroes were bought, and these excessively dear.

It happened, being in company with some merchants and planters of my acquaintance, and talking of those things very earnestly, three of them came to me next morning, and told me they had been musing very much upon what I had discoursed with them of the last night, and they came to make a secret proposal to me; and, after enjoining me to secrecy, they told me that they had a mind to fit out a ship to go to Guinea; that they had all plantations as well as I, and were straitened[54] for nothing so much as servants; that as it was a trade that could not be carried on, because they could not publicly sell the negroes when they came home, so they desired to make but one voyage, to bring the negroes on shore privately, and divide them among their own plantations; and, in a word, the question was whether I would go their super-cargo in the ship, to manage the trading part upon the coast of Guinea; and they offered me that I should have my equal share of the negroes, without providing any part of the stock.

This was a fair proposal, it must be confessed, had it been made to any one that had not had a settlement and a plantation of his own to look after, which was in a fair way of coming to be very considerable, and with a good stock upon it; but for me, that was thus entered and established, and had nothing to do but to go on as I had begun, for three or four years more, and to have sent for the other hundred pounds from England; and who in that time, and with that little addition, could scarce have failed of being worth three or four thousand pounds sterling,[55] and that increasing too—for me to think of such a voyage was the most preposterous thing that ever man in such circumstances could be guilty of.

But I, that was born to be my own destroyer, could no more resist the offer than I could restrain my first rambling designs when my father's good counsel was lost upon me. In a word, I told them I would go with all my

---

[54] lacking
[55] In our day this would have made Robinson Crusoe the equivalent of a multimillionaire.

heart, if they would undertake to look after my plantation in my absence, and would dispose of it to such as I should direct, if I miscarried. This they all engaged to do, and entered into writings or covenants to do so; and I made a formal will, disposing of my plantation and effects in case of my death, making the captain of the ship that had saved my life, as before, my universal heir, but obliging him to dispose of my effects as I had directed in my will; one half of the produce being to himself, and the other to be shipped to England.

In short, I took all possible caution to preserve my effects and to keep up my plantation. Had I used half as much prudence to have looked into my own interest, and have made a judgment of what I ought to have done and not to have done, I had certainly never gone away from so prosperous an undertaking, leaving all the probable views of a thriving circumstance, and gone upon a voyage to sea, attended with all its common hazards, to say nothing of the reasons I had to expect particular misfortunes to myself.

But I was hurried on, and obeyed blindly the dictates of my fancy rather than my reason; and, accordingly, the ship being fitted out, and the cargo furnished, and all things done, as by agreement, by my partners in the voyage, I went on board in an evil hour, the 1st September 1659, being the same day eight years that I went from my father and mother at Hull, in order to act the rebel to their authority, and the fool to my own interests.

Our ship was about one hundred and twenty tons burden, carried six guns and fourteen men, besides the master, his boy, and myself. We had on board no large cargo of goods, except of such toys as were fit for our trade with the negroes, such as beads, bits of glass, shells, and other trifles, especially little looking-glasses, knives, scissors, hatchets, and the like.

The same day I went on board we set sail, standing away to the northward upon our own coast, with design to stretch over for the African coast when we came about ten or twelve degrees of northern latitude, which, it seems, was the manner of course in those days. We had very good weather, only excessively hot, all the way upon our own coast, till we came to the height of Cape St. Augustino; from whence, keeping further off at sea, we lost sight of land, and steered as if we were bound for the isle Fernando de Noronha, holding our course N.E. by N., and leaving those isles on the east. In this course we passed the line in about twelve days' time, and were, by our last observation, in seven degrees twenty-two minutes northern latitude, when a violent tornado, or hurricane, took us quite out of our knowledge. It began from the south-east, came about to the north-west, and then settled in the north-east; from whence it blew in such a terrible manner, that for twelve days together we could do nothing but drive, and, scudding away before it, let it carry us whither fate and the fury of the winds directed; and, during these twelve days, I need not say that I expected every day to be swallowed up; nor, indeed, did any in the ship expect to save their lives.

In this distress we had, besides the terror of the storm, one of our men died of the calenture,[56] and one man and the boy washed overboard. About the twelfth day, the weather abating a little, the master made an observation as well as he could, and found that he was in about eleven degrees north latitude, but that he was twenty-two degrees of longitude difference west from Cape St. Augustino; so that he found he was upon the coast of Guiana, or the north part of Brazil, beyond the river Amazon, toward that of the river Orinoco, commonly called the Great River; and began to consult with me what course he should take, for the ship was leaky, and very much disabled, and he was going directly back to the coast of Brazil.

I was positively against that; and looking over the charts of the sea-coast of America with him, we concluded there was no inhabited country for us to have recourse to till we came within the circle of the Caribbee Islands, and therefore resolved to stand away for Barbadoes; which, by keeping off at sea, to avoid the indraft of the Bay or Gulf of Mexico, we might easily perform, as we hoped, in about fifteen days' sail; whereas we could not possibly make our voyage to the coast of Africa without some assistance both to our ship and to ourselves.

With this design we changed our course, and steered away N.W. by W., in order to reach some of our English islands, where I hoped for relief. But our voyage was otherwise determined; for, being in the latitude of twelve degrees eighteen minutes, a second storm came upon us, which carried us away with the same impetuosity[57] westward, and drove us so out of the way of all human commerce, that, had all our lives been saved as to the sea, we were rather in danger of being devoured by savages than ever returning to our own country.

In this distress, the wind still blowing very hard, one of our men early in the morning cried out, "Land!" and we had no sooner run out of the cabin to look out, in hopes of seeing whereabouts in the world we were, than the ship struck upon a sand, and in a moment her motion being so stopped, the sea broke over her in such a manner that we expected we should all have perished immediately; and we were immediately driven into our close quarters, to shelter us from the very foam and spray of the sea.

It is not easy for any one who has not been in the like condition to describe or conceive the consternation of men in such circumstances. We knew nothing where we were, or upon what land it was we were driven—whether an island or the main, whether inhabited or not inhabited. As the rage of the wind was still great, though rather less than at first, we could not

---

[56] heat stroke or fever
[57] suddenness

so much as hope to have the ship hold many minutes without breaking into pieces, unless the winds, by a kind of miracle, should turn immediately about. In a word, we sat looking upon one another, and expecting death every moment, and every man, accordingly, preparing for another world; for there was little or nothing more for us to do in this. That which was our present comfort, and all the comfort we had, was that, contrary to our expectation, the ship did not break yet, and that the master said the wind began to abate.

Now, though we thought that the wind did a little abate, yet the ship having thus struck upon the sand, and sticking too fast for us to expect her getting off, we were in a dreadful condition indeed, and had nothing to do but to think of saving our lives as well as we could. We had a boat at our stern just before the storm, but she was first staved by dashing against the ship's rudder, and in the next place she broke away, and either sunk or was driven off to sea; so there was no hope from her. We had another boat on board, but how to get her off into the sea was a doubtful thing. However, there was no time to debate, for we fancied that the ship would break in pieces every minute, and some told us she was actually broken already.

In this distress the mate of our vessel laid hold of the boat, and with the help of the rest of the men got her slung over the ship's side; and getting all into her, let go, and committed ourselves, being eleven in number, to God's mercy and the wild sea; for though the storm was abated considerably, yet the sea ran dreadfully high upon the shore, and might be well called *den wild zee*, as the Dutch call the sea in a storm.

And now our case was very dismal indeed; for we all saw plainly that the sea went so high that the boat could not live, and that we should be inevitably drowned. As to making sail, we had none, nor if we had could we have done anything with it; so we worked at the oar towards the land, though with heavy hearts, like men going to execution; for we all knew that when the boat came near the shore she would be dashed in a thousand pieces by the breach of the sea. However, we committed our souls to God in the most earnest manner; and the wind driving us towards the shore, we hastened our destruction with our own hands, pulling as well as we could towards land.

What the shore was, whether rock or sand, whether steep or shoal,[58] we knew not. The only hope that could rationally give us the least shadow of expectation was, if we might find some bay or gulf, or the mouth of some river, where by great chance we might have run our boat in, or got under the lee of the land, and perhaps made smooth water. But there was nothing like this appeared; but as we made nearer and nearer the shore, the land looked more frightful than the sea.

---

[58] shallow

After we had rowed, or rather driven about a league and a half, as we reckoned it, a raging wave, mountain-like, came rolling astern of us, and plainly bade us expect the *coup de grâce*.[59] It took us with such a fury, that it overset the boat at once; and separating us as well from the boat as from one another, gave us no time to say, "O God!" for we were all swallowed up in a moment.

Nothing can describe the confusion of thought which I felt when I sank into the water; for though I swam very well, yet I could not deliver myself from the waves so as to draw breath, till that wave having driven me, or rather carried me, a vast way on towards the shore, and having spent itself, went back, and left me upon the land almost dry, but half dead with the water I took in. I had so much presence of mind, as well as breath left, that seeing myself nearer the mainland than I expected, I got upon my feet, and endeavoured to make on towards the land as fast as I could before another wave should return and take me up again; but I soon found it was impossible to avoid it; for I saw the sea come after me as high as a great hill, and as furious as an enemy, which I had no means or strength to contend with: my business was to hold my breath, and raise myself upon the water if I could; and so, by swimming, to preserve my breathing, and pilot myself towards the shore, if possible, my greatest concern now being that the sea, as it would carry me a great way towards the shore when it came on, might not carry me back again with it when it gave back towards the sea.

The wave that came upon me again buried me at once twenty or thirty feet deep in its own body, and I could feel myself carried with a mighty force and swiftness towards the shore—a very great way; but I held my breath, and assisted myself to swim still forward with all my might. I was ready to burst with holding my breath, when, as I felt myself rising up, so, to my immediate relief, I found my head and hands shoot out above the surface of the water; and though it was not two seconds of time that I could keep myself so, yet it relieved me greatly, gave me breath, and new courage. I was covered again with water a good while, but not so long but I held it out; and finding the water had spent itself, and began to return, I struck forward against the return of the waves, and felt ground again with my feet. I stood still a few moments to recover breath, and till the waters went from me, and then took to my heels and ran with what strength I had further towards the shore. But neither would this deliver me from the fury of the sea, which came pouring in after me again; and twice more I was lifted up by the waves and carried forward as before, the shore being very flat.

The last time of these two had well-nigh been fatal to me, for the sea having hurried me along as before, landed me, or rather dashed me, against

---

[59] final death blow

a piece of rock, and that with such force, that it left me senseless, and indeed helpless, as to my own deliverance; for the blow taking my side and breast, beat the breath as it were quite out of my body; and had it returned again immediately, I must have been strangled in the water; but I recovered a little before the return of the waves, and seeing I should be covered again with the water, I resolved to hold fast by a piece of the rock, and so to hold my breath, if possible, till the wave went back. Now, as the waves were not so high as at first, being nearer land, I held my hold till the wave abated, and then fetched another run, which brought me so near the shore that the next wave, though it went over me, yet did not so swallow me up as to carry me away; and the next run I took, I got to the mainland, where, to my great comfort, I clambered up the cliffs of the shore and sat me down upon the grass, free from danger and quite out of the reach of the water.

I was now landed and safe on shore, and began to look up and thank God that my life was saved, in a case wherein there was some minutes before scarce any room to hope. I believe it is impossible to express, to the life, what the ecstasies and transports of the soul are, when it is so saved, as I may say, out of the very grave: and I do not wonder now at the custom, when a malefactor, who has the halter about his neck, is tied up, and just going to be turned off, and has a reprieve brought to him—I say, I do not wonder that they bring a surgeon with it, to let him blood that very moment they tell him of it, that the surprise may not drive the animal spirits from the heart and overwhelm him.

"For sudden joys, like griefs, confound at first."

I walked about on the shore lifting up my hands, and my whole being, as I may say, wrapped up in a contemplation of my deliverance; making a thousand gestures and motions, which I cannot describe; reflecting upon all my comrades that were drowned, and that there should not be one soul saved but myself; for, as for them, I never saw them afterwards, or any sign of them, except three of their hats, one cap, and two shoes that were not fellows.[60]

I cast my eye to the stranded vessel, when, the breach and froth of the sea being so big, I could hardly see it, it lay so far of; and considered, Lord! how was it possible I could get on shore?

After I had solaced my mind with the comfortable part of my condition, I began to look round me, to see what kind of place I was in, and what was next to be done; and I soon found my comforts abate, and that, in a word, I had a dreadful deliverance; for I was wet, had no clothes to shift me, nor anything either to eat or drink to comfort me; neither did I see any prospect before me but that of perishing with hunger or being devoured by wild

---

[60] "were not fellows": did not match

beasts; and that which was particularly afflicting to me was, that I had no weapon, either to hunt and kill any creature for my sustenance, or to defend myself against any other creature that might desire to kill me for theirs. In a word, I had nothing about me but a knife, a tobacco-pipe, and a little tobacco in a box. This was all my provisions; and this threw me into such terrible agonies of mind, that for a while I ran about like a madman. Night coming upon me, I began with a heavy heart to consider what would be my lot if there were any ravenous beasts in that country, as at night they always come abroad for their prey.

All the remedy that offered to my thoughts at that time was to get up into a thick bushy tree like a fir, but thorny, which grew near me, and where I resolved to sit all night, and consider the next day what death I should die, for as yet I saw no prospect of life. I walked about a furlong[61] from the shore, to see if I could find any fresh water to drink, which I did, to my great joy; and having drank, and put a little tobacco into my mouth to prevent hunger, I went to the tree, and getting up into it, endeavoured to place myself so that if I should sleep I might not fall. And having cut me a short stick, like a truncheon,[62] for my defence, I took up my lodging; and having been excessively fatigued, I fell fast asleep, and slept as comfortably as, I believe, few could have done in my condition, and found myself more refreshed with it than, I think, I ever was on such an occasion.

Questions for Review:

1. Describe Robinson Crusoe's encounters with the islanders.

2. How does the Portuguese captain treat him and Xury?

3. Sum up Robinson Crusoe's activity in Brazil. What does he come to decide about life in Brazil? What kind of man does he say he lives like?

4. How does Robinson Crusoe prosper in Brazil? What does he say he should have done in regards to this prosperity?

5. Why does Robinson Crusoe set sail again? What is significant about the date he sails? Describe what happens to his ship and lifeboat.

6. Give several reasons why Robinson Crusoe's decision to sail for Africa for slaves is foolish and wrong.

---

[61] 220 yards (one-eighth of a mile)
[62] club

CHAPTER IV: FIRST WEEKS ON THE ISLAND

When I waked it was broad day, the weather clear, and the storm abated, so that the sea did not rage and swell as before. But that which surprised me most was, that the ship was lifted off in the night from the sand where she lay by the swelling of the tide, and was driven up almost as far as the rock which I at first mentioned, where I had been so bruised by the wave dashing me against it. This being within about a mile from the shore where I was, and the ship seeming to stand upright still, I wished myself on board, that at least I might save some necessary things for my use.

When I came down from my apartment in the tree, I looked about me again, and the first thing I found was the boat, which lay, as the wind and the sea had tossed her up, upon the land, about two miles on my right hand. I walked as far as I could upon the shore to have got to her; but found a neck or inlet of water between me and the boat which was about half a mile broad; so I came back for the present, being more intent upon getting at the ship, where I hoped to find something for my present subsistence.[63]

A little after noon I found the sea very calm, and the tide ebbed so far out that I could come within a quarter of a mile of the ship. And here I found a fresh renewing of my grief; for I saw evidently that if we had kept on board we had been all safe—that is to say, we had all got safe on shore, and I had not been so miserable as to be left entirely destitute of all comfort and company as I now was. This forced tears to my eyes again; but as there was little relief in that, I resolved, if possible, to get to the ship; so I pulled off my clothes—for the weather was hot to extremity—and took the water. But when I came to the ship my difficulty was still greater to know how to get on board; for, as she lay aground, and high out of the water, there was nothing within my reach to lay hold of. I swam round her twice, and the second time I spied a small piece of rope, which I wondered I did not see at first, hung down by the fore-chains so low, as that with great difficulty I got hold of it, and by the help of that rope I got up into the forecastle of the ship. Here I found that the ship was bulged, and had a great deal of water in her hold,

---

[63] that is, something to eat

but that she lay so on the side of a bank of hard sand, or, rather earth, that her stern lay lifted up upon the bank, and her head low, almost to the water. By this means all her quarter was free, and all that was in that part was dry; for you may be sure my first work was to search, and to see what was spoiled and what was free. And, first, I found that all the ship's provisions were dry and untouched by the water, and being very well disposed to eat, I went to the bread room and filled my pockets with biscuit, and ate it as I went about other things, for I had no time to lose. I also found some rum in the great cabin, of which I took a large dram, and which I had, indeed, need enough of to spirit me for what was before me. Now I wanted nothing but a boat to furnish myself with many things which I foresaw would be very necessary to me.

It was in vain to sit still and wish for what was not to be had; and this extremity roused my application. We had several spare yards, and two or three large spars of wood, and a spare topmast or two in the ship; I resolved to fall to work with these, and I flung as many of them overboard as I could manage for their weight, tying every one with a rope, that they might not drive away. When this was done I went down the ship's side, and pulling them to me, I tied four of them together at both ends as well as I could, in the form of a raft, and laying two or three short pieces of plank upon them crossways, I found I could walk upon it very well, but that it was not able to bear any great weight, the pieces being too light. So I went to work, and with a carpenter's saw I cut a spare topmast into three lengths, and added them to my raft, with a great deal of labour and pains. But the hope of furnishing myself with necessaries encouraged me to go beyond what I should have been able to have done upon another occasion.

My raft was now strong enough to bear any reasonable weight. My next care was what to load it with, and how to preserve what I laid upon it from the surf of the sea; but I was not long considering this. I first laid all the planks or boards upon it that I could get, and having considered well what I most wanted, I got three of the seamen's chests, which I had broken open, and emptied, and lowered them down upon my raft; the first of these I filled with provisions—viz. bread, rice, three Dutch cheeses, five pieces of dried goat's flesh (which we lived much upon), and a little remainder of European corn, which had been laid by for some fowls which we brought to sea with us, but the fowls were killed. There had been some barley and wheat together; but, to my great disappointment, I found afterwards that the rats had eaten or spoiled it all. As for liquors, I found several, cases of bottles belonging to our skipper, in which were some cordial waters; and, in all, about five or six gallons of rack. These I stowed by themselves, there being no need to put them into the chest, nor any room for them. While I was doing this, I found the tide begin to flow, though very calm; and I had the mortification[64] to see my coat, shirt, and waistcoat, which I had left on the shore, upon the sand, swim away. As for my breeches, which were only linen, and open-kneed, I swam on board in them and my stockings. However, this set me on rummaging for clothes, of which I found enough, but took no more than I wanted for present use, for I had others things which my eye was more upon—as, first, tools to work with on shore. And it was after long searching that I found out the carpenter's chest, which was, indeed, a very useful prize to me, and much more valuable than a shipload of gold would have been at that time. I got it down to my raft, whole as it was, without losing time to look into it, for I knew in general what it contained.

My next care was for some ammunition and arms. There were two very good fowling-pieces in the great cabin, and two pistols. These I secured first, with some powder-horns and a small bag of shot, and two old rusty swords. I knew there were three barrels of powder in the ship, but knew not where our gunner had stowed them; but with much search I found them, two of them dry and good, the third had taken water. Those two I got to my raft with the arms. And now I thought myself pretty well freighted, and began to think how I should get to shore with them, having neither sail, oar, nor rudder; and the least capful of wind would have overset all my navigation.

I had three encouragements—1st, a smooth, calm sea; 2ndly, the tide rising, and setting in to the shore; 3rdly, what little wind there was blew me towards the land. And thus, having found two or three broken oars belonging to the boat—and, besides the tools which were in the chest, I found two saws, an axe, and a hammer; with this cargo I put to sea. For a mile or thereabouts my raft went very well, only that I found it drive a little distant from the place where I had landed before; by which I perceived that there was some indraft of the water, and consequently I hoped to find some creek or river there, which I might make use of as a port to get to land with my cargo.

As I imagined, so it was. There appeared before me a little opening of the land, and I found a strong current of the tide set into it; so I guided my raft as well as I could, to keep in the middle of the stream.

But here I had like to have suffered a second shipwreck, which, if I had, I think verily would have broken my heart; for, knowing nothing of the coast, my raft ran aground at one end of it upon a shoal, and not being aground at the other end, it wanted but a little that all my cargo had slipped off towards the end that was afloat, and to fallen into the water. I did my utmost, by setting my back against the chests, to keep them in their places, but could not thrust off the raft with all my strength; neither durst I stir from

---

[64] embarrassment, humiliation

the posture I was in; but holding up the chests with all my might, I stood in that manner near half-an-hour, in which time the rising of the water brought me a little more upon a level; and a little after, the water still-rising, my raft floated again, and I thrust her off with the oar I had into the channel, and then driving up higher, I at length found myself in the mouth of a little river, with land on both sides, and a strong current of tide running up. I looked on both sides for a proper place to get to shore, for I was not willing to be driven too high up the river: hoping in time to see some ships at sea, and therefore resolved to place myself as near the coast as I could.

At length I spied a little cove on the right shore of the creek, to which with great pain and difficulty I guided my raft, and at last got so near that, reaching ground with my oar, I could thrust her directly in. But here I had like to have dipped all my cargo into the sea again; for that shore lying pretty steep—that is to say sloping—there was no place to land, but where one end of my float, if it ran on shore, would lie so high, and the other sink lower, as before, that it would endanger my cargo again. All that I could do was to wait till the tide was at the highest, keeping the raft with my oar like an anchor, to hold the side of it fast to the shore, near a flat piece of ground, which I expected the water would flow over; and so it did. As soon as I found water enough—for my raft drew about a foot of water—I thrust her upon that flat piece of ground, and there fastened or moored her, by sticking my two broken oars into the ground, one on one side near one end, and one on the other side near the other end; and thus I lay till the water ebbed away, and left my raft and all my cargo safe on shore.

My next work was to view the country, and seek a proper place for my habitation, and where to stow my goods to secure them from whatever might happen. Where I was, I yet knew not; whether on the continent or on an island; whether inhabited or not inhabited; whether in danger of wild beasts or not. There was a hill not above a mile from me, which rose up very steep and high, and which seemed to overtop some other hills, which lay as in a ridge from it northward. I took out one of the fowling-pieces, and one of the pistols, and a horn of powder; and thus armed, I travelled for discovery up to the top of that hill, where, after I had with great labour and difficulty got to the top, I saw my fate, to my great affliction—viz. that I was in an island environed every way with the sea: no land to be seen except some rocks, which lay a great way off; and two small islands, less than this, which lay about three leagues to the west.

I found also that the island I was in was barren, and, as I saw good reason to believe, uninhabited except by wild beasts, of whom, however, I saw none. Yet I saw abundance of fowls, but knew not their kinds; neither when I killed them could I tell what was fit for food, and what not. At my coming back, I shot at a great bird which I saw sitting upon a tree on the side of a great wood. I believe it was the first gun that had been fired there since the creation of the world. I had no sooner fired, than from all parts of the wood there arose an innumerable number of fowls, of many sorts, making a confused screaming and crying, and every one according to his usual note, but not one of them of any kind that I knew. As for the creature I killed, I took it to be a kind of hawk, its colour and beak resembling it, but it had no talons or claws more than common. Its flesh was carrion, and fit for nothing.

Contented with this discovery, I came back to my raft, and fell to work to bring my cargo on shore, which took me up the rest of that day. What to do with myself at night I knew not, nor indeed where to rest, for I was afraid to lie down on the ground, not knowing but some wild beast might devour me, though, as I afterwards found, there was really no need for those fears.

However, as well as I could, I barricaded myself round with the chest and boards that I had brought on shore, and made a kind of hut for that night's lodging. As for food, I yet saw not which way to supply myself, except that I had seen two or three creatures like hares run out of the wood where I shot the fowl.

I now began to consider that I might yet get a great many things out of the ship which would be useful to me, and particularly some of the rigging and sails, and such other things as might come to land; and I resolved to make another voyage on board the vessel, if possible. And as I knew that the first storm that blew must necessarily break her all in pieces, I resolved to set all other things apart till I had got everything out of the ship that I could get. Then I called a council—that is to say in my thoughts—whether I should take back the raft; but this appeared impracticable: so I resolved to go as before, when the tide was down; and I did so, only that I stripped before I went from my hut, having nothing on but my chequered shirt, a pair of linen drawers, and a pair of pumps on my feet.

I got on board the ship as before, and prepared a second raft; and, having had experience of the first, I neither made this so unwieldy, nor loaded it so hard, but yet I brought away several things very useful to me; as first, in the carpenters stores I found two or three bags full of nails and spikes, a great screw-jack, a dozen or two of hatchets, and, above all, that most useful thing called a grindstone. All these I secured, together with several things belonging to the gunner, particularly two or three iron crows,[65] and two barrels of musket bullets, seven muskets, another fowling-piece, with some small quantity of powder more; a large bagful of small shot, and a great roll of sheet-lead; but this last was so heavy, I could not hoist it up to get it over the ship's side.

Besides these things, I took all the men's clothes that I could find, and a

---

[65] crowbars

spare fore-topsail, a hammock, and some bedding; and with this I loaded my second raft, and brought them all safe on shore, to my very great comfort.

I was under some apprehension, during my absence from the land, that at least my provisions might be devoured on shore: but when I came back I found no sign of any visitor; only there sat a creature like a wild cat upon one of the chests, which, when I came towards it, ran away a little distance, and then stood still. She sat very composed and unconcerned, and looked full in my face, as if she had a mind to be acquainted with me. I presented my gun at her, but, as she did not understand it, she was perfectly unconcerned at it, nor did she offer to stir away; upon which I tossed her a bit of biscuit, though by the way, I was not very free of it, for my store was not great: however, I spared her a bit, I say, and she went to it, smelled at it, and ate it, and looked (as if pleased) for more; but I thanked her, and could spare no more: so she marched off.

Having got my second cargo on shore—though I was fain[66] to open the barrels of powder, and bring them by parcels, for they were too heavy, being large casks—I went to work to make me a little tent with the sail and some poles which I cut for that purpose: and into this tent I brought everything that I knew would spoil either with rain or sun; and I piled all the empty chests and casks up in a circle round the tent, to fortify it from any sudden attempt, either from man or beast.

When I had done this, I blocked up the door of the tent with some boards within, and an empty chest set up on end without; and spreading one of the beds upon the ground, laying my two pistols just at my head, and my gun at length by me, I went to bed for the first time, and slept very quietly all night, for I was very weary and heavy; for the night before I had slept little, and had laboured very hard all day to fetch all those things from the ship, and to get them on shore.

I had the biggest magazine[67] of all kinds now that ever was laid up, I believe, for one man: but I was not satisfied still, for while the ship sat upright in that posture, I thought I ought to get everything out of her that I could; so every day at low water I went on board, and brought away something or other; but particularly the third time I went I brought away as much of the rigging as I could, as also all the small ropes and rope-twine I could get, with a piece of spare canvas, which was to mend the sails upon occasion, and the barrel of wet gunpowder. In a word, I brought away all the sails, first and last; only that I was fain to cut them in pieces, and bring as much at a time as I could, for they were no more useful to be sails, but as mere

---

[66] glad, pleased
[67] collection of arms, ammunition, or both

canvas only.

But that which comforted me more still, was, that last of all, after I had made five or six such voyages as these, and thought I had nothing more to expect from the ship that was worth my meddling with—I say, after all this, I found a great hogshead of bread, three large runlets of rum, or spirits, a box of sugar, and a barrel of fine flour; this was surprising to me, because I had given over expecting any more provisions, except what was spoiled by the water. I soon emptied the hogshead of the bread, and wrapped it up, parcel by parcel, in pieces of the sails, which I cut out; and, in a word, I got all this safe on shore also.

The next day I made another voyage, and now, having plundered the ship of what was portable and fit to hand out, I began with the cables. Cutting the great cable into pieces, such as I could move, I got two cables and a hawser[68] on shore, with all the ironwork I could get; and having cut down the spritsail-yard, and the mizzen-yard, and everything I could, to make a large raft, I loaded it with all these heavy goods, and came away. But my good luck began now to leave me; for this raft was so unwieldy, and so overladen, that, after I had entered the little cove where I had landed the rest of my goods, not being able to guide it so handily as I did the other, it overset, and threw me and all my cargo into the water. As for myself, it was no great harm, for I was near the shore; but as to my cargo, it was a great part of it lost, especially the iron, which I expected would have been of great use to me; however, when the tide was out, I got most of the pieces of the cable ashore, and some of the iron, though with infinite labour; for I was fain to dip for it into the water, a work which fatigued me very much. After this, I went every day on board, and brought away what I could get.

I had been now thirteen days on shore, and had been eleven times on board the ship, in which time I had brought away all that one pair of hands could well be supposed capable to bring; though I believe verily,[69] had the calm weather held, I should have brought away the whole ship, piece by piece. But preparing the twelfth time to go on board, I found the wind began to rise: however, at low water I went on board, and though I thought I had rummaged the cabin so effectually that nothing more could be found, yet I discovered a locker with drawers in it, in one of which I found two or three razors, and one pair of large scissors, with some ten or a dozen of good knives and forks: in another I found about thirty-six pounds value in money—some European coin, some Brazil, some pieces of eight, some gold, and some silver.

I smiled to myself at the sight of this money: "O drug!" said I, aloud,

---

[68] heavy rope used to tow a ship
[69] truly

"what art thou good for? Thou art not worth to me—no, not the taking off the ground; one of those knives is worth all this heap; I have no manner of use for thee—e'en[70] remain where thou art, and go to the bottom as a creature whose life is not worth saying." However, upon second thoughts I took it away; and wrapping all this in a piece of canvas, I began to think of making another raft; but while I was preparing this, I found the sky overcast, and the wind began to rise, and in a quarter of an hour it blew a fresh gale from the shore. It presently occurred to me that it was in vain to pretend to make a raft with the wind offshore; and that it was my business to be gone before the tide of flood began, otherwise I might not be able to reach the shore at all. Accordingly, I let myself down into the water, and swam across the channel, which lay between the ship and the sands, and even that with difficulty enough, partly with the weight of the things I had about me, and partly the roughness of the water; for the wind rose very hastily, and before it was quite high water it blew a storm.

But I had got home to my little tent, where I lay, with all my wealth about me, very secure. It blew very hard all night, and in the morning, when I looked out, behold, no more ship was to be seen! I was a little surprised, but recovered myself with the satisfactory reflection that I had lost no time, nor abated any diligence, to get everything out of her that could be useful to me; and that, indeed, there was little left in her that I was able to bring away, if I had had more time.

I now gave over any more thoughts of the ship, or of anything out of her, except what might drive on shore from her wreck; as, indeed, divers pieces of her afterwards did; but those things were of small use to me.

My thoughts were now wholly employed about securing myself against either savages, if any should appear, or wild beasts, if any were in the island; and I had many thoughts of the method how to do this, and what kind of dwelling to make—whether I should make me a cave in the earth, or a tent upon the earth; and, in short, I resolved upon both; the manner and description of which, it may not be improper to give an account of.

I soon found the place I was in was not fit for my settlement, because it was upon a low, moorish ground, near the sea, and I believed it would not be wholesome, and more particularly because there was no fresh water near it; so I resolved to find a more healthy and more convenient spot of ground.

I consulted several things in my situation, which I found would be proper for me: 1st, health and fresh water, I just now mentioned; 2ndly, shelter from the heat of the sun; 3rdly, security from ravenous creatures, whether man or beast; 4thly, a view to the sea, that if God sent any ship in sight, I might not lose any advantage for my deliverance, of which I was not willing

---

[70] even

to banish all my expectation yet.

In search of a place proper for this, I found a little plain on the side of a rising hill, whose front towards this little plain was steep as a house-side, so that nothing could come down upon me from the top. On the one side of the rock there was a hollow place, worn a little way in, like the entrance or door of a cave but there was not really any cave or way into the rock at all.

On the flat of the green, just before this hollow place, I resolved to pitch my tent. This plain was not above a hundred yards broad, and about twice as long, and lay like a green before my door; and, at the end of it, descended irregularly every way down into the low ground by the seaside. It was on the N.N.W. side of the hill; so that it was sheltered from the heat every day, till it came to a W. and by S. sun, or thereabouts, which, in those countries, is near the setting.

Before I set up my tent I drew a half-circle before the hollow place, which took in about ten yards in its semi-diameter from the rock, and twenty yards in its diameter from its beginning and ending.

In this half-circle I pitched two rows of strong stakes, driving them into the ground till they stood very firm like piles, the biggest end being out of the ground above five feet and a half, and sharpened on the top. The two rows did not stand above six inches from one another.

Then I took the pieces of cable which I had cut in the ship, and laid them in rows, one upon another, within the circle, between these two rows of stakes, up to the top, placing other stakes in the inside, leaning against them, about two feet and a half high, like a spur to a post; and this fence was so strong, that neither man nor beast could get into it or over it. This cost me a great deal of time and labour, especially to cut the piles in the woods, bring them to the place, and drive them into the earth.

The entrance into this place I made to be, not by a door, but by a short ladder to go over the top; which ladder, when I was in, I lifted over after me; and so I was completely fenced in and fortified, as I thought, from all the world, and consequently slept secure in the night, which otherwise I could not have done; though, as it appeared afterwards, there was no need of all this caution from the enemies that I apprehended danger from.

Into this fence or fortress, with infinite labour, I carried all my riches, all my provisions, ammunition, and stores, of which you have the account above; and I made a large tent, which to preserve me from the rains that in one part of the year are very violent there, I made double—one smaller tent within, and one larger tent above it; and covered the uppermost with a large tarpaulin, which I had saved among the sails.

And now I lay no more for a while in the bed which I had brought on shore, but in a hammock, which was indeed a very good one, and belonged to the mate of the ship.

Into this tent I brought all my provisions, and everything that would spoil by the wet; and having thus enclosed all my goods, I made up the entrance, which till now I had left open, and so passed and re-passed, as I said, by a short ladder.

When I had done this, I began to work my way into the rock, and bringing all the earth and stones that I dug down out through my tent, I laid them up within my fence, in the nature of a terrace, so that it raised the ground within about a foot and a half; and thus I made me a cave, just behind my tent, which served me like a cellar to my house.

It cost me much labour and many days before all these things were brought to perfection; and therefore I must go back to some other things which took up some of my thoughts. At the same time it happened, after I had laid my scheme for the setting up my tent, and making the cave, that a storm of rain falling from a thick, dark cloud, a sudden flash of lightning happened, and after that a great clap of thunder, as is naturally the effect of it. I was not so much surprised with the lightning as I was with the thought which darted into my mind as swift as the lightning itself—Oh, my powder! My very heart sank within me when I thought that, at one blast, all my powder might be destroyed; on which, not my defence only, but the providing my food, as I thought, entirely depended. I was nothing near so anxious about my own danger, though, had the powder took fire, I should never have known who had hurt me.

Such impression did this make upon me, that after the storm was over I laid aside all my works, my building and fortifying, and applied myself to make bags and boxes, to separate the powder, and to keep it a little and a little in a parcel, in the hope that, whatever might come, it might not all take fire at once; and to keep it so apart that it should not be possible to make one part fire another. I finished this work in about a fortnight;[71] and I think my powder, which in all was about two hundred and forty pounds weight, was divided in not less than a hundred parcels. As to the barrel that had been wet, I did not apprehend any danger from that; so I placed it in my new cave, which, in my fancy, I called my kitchen; and the rest I hid up and down in holes among the rocks, so that no wet might come to it, marking very carefully where I laid it.

In the interval of time while this was doing, I went out once at least every day with my gun, as well to divert myself as to see if I could kill anything fit for food; and, as near as I could, to acquaint myself with what the island produced. The first time I went out, I presently discovered that there were goats in the island, which was a great satisfaction to me; but then it was attended with this misfortune to me—viz. that they were so shy, so subtle,

---

[71] "fourteen nights": two weeks

and so swift of foot, that it was the most difficult thing in the world to come at them; but I was not discouraged at this, not doubting but I might now and then shoot one, as it soon happened; for after I had found their haunts a little, I laid wait in this manner for them: I observed if they saw me in the valleys, though they were upon the rocks, they would run away, as in a terrible fright; but if they were feeding in the valleys, and I was upon the rocks, they took no notice of me; from whence I concluded that, by the position of their optics, their sight was so directed downward that they did not readily see objects that were above them; so afterwards I took this method—I always climbed the rocks first, to get above them, and then had frequently a fair mark.

The first shot I made among these creatures, I killed a she-goat, which had a little kid by her, which she gave suck to, which grieved me heartily; for when the old one fell, the kid stood stock still by her, till I came and took her up; and not only so, but when I carried the old one with me, upon my shoulders, the kid followed me quite to my enclosure; upon which I laid down the dam, and took the kid in my arms, and carried it over my pale, in hopes to have bred it up tame; but it would not eat; so I was forced to kill it and eat it myself. These two supplied me with flesh a great while, for I ate sparingly, and saved my provisions, my bread especially, as much as possibly I could.

Having now fixed my habitation, I found it absolutely necessary to provide a place to make a fire in, and fuel to burn: and what I did for that, and also how I enlarged my cave, and what conveniences I made, I shall give a full account of in its place; but I must now give some little account of myself, and of my thoughts about living, which, it may well be supposed, were not a few.

I had a dismal prospect of my condition; for as I was not cast away upon that island without being driven, as is said, by a violent storm, quite out of the course of our intended voyage, and a great way, viz. some hundreds of leagues, out of the ordinary course of the trade of mankind, I had great reason to consider it as a determination of Heaven, that in this desolate place, and in this desolate manner, I should end my life. The tears would run plentifully down my face when I made these reflections; and sometimes I would expostulate with myself why Providence should thus completely ruin His creatures, and render them so absolutely miserable; so without help, abandoned, so entirely depressed, that it could hardly be rational to be thankful for such a life.

But something always returned swift upon me to check these thoughts, and to reprove me; and particularly one day, walking with my gun in my hand by the seaside, I was very pensive upon the subject of my present condition, when reason, as it were, expostulated with me the other way, thus:

"Well, you are in a desolate condition, it is true; but, pray remember, where are the rest of you? Did not you come, eleven of you in the boat? Where are the ten? Why were they not saved, and you lost? Why were you singled out? Is it better to be here or there?" And then I pointed to the sea. All evils are to be considered with the good that is in them, and with what worse attends them.

Then it occurred to me again, how well I was furnished for my subsistence, and what would have been my case if it had not happened (which was a hundred thousand to one) that the ship floated from the place where she first struck, and was driven so near to the shore that I had time to get all these things out of her; what would have been my case, if I had been forced to have lived in the condition in which I at first came on shore, without necessaries of life, or necessaries to supply and procure them? "Particularly," said I, aloud (though to myself), "what should I have done without a gun, without ammunition, without any tools to make anything, or to work with, without clothes, bedding, a tent, or any manner of covering?" and that now I had all these to sufficient quantity, and was in a fair way to provide myself in such a manner as to live without my gun, when my ammunition was spent: so that I had a tolerable view of subsisting, without any want, as long as I lived; for I considered from the beginning how I would provide for the accidents that might happen, and for the time that was to come, even not only after my ammunition should be spent, but even after my health and strength should decay.

I confess I had not entertained any notion of my ammunition being destroyed at one blast—I mean my powder being blown up by lightning; and this made the thoughts of it so surprising to me, when it lightened and thundered, as I observed just now.

And now being about to enter into a melancholy relation of a scene of silent life, such, perhaps, as was never heard of in the world before, I shall take it from its beginning, and continue it in its order. It was by my account the 30th of September, when, in the manner as above said, I first set foot upon this horrid island; when the sun, being to us in its autumnal equinox, was almost over my head; for I reckoned myself, by observation, to be in the latitude of nine degrees twenty-two minutes north of the line.

After I had been there about ten or twelve days, it came into my thoughts that I should lose my reckoning of time for want of books, and pen and ink, and should even forget the Sabbath days; but to prevent this, I cut with my knife upon a large post, in capital letters—and making it into a great cross, I set it up on the shore where I first landed—"I came on shore here on the 30th September 1659."

Upon the sides of this square post I cut every day a notch with my knife, and every seventh notch was as long again as the rest, and every first day of the month as long again as that long one; and thus I kept my calendar, or weekly, monthly, and yearly reckoning of time.

In the next place, we are to observe that among the many things which I brought out of the ship, in the several voyages which, as above mentioned, I made to it, I got several things of less value, but not at all less useful to me, which I omitted setting down before; as, in particular, pens, ink, and paper, several parcels in the captain's, mate's, gunner's and carpenter's keeping; three or four compasses, some mathematical instruments, dials, perspectives, charts, and books of navigation, all which I huddled together, whether I might want them or no; also, I found three very good Bibles, which came to me in my cargo from England, and which I had packed up among my things; some Portuguese books also; and among them two or three Popish prayer-books, and several other books, all which I carefully secured. And I must not forget that we had in the ship a dog and two cats, of whose eminent history I may have occasion to say something in its place; for I carried both the cats with me; and as for the dog, he jumped out of the ship of himself, and swam on shore to me the day after I went on shore with my first cargo, and was a trusty servant to me many years; I wanted nothing that he could fetch me, nor any company that he could make up to me; I only wanted to have him talk to me, but that would not do. As I observed before, I found pens, ink, and paper, and I husbanded them to the utmost; and I shall show that while my ink lasted, I kept things very exact, but after that was gone I could not, for I could not make any ink by any means that I could devise.

And this put me in mind that I wanted many things notwithstanding all that I had amassed together; and of these, ink was one; as also a spade, pickaxe, and shovel, to dig or remove the earth; needles, pins, and thread; as for linen, I soon learned to want[72] that without much difficulty.

This want of tools made every work I did go on heavily; and it was near a whole year before I had entirely finished my little pale, or surrounded my habitation. The piles, or stakes, which were as heavy as I could well lift, were a long time in cutting and preparing in the woods, and more, by far, in bringing home; so that I spent sometimes two days in cutting and bringing home one of those posts, and a third day in driving it into the ground; for which purpose I got a heavy piece of wood at first, but at last bethought myself of one of the iron crows; which, however, though I found it, made driving those posts or piles very laborious and tedious work. But what need I have been concerned at the tediousness of anything I had to do, seeing I had time enough to do it in? nor had I any other employment, if that had been over, at least that I could foresee, except the ranging the island to seek for food, which I did, more or less, every day.

I now began to consider seriously my condition, and the circumstances I was reduced to; and I drew up the state of my affairs in writing, not so much to leave them to any that were to come after me—for I was likely to have but few heirs—as to deliver my thoughts from daily poring over them, and afflicting my mind; and as my reason began now to master my despondency, I began to comfort myself as well as I could, and to set the good against the evil, that I might have something to distinguish my case from worse; and I stated very impartially, like debtor and creditor, the comforts I enjoyed against the miseries I suffered, thus:

Evil.	*Good.*
I am cast upon a horrible, desolate island, void of all hope of recovery.	But I am alive; and not drowned, as all my ship's company were.
I am singled out and separated,	But I am singled out, too, from all the ship's crew, to be spared from death;

---

[72] lack, go without

as it were, from all the world, to be miserable.

and He that miraculously saved me from death can deliver me from this condition.

I am divided from mankind—a solitaire; one banished from human society.

But I am not starved, and perishing on a barren place, affording no sustenance.

I have no clothes to cover me.

But I am in a hot climate, where, if I had clothes, I could hardly wear them.

I am without any defence, or means to resist any violence of man or beast.

But I am cast on an island where I see no wild beasts to hurt me, as I saw on the coast of Africa; and what if I had been shipwrecked there?

I have no soul to speak to or relieve me.

But God wonderfully sent the ship in near enough to the shore, that I have got out as many necessary things as will either supply my wants or enable me to supply myself, even as long as I live.

Upon the whole, here was an undoubted testimony that there was scarce any condition in the world so miserable but there was something negative or something positive to be thankful for in it; and let this stand as a direction from the experience of the most miserable of all conditions in this world: that we may always find in it something to comfort ourselves from, and to set, in the description of good and evil, on the credit side of the account.

Having now brought my mind a little to relish my condition, and given over looking out to sea, to see if I could spy a ship—I say, giving over these things, I began to apply myself to arrange my way of living, and to make things as easy to me as I could.

I have already described my habitation, which was a tent under the side of a rock, surrounded with a strong pale[73] of posts and cables: but I might now rather call it a wall, for I raised a kind of wall up against it of turfs, about two feet thick on the outside; and after some time (I think it was a year and a half) I raised rafters from it, leaning to the rock, and thatched or covered it with boughs of trees, and such things as I could get, to keep out the rain; which I found at some times of the year very violent.

---

[73] fence

I have already observed how I brought all my goods into this pale, and into the cave which I had made behind me. But I must observe, too, that at first this was a confused heap of goods, which, as they lay in no order, so they took up all my place; I had no room to turn myself: so I set myself to enlarge my cave, and work farther into the earth; for it was a loose sandy rock, which yielded easily to the labour I bestowed on it: and so when I found I was pretty safe as to beasts of prey, I worked sideways, to the right hand, into the rock; and then, turning to the right again, worked quite out, and made me a door to come out on the outside of my pale or fortification. This gave me not only egress and regress,[74] as it was a back way to my tent and to my storehouse, but gave me room to store my goods.

And now I began to apply myself to make such necessary things as I found I most wanted, particularly a chair and a table; for without these I was not able to enjoy the few comforts I had in the world; I could not write or eat, or do several things, with so much pleasure without a table: so I went to work. And here I must needs observe, that as reason is the substance and origin of the mathematics, so by stating and squaring everything by reason, and by making the most rational judgment of things, every man may be, in time, master of every mechanic art. I had never handled a tool in my life; and yet, in time, by labour, application, and contrivance, I found at last that I wanted nothing but I could have made it, especially if I had had tools. However, I made abundance of things, even without tools; and some with no more tools than an adze[75] and a hatchet, which perhaps were never made that way before, and that with infinite labour. For example, if I wanted a board, I had no other way but to cut down a tree, set it on an edge before me, and hew it flat on either side with my axe, till I brought it to be thin as a plank, and then dub it smooth with my adze. It is true, by this method I could make but one board out of a whole tree; but this I had no remedy for but patience, any more than I had for the prodigious deal of time and labour which it took me up to make a plank or board: but my time or labour was little worth, and so it was as well employed one way as another.

However, I made me a table and a chair, as I observed above, in the first place; and this I did out of the short pieces of boards that I brought on my raft from the ship. But when I had wrought out some boards as above, I made large shelves, of the breadth of a foot and a half, one over another all along one side of my cave, to lay all my tools, nails and ironwork on; and, in a word, to separate everything at large into their places, that I might come easily at them. I knocked pieces into the wall of the rock to hang my guns and all things that would hang up; so that, had my cave been to be seen, it

---

[74] "egress and regress": a way out and in
[75] cutting tool

looked like a general magazine of all necessary things; and had everything so ready at my hand, that it was a great pleasure to me to see all my goods in such order, and especially to find my stock of all necessaries so great.

And now it was that I began to keep a journal of every day's employment; for, indeed, at first I was in too much hurry, and not only hurry as to labour, but in too much discomposure of mind; and my journal would have been full of many dull things; for example, I must have said thus: "30*th.*—After I had got to shore, and escaped drowning, instead of being thankful to God for my deliverance, having first vomited, with the great quantity of salt water which had got into my stomach, and recovering myself a little, I ran about the shore wringing my hands and beating my head and face, exclaiming at my misery, and crying out, 'I was undone, undone!' till, tired and faint, I was forced to lie down on the ground to repose, but durst not sleep for fear of being devoured."

Some days after this, and after I had been on board the ship, and got all that I could out of her, yet I could not forbear[76] getting up to the top of a little mountain and looking out to sea, in hopes of seeing a ship; then fancy at a vast distance I spied a sail, please myself with the hopes of it, and then after looking steadily, till I was almost blind, lose it quite, and sit down and weep like a child, and thus increase my misery by my folly.

But having gotten over these things in some measure, and having settled my household staff and habitation, made me a table and a chair, and all as handsome about me as I could, I began to keep my journal; of which I shall here give you the copy (though in it will be told all these particulars over again) as long as it lasted; for having no more ink, I was forced to leave it off.

Questions for Review:

1. Why does Robinson Crusoe return to the ship?

2. Describe the island.

3. List the items Robinson Crusoe brings from the ship. In what general order does he bring them, and why? What does he say to the money, and why?

4. List his four key concerns for how and where he should set himself up.

5. What spiritual thoughts does Robinson Crusoe have? Why is he thankful?

---

[76] refrain from

6.   Give some other details of helpful items not listed before that Robinson Crusoe is able to take from the ship to the island. What things does he lack?

7.   Sum up Robinson Crusoe's "Evil" vs. "Good" list as he marks one year on the island.

8.   What has Robinson Crusoe completed on the island by the end of Chapter IV?

CHAPTER V: BUILDS A HOUSE... THE JOURNAL

Septomber 30, 1659.—I, poor miserable Robinson Crusoe, being ship-wrecked during a dreadful storm in the offing, came on shore on this dismal, unfortunate island, which I called "The Island of Despair"; all the rest of the ship's company being drowned, and myself almost dead.

All the rest of the day I spent in afflicting myself at the dismal circumstances I was brought to—viz. I had neither food, house, clothes, weapon, nor place to fly to; and in despair of any relief, saw nothing but death before me—either that I should be devoured by wild beasts, murdered by savages, or starved to death for want of food. At the approach of night I slept in a tree, for fear of wild creatures; but slept soundly, though it rained all night.

October 1.—In the morning I saw, to my great surprise, the ship had floated with the high tide, and was driven on shore again much nearer the island; which, as it was some comfort, on one hand—for, seeing her set upright, and not broken to pieces, I hoped, if the wind abated, I might get on board, and get some food and necessaries out of her for my relief—so, on the other hand, it renewed my grief at the loss of my comrades, who, I imagined, if we had all stayed on board, might have saved the ship, or, at least, that they would not have been all drowned as they were; and that, had the men been saved, we might perhaps have built us a boat out of the ruins of the ship to have carried us to some other part of the world. I spent great part of this day in perplexing myself on these things; but at length, seeing the ship almost dry, I went upon the sand as near as I could, and then swam on board. This day also it continued raining, though with no wind at all.

From the 1st of October to the 24th.—All these days entirely spent in many several voyages to get all I could out of the ship, which I brought on shore every tide of flood upon rafts. Much rain also in the days, though with some intervals of fair weather; but it seems this was the rainy season.

Oct. 20.—I overset my raft, and all the goods I had got upon it; but, being in shoal water, and the things being chiefly heavy, I recovered many of them when the tide was out.

Oct. 25.—It rained all night and all day, with some gusts of wind; during which time the ship broke in pieces, the wind blowing a little harder than before, and was no more to be seen, except the wreck of her, and that only at low water. I spent this day in covering and securing the goods which I had saved, that the rain might not spoil them.

Oct. 26.—I walked about the shore almost all day, to find out a place to fix my habitation, greatly concerned to secure myself from any attack in the night, either from wild beasts or men. Towards night, I fixed upon a proper place, under a rock, and marked out a semicircle for my encampment; which I resolved to strengthen with a work, wall, or fortification, made of double piles, lined within with cables, and without with turf.

From the 26th to the 30th I worked very hard in carrying all my goods to my new habitation, though some part of the time it rained exceedingly hard.

The 31st, in the morning, I went out into the island with my gun, to seek for some food, and discover the country; when I killed a she-goat, and her kid followed me home, which I afterwards killed also, because it would not feed.

November 1.—I set up my tent under a rock, and lay there for the first night; making it as large as I could, with stakes driven in to swing my hammock upon.

Nov. 2.—I set up all my chests and boards, and the pieces of timber which made my rafts, and with them formed a fence round me, a little within the place I had marked out for my fortification.

Nov. 3.—I went out with my gun, and killed two fowls like ducks, which were very good food. In the afternoon went to work to make me a table.

Nov. 4.—This morning I began to order my times of work, of going out with my gun, time of sleep, and time of diversion—viz. every morning I walked out with my gun for two or three hours, if it did not rain; then employed myself to work till about eleven o'clock; then eat what I had to live on; and from twelve to two I lay down to sleep, the weather being excessively hot; and then, in the evening, to work again. The working part of this day and of the next were wholly employed in making my table, for I was yet but a very sorry workman, though time and necessity made me a complete natural mechanic soon after, as I believe they would do any one else.

Nov. 5.—This day went abroad with my gun and my dog, and killed a wild cat; her skin pretty soft, but her flesh good for nothing; every creature that I killed I took of the skins and preserved them. Coming back by the sea-shore, I saw many sorts of sea-fowls, which I did not understand; but was surprised, and almost frightened, with two or three seals, which, while I was gazing at, not well knowing what they were, got into the sea, and escaped me for that time.

Nov. 6.—After my morning walk I went to work with my table again, and finished it, though not to my liking; nor was it long before I learned to mend it.

Nov. 7.—Now it began to be settled fair weather. The 7th, 8th, 9th, 10th, and part of the 12th (for the 11th was Sunday) I took wholly up to make me a chair, and with much ado brought it to a tolerable shape, but never to please me; and even in the making I pulled it in pieces several times.

Note.—I soon neglected my keeping Sundays; for, omitting my mark for them on my post, I forgot which was which.

Nov. 13.—This day it rained, which refreshed me exceedingly, and cooled the earth; but it was accompanied with terrible thunder and lightning, which frightened me dreadfully, for fear of my powder. As soon as it was over, I resolved to separate my stock of powder into as many little parcels as possible, that it might not be in danger.

Nov. 14, 15, 16.—These three days I spent in making little square chests, or boxes, which might hold about a pound, or two pounds at most, of powder; and so, putting the powder in, I stowed it in places as secure and remote from one another as possible. On one of these three days I killed a large bird that was good to eat, but I knew not what to call it.

Nov. 17.—This day I began to dig behind my tent into the rock, to make room for my further conveniency.

Note.—Three things I wanted exceedingly for this work—viz. a pickaxe, a shovel, and a wheelbarrow or basket; so I desisted from my work, and began to consider how to supply that want, and make me some tools. As for the pickaxe, I made use of the iron crows, which were proper enough, though heavy; but the next thing was a shovel or spade; this was so absolutely necessary, that, indeed, I could do nothing effectually without it; but what kind of one to make I knew not.

Nov. 18.—The next day, in searching the woods, I found a tree of that wood, or like it, which in the Brazils they call the iron-tree, for its exceeding hardness. Of this, with great labour, and almost spoiling my axe, I cut a piece, and brought it home, too, with difficulty enough, for it was exceeding heavy. The excessive hardness of the wood, and my having no other way, made me a long while upon this machine, for I worked it effectually by little and little into the form of a shovel or spade; the handle exactly shaped like ours in England, only that the board part having no iron shod upon it at bottom, it would not last me so long; however, it served well enough for the uses which I had occasion to put it to; but never was a shovel, I believe, made after that fashion, or so long in making.

I was still deficient, for I wanted a basket or a wheelbarrow. A basket I could not make by any means, having no such things as twigs that would bend to make wicker-ware—at least, none yet found out; and as to a wheelbarrow, I fancied I could make all but the wheel; but that I had no notion of; neither did I know how to go about it; besides, I had no possible way to make the iron gudgeons for the spindle or axis of the wheel to run in; so I gave it over, and so, for carrying away the earth which I dug out of the cave, I made me a thing like a hod which the labourers carry mortar in when they serve the bricklayers. This was not so difficult to me as the making the shovel: and yet this and the shovel, and the attempt which I made in vain to make a wheelbarrow, took me up no less than four days—I mean always excepting my morning walk with my gun, which I seldom failed, and very seldom failed also bringing home something fit to eat.

Nov. 23.—My other work having now stood still, because of my making these tools, when they were finished I went on, and working every day, as my strength and time allowed, I spent eighteen days entirely in widening and deepening my cave, that it might hold my goods commodiously.

Note.—During all this time I worked to make this room or cave spacious enough to accommodate me as a warehouse or magazine, a kitchen, a dining-room, and a cellar. As for my lodging, I kept to the tent; except that sometimes, in the wet season of the year, it rained so hard that I could not keep myself dry, which caused me afterwards to cover all my place within my pale with long poles, in the form of rafters, leaning against the rock, and load them with flags and large leaves of trees, like a thatch.

December 10.—I began now to think my cave or vault finished, when on a sudden (it seems I had made it too large) a great quantity of earth fell down from the top on one side; so much that, in short, it frighted me, and not without reason, too, for if I had been under it, I had never wanted a gravedigger. I had now a great deal of work to do over again, for I had the loose earth to carry out; and, which was of more importance, I had the ceiling to prop up, so that I might be sure no more would come down.

Dec. 11.—This day I went to work with it accordingly, and got two shores or posts pitched upright to the top, with two pieces of boards across over each post; this I finished the next day; and setting more posts up with boards, in about a week more I had the roof secured, and the posts, standing in rows, served me for partitions to part off the house.

Dec. 17.—From this day to the 20th I placed shelves, and knocked up nails on the posts, to hang everything up that could be hung up; and now I began to be in some order within doors.

Dec. 20.—Now I carried everything into the cave, and began to furnish my house, and set up some pieces of boards like a dresser, to order my victuals[77] upon; but boards began to be very scarce with me; also, I made me another table.

Dec. 24.—Much rain all night and all day. No stirring out.

Dec. 25.—Rain all day.

Dec. 26.—No rain, and the earth much cooler than before, and pleasanter.

Dec. 27.—Killed a young goat, and lamed another, so that I caught it and led it home in a string; when I had it at home, I bound and splintered up its leg, which was broke.

N.B.[78]—I took such care of it that it lived, and the leg grew well and as strong as ever; but, by my nursing it so long, it grew tame, and fed upon the little green at my door, and would not go away. This was the first time that I entertained a thought of breeding up some tame creatures, that I might have food when my powder and shot was all spent.

Dec. 28, 29, 30, 31.—Great heats, and no breeze, so that there was no stirring abroad, except in the evening, for food; this time I spent in putting all my things in order within doors.

January 1.—Very hot still: but I went abroad early and late with my gun, and lay still in the middle of the day. This evening, going farther into the valleys which lay towards the centre of the island, I found there were plenty of goats, though exceedingly shy, and hard to come at; however, I resolved to try if I could not bring my dog to hunt them down.

Jan. 2.—Accordingly, the next day I went out with my dog, and set him upon the goats, but I was mistaken, for they all faced about upon the dog, and he knew his danger too well, for he would not come near them.

Jan. 3.—I began my fence or wall; which, being still jealous of my being attacked by somebody, I resolved to make very thick and strong.

N.B.—This wall being described before, I purposely omit what was said in the journal; it is sufficient to observe, that I was no less time than from the 2nd of January to the 14th of April working, finishing, and perfecting this wall, though it was no more than about twenty-four yards in length, being a half-circle from one place in the rock to another place, about eight yards from it, the door of the cave being in the centre behind it.

All this time I worked very hard, the rains hindering me many days, nay, sometimes weeks together; but I thought I should never be perfectly secure till this wall was finished; and it is scarce credible what inexpressible labour everything was done with, especially the bringing piles out of the woods and driving them into the ground; for I made them much bigger than I

---

[77] food (pronounced "vittles")
[78] initials of *nota bene*, or "Note:"

needed to have done.

When this wall was finished, and the outside double fenced, with a turf wall raised up close to it, I perceived myself that if any people were to come on shore there, they would not perceive anything like a habitation; and it was very well I did so, as may be observed hereafter, upon a very remarkable occasion.

During this time I made my rounds in the woods for game every day when the rain permitted me, and made frequent discoveries in these walks of something or other to my advantage; particularly, I found a kind of wild pigeons, which build, not as wood-pigeons in a tree, but rather as house-pigeons, in the holes of the rocks; and taking some young ones, I endeavoured to breed them up tame, and did so; but when they grew older they flew away, which perhaps was at first for want of feeding them, for I had nothing to give them; however, I frequently found their nests, and got their young ones, which were very good meat. And now, in the managing my household affairs, I found myself wanting in many things, which I thought at first it was impossible for me to make; as, indeed, with some of them it was: for instance, I could never make a cask to be hooped. I had a small runlet or two, as I observed before; but I could never arrive at the capacity of making one by them, though I spent many weeks about it; I could neither put in the heads, or join the staves so true to one another as to make them hold water; so I gave that also over. In the next place, I was at a great loss for candles; so that as soon as ever it was dark, which was generally by seven o'clock, I was obliged to go to bed. I remembered the lump of bees-wax with which I made candles in my African adventure; but I had none of that now; the only remedy I had was, that when I had killed a goat I saved the tallow, and with a little dish made of clay, which I baked in the sun, to which I added a wick of some oakum, I made me a lamp; and this gave me light, though not a clear, steady light, like a candle. In the middle of all my labours it happened that, rummaging my things, I found a little bag which, as I hinted before, had been filled with corn for the feeding of poultry—not for this voyage, but before, as I suppose, when the ship came from Lisbon. The little remainder of corn that had been in the bag was all devoured by the rats, and I saw nothing in the bag but husks and dust; and being willing to have the bag for some other use (I think it was to put powder in, when I divided it for fear of the lightning, or some such use), I shook the husks of corn out of it on one side of my fortification, under the rock.

It was a little before the great rains just now mentioned that I threw this stuff away, taking no notice, and not so much as remembering that I had thrown anything there, when, about a month after, or thereabouts, I saw some few stalks of something green shooting out of the ground, which I fancied might be some plant I had not seen; but I was surprised, and perfectly astonished, when, after a little longer time, I saw about ten or twelve ears come out, which were perfect green barley, of the same kind as our European—nay, as our English barley.

It is impossible to express the astonishment and confusion of my thoughts on this occasion. I had hitherto[79] acted upon no religious foundation at all; indeed, I had very few notions of religion in my head, nor had entertained any sense of anything that had befallen me otherwise than as chance, or, as we lightly say, what pleases God, without so much as inquiring into the end of Providence in these things, or His order in governing events for the world. But after I saw barley grow there, in a climate which I knew was not proper for corn, and especially that I knew not how it came there, it startled me strangely, and I began to suggest that God had miraculously caused His grain to grow without any help of seed sown, and that it was so directed purely for my sustenance on that wild, miserable place.

This touched my heart a little, and brought tears out of my eyes, and I began to bless myself that such a prodigy[80] of nature should happen upon my account; and this was the more strange to me, because I saw near it still, all along by the side of the rock, some other straggling stalks, which proved to be stalks of rice, and which I knew, because I had seen it grow in Africa when I was ashore there.

I not only thought these the pure productions of Providence for my support, but not doubting that there was more in the place, I went all over that part of the island, where I had been before, peering in every corner, and under every rock, to see for more of it, but I could not find any. At last it occurred to my thoughts that I shook a bag of chickens' meat out in that place; and then the wonder began to cease; and I must confess my religious thankfulness to God's providence began to abate, too, upon the discovering that all this was nothing but what was common; though I ought to have been as thankful for so strange and unforeseen a providence as if it had been miraculous; for it was really the work of Providence to me, that should order or appoint that ten or twelve grains of corn should remain unspoiled, when the rats had destroyed all the rest, as if it had been dropped from heaven; as also, that I should throw it out in that particular place, where, it being in the shade of a high rock, it sprang up immediately; whereas, if I had thrown it anywhere else at that time, it had been burnt up and destroyed.

I carefully saved the ears of this corn, you may be sure, in their season, which was about the end of June; and, laying up every corn, I resolved to sow them all again, hoping in time to have some quantity sufficient to supply me with bread. But it was not till the fourth year that I could allow

---

[79] up to that point
[80] wonder, phenomenon

myself the least grain of this corn to eat, and even then but sparingly, as I shall say afterwards, in its order; for I lost all that I sowed the first season by not observing the proper time; for I sowed it just before the dry season, so that it never came up at all, at least not as it would have done; of which in its place.

Besides this barley, there were, as above, twenty or thirty stalks of rice, which I preserved with the same care and for the same use, or to the same purpose—to make me bread, or rather food; for I found ways to cook it without baking, though I did that also after some time.

But to return to my Journal.

I worked excessive hard these three or four months to get my wall done; and the 14th of April I closed it up, contriving to go into it, not by a door but over the wall, by a ladder, that there might be no sign on the outside of my habitation.

April 16.—I finished the ladder; so I went up the ladder to the top, and then pulled it up after me, and let it down in the inside. This was a complete enclosure to me; for within I had room enough, and nothing could come at me from without, unless it could first mount my wall.

The very next day after this wall was finished I had almost had all my labour overthrown at once, and myself killed. The case was thus: As I was busy in the inside, behind my tent, just at the entrance into my cave, I was terribly frighted with a most dreadful, surprising thing indeed; for all on a sudden I found the earth come crumbling down from the roof of my cave, and from the edge of the hill over my head, and two of the posts I had set up in the cave cracked in a frightful manner. I was heartily scared; but thought nothing of what was really the cause, only thinking that the top of my cave was fallen in, as some of it had done before: and for fear I should be buried in it I ran forward to my ladder, and not thinking myself safe there neither, I got over my wall for fear of the pieces of the hill, which I expected might roll down upon me. I had no sooner stepped do ground, than I plainly saw it was a terrible earthquake, for the ground I stood on shook three times at about eight minutes' distance, with three such shocks as would have over-turned the strongest building that could be supposed to have stood on the earth; and a great piece of the top of a rock which stood about half a mile from me next the sea fell down with such a terrible noise as I never heard in all my life. I perceived also the very sea was put into violent motion by it; and I believe the shocks were stronger under the water than on the island.

I was so much amazed with the thing itself, having never felt the like, nor discoursed with any one that had, that I was like one dead or stupefied; and the motion of the earth made my stomach sick, like one that was tossed at sea; but the noise of the falling of the rock awakened me, as it were, and rousing me from the stupefied condition I was in, filled me with horror; and

I thought of nothing then but the hill falling upon my tent and all my household goods, and burying all at once; and this sunk my very soul within me a second time.

After the third shock was over, and I felt no more for some time, I began to take courage; and yet I had not heart enough to go over my wall again, for fear of being buried alive, but sat still upon the ground greatly cast down and disconsolate, not knowing what to do. All this while I had not the least serious religious thought; nothing but the common "Lord have mercy upon me!" and when it was over that went away too.

While I sat thus, I found the air overcast and grow cloudy, as if it would rain. Soon after that the wind arose by little and little, so that in less than half-an-hour it blew a most dreadful hurricane; the sea was all on a sudden covered over with foam and froth; the shore was covered with the breach of the water, the trees were torn up by the roots, and a terrible storm it was. This held about three hours, and then began to abate; and in two hours more it was quite calm, and began to rain very hard. All this while I sat upon the ground very much terrified and dejected; when on a sudden it came into my thoughts, that these winds and rain being the consequences of the earth-quake, the earthquake itself was spent and over, and I might venture into my cave again. With this thought my spirits began to revive; and the rain also helping to persuade me, I went in and sat down in my tent. But the rain was so violent that my tent was ready to be beaten down with it; and I was forced to go into my cave, though very much afraid and uneasy, for fear it should fall on my head. This violent rain forced me to a new work—viz. to cut a hole through my new fortification, like a sink, to let the water go out, which would else have flooded my cave. After I had been in my cave for some time, and found still no more shocks of the earthquake follow, I began to be more composed. And now, to support my spirits, which indeed wanted it very much, I went to my little store, and took a small sup of rum; which, however, I did then and always very sparingly, knowing I could have no more when that was gone. It continued raining all that night and great part of the next day, so that I could not stir abroad; but my mind being more composed, I began to think of what I had best do; concluding that if the island was subject to these earthquakes, there would be no living for me in a cave, but I must consider of building a little hut in an open place which I might surround with a wall, as I had done here, and so make myself secure from wild beasts or men; for I concluded, if I stayed where I was, I should certainly one time or other be buried alive.

With these thoughts, I resolved to remove my tent from the place where it stood, which was just under the hanging precipice of the hill; and which, if it should be shaken again, would certainly fall upon my tent; and I spent the two next days, being the 19th and 20th of April, in contriving where and how to remove my habitation. The fear of being swallowed up alive made me that I never slept in quiet; and yet the apprehension of lying abroad without any fence was almost equal to it; but still, when I looked about, and saw how everything was put in order, how pleasantly concealed I was, and how safe from danger, it made me very loath to remove. In the meantime, it occurred to me that it would require a vast deal of time for me to do this, and that I must be contented to venture where I was, till I had formed a camp for myself, and had secured it so as to remove to it. So with this resolution I composed myself for a time, and resolved that I would go to work with all speed to build me a wall with piles and cables, &c., in a circle, as before, and set my tent up in it when it was finished; but that I would venture to stay where I was till it was finished, and fit to remove. This was the 21st.

April 22.—The next morning I begin to consider of means to put this resolve into execution; but I was at a great loss about my tools. I had three large axes, and abundance of hatchets (for we carried the hatchets for traffic with the Indians); but with much chopping and cutting knotty hard wood, they were all full of notches, and dull; and though I had a grindstone, I could not turn it and grind my tools too. This cost me as much thought as a states-man would have bestowed upon a grand point of politics, or a judge upon the life and death of a man. At length I contrived a wheel with a string, to turn it with my foot, that I might have both my hands at liberty. *Note.*—I had never seen any such thing in England, or at least, not to take notice how it was done, though since I have observed, it is very common there; besides that, my grindstone was very large and heavy. This machine cost me a full week's work to bring it to perfection.

April 28, 29.—These two whole days I took up in grinding my tools, my machine for turning my grindstone performing very well.

April 30.—Having perceived my bread had been low a great while, now I took a survey of it, and reduced myself to one biscuit cake a day, which made my heart very heavy.

May 1.—In the morning, looking towards the sea side, the tide being low, I saw something lie on the shore bigger than ordinary, and it looked like a cask; when I came to it, I found a small barrel, and two or three pieces of the wreck of the ship, which were driven on shore by the late hurricane; and looking towards the wreck itself, I thought it seemed to lie higher out of the water than it used to do. I examined the barrel which was driven on shore, and soon found it was a barrel of gunpowder; but it had taken water, and the powder was caked as hard as a stone; however, I rolled it farther on shore for the present, and went on upon the sands, as near as I could to the wreck of the ship, to look for more.

Questions for Review:

1. What saddens Robinson Crusoe about the fact that all the men left the ship during storm?

2. What does Robinson Crusoe do about his powder when he hears thunder and lightning?

3. How does Robinson Crusoe use the "iron-tree"? What else useful does he make, and what else does he wish he had?

4. How does Robinson Crusoe improve his home? What does he realize after his encounter with the goats?

5. How does the wall doubly provide security?

6. How does the thrown-away corn affect Robinson Crusoe spiritually?

7. Explain the terrible weather's effects on Robinson Crusoe.

CHAPTER VI: ILL AND CONSCIENCE-STRICKEN

When I came down to the ship I found it strangely removed. The forecastle, which lay before buried in sand, was heaved up at least six feet, and the stern, which was broke in pieces and parted from the rest by the force of the sea, soon after I had left rummaging her, was tossed as it were up, and cast on one side; and the sand was thrown so high on that side next her stern, that whereas there was a great place of water before, so that I could not come within a quarter of a mile of the wreck without swimming I could now walk quite up to her when the tide was out. I was surprised with this at first, but soon concluded it must be done by the earthquake; and as by this violence the ship was more broke open than formerly, so many things came daily on shore, which the sea had loosened, and which the winds and water rolled by degrees to the land.

This wholly diverted my thoughts from the design of removing my habitation, and I busied myself mightily, that day especially, in searching whether I could make any way into the ship; but I found nothing was to be expected of that kind, for all the inside of the ship was choked up with sand. However, as I had learned not to despair of anything, I resolved to pull everything to pieces that I could of the ship, concluding that everything I could get from her would be of some use or other to me.

May 3.—I began with my saw, and cut a piece of a beam through, which I thought held some of the upper part or quarter-deck together, and when I had cut it through, I cleared away the sand as well as I could from the side which lay highest; but the tide coming in, I was obliged to give over for that time.

May 4.—I went a-fishing, but caught not one fish that I durst eat of, till I was weary of my sport; when, just going to leave off, I caught a young dolphin. I had made me a long line of some rope-yarn, but I had no hooks; yet I frequently caught fish enough, as much as I cared to eat; all which I dried in the sun, and ate them dry.

May 5.—Worked on the wreck; cut another beam asunder, and brought three great fir planks off from the decks, which I tied together, and made to float on shore when the tide of flood came on.

May 6.—Worked on the wreck; got several iron bolts out of her and other pieces of ironwork. Worked very hard, and came home very much tired, and had thoughts of giving it over.[81]

May 7.—Went to the wreck again, not with an intent to work, but found the weight of the wreck had broke itself down, the beams being cut; that several pieces of the ship seemed to lie loose, and the inside of the hold lay so open that I could see into it; but it was almost full of water and sand.

May 8.—Went to the wreck, and carried an iron crow to wrench up the deck, which lay now quite clear of the water or sand. I wrenched open two planks, and brought them on shore also with the tide. I left the iron crow in the wreck for next day.

May 9.—Went to the wreck, and with the crow made way into the body of the wreck, and felt several casks, and loosened them with the crow, but could not break them up. I felt also a roll of English lead, and could stir it, but it was too heavy to remove.

May 10–14.—Went every day to the wreck; and got a great many pieces of timber, and boards, or plank, and two or three hundredweight of iron.

May 15.—I carried two hatchets, to try if I could not cut a piece off the roll of lead by placing the edge of one hatchet and driving it with the other; but as it lay about a foot and a half in the water, I could not make any blow

---

[81] "giving it over": giving up

to drive the hatchet.

May 16.—It had blown hard in the night, and the wreck appeared more broken by the force of the water; but I stayed so long in the woods, to get pigeons for food, that the tide prevented my going to the wreck that day.

May 17.—I saw some pieces of the wreck blown on shore, at a great distance, near two miles off me, but resolved to see what they were, and found it was a piece of the head, but too heavy for me to bring away.

May 24.—Every day, to this day, I worked on the wreck; and with hard labour I loosened some things so much with the crow, that the first flowing tide several casks floated out, and two of the seamen's chests; but the wind blowing from the shore, nothing came to land that day but pieces of timber, and a hogshead, which had some Brazil pork in it; but the salt water and the sand had spoiled it. I continued this work every day to the 15th of June, except the time necessary to get food, which I always appointed, during this part of my employment, to be when the tide was up, that I might be ready when it was ebbed out; and by this time I had got timber and plank and ironwork enough to have built a good boat, if I had known how; and also I got, at several times and in several pieces, near one hundredweight of the sheet lead.

June 16.—Going down to the seaside, I found a large tortoise or turtle. This was the first I had seen, which, it seems, was only my misfortune, not any defect of the place, or scarcity; for had I happened to be on the other side of the island, I might have had hundreds of them every day, as I found afterwards; but perhaps had paid dear enough for them.

June 17.—I spent in cooking the turtle. I found in her three-score eggs; and her flesh was to me, at that time, the most savoury and pleasant that ever I tasted in my life, having had no flesh, but of goats and fowls, since I landed in this horrid place.

June 18.—Rained all day, and I stayed within. I thought at this time the rain felt cold, and I was something chilly; which I knew was not usual in that latitude.

June 19.—Very ill, and shivering, as if the weather had been cold.

June 20.—No rest all night; violent pains in my head, and feverish.

June 21.—Very ill; frighted almost to death with the apprehensions of my sad condition—to be sick, and no help. Prayed to God, for the first time since the storm off Hull, but scarce knew what I said, or why, my thoughts being all confused.

June 22.—A little better; but under dreadful apprehensions of sickness.

June 23.—Very bad again; cold and shivering, and then a violent headache.

June 24.—Much better.

June 25.—An ague[82] very violent; the fit held me seven hours; cold fit and hot, with faint sweats after it.

June 26.—Better; and having no victuals to eat, took my gun, but found myself very weak. However, I killed a she-goat, and with much difficulty got it home, and broiled some of it, and ate, I would fain have stewed it, and made some broth, but had no pot.

June 27.—The ague again so violent that I lay a-bed all day, and neither ate nor drank. I was ready to perish for thirst; but so weak, I had not strength to stand up, or to get myself any water to drink. Prayed to God again, but was light-headed; and when I was not, I was so ignorant that I knew not what to say; only I lay and cried, "Lord, look upon me! Lord, pity me! Lord, have mercy upon me!" I suppose I did nothing else for two or three hours; till, the fit wearing off, I fell asleep, and did not wake till far in the night. When I awoke, I found myself much refreshed, but weak, and exceeding thirsty. However, as I had no water in my habitation, I was forced to lie till morning, and went to sleep again. In this second sleep I had this terrible dream: I thought that I was sitting on the ground, on the outside of my wall, where I sat when the storm blew after the earthquake, and that I saw a man descend from a great black cloud, in a bright flame of fire, and light upon the ground. He was all over as bright as a flame, so that I could but just bear to look towards him; his countenance was most inexpressibly dreadful, impossible for words to describe. When he stepped upon the ground with his feet, I thought the earth trembled, just as it had done before in the earthquake, and all the air looked, to my apprehension, as if it had been filled with flashes of fire. He was no sooner landed upon the earth, but he moved forward towards me, with a long spear or weapon in his hand, to kill me; and when he came to a rising ground, at some distance, he spoke to me—or I heard a voice so terrible that it is impossible to express the terror of it. All that I can say I understood was this: "Seeing all these things have not brought thee to repentance, now thou shalt die;" at which words, I thought he lifted up the spear that was in his hand to kill me.

No one that shall ever read this account will expect that I should be able to describe the horrors of my soul at this terrible vision. I mean, that even while it was a dream, I even dreamed of those horrors. Nor is it any more possible to describe the impression that remained upon my mind when I awaked, and found it was but a dream.

I had, alas! no divine knowledge. What I had received by the good instruction of my father was then worn out by an uninterrupted series, for eight years, of seafaring wickedness, and a constant conversation with none but such as were, like myself, wicked and profane to the last degree. I do

---

[82] fever or chills

not remember that I had, in all that time, one thought that so much as tended either to looking upwards towards God, or inwards towards a reflection upon my own ways; but a certain stupidity[83] of soul, without desire of good, or conscience of evil, had entirely overwhelmed me; and I was all that the most hardened, unthinking, wicked creature among our common sailors can be supposed to be; not having the least sense, either of the fear of God in danger, or of thankfulness to God in deliverance.

In the relating what is already past of my story, this will be the more easily believed when I shall add, that through all the variety of miseries that had to this day befallen me, I never had so much as one thought of it being the hand of God, or that it was a just punishment for my sin—my rebellious behaviour against my father—or my present sins, which were great—or so much as a punishment for the general course of my wicked life. When I was on the desperate expedition on the desert shores of Africa, I never had so much as one thought of what would become of me, or one wish to God to direct me whither I should go, or to keep me from the danger which apparently surrounded me, as well from voracious creatures as cruel savages. But I was merely thoughtless of a God or a Providence, acted like a mere brute, from the principles of nature, and by the dictates of common sense only, and, indeed, hardly that. When I was delivered and taken up at sea by the Portugal captain, well used, and dealt justly and honourably with, as well as charitably, I had not the least thankfulness in my thoughts. When, again, I was shipwrecked, ruined, and in danger of drowning on this island, I was as far from remorse, or looking on it as a judgment. I only said to myself often, that I was an unfortunate dog, and born to be always miserable.

It is true, when I got on shore first here, and found all my ship's crew drowned and myself spared, I was surprised with a kind of ecstasy, and some transports of soul, which, had the grace of God assisted, might have come up to true thankfulness; but it ended where it began, in a mere common flight of joy, or, as I may say, being glad I was alive, without the least reflection upon the distinguished goodness of the hand which had preserved me, and had singled me out to be preserved when all the rest were destroyed, or an inquiry why Providence had been thus merciful unto me. Even just the same common sort of joy which seamen generally have, after they are got safe ashore from a shipwreck, which they drown all in the next bowl of punch, and forget almost as soon as it is over; and all the rest of my life was like it. Even when I was afterwards, on due consideration, made sensible of my condition, how I was cast on this dreadful place, out of the reach of human kind, out of all hope of relief, or prospect of redemption, as soon as I saw but a prospect of living and that I should not starve and perish for hun-

---

[83] dullness, lifelessness

ger, all the sense of my affliction wore off; and I began to be very easy, applied myself to the works proper for my preservation and supply, and was far enough from being afflicted at my condition, as a judgment from heaven, or as the hand of God against me: these were thoughts which very seldom entered my head.

The growing up of the corn, as is hinted in my Journal, had at first some little influence upon me, and began to affect me with seriousness, as long as I thought it had something miraculous in it; but as soon as ever that part of the thought was removed, all the impression that was raised from it wore off also, as I have noted already. Even the earthquake, though nothing could be more terrible in its nature, or more immediately directing to the invisible Power which alone directs such things, yet no sooner was the first fright over, but the impression it had made went off also. I had no more sense of God or His judgments—much less of the present affliction of my circumstances being from His hand—than if I had been in the most prosperous condition of life. But now, when I began to be sick, and a leisurely view of the miseries of death came to place itself before me; when my spirits began to sink under the burden of a strong distemper, and nature was exhausted with the violence of the fever; conscience, that had slept so long, began to awake, and I began to reproach myself with my past life, in which I had so evidently, by uncommon wickedness, provoked the justice of God to lay me under uncommon strokes, and to deal with me in so vindictive a manner. These reflections oppressed me for the second or third day of my distemper; and in the violence, as well of the fever as of the dreadful reproaches of my conscience, extorted some words from me like praying to God, though I cannot say they were either a prayer attended with desires or with hopes: it was rather the voice of mere fright and distress. My thoughts were confused, the convictions great upon my mind, and the horror of dying in such a miserable condition raised vapours into my head with the mere apprehensions; and in these hurries of my soul I knew not what my tongue might express. But it was rather exclamation, such as, "Lord, what a miserable creature am I! If I should be sick, I shall certainly die for want of help; and what will become of me!" Then the tears burst out of my eyes, and I could say no more for a good while. In this interval the good advice of my father came to my mind, and presently his prediction, which I mentioned at the beginning of this story—viz. that if I did take this foolish step, God would not bless me, and I would have leisure hereafter to reflect upon having neglected his counsel when there might be none to assist in my recovery. "Now," said I, aloud, "my dear father's words are come to pass; God's justice has overtaken me, and I have none to help or hear me. I rejected the voice of Providence, which had mercifully put me in a posture or station of life wherein I might have been happy and easy; but I would neither see it myself nor learn to know the blessing of it from my parents. I left them to mourn over my folly, and now I am left to mourn under the consequences of it. I abused their help and assistance, who would have lifted me in the world, and would have made everything easy to me; and now I have difficulties to struggle with, too great for even nature itself to support, and no assistance, no help, no comfort, no advice." Then I cried out, "Lord, be my help, for I am in great distress." This was the first prayer, if I may call it so, that I had made for many years.

But to return to my Journal.

June 28.—Having been somewhat refreshed with the sleep I had had, and the fit being entirely off, I got up; and though the fright and terror of my dream was very great, yet I considered that the fit of the ague would return again the next day, and now was my time to get something to refresh and support myself when I should be ill; and the first thing I did, I filled a large square case-bottle with water, and set it upon my table, in reach of my bed; and to take off the chill or aguish disposition of the water, I put about a quarter of a pint of rum into it, and mixed them together. Then I got me a piece of the goat's flesh and broiled it on the coals, but could eat very little. I walked about, but was very weak, and withal very sad and heavy-hearted under a sense of my miserable condition, dreading, the return of my distemper the next day. At night I made my supper of three of the turtle's eggs, which I roasted in the ashes, and ate, as we call it, in the shell, and this was the first bit of meat I had ever asked God's blessing to, that I could remember, in my whole life. After I had eaten I tried to walk, but found myself so weak that I could hardly carry a gun, for I never went out without that; so I went but a little way, and sat down upon the ground, looking out upon the sea, which was just before me, and very calm and smooth. As I sat here some such thoughts as these occurred to me: What is this earth and sea, of which I have seen so much? Whence is it produced? And what am I, and all the other creatures wild and tame, human and brutal? Whence[84] are we? Sure we are all made by some secret Power, who formed the earth and sea, the air and sky. And who is that? Then it followed most naturally, it is God that has made all. Well, but then it came on strangely, if God has made all these things, He guides and governs them all, and all things that concern them; for the Power that could make all things must certainly have power to guide and direct them. If so, nothing can happen in the great circuit of His works, either without His knowledge or appointment.

And if nothing happens without His knowledge, He knows that I am here, and am in this dreadful condition; and if nothing happens without His appointment, He has appointed all this to befall me. Nothing occurred to my

---

[84] from where

thought to contradict any of these conclusions, and therefore it rested upon me with the greater force, that it must needs be that God had appointed all this to befall me; that I was brought into this miserable circumstance by His direction, He having the sole power, not of me only, but of everything that happened in the world. Immediately it followed: Why has God done this to me? What have I done to be thus used? My conscience presently checked me in that inquiry, as if I had blasphemed, and methought it spoke to me like a voice: "Wretch! dost thou ask what thou hast done? Look back upon a dreadful misspent life, and ask thyself what thou hast not done? Ask, why is it that thou wert not long ago destroyed? Why wert thou not drowned in Yarmouth Roads; killed in the fight when the ship was taken by the Sallee man-of-war; devoured by the wild beasts on the coast of Africa; or drowned here, when all the crew perished but thyself? Dost thou ask, what have I done?" I was struck dumb with these reflections, as one astonished, and had not a word to say—no, not to answer to myself, but rose up pensive and sad, walked back to my retreat, and went up over my wall, as if I had been going to bed; but my thoughts were sadly disturbed, and I had no inclination to sleep; so I sat down in my chair, and lighted my lamp, for it began to be dark. Now, as the apprehension of the return of my distemper terrified me very much, it occurred to my thought that the Brazilians take no physic[85] but their tobacco for almost all distempers, and I had a piece of a roll of tobacco in one of the chests, which was quite cured, and some also that was green, and not quite cured.

I went, directed by Heaven no doubt; for in this chest I found a cure both for soul and body. I opened the chest, and found what I looked for, the tobacco; and as the few books I had saved lay there too, I took out one of the Bibles which I mentioned before, and which to this time I had not found leisure or inclination to look into. I say, I took it out, and brought both that and the tobacco with me to the table. What use to make of the tobacco I knew not, in my distemper, or whether it was good for it or no: but I tried several experiments with it, as if I was resolved it should hit one way or other. I first took a piece of leaf, and chewed it in my mouth, which, indeed, at first almost stupefied my brain, the tobacco being green and strong, and that I had not been much used to. Then I took some and steeped it an hour or two in some rum, and resolved to take a dose of it when I lay down; and lastly, I burnt some upon a pan of coals, and held my nose close over the smoke of it as long as I could bear it, as well for the heat as almost for suffocation. In the interval of this operation I took up the Bible and began to read; but my head was too much disturbed with the tobacco to bear reading, at least at that time; only, having opened the book casually, the first words that

---

[85] medicine, drug

occurred to me were these: "Call on Me in the day of trouble, and I will deliver thee, and thou shalt glorify Me."[86] These words were very apt to my case, and made some impression upon my thoughts at the time of reading them, though not so much as they did afterwards; for, as for being delivered, the word had no sound, as I may say, to me; the thing was so remote, so impossible in my apprehension of things, that I began to say, as the children of Israel did when they were promised flesh to eat, "Can God spread a table in the wilderness?" so I began to say, "Can God Himself deliver me from this place?" And as it was not for many years that any hopes appeared, this prevailed very often upon my thoughts; but, however, the words made a great impression upon me, and I mused upon them very often. It grew now late, and the tobacco had, as I said, dozed my head so much that I inclined to sleep; so I left my lamp burning in the cave, lest I should want anything in the night, and went to bed. But before I lay down, I did what I never had done in all my life—I kneeled down, and prayed to God to fulfil the promise to me, that if I called upon Him in the day of trouble, He would deliver me. After my broken and imperfect prayer was over, I drank the rum in which I had steeped the tobacco, which was so strong and rank of the tobacco that I could scarcely get it down; immediately upon this I went to bed. I found presently it flew up into my head violently; but I fell into a sound sleep, and waked no more till, by the sun, it must necessarily be near three o'clock in the afternoon the next day—nay, to this hour I am partly of opinion that I slept all the next day and night, and till almost three the day after; for otherwise I know not how I should lose a day out of my reckoning in the days of the week, as it appeared some years after I had done; for if I had lost it by crossing and recrossing the line, I should have lost more than one day; but certainly I lost a day in my account, and never knew which way. Be that, however, one way or the other, when I awaked I found myself exceedingly refreshed, and my spirits lively and cheerful; when I got up I was stronger than I was the day before, and my stomach better, for I was hungry; and, in short, I had no fit the next day, but continued much altered for the better. This was the 29th.

The 30th was my well day, of course, and I went abroad with my gun, but did not care to travel too far. I killed a sea-fowl or two, something like a brandgoose, and brought them home, but was not very forward to eat them; so I ate some more of the turtle's eggs, which were very good. This evening I renewed the medicine, which I had supposed did me good the day before—the tobacco steeped in rum; only I did not take so much as before, nor did I chew any of the leaf, or hold my head over the smoke; however, I was not so well the next day, which was the first of July, as I hoped I should

---

[86] Psalm 50:15

have been; for I had a little spice of the cold fit, but it was not much.

July 2.—I renewed the medicine all the three ways; and dosed myself with it as at first, and doubled the quantity which I drank.

July 3.—I missed the fit for good and all, though I did not recover my full strength for some weeks after. While I was thus gathering strength, my thoughts ran exceedingly upon this Scripture, "I will deliver thee"; and the impossibility of my deliverance lay much upon my mind, in bar of my ever expecting it; but as I was discouraging myself with such thoughts, it occurred to my mind that I pored so much upon my deliverance from the main affliction, that I disregarded the deliverance I had received, and I was as it were made to ask myself such questions as these—viz. Have I not been delivered, and wonderfully too, from sickness—from the most distressed condition that could be, and that was so frightful to me? and what notice had I taken of it? Had I done my part? God had delivered me, but I had not glorified Him—that is to say, I had not owned and been thankful for that as a deliverance; and how could I expect greater deliverance? This touched my heart very much; and immediately I knelt down and gave God thanks aloud for my recovery from my sickness.

July 4.—In the morning I took the Bible; and beginning at the New Testament, I began seriously to read it, and imposed upon myself to read a while every morning and every night; not tying myself to the number of chapters, but long as my thoughts should engage me. It was not long after I set seriously to this work till I found my heart more deeply and sincerely affected with the wickedness of my past life. The impression of my dream revived; and the words, "All these things have not brought thee to repentance," ran seriously through my thoughts. I was earnestly begging of God to give me repentance, when it happened providentially, the very day, that, reading the Scripture, I came to these words: "He is exalted a Prince and a Saviour, to give repentance and to give remission."[87] I threw down the book; and with my heart as well as my hands lifted up to heaven, in a kind of ecstasy of joy, I cried out aloud, "Jesus, thou son of David! Jesus, thou exalted Prince and Saviour! give me repentance!" This was the first time I could say, in the true sense of the words, that I prayed in all my life; for now I prayed with a sense of my condition, and a true Scripture view of hope, founded on the encouragement of the Word of God; and from this time, I may say, I began to hope that God would hear me.

Now I began to construe the words mentioned above, "Call on Me, and I will deliver thee," in a different sense from what I had ever done before;

---

[87] "The God of our fathers raised up Jesus, whom ye slew and hanged on a tree. Him hath God exalted with his right hand *to be* a Prince and a Saviour, for to give repentance to Israel, and forgiveness of sins" (Acts 5:30-31).

for then I had no notion of anything being called deliverance, but my being delivered from the captivity I was in; for though I was indeed at large in the place, yet the island was certainly a prison to me, and that in the worse sense in the world. But now I learned to take it in another sense: now I looked back upon my past life with such horror, and my sins appeared so dreadful, that my soul sought nothing of God but deliverance from the load of guilt that bore down all my comfort. As for my solitary life, it was nothing. I did not so much as pray to be delivered from it or think of it; it was all of no consideration in comparison to this. And I add this part here, to hint to whoever shall read it, that whenever they come to a true sense of things, they will find deliverance from sin a much greater blessing than deliverance from affliction.

But, leaving this part, I return to my Journal.

My condition began now to be, though not less miserable as to my way of living, yet much easier to my mind: and my thoughts being directed, by a constant reading the Scripture and praying to God, to things of a higher nature, I had a great deal of comfort within, which till now I knew nothing of; also, my health and strength returned, I bestirred myself to furnish myself with everything that I wanted, and make my way of living as regular as I could.

From the 4th of July to the 14th I was chiefly employed in walking about with my gun in my hand, a little and a little at a time, as a man that was gathering up his strength after a fit of sickness; for it is hardly to be imagined how low I was, and to what weakness I was reduced. The application which I made use of was perfectly new, and perhaps which had never cured an ague before; neither can I recommend it to any to practise, by this experiment: and though it did carry off the fit, yet it rather contributed to weakening me; for I had frequent convulsions in my nerves and limbs for some time. I learned from it also this, in particular, that being abroad in the rainy season was the most pernicious[88] thing to my health that could be, especially in those rains which came attended with storms and hurricanes of wind; for as the rain which came in the dry season was almost always accompanied with such storms, so I found that rain was much more dangerous than the rain which fell in September and October.

---

[88] destructive, harmful

CHAPTER VII: AGRICULTURAL EXPERIENCE

I had now been in this unhappy island above ten months. All possibility of deliverance from this condition seemed to be entirely taken from me; and I firmly believe that no human shape had ever set foot upon that place. Having now secured my habitation, as I thought, fully to my mind, I had a great desire to make a more perfect discovery of the island, and to see what other productions I might find, which I yet knew nothing of.

It was on the 15th of July that I began to take a more particular survey of the island itself. I went up the creek first, where, as I hinted, I brought my rafts on shore. I found after I came about two miles up, that the tide did not flow any higher, and that it was no more than a little brook of running water, very fresh and good; but this being the dry season, there was hardly any water in some parts of it—at least not enough to run in any stream, so as it could be perceived. On the banks of this brook I found many pleasant savannahs or meadows, plain, smooth, and covered with grass; and on the rising parts of them, next to the higher grounds, where the water, as might be supposed, never overflowed, I found a great deal of tobacco, green, and growing to a great and very strong stalk. There were divers other plants, which I had no notion of or understanding about, that might, perhaps, have virtues of their own, which I could not find out. I searched for the cassava root, which the Indians, in all that climate, make their bread of, but I could find none. I saw large plants of aloes, but did not understand them. I saw several sugar-canes, but wild, and, for want of cultivation, imperfect. I contented myself with these discoveries for this time, and came back, musing with myself what course I might take to know the virtue and goodness of any of the fruits or plants which I should discover, but could bring it to no conclusion; for, in short, I had made so little observation while I was in the Brazils, that I knew little of the plants in the field; at least, very little that might serve to any purpose now in my distress.

The next day, the sixteenth, I went up the same way again; and after going something further than I had gone the day before, I found the brook and the savannahs cease, and the country become more woody than before. In this part I found different fruits, and particularly I found melons upon the ground, in great abundance, and grapes upon the trees. The vines had spread, indeed, over the trees, and the clusters of grapes were just now in their prime, very ripe and rich. This was a surprising discovery, and I was exceeding glad of them; but I was warned by my experience to eat sparingly of them; remembering that when I was ashore in Barbary, the eating of grapes killed several of our Englishmen, who were slaves there, by throwing them into fluxes and fevers. But I found an excellent use for these grapes; and that was, to cure or dry them in the sun, and keep them as dried grapes or raisins are kept, which I thought would be, as indeed they were, wholesome and agreeable to eat when no grapes could be had.

I spent all that evening there, and went not back to my habitation; which, by the way, was the first night, as I might say, I had lain from home. In the night, I took my first contrivance, and got up in a tree, where I slept well; and the next morning proceeded upon my discovery; travelling nearly four miles, as I might judge by the length of the valley, keeping still due north, with a ridge of hills on the south and north side of me. At the end of this march I came to an opening where the country seemed to descend to the west; and a little spring of fresh water, which issued out of the side of the hill by me, ran the other way, that is, due east; and the country appeared so fresh, so green, so flourishing, everything being in a constant verdure or flourish of spring that it looked like a planted garden. I descended a little on the side of that delicious vale, surveying it with a secret kind of pleasure, though mixed with my other afflicting thoughts, to think that this was all my own; that I was king and lord of all this country indefensibly, and had a right of possession; and if I could convey it, I might have it in inheritance as completely as any lord of a manor in England. I saw here abundance of cocoa trees, orange, and lemon, and citron[89] trees; but all wild, and very few bearing any fruit, at least not then. However, the green limes that I gathered were not only pleasant to eat, but very wholesome; and I mixed their juice afterwards with water, which made it very wholesome, and very cool and refreshing. I found now I had business enough to gather and carry home; and I resolved to lay up a store as well of grapes as limes and lemons, to furnish myself for the wet season, which I knew was approaching. In order to do this, I gathered a great heap of grapes in one place, a lesser heap in another place, and a great parcel of limes and lemons in another place; and taking a few of each with me, I travelled homewards; resolving to come again, and bring a bag or sack, or what I could make, to carry the rest home. Accordingly, having spent three days in this journey, I came home (so I must now call my tent and my cave); but before I got thither the grapes were spoiled; the richness of the fruit and the weight of the juice having broken them and bruised them, they were good for little or nothing; as to the limes,

---

[89] yellow-green citrus fruit

they were good, but I could bring but a few.

The next day, being the nineteenth, I went back, having made me two small bags to bring home my harvest; but I was surprised, when coming to my heap of grapes, which were so rich and fine when I gathered them, to find them all spread about, trod to pieces, and dragged about, some here, some there, and abundance eaten and devoured. By this I concluded there were some wild creatures thereabouts, which had done this; but what they were I knew not. However, as I found there was no laying them up on heaps, and no carrying them away in a sack, but that one way they would be destroyed, and the other way they would be crushed with their own weight, I took another course; for I gathered a large quantity of the grapes, and hung upon the out-branches of the trees, that they might cure and dry in the sun; and as for the limes and lemons, I carried as many back as I could well stand under.

When I came home from this journey, I contemplated with great pleasure the fruitfulness of that valley, and the pleasantness of the situation; the security from storms on that side of the water, and the wood: and concluded that I had pitched upon a place to fix my abode which was by far the worst part of the country. Upon the whole, I began to consider of removing my habitation, and looking out for a place equally safe as where now I was situate, if possible, in that pleasant, fruitful part of the island.

This thought ran long in my head, and I was exceeding fond of it for some time, the pleasantness of the place tempting me; but when I came to a nearer view of it, I considered that I was now by the seaside, where it was at least possible that something might happen to my advantage, and, by the same ill fate that brought me hither might bring some other unhappy wretches to the same place; and though it was scarce probable that any such thing should ever happen, yet to enclose myself among the hills and woods in the centre of the island was to anticipate my bondage, and to render such an affair not only improbable, but impossible; and that therefore I ought not by any means to remove. However, I was so enamoured of this place, that I spent much of my time there for the whole of the remaining part of the month of July; and though upon second thoughts, I resolved not to remove, yet I built me a little kind of a bower,[90] and surrounded it at a distance with a strong fence, being a double hedge, as high as I could reach, well staked and filled between with brushwood; and here I lay very secure, sometimes two or three nights together; always going over it with a ladder; so that I fancied now I had my country house and my sea-coast house; and this work took me up to the beginning of August.

I had but newly finished my fence, and began to enjoy my labour, when

---

[90] hideaway, den

the rains came on, and made me stick close to my first habitation; for though I had made me a tent like the other, with a piece of a sail, and spread it very well, yet I had not the shelter of a hill to keep me from storms, nor a cave behind me to retreat into when the rains were extraordinary.

About the beginning of August, as I said, I had finished my bower, and began to enjoy myself. The 3rd of August, I found the grapes I had hung up perfectly dried, and, indeed, were excellent good raisins of the sun; so I began to take them down from the trees, and it was very happy that I did so, for the rains which followed would have spoiled them, and I had lost the best part of my winter food; for I had above two hundred large bunches of them. No sooner had I taken them all down, and carried the most of them home to my cave, than it began to rain; and from hence, which was the 14th of August, it rained, more or less, every day till the middle of October; and sometimes so violently, that I could not stir out of my cave for several days.

In this season I was much surprised with the increase of my family; I had been concerned for the loss of one of my cats, who ran away from me, or, as I thought, had been dead, and I heard no more tidings of her till, to my astonishment, she came home about the end of August with three kittens. This was the more strange to me because, though I had killed a wild cat, as I called it, with my gun, yet I thought it was quite a different kind from our European cats; but the young cats were the same kind of house-breed as the old one; and both my cats being females, I thought it very strange. But from these three cats I afterwards came to be so pestered with cats that I was forced to kill them like vermin or wild beasts, and to drive them from my house as much as possible.

From the 14th of August to the 26th, incessant rain, so that I could not stir, and was now very careful not to be much wet. In this confinement, I began to be straitened for food: but venturing out twice, I one day killed a goat; and the last day, which was the 26th, found a very large tortoise, which was a treat to me, and my food was regulated thus: I ate a bunch of raisins for my breakfast; a piece of the goat's flesh, or of the turtle, for my dinner, broiled—for, to my great misfortune, I had no vessel to boil or stew anything; and two or three of the turtle's eggs for my supper.

During this confinement in my cover by the rain, I worked daily two or three hours at enlarging my cave, and by degrees worked it on towards one side, till I came to the outside of the hill, and made a door or way out, which came beyond my fence or wall; and so I came in and out this way. But I was not perfectly easy at lying so open; for, as I had managed myself before, I was in a perfect enclosure; whereas now I thought I lay exposed, and open for anything to come in upon me; and yet I could not perceive that there was any living thing to fear, the biggest creature that I had yet seen upon the island being a goat.

Sept. 30.—I was now come to the unhappy anniversary of my landing. I cast up the notches on my post, and found I had been on shore three hundred and sixty-five days. I kept this day as a solemn fast, setting it apart for religious exercise, prostrating myself on the ground[91] with the most serious humiliation, confessing my sins to God, acknowledging His righteous judgments upon me, and praying to Him to have mercy on me through Jesus Christ; and not having tasted the least refreshment for twelve hours, even till the going down of the sun, I then ate a biscuit-cake and a bunch of grapes, and went to bed, finishing the day as I began it. I had all this time observed no Sabbath day; for as at first I had no sense of religion upon my mind, I had, after some time, omitted to distinguish the weeks, by making a longer notch than ordinary for the Sabbath day, and so did not really know what any of the days were; but now, having cast up the days as above, I found I had been there a year; so I divided it into weeks, and set apart every seventh day for a Sabbath; though I found at the end of my account I had lost a day or two in my reckoning. A little after this, my ink began to fail me, and so I contented myself to use it more sparingly, and to write down only the most remarkable events of my life, without continuing a daily memorandum of other things.

The rainy season and the dry season began now to appear regular to me, and I learned to divide them so as to provide for them accordingly; but I bought all my experience before I had it, and this I am going to relate was one of the most discouraging experiments that I made.

I have mentioned that I had saved the few ears of barley and rice, which I had so surprisingly found spring up, as I thought, of themselves, and I believe there were about thirty stalks of rice, and about twenty of barley; and now I thought it a proper time to sow it, after the rains, the sun being in its southern position, going from me. Accordingly, I dug up a piece of ground as well as I could with my wooden spade, and dividing it into two parts, I sowed my grain; but as I was sowing, it casually occurred to my thoughts that I would not sow it all at first, because I did not know when was the proper time for it, so I sowed about two-thirds of the seed, leaving about a handful of each. It was a great comfort to me afterwards that I did so, for not one grain of what I sowed this time came to anything: for the dry months following, the earth having had no rain after the seed was sown, it had no moisture to assist its growth, and never came up at all till the wet season had come again, and then it grew as if it had been but newly sown. Finding my first seed did not grow, which I easily imagined was by the drought, I sought for a moister piece of ground to make another trial in, and I dug up a piece of ground near my new bower, and sowed the rest of my seed in

---

[91] lying face down

February, a little before the vernal equinox; and this having the rainy months of March and April to water it, sprung up very pleasantly, and yielded a very good crop; but having part of the seed left only, and not daring to sow all that I had, I had but a small quantity at last, my whole crop not amounting to above half a peck[92] of each kind. But by this experiment I was made master of my business, and knew exactly when the proper season was to sow, and that I might expect two seed-times and two harvests every year.

While this corn was growing I made a little discovery, which was of use to me afterwards. As soon as the rains were over, and the weather began to settle, which was about the month of November, I made a visit up the country to my bower, where, though I had not been some months, yet I found all things just as I left them. The circle or double hedge that I had made was not only firm and entire, but the stakes which I had cut out of some trees that grew thereabouts were all shot out and grown with long branches, as much as a willow-tree usually shoots the first year after lopping its head. I could not tell what tree to call it that these stakes were cut from. I was surprised, and yet very well pleased, to see the young trees grow; and I pruned them, and led them up to grow as much alike as I could; and it is scarce credible how beautiful a figure they grew into in three years; so that though the hedge made a circle of about twenty-five yards in diameter, yet the trees, for such I might now call them, soon covered it, and it was a complete shade, sufficient to lodge under all the dry season. This made me resolve to cut some more stakes, and make me a hedge like this, in a semi-circle round my wall (I mean that of my first dwelling), which I did; and placing the trees or stakes in a double row, at about eight yards distance from my first fence, they grew presently, and were at first a fine cover to my habitation, and afterwards served for a defence also, as I shall observe in its order.

I found now that the seasons of the year might generally be divided, not into summer and winter, as in Europe, but into the rainy seasons and the dry seasons, which were generally thus:—

The half of February, the whole of March, and the half of April—rainy, the sun being then on or near the equinox.

The half of April, the whole of May, June, and July, and the half of August—dry, the sun being then to the north of the line.

The half of August, the whole of September, and the half of October—rainy, the sun being then come back.

The half of October, the whole of November, December, and January, and the half of February—dry, the sun being then to the south of the line.

The rainy seasons sometimes held longer or shorter as the winds hap-

---

[92] a quarter of a bushel, or eight quarts

pened to blow, but this was the general observation I made. After I had found by experience the ill consequences of being abroad in the rain, I took care to furnish myself with provisions beforehand, that I might not be obliged to go out, and I sat within doors as much as possible during the wet months. This time I found much employment, and very suitable also to the time, for I found great occasion for many things which I had no way to furnish myself with but by hard labour and constant application; particularly I tried many ways to make myself a basket, but all the twigs I could get for the purpose proved so brittle that they would do nothing. It proved of excellent advantage to me now, that when I was a boy, I used to take great delight in standing at a basket-maker's, in the town where my father lived, to see them make their wicker-ware; and being, as boys usually are, very officious to help, and a great observer of the manner in which they worked those things, and sometimes lending a hand, I had by these means full knowledge of the methods of it, and I wanted nothing but the materials, when it came into my mind that the twigs of that tree from whence I cut my stakes that grew might possibly be as tough as the sallows, willows, and osiers in England, and I resolved to try. Accordingly, the next day I went to my country house, as I called it, and cutting some of the smaller twigs, I found them to my purpose as much as I could desire; whereupon I came the next time prepared with a hatchet to cut down a quantity, which I soon found, for there was great plenty of them. These I set up to dry within my circle or hedge, and when they were fit for use I carried them to my cave; and here, during the next season, I employed myself in making, as well as I could, a great many baskets, both to carry earth or to carry or lay up anything, as I had occasion; and though I did not finish them very handsomely, yet I made them sufficiently serviceable for my purpose; thus, afterwards, I took care never to be without them; and as my wicker-ware decayed, I made more, especially strong, deep baskets to place my corn in, instead of sacks, when I should come to have any quantity of it.

Having mastered this difficulty, and employed a world of time about it, I bestirred myself to see, if possible, how to supply two wants. I had no vessels to hold anything that was liquid, except two runlets, which were almost full of rum, and some glass bottles—some of the common size, and others which were case bottles, square, for the holding of water, spirits, &c. I had not so much as a pot to boil anything, except a great kettle, which I saved out of the ship, and which was too big for such as I desired it—viz. to make broth, and stew a bit of meat by itself. The second thing I fain would have had was a tobacco-pipe, but it was impossible to me to make one; however, I found a contrivance for that, too, at last. I employed myself in planting my second rows of stakes or piles, and in this wicker-working all the summer or dry season, when another business took me up more time than it could be imagined I could spare.

Questions for Review:

1. Sum up Robinson Crusoe's next batch of work on the wreckage.

2. What is the effect upon the reader in reading about Robinson Crusoe's illness in a journal format? How does his illness affect him?

3. What key thoughts does Crusoe have while sitting by the sea?

4. Explain his finding of bodily and spiritual cures.

5. How does Robinson Crusoe's Bible reading affect him?

6. What does Robinson Crusoe learn on his trip around the island? What decision does he make?

7. How does Robinson Crusoe spend his year anniversary?

8. What does Robinson Crusoe learn about planting and the island's seasons? What does he learn to make with his hands, and what does he wish for?

CHAPTER VIII: SURVEYS HIS POSITION

I mentioned before that I had a great mind to see the whole island, and that I had travelled up the brook, and so on to where I built my bower, and where I had an opening quite to the sea, on the other side of the island. I now resolved to travel quite across to the sea-shore on that side; so, taking my gun, a hatchet, and my dog, and a larger quantity of powder and shot than usual, with two biscuit-cakes and a great bunch of raisins in my pouch for my store, I began my journey. When I had passed the vale where my bower stood, as above, I came within view of the sea to the west, and it being a very clear day, I fairly descried land—whether an island or a continent I could not tell; but it lay very high, extending from the W. to the W.S.W. at a very great distance; by my guess it could not be less than fifteen or twenty leagues off.

I could not tell what part of the world this might be, otherwise than that I knew it must be part of America, and, as I concluded by all my observations, must be near the Spanish dominions, and perhaps was all inhabited by savages, where, if I had landed, I had been in a worse condition than I was now; and therefore I acquiesced[93] in the dispositions of Providence, which I began now to own and to believe ordered everything for the best; I say I quieted my mind with this, and left off afflicting myself with fruitless wishes of being there.

Besides, after some thought upon this affair, I considered that if this land was the Spanish coast, I should certainly, one time or other, see some vessel pass or repass one way or other; but if not, then it was the savage coast between the Spanish country and Brazils, where are found the worst of savages; for they are cannibals or men-eaters, and fail not to murder and devour all the human bodies that fall into their hands.

With these considerations, I walked very leisurely forward. I found that side of the island where I now was much pleasanter than mine—the open or savannah fields sweet, adorned with flowers and grass, and full of very fine woods. I saw abundance of parrots, and fain I would have caught one, if possible, to have kept it to be tame, and taught it to speak to me. I did, after some painstaking, catch a young parrot, for I knocked it down with a stick, and having recovered it, I brought it home; but it was some years before I could make him speak; however, at last I taught him to call me by name very familiarly. But the accident that followed, though it be a trifle, will be very diverting in its place.

I was exceedingly diverted with this journey. I found in the low grounds hares (as I thought them to be) and foxes; but they differed greatly from all the other kinds I had met with, nor could I satisfy myself to eat them, though I killed several. But I had no need to be venturous, for I had no want of food, and of that which was very good too, especially these three sorts, viz. goats, pigeons, and turtle, or tortoise, which added to my grapes, Leadenhall Market[94] could not have furnished a table better than I, in proportion to the company; and though my case was deplorable enough, yet I had great cause for thankfulness that I was not driven to any extremities for food, but had rather plenty, even to dainties.[95]

I never travelled in this journey above two miles outright in a day, or thereabouts; but I took so many turns and returns to see what discoveries I could make, that I came weary enough to the place where I resolved to sit down all night; and then I either reposed myself in a tree, or surrounded my-

[93] submitted
[94] famous market in London
[95] high-class foods, delicacies

self with a row of stakes set upright in the ground, either from one tree to another, or so as no wild creature could come at me without waking me.

As soon as I came to the sea-shore, I was surprised to see that I had taken up my lot on the worst side of the island, for here, indeed, the shore was covered with innumerable turtles, whereas on the other side I had found but three in a year and a half. Here was also an infinite number of fowls of many kinds, some which I had seen, and some which I had not seen before, and many of them very good meat, but such as I knew not the names of, except those called penguins.

I could have shot as many as I pleased, but was very sparing of my powder and shot, and therefore had more mind to kill a she-goat if I could, which I could better feed on; and though there were many goats here, more than on my side the island, yet it was with much more difficulty that I could come near them, the country being flat and even, and they saw me much sooner than when I was on the hills.

I confess this side of the country was much pleasanter than mine; but yet I had not the least inclination to remove, for as I was fixed in my habitation it became natural to me, and I seemed all the while I was here to be as it were upon a journey, and from home. However, I travelled along the shore of the sea towards the east, I suppose about twelve miles, and then setting up a great pole upon the shore for a mark, I concluded I would go home again, and that the next journey I took should be on the other side of the island east from my dwelling, and so round till I came to my post again.

I took another way to come back than that I went, thinking I could easily keep all the island so much in my view that I could not miss finding my first dwelling by viewing the country; but I found myself mistaken, for being come about two or three miles, I found myself descended into a very large valley, but so surrounded with hills, and those hills covered with wood, that I could not see which was my way by any direction but that of the sun, nor even then, unless I knew very well the position of the sun at that time of the day. It happened, to my further misfortune, that the weather proved hazy for three or four days while I was in the valley, and not being able to see the sun, I wandered about very uncomfortably, and at last was obliged to find the seaside, look for my post, and come back the same way I went: and then, by easy journeys, I turned homeward, the weather being exceeding hot, and my gun, ammunition, hatchet, and other things very heavy.

In this journey my dog surprised a young kid, and seized upon it; and I, running in to take hold of it, caught it, and saved it alive from the dog. I had a great mind to bring it home if I could, for I had often been musing whether it might not be possible to get a kid or two, and so raise a breed of tame goats, which might supply me when my powder and shot should be all spent. I made a collar for this little creature, and with a string, which I made of some rope-yam, which I always carried about me, I led him along, though with some difficulty, till I came to my bower, and there I enclosed him and left him, for I was very impatient to be at home, from whence I had been absent above a month.

I cannot express what a satisfaction it was to me to come into my old hutch, and lie down in my hammock-bed. This little wandering journey, without settled place of abode, had been so unpleasant to me, that my own house, as I called it to myself, was a perfect settlement to me compared to that; and it rendered everything about me so comfortable, that I resolved I would never go a great way from it again while it should be my lot to stay on the island.

I reposed myself here a week, to rest and regale[96] myself after my long journey; during which most of the time was taken up in the weighty affair of making a cage for my Poll, who began now to be a mere domestic, and to be well acquainted with me. Then I began to think of the poor kid which I had penned in within my little circle, and resolved to go and fetch it home, or give it some food; accordingly I went, and found it where I left it, for indeed it could not get out, but was almost starved for want of food. I went and cut boughs of trees, and branches of such shrubs as I could find, and threw it over, and having fed it, I tied it as I did before, to lead it away; but it was so tame with being hungry, that I had no need to have tied it, for it followed me like a dog: and as I continually fed it, the creature became so loving, so gentle, and so fond, that it became from that time one of my domestics also, and would never leave me afterwards.

The rainy season of the autumnal equinox was now come, and I kept the 30th of September in the same solemn manner as before, being the anniversary of my landing on the island, having now been there two years, and no more prospect of being delivered than the first day I came there, I spent the whole day in humble and thankful acknowledgments of the many wonderful mercies which my solitary condition was attended with, and without which it might have been infinitely more miserable. I gave humble and hearty thanks that God had been pleased to discover to me that it was possible I might be more happy in this solitary condition than I should have been in the liberty of society, and in all the pleasures of the world; that He could fully make up to me the deficiencies of my solitary state, and the want of human society, by His presence and the communications of His grace to my soul; supporting, comforting, and encouraging me to depend upon His providence here, and hope for His eternal presence hereafter.

It was now that I began sensibly to feel how much more happy this life I now led was, with all its miserable circumstances, than the wicked, cursed,

---

[96] amuse, entertain

abominable life I led all the past part of my days; and now I changed both my sorrows and my joys; my very desires altered, my affections changed their gusts, and my delights were perfectly new from what they were at my first coming, or, indeed, for the two years past.

Before, as I walked about, either on my hunting or for viewing the country, the anguish of my soul at my condition would break out upon me on a sudden, and my very heart would die within me, to think of the woods, the mountains, the deserts I was in, and how I was a prisoner, locked up with the eternal bars and bolts of the ocean, in an uninhabited wilderness, without redemption. In the midst of the greatest composure of my mind, this would break out upon me like a storm, and make me wring my hands and weep like a child. Sometimes it would take me in the middle of my work, and I would immediately sit down and sigh, and look upon the ground for an hour or two together; and this was still worse to me, for if I could burst out into tears, or vent myself by words, it would go off, and the grief, having exhausted itself, would abate.

But now I began to exercise myself with new thoughts: I daily read the word of God, and applied all the comforts of it to my present state. One morning, being very sad, I opened the Bible upon these words, "I will never, never leave thee, nor forsake thee." Immediately it occurred that these words were to me; why else should they be directed in such a manner, just at the moment when I was mourning over my condition, as one forsaken of God and man? "Well, then," said I, "if God does not forsake me, of what ill consequence can it be, or what matters it, though the world should all forsake me, seeing on the other hand, if I had all the world, and should lose the favour and blessing of God, there would be no comparison in the loss?"

From this moment I began to conclude in my mind that it was possible for me to be more happy in this forsaken, solitary condition than it was probable I should ever have been in any other particular state in the world; and with this thought I was going to give thanks to God for bringing me to this place. I know not what it was, but something shocked my mind at that thought, and I durst not speak the words. "How canst thou become such a hypocrite," said I, even audibly, "to pretend to be thankful for a condition which, however thou mayest endeavour to be contented with, thou wouldst rather pray heartily to be delivered from?" So I stopped there; but though I could not say I thanked God for being there, yet I sincerely gave thanks to God for opening my eyes, by whatever afflicting providences, to see the former condition of my life, and to mourn for my wickedness, and repent. I never opened the Bible, or shut it, but my very soul within me blessed God for directing my friend in England, without any order of mine, to pack it up among my goods, and for assisting me afterwards to save it out of the wreck of the ship.

Thus, and in this disposition of mind, I began my third year; and though I have not given the reader the trouble of so particular an account of my works this year as the first, yet in general it may be observed that I was very seldom idle, but having regularly divided my time according to the several daily employments that were before me, such as: first, my duty to God, and the reading the Scriptures, which I constantly set apart some time for thrice every day; secondly, the going abroad with my gun for food, which generally took me up three hours in every morning, when it did not rain; thirdly, the ordering, cutting, preserving, and cooking what I had killed or caught for my supply; these took up great part of the day. Also, it is to be considered, that in the middle of the day, when the sun was in the zenith, the violence of the heat was too great to stir out; so that about four hours in the evening was all the time I could be supposed to work in, with this exception, that sometimes I changed my hours of hunting and working, and went to work in the morning, and abroad with my gun in the afternoon.

To this short time allowed for labour I desire may be added the exceeding laboriousness of my work; the many hours which, for want of tools, want of help, and want of skill, everything I did took up out of my time. For example, I was full two and forty days in making a board for a long shelf, which I wanted in my cave; whereas, two sawyers,[97] with their tools and a saw-pit, would have cut six of them out of the same tree in half a day.

My case was this: it was to be a large tree which was to be cut down, because my board was to be a broad one. This tree I was three days in cutting down, and two more cutting off the boughs, and reducing it to a log or piece of timber. With inexpressible hacking and hewing I reduced both the sides of it into chips till it began to be light enough to move; then I turned it, and made one side of it smooth and flat as a board from end to end; then, turning that side downward, cut the other side til I brought the plank to be about three inches thick, and smooth on both sides. Any one may judge the labour of my hands in such a piece of work; but labour and patience carried me through that, and many other things. I only observe this in particular, to show the reason why so much of my time went away with so little work— viz. that what might be a little to be done with help and tools, was a vast labour and required a prodigious time to do alone, and by hand. But notwithstanding this, with patience and labour I got through everything that my circumstances made necessary to me to do, as will appear by what follows.

I was now, in the months of November and December, expecting my crop of barley and rice. The ground I had manured and dug up for them was not great; for, as I observed, my seed of each was not above the quantity of half a peck, for I had lost one whole crop by sowing in the dry season. But

---

[97] someone who saws wood

now my crop promised very well, when on a sudden I found I was in danger of losing it all again by enemies of several sorts, which it was scarcely possible to keep from it; as, first, the goats, and wild creatures which I called hares, who, tasting the sweetness of the blade, lay in it night and day, as soon as it came up, and eat it so close, that it could get no time to shoot up into stalk.

This I saw no remedy for but by making an enclosure about it with a hedge; which I did with a great deal of toil, and the more, because it required speed. However, as my arable[98] land was but small, suited to my crop, I got it totally well fenced in about three weeks' time; and shooting some of the creatures in the daytime, I set my dog to guard it in the night, tying him up to a stake at the gate, where he would stand and bark all night long; so in a little time the enemies forsook the place, and the corn grew very strong and well, and began to ripen apace.

But as the beasts ruined me before, while my corn was in the blade, so the birds were as likely to ruin me now, when it was in the ear; for, going along by the place to see how it throve, I saw my little crop surrounded with fowls, of I know not how many sorts, who stood, as it were, watching till I should be gone. I immediately let fly among them, for I always had my gun with me. I had no sooner shot, but there rose up a little cloud of fowls, which I had not seen at all, from among the corn itself.

This touched me sensibly, for I foresaw that in a few days they would devour all my hopes; that I should be starved, and never be able to raise a crop at all; and what to do I could not tell; however, I resolved not to lose my corn, if possible, though I should watch it night and day. In the first place, I went among it to see what damage was already done, and found they had spoiled a good deal of it; but that as it was yet too green for them, the loss was not so great but that the remainder was likely to be a good crop if it could be saved.

I stayed by it to load my gun, and then coming away, I could easily see the thieves sitting upon all the trees about me, as if they only waited till I was gone away, and the event proved it to be so; for as I walked off, as if I was gone, I was no sooner out of their sight than they dropped down one by one into the corn again. I was so provoked, that I could not have patience to stay till more came on, knowing that every grain that they ate now was, as it might be said, a peck-loaf to me in the consequence; but coming up to the hedge, I fired again, and killed three of them. This was what I wished for; so I took them up, and served them as we serve notorious thieves in Eng-land—hanged them in chains, for a terror to others. It is impossible to imag-ine that this should have such an effect as it had, for the fowls would not

---

[98] usable for growing crops

only not come at the corn, but, in short, they forsook all that part of the island, and I could never see a bird near the place as long as my scarecrows hung there. This I was very glad of, you may be sure, and about the latter end of December, which was our second harvest of the year, I reaped my corn.

I was sadly put to it for a scythe or sickle to cut it down, and all I could do was to make one, as well as I could, out of one of the broad-swords, or cutlasses, which I saved among the arms out of the ship. However, as my first crop was but small, I had no great difficulty to cut it down; in short, I reaped it in my way, for I cut nothing off but the ears, and carried it away in a great basket which I had made, and so rubbed it out with my hands; and at the end of all my harvesting, I found that out of my half-peck of seed I had near two bushels of rice, and about two bushels and a half of barley; that is to say, by my guess, for I had no measure at that time.

However, this was a great encouragement to me, and I foresaw that, in time, it would please God to supply me with bread. And yet here I was perplexed again, for I neither knew how to grind or make meal of my corn, or indeed how to clean it and part it; nor, if made into meal, how to make bread of it; and if how to make it, yet I knew not how to bake it. These things being added to my desire of having a good quantity for store, and to secure a constant supply, I resolved not to taste any of this crop, but to preserve it all for seed against the next season; and in the meantime to employ all my study and hours of working to accomplish this great work of providing myself with corn and bread.

It might be truly said, that now I worked for my bread. I believe few people have thought much upon the strange multitude of little things necessary in the providing, producing, curing, dressing, making, and finishing this one article of bread.

I, that was reduced to a mere state of nature, found this to my daily discouragement; and was made more sensible of it every hour, even after I had got the first handful of seed-corn, which, as I have said, came up unexpectedly, and indeed to a surprise.

First, I had no plough to turn up the earth—no spade or shovel to dig it.

Well, this I conquered by making me a wooden spade, as I observed before; but this did my work but in a wooden manner; and though it cost me a great many days to make it, yet, for want of iron, it not only wore out soon, but made my work the harder, and made it be performed much worse. However, this I bore with, and was content to work it out with patience, and bear with the badness of the performance. When the corn was sown, I had no harrow, but was forced to go over it myself, and drag a great heavy bough of a tree over it, to scratch it, as it may be called, rather than rake or harrow it. When it was growing, and grown, I have observed already how many things I wanted to fence it, secure it, mow or reap it, cure and carry it home, thrash, part it from the chaff, and save it. Then I wanted a mill to grind it sieves to dress it, yeast and salt to make it into bread, and an oven to bake it; but all these things I did without, as shall be observed; and yet the corn was an inestimable comfort and advantage to me too. All this, as I said, made everything laborious and tedious to me; but that there was no help for. Neither was my time so much loss to me, because, as I had divided it, a certain part of it was every day appointed to these works; and as I had resolved to use none of the corn for bread till I had a greater quantity by me, I had the next six months to apply myself wholly, by labour and invention, to furnish myself with utensils proper for the performing all the operations necessary for making the corn, when I had it, fit for my use.

Questions for Review:

1. Sum up Robinson Crusoe's exploration of the islands, what he gains from the exploration, his impressions, and what he decides.

2. What does September 30 mark? How does Robinson Crusoe spend the day?

3. Sum up Robinson Crusoe's spiritual journey, and how it has changed his outlook on his life, and his behavior.

4. What are Robinson Crusoe's daily tasks, in order? What is praiseworthy about this order?

5. List what Robinson Crusoe works on during this time on the island. What character traits are brought to light by these descriptions of his work?

CHAPTER IX:
A BOAT

But first I was to prepare more land, for I had now seed enough to sow above an acre of ground. Before I did this, I had a week's work at least to make me a spade, which, when it was done, was but a sorry one indeed, and very heavy, and required double labour to work with it. However, I got through that, and sowed my seed in two large flat pieces of ground, as near my house as I could find them to my mind, and fenced them in with a good hedge, the stakes of which were all cut off that wood which I had set before, and knew it would grow; so that, in a year's time, I knew I should have a quick or living hedge, that would want but little repair. This work did not take me up less than three months, because a great part of that time was the wet season, when I could not go abroad. Within-doors, that is, when it rained and I could not go out, I found employment in the following occupations—always observing, that all the while I was at work I diverted myself with talking to my parrot, and teaching him to speak; and I quickly taught him to know his own name, and at last to speak it out pretty loud, "Poll," which was the first word I ever heard spoken in the island by any mouth but my own. This, therefore, was not my work, but an assistance to my work; for now, as I said, I had a great employment upon my hands, as follows: I had long studied to make, by some means or other, some earthen vessels, which, indeed, I wanted sorely, but knew not where to come at them. However, considering the heat of the climate, I did not doubt but if I could find out any clay, I might make some pots that might, being dried in the sun, be hard enough and strong enough to bear handling, and to hold anything that was dry, and required to be kept so; and as this was necessary in the preparing corn, meal, &c., which was the thing I was doing, I resolved to make some as large as I could, and fit only to stand like jars, to hold what should be put into them.

It would make the reader pity me, or rather laugh at me, to tell how many awkward ways I took to raise this paste; what odd, misshapen, ugly things I made; how many of them fell in and how many fell out, the clay not being stiff enough to bear its own weight; how many cracked by the over-violent heat of the sun, being set out too hastily; and how many fell in pieces with only removing, as well before as after they were dried; and, in a word, how, after having laboured hard to find the clay—to dig it, to temper it, to bring it home, and work it—I could not make above two large earthen ugly things (I cannot call them jars) in about two months' labour.

However, as the sun baked these two very dry and hard, I lifted them very gently up, and set them down again in two great wicker baskets, which I had made on purpose for them, that they might not break; and as between the pot and the basket there was a little room to spare, I stuffed it full of the rice and barley straw; and these two pots being to stand always dry I thought would hold my dry corn, and perhaps the meal, when the corn was bruised.

Though I miscarried so much in my design for large pots, yet I made several smaller things with better success; such as little round pots, flat dishes, pitchers, and pipkins,[99] and any things my hand turned to; and the heat of the sun baked them quite hard.

But all this would not answer my end, which was to get an earthen pot to hold what was liquid, and bear the fire, which none of these could do. It happened after some time, making a pretty large fire for cooking my meat, when I went to put it out after I had done with it, I found a broken piece of one of my earthenware vessels in the fire, burnt as hard as a stone, and red as a tile. I was agreeably surprised to see it, and said to myself, that certainly they might be made to burn whole, if they would burn broken.

This set me to study how to order my fire, so as to make it burn some pots. I had no notion of a kiln, such as the potters burn in, or of glazing them with lead, though I had some lead to do it with; but I placed three large pipkins and two or three pots in a pile, one upon another, and placed my firewood all round it, with a great heap of embers under them. I plied the fire with fresh fuel round the outside and upon the top, till I saw the pots in the inside red-hot quite through, and observed that they did not crack at all. When I saw them clear red, I let them stand in that heat about five or six hours, till I found one of them, though it did not crack, did melt or run; for the sand which was mixed with the clay melted by the violence of the heat, and would have run into glass if I had gone on; so I slacked my fire gradually till the pots began to abate of the red colour; and watching them all night, that I might not let the fire abate too fast, in the morning I had three very good (I will not say handsome) pipkins, and two other earthen pots, as hard burnt as could be desired, and one of them perfectly glazed with the running of the sand.

After this experiment, I need not say that I wanted no sort of earthenware for my use; but I must needs say as to the shapes of them, they were very indifferent, as any one may suppose, when I had no way of making them but as the children make dirt pies, or as a woman would make pies that never learned to raise paste.

No joy at a thing of so mean a nature was ever equal to mine, when I found I had made an earthen pot that would bear the fire; and I had hardly

---

[99] small vessels for boiling

patience to stay till they were cold before I set one on the fire again with some water in it to boil me some meat, which it did admirably well; and with a piece of a kid I made some very good broth, though I wanted oatmeal, and several other ingredients requisite to make it as good as I would have had it been.

My next concern was to get me a stone mortar to stamp or beat some corn in; for as to the mill, there was no thought of arriving at that perfection of art with one pair of hands. To supply this want, I was at a great loss; for, of all the trades in the world, I was as perfectly unqualified for a stone-cutter as for any whatever; neither had I any tools to go about it with. I spent many a day to find out a great stone big enough to cut hollow, and make fit for a mortar, and could find none at all, except what was in the solid rock, and which I had no way to dig or cut out; nor indeed were the rocks in the island of hardness sufficient, but were all of a sandy, crumbling stone, which neither would bear the weight of a heavy pestle, nor would break the corn without filling it with sand. So, after a great deal of time lost in searching for a stone, I gave it over, and resolved to look out for a great block of hard wood, which I found, indeed, much easier; and getting one as big as I had strength to stir, I rounded it, and formed it on the outside with my axe and hatchet, and then with the help of fire and infinite labour, made a hollow place in it, as the Indians in Brazil make their canoes. After this, I made a great heavy pestle or beater of the wood called the iron-wood; and this I prepared and laid by against I had my next crop of corn, which I proposed to myself to grind, or rather pound into meal to make bread.

My next difficulty was to make a sieve or searce, to dress my meal, and to part it from the bran and the husk; without which I did not see it possible I could have any bread. This was a most difficult thing even to think on, for to be sure I had nothing like the necessary thing to make it—I mean fine thin canvas or stuff to searce the meal through. And here I was at a full stop for many months; nor did I really know what to do. Linen I had none left but what was mere rags; I had goat's hair, but neither knew how to weave it or spin it; and had I known how, here were no tools to work it with. All the remedy that I found for this was, that at last I did remember I had, among the seamen's clothes which were saved out of the ship, some neckcloths of calico or muslin; and with some pieces of these I made three small sieves proper enough for the work; and thus I made shift for some years: how I did afterwards, I shall show in its place.

The baking part was the next thing to be considered, and how I should make bread when I came to have corn; for first, I had no yeast. As to that part, there was no supplying the want, so I did not concern myself much about it. But for an oven I was indeed in great pain. At length I found out an experiment for that also, which was this: I made some earthen-vessels very broad but not deep, that is to say, about two feet diameter, and not above nine inches deep. These I burned in the fire, as I had done the other, and laid them by; and when I wanted to bake, I made a great fire upon my hearth, which I had paved with some square tiles of my own baking and burning also; but I should not call them square.

When the firewood was burned pretty much into embers or live coals, I drew them forward upon this hearth, so as to cover it all over, and there I let them lie till the hearth was very hot. Then sweeping away all the embers, I set down my loaf or loaves, and whelming down the earthen pot upon them, drew the embers all round the outside of the pot, to keep in and add to the heat; and thus as well as in the best oven in the world, I baked my barley-loaves, and became in little time a good pastrycook into the bargain; for I made myself several cakes and puddings of the rice; but I made no pies, neither had I anything to put into them supposing I had, except the flesh either of fowls or goats.

It need not be wondered at if all these things took me up most part of the third year of my abode here; for it is to be observed that in the intervals of these things I had my new harvest and husbandry to manage; for I reaped my corn in its season, and carried it home as well as I could, and laid it up in the ear, in my large baskets, till I had time to rub it out, for I had no floor to thrash it on, or instrument to thrash it with.

And now, indeed, my stock of corn increasing, I really wanted to build my barns bigger; I wanted a place to lay it up in, for the increase of the corn now yielded me so much, that I had of the barley about twenty bushels, and of the rice as much or more; insomuch that now I resolved to begin to use it freely; for my bread had been quite gone a great while; also I resolved to see what quantity would be sufficient for me a whole year, and to sow but once a year.

Upon the whole, I found that the forty bushels of barley and rice were much more than I could consume in a year; so I resolved to sow just the same quantity every year that I sowed the last, in hopes that such a quantity would fully provide me with bread, &c.

All the while these things were doing, you may be sure my thoughts ran many times upon the prospect of land which I had seen from the other side of the island; and I was not without secret wishes that I were on shore there, fancying that, seeing the mainland, and an inhabited country, I might find some way or other to convey myself further, and perhaps at last find some means of escape.

But all this while I made no allowance for the dangers of such an under-taking, and how I might fall into the hands of savages, and perhaps such as I might have reason to think far worse than the lions and tigers of Africa: that if I once came in their power, I should run a hazard of more than a thousand to one of being killed, and perhaps of being eaten; for I had heard that the people of the Caribbean coast were cannibals or man-eaters, and I knew by the latitude that I could not be far from that shore. Then, supposing they were not cannibals, yet they might kill me, as many Europeans who had fallen into their hands had been served, even when they had been ten or twenty together—much more I, that was but one, and could make little or no defence; all these things, I say, which I ought to have considered well; and did come into my thoughts afterwards, yet gave me no apprehensions at first, and my head ran mightily upon the thought of getting over to the shore.

Now I wished for my boy Xury, and the long-boat with shoulder-of-mutton sail, with which I sailed above a thousand miles on the coast of Africa; but this was in vain: then I thought I would go and look at our ship's boat, which, as I have said, was blown up upon the shore a great way, in the storm, when we were first cast away. She lay almost where she did at first, but not quite; and was turned, by the force of the waves and the winds, almost bottom upward, against a high ridge of beachy, rough sand, but no water about her. If I had had hands to have refitted her, and to have launched her into the water, the boat would have done well enough, and I might have gone back into the Brazils with her easily enough; but I might have foreseen that I could no more turn her and set her upright upon her bottom than I could remove the island; however, I went to the woods, and cut levers and rollers, and brought them to the boat resolving to try what I could do; suggesting to myself that if I could but turn her down, I might repair the damage she had received, and she would be a very good boat, and I might go to sea in her very easily.

I spared no pains, indeed, in this piece of fruitless toil, and spent, I think, three or four weeks about it; at last finding it impossible to heave it up with my little strength, I fell to digging away the sand, to undermine it, and so to make it fall down, setting pieces of wood to thrust and guide it right in the fall.

But when I had done this, I was unable to stir it up again, or to get under it, much less to move it forward towards the water; so I was forced to give it over; and yet, though I gave over the hopes of the boat, my desire to venture over for the main increased, rather than decreased, as the means for it seemed impossible.

This at length put me upon thinking whether it was not possible to make myself a canoe, or periagua, such as the natives of those climates make, even without tools, or, as I might say, without hands, of the trunk of a great tree. This I not only thought possible, but easy, and pleased myself extremely with the thoughts of making it, and with my having much more convenience for it than any of the negroes or Indians; but not at all considering the particular inconveniences which I lay under more than the Indians did—viz. want of hands to move it, when it was made, into the water—a difficulty much harder for me to surmount than all the consequences of want of tools could be to them; for what was it to me, if when I had chosen a vast tree in the woods, and with much trouble cut it down, if I had been able with my tools to hew and dub the outside into the proper shape of a boat, and burn or cut out the inside to make it hollow, so as to make a boat of it—if, after all this, I must leave it just there where I found it, and not be able to launch it into the water?

One would have thought I could not have had the least reflection upon my mind of my circumstances while I was making this boat, but I should have immediately thought how I should get it into the sea; but my thoughts were so intent upon my voyage over the sea in it, that I never once considered how I should get it off the land: and it was really, in its own nature, more easy for me to guide it over forty-five miles of sea than about forty-five fathoms of land, where it lay, to set it afloat in the water.

I went to work upon this boat the most like a fool that ever man did who had any of his senses awake. I pleased myself with the design, without determining whether I was ever able to undertake it; not but that the difficulty of launching my boat came often into my head; but I put a stop to my inquiries into it by this foolish answer which I gave myself—"Let me first make it; I warrant I will find some way or other to get it along when it is done."

This was a most preposterous method; but the eagerness of my fancy prevailed, and to work I went. I felled a cedar-tree, and I question much whether Solomon ever had such a one for the building of the Temple of Jerusalem;[100] it was five feet ten inches diameter at the lower part next the stump, and four feet eleven inches diameter at the end of twenty-two feet; after which it lessened for a while, and then parted into branches. It was not without infinite labour that I felled this tree; I was twenty days hacking and hewing at it at the bottom; I was fourteen more getting the branches and limbs and the vast spreading head cut off, which I hacked and hewed through with axe and hatchet, and inexpressible labour; after this, it cost me a month to shape it and dub it to a proportion, and to something like the bottom of a boat, that it might swim upright as it ought to do. It cost me near three months more to clear the inside, and work it out so as to make an exact boat of it; this I did, indeed, without fire, by mere mallet and chisel, and by the dint of hard labour, till I had brought it to be a very handsome periagua, and big enough to have carried six-and-twenty men, and consequently big enough to have carried me and all my cargo.

---

[100] See 1 Kings 5:1-10.

When I had gone through this work I was extremely delighted with it. The boat was really much bigger than ever I saw a canoe or periagua, that was made of one tree, in my life. Many a weary stroke it had cost, you may be sure; and had I gotten it into the water, I make no question, but I should have begun the maddest voyage, and the most unlikely to be performed, that ever was undertaken.

But all my devices to get it into the water failed me; though they cost me infinite labour too. It lay about one hundred yards from the water, and not more; but the first inconvenience was, it was up hill towards the creek. Well, to take away this discouragement, I resolved to dig into the surface of the earth, and so make a declivity:[101] this I began, and it cost me a prodigious deal of pains (but who grudge pains who have their deliverance in view?); but when this was worked through, and this difficulty managed, it was still much the same, for I could no more stir the canoe than I could the other boat. Then I measured the distance of ground, and resolved to cut a dock or canal, to bring the water up to the canoe, seeing I could not bring the canoe down to the water. Well, I began this work; and when I began to enter upon it, and calculate how deep it was to be dug, how broad, how the stuff was to be thrown out, I found that, by the number of hands I had, being none but my own, it must have been ten or twelve years before I could have gone through with it; for the shore lay so high, that at the upper end it must have been at least twenty feet deep; so at length, though with great reluctancy, I gave this attempt over also.

This grieved me heartily; and now I saw, though too late, the folly of beginning a work before we count the cost,[102] and before we judge rightly of our own strength to go through with it.

In the middle of this work I finished my fourth year in this place, and kept my anniversary with the same devotion, and with as much comfort as ever before; for, by a constant study and serious application to the Word of God, and by the assistance of His grace, I gained a different knowledge from what I had before. I entertained different notions of things. I looked now upon the world as a thing remote, which I had nothing to do with, no expectations from, and, indeed, no desires about: in a word, I had nothing indeed to do with it, nor was ever likely to have, so I thought it looked, as we may perhaps look upon it hereafter—viz. as a place I had lived in, but was come out of it; and well might I say, as Father Abraham to Dives,

---

[101] incline, slope

[102] "And whosoever doth not bear his cross, and come after me, cannot be my disciple. For which of you, intending to build a tower, sitteth not down first, and counteth the cost, whether he have sufficient to finish it? Lest haply, after he hath laid the foundation, and is not able to finish it, all that behold it begin to mock him, Saying, This man began to build, and was not able to finish" (Jesus speaking in Luke 14:27-30).

"Between me and thee is a great gulf fixed."[103]

In the first place, I was removed from all the wickedness of the world here; I had neither the lusts of the flesh, the lusts of the eye, nor the pride of life.[104] I had nothing to covet, for I had all that I was now capable of enjoying; I was lord of the whole manor; or, if I pleased, I might call myself king or emperor over the whole country which I had possession of: there were no rivals; I had no competitor, none to dispute sovereignty or command with me: I might have raised ship-loadings of corn, but I had no use for it; so I let as little grow as I thought enough for my occasion. I had tortoise or turtle enough, but now and then one was as much as I could put to any use: I had timber enough to have built a fleet of ships; and I had grapes enough to have made wine, or to have cured into raisins, to have loaded that fleet when it had been built.

But all I could make use of was all that was valuable: I had enough to eat and supply my wants, and what was all the rest to me? If I killed more flesh than I could eat, the dog must eat it, or vermin; if I sowed more corn than I could eat, it must be spoiled; the trees that I cut down were lying to rot on the ground; I could make no more use of them but for fuel, and that I had no occasion for but to dress my food.

In a word, the nature and experience of things dictated to me, upon just reflection, that all the good things of this world are no farther good to us than they are for our use; and that, whatever we may heap up to give others, we enjoy just as much as we can use, and no more. The most covetous, griping miser[105] in the world would have been cured of the vice of covetousness if he had been in my case; for I possessed infinitely more than I knew what to do with. I had no room for desire, except it was of things which I had not, and they were but trifles, though, indeed, of great use to me. I had, as I hinted before, a parcel of money, as well gold as silver, about thirty-six pounds sterling. Alas! there the sorry, useless stuff lay; I had no more manner of business for it; and often thought with myself that I would have given a handful of it for a gross of tobacco-pipes;[106] or for a hand-mill to grind my corn; nay, I would have given it all for a sixpenny-worth of turnip and carrot seed out of England, or for a handful of peas and beans, and a bottle of ink. As it was, I had not the least advantage by it or benefit from it; but there

---

[103] See Luke 16:19-31. The rich man in this account has sometimes been called "Dives" (from the Latin *dives, divitis*, which means "rich man").

[104] 1 John 2:15-17: "Love not the world, neither the things *that are* in the world. If any man love the world, the love of the Father is not in him. For all that *is* in the world, the lust of the flesh, and the lust of the eyes, and the pride of life, is not of the Father, but is of the world. And the world passeth away, and the lust thereof: but he that doeth the will of God abideth for ever."

[105] cheapskate, hoarder

[106] that is, 144 tobacco-pipes

it lay in a drawer, and grew mouldy with the damp of the cave in the wet seasons; and if I had had the drawer full of diamonds, it had been the same case—they had been of no manner of value to me, because of no use.

I had now brought my state of life to be much easier in itself than it was at first, and much easier to my mind, as well as to my body. I frequently sat down to meat with thankfulness, and admired the hand of God's providence, which had thus spread my table in the wilderness.[107] I learned to look more upon the bright side of my condition, and less upon the dark side, and to consider what I enjoyed rather than what I wanted; and this gave me sometimes such secret comforts, that I cannot express them; and which I take notice of here, to put those discontented people in mind of it, who cannot enjoy comfortably what God has given them, because they see and covet something that He has not given them. All our discontents about what we want appeared to me to spring from the want of thankfulness for what we have.

Another reflection was of great use to me, and doubtless would be so to any one that should fall into such distress as mine was; and this was, to compare my present condition with what I at first expected it would be; nay, with what it would certainly have been, if the good providence of God had not wonderfully ordered the ship to be cast up nearer to the shore, where I not only could come at her, but could bring what I got out of her to the shore, for my relief and comfort; without which, I had wanted for tools to work, weapons for defence, and gunpowder and shot for getting my food.

I spent whole hours, I may say whole days, in representing to myself, in the most lively colours, how I must have acted if I had got nothing out of the ship. How I could not have so much as got any food, except fish and turtles; and that, as it was long before I found any of them, I must have perished first; that I should have lived, if I had not perished, like a mere savage; that if I had killed a goat or a fowl, by any contrivance, I had no way to flay or open it, or part the flesh from the skin and the bowels, or to cut it up; but must gnaw it with my teeth, and pull it with my claws, like a beast.

These reflections made me very sensible of the goodness of Providence to me, and very thankful for my present condition, with all its hardships and misfortunes; and this part also I cannot but recommend to the reflection of those who are apt, in their misery, to say, "Is any affliction like mine?" Let them consider how much worse the cases of some people are, and their case might have been, if Providence had thought fit.

I had another reflection, which assisted me also to comfort my mind with hopes; and this was comparing my present situation with what I had de-

---

[107] This refers to the rebellious Israelites who grumbled, "Can God furnish a table in the wilderness?" when they were brought out of Egypt. See Psalm 78:1-19.

served, and had therefore reason to expect from the hand of Providence. I had lived a dreadful life, perfectly destitute of the knowledge and fear of God. I had been well instructed by father and mother; neither had they been wanting to me in their early endeavours to infuse a religious awe of God into my mind, a sense of my duty, and what the nature and end of my being required of me. But, alas! falling early into the seafaring life, which of all lives is the most destitute of the fear of God, though His terrors are always before them; I say, falling early into the seafaring life, and into seafaring company, all that little sense of religion which I had entertained was laughed out of me by my mess-mates; by a hardened despising of dangers, and the views of death, which grew habitual to me by my long absence from all manner of opportunities to converse with anything but what was like myself, or to hear anything that was good or tended towards it.

So void was I of everything that was good, or the least sense of what I was, or was to be, that, in the greatest deliverances I enjoyed—such as my escape from Sallee; my being taken up by the Portuguese master of the ship; my being planted so well in the Brazils; my receiving the cargo from England, and the like—I never had once the words "Thank God!" so much as on my mind, or in my mouth; nor in the greatest distress had I so much as a thought to pray to Him, or so much as to say, "Lord, have mercy upon me!" no, nor to mention the name of God, unless it was to swear by, and blaspheme it.

I had terrible reflections upon my mind for many months, as I have already observed, on account of my wicked and hardened life past; and when I looked about me, and considered what particular providences had attended me since my coming into this place, and how God had dealt bountifully with me—had not only punished me less than my iniquity had deserved, but had so plentifully provided for me—this gave me great hopes that my repentance was accepted, and that God had yet mercy in store for me.

With these reflections I worked my mind up, not only to a resignation to the will of God in the present disposition of my circumstances, but even to a sincere thankfulness for my condition; and that I, who was yet a living man, ought not to complain, seeing I had not the due punishment of my sins; that I enjoyed so many mercies which I had no reason to have expected in that place; that I ought never more to repine at my condition, but to rejoice, and to give daily thanks for that daily bread, which nothing but a crowd of wonders could have brought; that I ought to consider I had been fed even by a miracle, even as great as that of feeding Elijah by ravens,[108] nay, by a long series of miracles; and that I could hardly have named a place in the uninhabitable part of the world where I could have been cast more to my

---

[108] See 1 Kings 17:1-6.

advantage; a place where, as I had no society, which was my affliction on one hand, so I found no ravenous beasts, no furious wolves or tigers, to threaten my life; no venomous creatures, or poisons, which I might feed on to my hurt; no savages to murder and devour me. In a word, as my life was a life of sorrow one way, so it was a life of mercy another; and I wanted nothing to make it a life of comfort but to be able to make my sense of God's goodness to me, and care over me in this condition, be my daily consolation; and after I did make a just improvement on these things, I went away, and was no more sad. I had now been here so long that many things which I had brought on shore for my help were either quite gone, or very much wasted and near spent.

My ink, as I observed, had been gone some time, all but a very little, which I eked out with water, a little and a little, till it was so pale, it scarce left any appearance of black upon the paper. As long as it lasted I made use of it to minute down the days of the month on which any remarkable thing happened to me; and first, by casting up times past, I remembered that there was a strange concurrence of days in the various providences which befell me, and which, if I had been superstitiously inclined to observe days as fatal or fortunate, I might have had reason to have looked upon with a great deal of curiosity.

First, I had observed that the same day that I broke away from my father and friends and ran away to Hull, in order to go to sea, the same day afterwards I was taken by the Sallee man-of-war, and made a slave; the same day of the year that I escaped out of the wreck of that ship in Yarmouth Roads, that same day-year afterwards I made my escape from Sallee in a boat; the same day of the year I was born on—viz. the 30th of September, that same day I had my life so miraculously saved twenty-six years after, when I was cast on shore in this island; so that my wicked life and my solitary life began both on a day.

The next thing to my ink being wasted was that of my bread—I mean the biscuit which I brought out of the ship; this I had husbanded to the last degree, allowing myself but one cake of bread a-day for above a year; and yet I was quite without bread for near a year before I got any corn of my own, and great reason I had to be thankful that I had any at all, the getting it being, as has been already observed, next to miraculous.

My clothes, too, began to decay; as to linen, I had had none a good while, except some chequered shirts which I found in the chests of the other seamen, and which I carefully preserved; because many times I could bear no other clothes on but a shirt; and it was a very great help to me that I had, among all the men's clothes of the ship, almost three dozen of shirts. There were also, indeed, several thick watch-coats of the seamen's which were left, but they were too hot to wear; and though it is true that the weather was so violently hot that there was no need of clothes, yet I could not go quite naked—no, though I had been inclined to it, which I was not—nor could I abide the thought of it, though I was alone. The reason why I could not go naked was, I could not bear the heat of the sun so well when quite naked as with some clothes on; nay, the very heat frequently blistered my skin: whereas, with a shirt on, the air itself made some motion, and whistling under the shirt, was twofold cooler than without it. No more could I ever bring myself to go out in the heat of the sun without a cap or a hat; the heat of the sun, beating with such violence as it does in that place, would give me the headache presently, by darting so directly on my head, without a cap or hat on, so that I could not bear it; whereas, if I put on my hat it would presently go away.

Upon these views I began to consider about putting the few rags I had, which I called clothes, into some order; I had worn out all the waistcoats I had, and my business was now to try if I could not make jackets out of the great watch-coats which I had by me, and with such other materials as I had; so I set to work, tailoring, or rather, indeed, botching, for I made most piteous work of it. However, I made shift to make two or three new waistcoats, which I hoped would serve me a great while: as for breeches or drawers, I made but a very sorry shift indeed till afterwards.

I have mentioned that I saved the skins of all the creatures that I killed, I mean four-footed ones, and I had them hung up, stretched out with sticks in the sun, by which means some of them were so dry and hard that they were fit for little, but others were very useful. The first thing I made of these was a great cap for my head, with the hair on the outside, to shoot off the rain; and this I performed so well, that after I made me a suit of clothes wholly of these skins—that is to say, a waist-coat, and breeches open at the knees, and both loose, for they were rather wanting to keep me cool than to keep me warm. I must not omit to acknowledge that they were wretchedly made; for if I was a bad carpenter, I was a worse tailor. However, they were such as I made very good shift with, and when I was out, if it happened to rain, the hair of my waistcoat and cap being outermost, I was kept very dry.

After this, I spent a great deal of time and pains to make an umbrella; I was, indeed, in great want of one, and had a great mind to make one; I had seen them made in the Brazils, where they are very useful in the great heats there, and I felt the heats every jot[109] as great here, and greater too, being nearer the equinox; besides, as I was obliged to be much abroad, it was a most useful thing to me, as well for the rains as the heats. I took a world of pains with it, and was a great while before I could make anything likely to hold: nay, after I had thought I had hit the way, I spoiled two or three before

---

[109] little bit

I made one to my mind: but at last I made one that answered indifferently well: the main difficulty I found was to make it let down. I could make it spread, but if it did not let down too, and draw in, it was not portable for me any way but just over my head, which would not do. However, at last, as I said, I made one to answer, and covered it with skins, the hair upwards, so that it cast off the rain like a pent-house, and kept off the sun so effectually, that I could walk out in the hottest of the weather with greater advantage than I could before in the coolest, and when I had no need of it could close it, and carry it under my arm. Thus I lived mighty comfortably, my mind being entirely composed by resigning myself to the will of God, and throwing myself wholly upon the disposal of His providence. This made my life better than sociable, for when I began to regret the want of conversation I would ask myself, whether thus conversing mutually with my own thoughts, and (as I hope I may say) with even God Himself, by ejaculations, was not better than the utmost enjoyment of human society in the world?

Questions for Review:

1. What projects does Robinson Crusoe undertake in this chapter? How do they benefit him?

2. What is Robinson Crusoe's grain situation? What does he think about escaping? How does he think the wreckage might help?

3. Describe Robinson Crusoe's work on the canoe. What lesson does he learn from his attempt?

4. Sum up Robinson Crusoe's fourth year service and the reflections he has on himself, on his world, and on God.

5. What needs does Robinson Crusoe face because of depletion and wear? How does he solve this? How does he comfort himself when he thinks of his situation?

CHAPTER X:
TAMES GOATS

I cannot say that after this, for five years, any extraordinary thing happened to me, but I lived on in the same course, in the same posture and place, as before; the chief things I was employed in, besides my yearly labour of planting my barley and rice, and curing my raisins, of both which I always kept up just enough to have sufficient stock of one year's provisions beforehand; I say, besides this yearly labour, and my daily pursuit of going out with my gun, I had one labour, to make a canoe, which at last I finished: so that, by digging a canal to it of six feet wide and four feet deep, I brought it into the creek, almost half a mile. As for the first, which was so vastly big, for I made it without considering beforehand, as I ought to have done, how I should be able to launch it, so, never being able to bring it into the water, or bring the water to it, I was obliged to let it lie where it was as a memorandum to teach me to be wiser the next time: indeed, the next time, though I could not get a tree proper for it, and was in a place where I could not get the water to it at any less distance than, as I have said, near half a mile, yet, as I saw it was practicable at last, I never gave it over; and though I was near two years about it, yet I never grudged my labour, in hopes of having a boat to go off to sea at last.

However, though my little periagua was finished, yet the size of it was not at all answerable to the design which I had in view when I made the first; I mean of venturing over to the terra firma,[110] where it was above forty miles broad; accordingly, the smallness of my boat assisted to put an end to that design, and now I thought no more of it. As I had a boat, my next design was to make a cruise round the island; for as I had been on the other side in one place, crossing, as I have already described it, over the land, so the discoveries I made in that little journey made me very eager to see other parts of the coast; and now I had a boat, I thought of nothing but sailing round the island.

For this purpose, that I might do everything with discretion and consideration, I fitted up a little mast in my boat, and made a sail too out of some of the pieces of the ship's sails which lay in store, and of which I had a great stock by me. Having fitted my mast and sail, and tried the boat, I found she would sail very well; then I made little lockers or boxes at each end of my boat, to put provisions, necessaries, ammunition, &c., into, to be kept dry,

---

[110] dry land, solid ground

either from rain or the spray of the sea; and a little, long, hollow place I cut in the inside of the boat, where I could lay my gun, making a flap to hang down over it to keep it dry.

I fixed my umbrella also in the step at the stern, like a mast, to stand over my head, and keep the heat of the sun off me, like an awning; and thus I every now and then took a little voyage upon the sea, but never went far out, nor far from the little creek. At last, being eager to view the circumference of my little kingdom, I resolved upon my cruise; and accordingly I victualled my ship for the voyage, putting in two dozen of loaves (cakes I should call them) of barley-bread, an earthen pot full of parched rice (a food I ate a good deal of), a little bottle of rum, half a goat, and powder and shot for killing more, and two large watch-coats, of those which, as I mentioned before, I had saved out of the seamen's chests; these I took, one to lie upon, and the other to cover me in the night.

It was the 6th of November, in the sixth year of my reign—or my captivity, which you please—that I set out on this voyage, and I found it much longer than I expected; for though the island itself was not very large, yet when I came to the east side of it, I found a great ledge of rocks lie out about two leagues into the sea, some above water, some under it; and beyond that a shoal of sand, lying dry half a league more, so that I was obliged to go a great way out to sea to double the point.

When I first discovered them, I was going to give over my enterprise, and come back again, not knowing how far it might oblige me to go out to sea; and above all, doubting how I should get back again: so I came to an anchor; for I had made a kind of an anchor with a piece of a broken grappling which I got out of the ship.

Having secured my boat, I took my gun and went on shore, climbing up a hill, which seemed to overlook that point where I saw the full extent of it, and resolved to venture.

In my viewing the sea from that hill where I stood, I perceived a strong, and indeed a most furious current, which ran to the east, and even came close to the point; and I took the more notice of it because I saw there might be some danger that when I came into it I might be carried out to sea by the strength of it, and not be able to make the island again; and indeed, had I not got first upon this hill, I believe it would have been so; for there was the same current on the other side the island, only that it set off at a further distance, and I saw there was a strong eddy[111] under the shore; so I had nothing to do but to get out of the first current, and I should presently be in an eddy.

I lay here, however, two days, because the wind blowing pretty fresh at

---

[111] whirling current

ESE., and that being just contrary to the current, made a great breach of the sea upon the point: so that it was not safe for me to keep too close to the shore for the breach, nor to go too far off, because of the stream.

The third day, in the morning, the wind having abated overnight, the sea was calm, and I ventured: but I am a warning to all rash and ignorant pilots; for no sooner was I come to the point, when I was not even my boat's length from the shore, but I found myself in a great depth of water, and a current like the sluice of a mill; it carried my boat along with it with such violence that all I could do could not keep her so much as on the edge of it; but I found it hurried me farther and farther out from the eddy, which was on my left hand. There was no wind stirring to help me, and all I could do with my paddles signified nothing: and now I began to give myself over for lost; for as the current was on both sides of the island, I knew in a few leagues distance they must join again, and then I was irrecoverably gone; nor did I see any possibility of avoiding it; so that I had no prospect before me but of perishing, not by the sea, for that was calm enough, but of starving from hunger. I had, indeed, found a tortoise on the shore, as big almost as I could lift, and had tossed it into the boat; and I had a great jar of fresh water, that is to say, one of my earthen pots; but what was all this to being driven into the vast ocean, where, to be sure, there was no shore, no mainland or island, for a thousand leagues at least?

And now I saw how easy it was for the providence of God to make even the most miserable condition of mankind worse. Now I looked back upon my desolate, solitary island as the most pleasant place in the world and all the happiness my heart could wish for was to be but there again. I stretched out my hands to it, with eager wishes—"O happy desert!" said I, "I shall never see thee more. O miserable creature! whither am I going?" Then I reproached myself with my unthankful temper, and that I had repined at my solitary condition; and now what would I give to be on shore there again! Thus, we never see the true state of our condition till it is illustrated to us by its contraries, nor know how to value what we enjoy, but by the want of it. It is scarcely possible to imagine the consternation[112] I was now in, being driven from my beloved island (for so it appeared to me now to be) into the wide ocean, almost two leagues, and in the utmost despair of ever recovering it again. However, I worked hard till, indeed, my strength was almost exhausted, and kept my boat as much to the northward, that is, towards the side of the current which the eddy lay on, as possibly I could; when about noon, as the sun passed the meridian, I thought I felt a little breeze of wind in my face, springing up from SSE. This cheered my heart a little, and especially when, in about half-an-hour more, it blew a pretty

---

[112] dread, anxiety

gentle gale. By this time I had got at a frightful distance from the island, and had the least cloudy or hazy weather intervened, I had been undone another way, too; for I had no compass on board, and should never have known how to have steered towards the island, if I had but once lost sight of it; but the weather continuing clear, I applied myself to get up my mast again, and spread my sail, standing away to the north as much as possible, to get out of the current.

Just as I had set my mast and sail, and the boat began to stretch away, I saw even by the clearness of the water some alteration of the current was near; for where the current was so strong the water was foul; but perceiving the water clear, I found the current abate; and presently I found to the east, at about half a mile, a breach of the sea upon some rocks: these rocks I found caused the current to part again, and as the main stress of it ran away more southerly, leaving the rocks to the north-east, so the other returned by the repulse of the rocks, and made a strong eddy, which ran back again to the north-west, with a very sharp stream.

They who know what it is to have a reprieve brought to them upon the ladder,[113] or to be rescued from thieves just going to murder them, or who have been in such extremities, may guess what my present surprise of joy was, and how gladly I put my boat into the stream of this eddy; and the wind also freshening, how gladly I spread my sail to it, running cheerfully before the wind, and with a strong tide or eddy underfoot.

This eddy carried me about a league on my way back again, directly towards the island, but about two leagues more to the northward than the current which carried me away at first; so that when I came near the island, I found myself open to the northern shore of it, that is to say, the other end of the island, opposite to that which I went out from.

When I had made something more than a league of way by the help of this current or eddy, I found it was spent, and served me no further. However, I found that being between two great currents—viz. that on the south side, which had hurried me away, and that on the north, which lay about a league on the other side; I say, between these two, in the wake of the island, I found the water at least still, and running no way; and having still a breeze of wind fair for me, I kept on steering directly for the island, though not making such fresh way as I did before.

About four o'clock in the evening, being then within a league of the island, I found the point of the rocks which occasioned this disaster stretching out, as is described before, to the southward, and casting off the current more southerly, had, of course, made another eddy to the north; and this I found very strong, but not directly setting the way my course lay, which

---

[113] that is, those who are making their way up the gallows to be hanged

178

was due west, but almost full north. However, having a fresh gale, I stretched across this eddy, slanting north-west; and in about an hour came within about a mile of the shore, where, it being smooth water, I soon got to land.

When I was on shore, I fell on my knees and gave God thanks for my deliverance, resolving to lay aside all thoughts of my deliverance by my boat; and refreshing myself with such things as I had, I brought my boat close to the shore, in a little cove that I had spied under some trees, and laid me down to sleep, being quite spent with the labour and fatigue of the voyage.

I was now at a great loss which way to get home with my boat! I had run so much hazard, and knew too much of the case, to think of attempting it by the way I went out; and what might be at the other side (I mean the west side) I knew not, nor had I any mind to run any more ventures; so I resolved on the next morning to make my way westward along the shore, and to see if there was no creek where I might lay up my frigate in safety, so as to have her again if I wanted her. In about three miles or thereabouts, coasting the shore, I came to a very good inlet or bay, about a mile over, which narrowed till it came to a very little rivulet or brook, where I found a very convenient harbour for my boat, and where she lay as if she had been in a little dock made on purpose for her. Here I put in, and having stowed my boat very safe, I went on shore to look about me, and see where I was.

I soon found I had but a little passed by the place where I had been before, when I travelled on foot to that shore; so taking nothing out of my boat but my gun and umbrella, for it was exceedingly hot, I began my march. The way was comfortable enough after such a voyage as I had been upon, and I reached my old bower in the evening, where I found everything standing as I left it; for I always kept it in good order, being, as I said before, my country house.

I got over the fence, and laid me down in the shade to rest my limbs, for I was very weary, and fell asleep; but judge you, if you can, that read my story, what a surprise I must be in when I was awaked out of my sleep by a voice calling me by my name several times, "Robin, Robin, Robin Crusoe: poor Robin Crusoe! Where are you, Robin Crusoe? Where are you? Where have you been?"

I was so dead asleep at first, being fatigued with rowing, or part of the day, and with walking the latter part, that I did not wake thoroughly; but dozing thought I dreamed that somebody spoke to me; but as the voice continued to repeat, "Robin Crusoe, Robin Crusoe," at last I began to wake more perfectly, and was at first dreadfully frightened, and started up in the utmost consternation; but no sooner were my eyes open, but I saw my Poll sitting on the top of the hedge; and immediately knew that it was he that spoke to me; for just in such bemoaning language I had used to talk to him and teach him; and he had learned it so perfectly that he would sit upon my finger, and lay his bill close to my face and cry, "Poor Robin Crusoe! Where are you? Where have you been? How came you here?" and such things as I had taught him.

However, even though I knew it was the parrot, and that indeed it could be nobody else, it was a good while before I could compose myself. First, I was amazed how the creature got thither; and then, how he should just keep about the place, and nowhere else; but as I was well satisfied it could be nobody but honest Poll, I got over it; and holding out my hand, and calling him by his name, "Poll," the sociable creature came to me, and sat upon my thumb, as he used to do, and continued talking to me, "Poor Robin Crusoe! and how did I come here? and where had I been?" just as if he had been overjoyed to see me again; and so I carried him home along with me.

I had now had enough of rambling to sea for some time, and had enough to do for many days to sit still and reflect upon the danger I had been in. I would have been very glad to have had my boat again on my side of the island; but I knew not how it was practicable to get it about. As to the east side of the island, which I had gone round, I knew well enough there was no venturing that way; my very heart would shrink, and my very blood run chill, but to think of it; and as to the other side of the island, I did not know how it might be there; but supposing the current ran with the same force against the shore at the east as it passed by it on the other, I might run the same risk of being driven down the stream, and carried by the island, as I had been before of being carried away from it: so with these thoughts, I contented myself to be without any boat, though it had been the product of so many months' labour to make it, and of so many more to get it into the sea.

In this government of my temper I remained near a year; and lived a very sedate, retired life, as you may well suppose; and my thoughts being very much composed as to my condition, and fully comforted in resigning myself to the dispositions of Providence, I thought I lived really very happily in all things except that of society.

I improved myself in this time in all the mechanic exercises which my necessities put me upon applying myself to; and I believe I should, upon occasion, have made a very good carpenter, especially considering how few tools I had.

Besides this, I arrived at an unexpected perfection in my earthen-ware, and contrived well enough to make them with a wheel, which I found infinitely easier and better; because I made things round and shaped, which before were filthy things indeed to look on. But I think I was never more vain of my own performance, or more joyful for anything I found out, than for my being able to make a tobacco-pipe; and though it was a very ugly, clumsy thing when it was done, and only burned red, like other earthenware, yet as it was hard and firm, and would draw the smoke, I was exceedingly comforted with it, for I had been always used to smoke; and there were pipes in the ship, but I forgot them at first, not thinking there was tobacco in the island; and afterwards, when I searched the ship again, I could not come at any pipes.

In my wicker-ware also I improved much, and made abundance of necessary baskets, as well as my invention showed me; though not very handsome, yet they were such as were very handy and convenient for laying things up in, or fetching things home. For example, if I killed a goat abroad, I could hang it up in a tree, flay it, dress it, and cut it in pieces, and bring it home in a basket; and the like by a turtle; I could cut it up, take out the eggs and a piece or two of the flesh, which was enough for me, and bring them home in a basket, and leave the rest behind me. Also, large deep baskets were the receivers of my corn, which I always rubbed out as soon as it was dry and cured, and kept it in great baskets.

I began now to perceive my powder abated considerably; this was a want which it was impossible for me to supply, and I began seriously to consider what I must do when I should have no more powder; that is to say, how I should kill any goats. I had, as is observed in the third year of my being here, kept a young kid, and bred her up tame, and I was in hopes of getting a he-goat; but I could not by any means bring it to pass, till my kid grew an old goat; and as I could never find in my heart to kill her, she died at last of mere age.

But being now in the eleventh year of my residence, and, as I have said, my ammunition growing low, I set myself to study some art to trap and snare the goats, to see whether I could not catch some of them alive; and particularly I wanted a she-goat great with young. For this purpose I made snares to hamper them; and I do believe they were more than once taken in them; but my tackle was not good, for I had no wire, and I always found them broken and my bait devoured. At length I resolved to try a pitfall; so I dug several large pits in the earth, in places where I had observed the goats used to feed, and over those pits I placed hurdles of my own making too, with a great weight upon them; and several times I put ears of barley and dry rice without setting the trap; and I could easily perceive that the goats had gone in and eaten up the corn, for I could see the marks of their feet. At length I set three traps in one night, and going the next morning I found them, all standing, and yet the bait eaten and gone; this was very discouraging. However, I altered my traps; and not to trouble you with particulars, going one morning to see my traps, I found in one of them a large old he-goat; and in one of the others three kids, a male and two females.

As to the old one, I knew not what to do with him; he was so fierce I durst not go into the pit to him; that is to say, to bring him away alive, which was what I wanted. I could have killed him, but that was not my business, nor would it answer my end; so I even let him out, and he ran away as if he had been frightened out of his wits. But I did not then know what I afterwards learned, that hunger will tame a lion. If I had let him stay three or four days without food, and then have carried him some water to drink and then a little corn, he would have been as tame as one of the kids; for they are mighty sagacious,[114] tractable[115] creatures, where they are well used.

However, for the present I let him go, knowing no better at that time: then I went to the three kids, and taking them one by one, I tied them with strings together, and with some difficulty brought them all home.

It was a good while before they would feed; but throwing them some sweet corn, it tempted them, and they began to be tame. And now I found that if I expected to supply myself with goats' flesh, when I had no powder or shot left, breeding some up tame was my only way, when, perhaps, I might have them about my house like a flock of sheep. But then it occurred to me that I must keep the tame from the wild, or else they would always run wild when they grew up; and the only way for this was to have some enclosed piece of ground, well fenced either with hedge or pale, to keep them in so effectually, that those within might not break out, or those without break in.

This was a great undertaking for one pair of hands yet, as I saw there was an absolute necessity for doing it, my first work was to find out a proper piece of ground, where there was likely to be herbage for them to eat, water for them to drink, and cover to keep them from the sun.

Those who understand such enclosures will think I had very little contrivance when I pitched upon a place very proper for all these (being a plain, open piece of meadow land, or savannah, as our people call it in the western colonies), which had two or three little drills of fresh water in it, and at one end was very woody—I say, they will smile at my forecast, when I shall tell them I began by enclosing this piece of ground in such a manner that, my hedge or pale must have been at least two miles about. Nor was the madness of it so great as to the compass, for if it was ten miles about, I was like to have time enough to do it in; but I did not consider that my goats would be as wild in so much compass as if they had had the whole island, and I should have so much room to chase them in that I should never catch them.

My hedge was begun and carried on, I believe, about fifty yards when this thought occurred to me; so I presently stopped short, and, for the beginning, I resolved to enclose a piece of about one hundred and fifty yards in

---

[114] intelligent
[115] manageable, controllable

length, and one hundred yards in breadth, which, as it would maintain as many as I should have in any reasonable time, so, as my stock increased, I could add more ground to my enclosure.

This was acting with some prudence, and I went to work with courage. I was about three months hedging in the first piece; and, till I had done it, I tethered the three kids in the best part of it, and used them to feed as near me as possible, to make them familiar; and very often I would go and carry them some ears of barley, or a handful of rice, and feed them out of my hand; so that after my enclosure was finished and I let them loose, they would follow me up and down, bleating after me for a handful of corn.

This answered my end, and in about a year and a half I had a flock of about twelve goats, kids and all; and in two years more I had three-and-forty, besides several that I took and killed for my food. After that, I enclosed five several pieces of ground to feed them in, with little pens to drive them to take them as I wanted, and gates out of one piece of ground into another.

But this was not all; for now I not only had goat's flesh to feed on when I pleased, but milk too—a thing which, indeed, in the beginning, I did not so much as think of, and which, when it came into my thoughts, was really an agreeable surprise, for now I set up my dairy, and had sometimes a gallon or two of milk in a day. And as Nature, who gives supplies of food to every creature, dictates even naturally how to make use of it, so I, that had never milked a cow, much less a goat, or seen butter or cheese made only when I was a boy, after a great many essays and miscarriages, made both butter and cheese at last, also salt (though I found it partly made to my hand by the heat of the sun upon some of the rocks of the sea), and never wanted it afterwards. How mercifully can our Creator treat His creatures, even in those conditions in which they seemed to be overwhelmed in destruction! How can He sweeten the bitterest providences, and give us cause to praise Him for dungeons and prisons! What a table was here spread for me in the wilderness, where I saw nothing at first but to perish for hunger!

Questions for Review:

1. Sum up Robinson Crusoe's second canoe and journey.

2. Explain what Robinson Crusoe means when he says this (while struggling to reach land again): "Thus, we never see the true state of our condition till it is illustrated to us by its contraries, nor know how to value what we enjoy, but by the want of it."

3. Describe Robinson Crusoe's second journey and his shock when he returns home. What does he spend the next year working on? (→)

4.   What major concern for the future does Robinson Crusoe have? How does he solve this looming problem? What unexpected blessings does this provide?

CHAPTER XI: FINDS PRINT OF MAN'S FOOT IN THE SAND

It would have made a Stoic[116] smile to have seen me and my little family sit down to dinner. There was my majesty the prince and lord of the whole island; I had the lives of all my subjects at my absolute command; I could hang, draw, give liberty, and take it away, and no rebels among all my subjects. Then, to see how like a king I dined, too, all alone, attended by my servants! Poll, as if he had been my favourite, was the only person permitted to talk to me. My dog, who was now grown old and crazy, and had found no species to multiply his kind upon, sat always at my right hand; and two cats, one on one side of the table and one on the other, expecting now and then a bit from my hand, as a mark of especial favour.

But these were not the two cats which I brought on shore at first, for they were both of them dead, and had been interred[117] near my habitation by my own hand; but one of them having multiplied by I know not what kind of creature, these were two which I had preserved tame; whereas the rest ran wild in the woods, and became indeed troublesome to me at last, for they would often come into my house, and plunder me too, till at last I was obliged to shoot them, and did kill a great many; at length they left me. With this attendance and in this plentiful manner I lived; neither could I be said to want anything but society; and of that, some time after this, I was likely to have too much.

I was something impatient, as I have observed, to have the use of my

---

[116] A Stoic is someone who subscribes to the philosophy of *stoicism* (the idea that one should be indifferent to pleasure or pain). Robinson Crusoe is saying that he and his "family" looked so funny that even a Stoic would have smiled at it!
[117] buried

boat, though very loath to run any more hazards; and therefore sometimes I sat contriving ways to get her about the island, and at other times I sat myself down contented enough without her. But I had a strange uneasiness in my mind to go down to the point of the island where, as I have said in my last ramble, I went up the hill to see how the shore lay, and how the current set, that I might see what I had to do: this inclination increased upon me every day, and at length I resolved to travel thither by land, following the edge of the shore. I did so; but had any one in England met such a man as I was, it must either have frightened him, or raised a great deal of laughter; and as I frequently stood still to look at myself, I could not but smile at the notion of my travelling through Yorkshire with such an equipage, and in such a dress. Be pleased to take a sketch of my figure, as follows.

I had a great high shapeless cap, made of a goat's skin, with a flap hanging down behind, as well to keep the sun from me as to shoot the rain off from running into my neck, nothing being so hurtful in these climates as the rain upon the flesh under the clothes.

I had a short jacket of goat's skin, the skirts coming down to about the middle of the thighs, and a pair of open-kneed breeches of the same; the breeches were made of the skin of an old he-goat, whose hair hung down such a length on either side that, like pantaloons, it reached to the middle of my legs; stockings and shoes I had none, but had made me a pair of somethings, I scarce knew what to call them, like buskins,[118] to flap over my legs, and lace on either side like spatterdashes,[119] but of a most barbarous shape, as indeed were all the rest of my clothes.

I had on a broad belt of goat's skin dried, which I drew together with two thongs of the same instead of buckles, and in a kind of a frog on either side of this, instead of a sword and dagger, hung a little saw and a hatchet, one on one side and one on the other. I had another belt not so broad, and fastened in the same manner, which hung over my shoulder, and at the end of it, under my left arm, hung two pouches, both made of goat's skin too, in one of which hung my powder, in the other my shot. At my back I carried my basket, and on my shoulder my gun, and over my head a great clumsy, ugly, goat's-skin umbrella, but which, after all, was the most necessary thing I had about me next to my gun. As for my face, the colour of it was really not so mulatto-like as one might expect from a man not at all careful of it, and living within nine or ten degrees of the equinox. My beard I had once suffered to grow till it was about a quarter of a yard long; but as I had both scissors and razors sufficient, I had cut it pretty short, except what grew on my upper lip, which I had trimmed into a large pair of Mahometan[120]

---

[118] half-boots

[119] shoe coverings (usually referred to as "spats")

[120] Mohammedan (Muslim)

whiskers, such as I had seen worn by some Turks at Sallee, for the Moors did not wear such, though the Turks did; of these moustachios, or whiskers, I will not say they were long enough to hang my hat upon them, but they were of a length and shape monstrous enough, and such as in England would have passed for frightful.

But all this is by-the-bye; for as to my figure, I had so few to observe me that it was of no manner of consequence, so I say no more of that. In this kind of dress I went my new journey, and was out five or six days. I travelled first along the sea-shore, directly to the place where I first brought my boat to an anchor to get upon the rocks; and having no boat now to take care of, I went over the land a nearer way to the same height that I was upon before, when, looking forward to the points of the rocks which lay out, and which I was obliged to double with my boat, as is said above, I was surprised to see the sea all smooth and quiet—no rippling, no motion, no current, any more there than in other places. I was at a strange loss to understand this, and resolved to spend some time in the observing it, to see if nothing from the sets of the tide had occasioned it; but I was presently convinced how it was—viz. that the tide of ebb setting from the west, and joining with the current of waters from some great river on the shore, must be the occasion of this current, and that, according as the wind blew more forcibly from the west or from the north, this current came nearer or went farther from the shore; for, waiting thereabouts till evening, I went up to the rock again, and then the tide of ebb being made, I plainly saw the current again as before, only that it ran farther off, being near half a league from the shore, whereas in my case it set close upon the shore, and hurried me and my canoe along with it, which at another time it would not have done.

This observation convinced me that I had nothing to do but to observe the ebbing and the flowing of the tide, and I might very easily bring my boat about the island again; but when I began to think of putting it in practice, I had such terror upon my spirits at the remembrance of the danger I had been in, that I could not think of it again with any patience, but, on the contrary, I took up another resolution, which was more safe, though more laborious—and this was, that I would build, or rather make, me another periagua or canoe, and so have one for one side of the island, and one for the other.

You are to understand that now I had, as I may call it, two plantations in the island—one my little fortification or tent, with the wall about it, under the rock, with the cave behind me, which by this time I had enlarged into several apartments or caves, one within another. One of these, which was the driest and largest, and had a door out beyond my wall or fortification—that is to say, beyond where my wall joined to the rock—was all filled up with the large earthen pots of which I have given an account, and with fourteen or fifteen great baskets, which would hold five or six bushels each, where I laid up my stores of provisions, especially my corn, some in the ear, cut off short from the straw, and the other rubbed out with my hand.

As for my wall, made, as before, with long stakes or piles, those piles grew all like trees, and were by this time grown so big, and spread so very much, that there was not the least appearance, to any one's view, of any habitation behind them.

Near this dwelling of mine, but a little farther within the land, and upon lower ground, lay my two pieces of corn land, which I kept duly cultivated and sowed, and which duly yielded me their harvest in its season; and whenever I had occasion for more corn, I had more land adjoining as fit as that.

Besides this, I had my country seat, and I had now a tolerable plantation there also; for, first, I had my little bower, as I called it, which I kept in re-pair—that is to say, I kept the hedge which encircled it in constantly fitted up to its usual height, the ladder standing always in the inside. I kept the trees, which at first were no more than stakes, but were now grown very firm and tall, always cut, so that they might spread and grow thick and wild, and make the more agreeable shade, which they did effectually to my mind. In the middle of this I had my tent always standing, being a piece of a sail spread over poles, set up for that purpose, and which never wanted any repair or renewing; and under this I had made me a squab or couch with the skins of the creatures I had killed, and with other soft things, and a blan-ket laid on them, such as belonged to our sea-bedding, which I had saved; and a great watch-coat to cover me. And here, whenever I had occasion to be absent from my chief seat, I took up my country habitation.

Adjoining to this I had my enclosures for my cattle, that is to say my goats, and I had taken an inconceivable deal of pains to fence and enclose this ground. I was so anxious to see it kept entire, lest the goats should break through, that I never left off till, with infinite labour, I had stuck the outside of the hedge so full of small stakes, and so near to one another, that it was rather a pale than a hedge, and there was scarce room to put a hand through between them; which afterwards, when those stakes grew, as they all did in the next rainy season, made the enclosure strong like a wall, indeed stron-ger than any wall.

This will testify for me that I was not idle, and that I spared no pains to bring to pass whatever appeared necessary for my comfortable support, for I considered the keeping up a breed of tame creatures thus at my hand would be a living magazine of flesh, milk, butter, and cheese for me as long as I lived in the place, if it were to be forty years; and that keeping them in my reach depended entirely upon my perfecting my enclosures to such a degree that I might be sure of keeping them together; which by this method, indeed, I so effectually secured, that when these little stakes began to grow, I had planted them so very thick that I was forced to pull some of them up again.

In this place also I had my grapes growing, which I principally depended on for my winter store of raisins, and which I never failed to preserve very carefully, as the best and most agreeable dainty of my whole diet; and indeed they were not only agreeable, but medicinal, wholesome, nourishing, and refreshing to the last degree.

As this was also about half-way between my other habitation and the place where I had laid up my boat, I generally stayed and lay here in my way thither, for I used frequently to visit my boat; and I kept all things about or belonging to her in very good order. Sometimes I went out in her to divert myself, but no more hazardous voyages would I go, scarcely ever above a stone's cast or two from the shore, I was so apprehensive of being hurried out of my knowledge again by the currents or winds, or any other accident. But now I come to a new scene of my life. It happened one day, about noon, going towards my boat, I was exceedingly surprised with the print of a man's naked foot on the shore, which was very plain to be seen on the sand. I stood like one thunderstruck, or as if I had seen an apparition.[121] I listened, I looked round me, but I could hear nothing, nor see anything; I went up to a rising ground to look farther; I went up the shore and down the shore, but it was all one; I could see no other impression but that one. I went to it again to see if there were any more, and to observe if it might not be my fancy; but there was no room for that, for there was exactly the print of a foot—toes, heel, and every part of a foot. How it came thither I knew not, nor could I in the least imagine; but after innumerable fluttering thoughts, like a man perfectly confused and out of myself, I came home to my fortification, not feeling, as we say, the ground I went on, but terrified to the last degree, looking behind me at every two or three steps, mistaking every bush and tree, and fancying every stump at a distance to be a man. Nor is it possible to describe how many various shapes my affrighted imagination represented things to me in, how many wild ideas were found every moment in my fancy, and what strange, unaccountable whimsies came into my thoughts by the way.

When I came to my castle (for so I think I called it ever after this), I fled into it like one pursued. Whether I went over by the ladder, as first contrived, or went in at the hole in the rock, which I had called a door, I cannot remember; no, nor could I remember the next morning, for never frightened hare fled to cover, or fox to earth, with more terror of mind than I to this retreat.

I slept none that night; the farther I was from the occasion of my fright, the greater my apprehensions were, which is something contrary to the

---

[121] ghost

nature of such things, and especially to the usual practice of all creatures in fear; but I was so embarrassed with my own frightful ideas of the thing, that I formed nothing but dismal imaginations to myself, even though I was now a great way off. Sometimes I fancied it must be the devil, and reason joined in with me in this supposition, for how should any other thing in human shape come into the place? Where was the vessel that brought them? What marks were there of any other foot-step? And how was it possible a man should come there? But then, to think that Satan should take human shape upon him in such a place, where there could be no manner of occasion for it, but to leave the print of his foot behind him, and that even for no purpose too, for he could not be sure I should see it—this was an amusement the other way. I considered that the devil might have found out abundance of other ways to have terrified me than this of the single print of a foot; that as I lived quite on the other side of the island, he would never have been so simple as to leave a mark in a place where it was ten thousand to one whether I should ever see it or not, and in the sand too, which the first surge of the sea, upon a high wind, would have defaced entirely. All this seemed inconsistent with the thing itself and with all the notions we usually entertain of the subtlety of the devil.

Abundance of such things as these assisted to argue me out of all apprehensions of its being the devil; and I presently concluded then that it must be some more dangerous creature—viz. that it must be some of the savages of the mainland opposite who had wandered out to sea in their canoes, and either driven by the currents or by contrary winds, had made the island, and had been on shore, but were gone away again to sea; being as loath, perhaps, to have stayed in this desolate island as I would have been to have had them.

While these reflections were rolling in my mind, I was very thankful in my thoughts that I was so happy as not to be thereabouts at that time, or that they did not see my boat, by which they would have concluded that some inhabitants had been in the place, and perhaps have searched farther for me. Then terrible thoughts racked my imagination about their having found out my boat, and that there were people here; and that, if so, I should certainly have them come again in greater numbers and devour me; that if it should happen that they should not find me, yet they would find my enclosure, destroy all my corn, and carry away all my flock of tame goats, and I should perish at last for mere want.

Thus my fear banished all my religious hope, all that former confidence in God, which was founded upon such wonderful experience as I had had of His goodness; as if He that had fed me by miracle hitherto could not preserve, by His power, the provision which He had made for me by His goodness. I reproached myself with my laziness, that would not sow any more corn one year than would just serve me till the next season, as if no accident

could intervene to prevent my enjoying the crop that was upon the
ground; and this I thought so just
a reproof, that I resolved for the
future to have two or three years'
corn beforehand; so that, whatever might come, I might not perish
for want of bread.

How strange a chequer-work of
Providence is the life of man! and
by what secret different springs
are the affections hurried about, as
different circumstances present!
To-day we love what to-morrow
we hate; to-day we seek what to-
morrow we shun; to-day we desire what to-morrow we fear, nay,
even tremble at the apprehensions
of. This was exemplified in me, at
this time, in the most lively man-

ner imaginable; for I, whose only affliction was that I seemed banished from
human society, that I was alone, circumscribed by the boundless ocean, cut
off from mankind, and condemned to what I call silent life; that I was as
one whom Heaven thought not worthy to be numbered among the living, or
to appear among the rest of His creatures; that to have seen one of my own
species would have seemed to me a raising me from death to life, and the
greatest blessing that Heaven itself, next to the supreme blessing of salvation, could bestow; I say, that I should now tremble at the very apprehensions of seeing a man, and was ready to sink into the ground at but the
shadow or silent appearance of a man having set his foot in the island.

Such is the uneven state of human life; and it afforded me a great many
curious speculations afterwards, when I had a little recovered my first surprise. I considered that this was the station of life the infinitely wise and
good providence of God had determined for me; that as I could not foresee
what the ends of Divine wisdom might be in all this, so I was not to dispute
His sovereignty; who, as I was His creature, had an undoubted right, by
creation, to govern and dispose of me absolutely as He thought fit; and who,
as I was a creature that had offended Him, had likewise a judicial right to
condemn me to what punishment He thought fit; and that it was my part to
submit to bear His indignation, because I had sinned against Him. I then reflected, that as God, who was not only righteous but omnipotent, had
thought fit thus to punish and afflict me, so He was able to deliver me: that

if He did not think fit to do so, it was my unquestioned duty to resign myself absolutely and entirely to His will; and, on the other hand, it was my duty also to hope in Him, pray to Him, and quietly to attend to the dictates and directions of His daily providence.

These thoughts took me up many hours, days, nay, I may say weeks and months: and one particular effect of my cogitations on this occasion I cannot omit. One morning early, lying in my bed, and filled with thoughts about my danger from the appearances of savages, I found it discomposed me very much; upon which these words of the Scripture came into my thoughts, "Call upon Me in the day of trouble, and I will deliver thee, and thou shalt glorify Me." Upon this, rising cheerfully out of my bed, my heart was not only comforted, but I was guided and encouraged to pray earnestly to God for deliverance: when I had done praying I took up my Bible, and opening it to read, the first words that presented to me were, "Wait on the Lord, and be of good cheer, and He shall strengthen thy heart; wait, I say, on the Lord."[122]

It is impossible to express the comfort this gave me. In answer, I thankfully laid down the book, and was no more sad, at least on that occasion.

In the middle of these cogitations,[123] apprehensions, and reflections, it came into my thoughts one day that all this might be a mere chimera[124] of my own, and that this foot might be the print of my own foot, when I came on shore from my boat: this cheered me up a little, too, and I began to persuade myself it was all a delusion; that it was nothing else but my own foot; and why might I not come that way from the boat, as well as I was going that way to the boat? Again, I considered also that I could by no means tell for certain where I had trod, and where I had not; and that if, at last, this was only the print of my own foot, I had played the part of those fools who try to make stories of spectres and apparitions, and then are frightened at them more than anybody.

Now I began to take courage, and to peep abroad again, for I had not stirred out of my castle for three days and nights, so that I began to starve for provisions; for I had little or nothing within doors but some barley-cakes and water; then I knew that my goats wanted to be milked too, which usually was my evening diversion: and the poor creatures were in great pain and inconvenience for want of it; and, indeed, it almost spoiled some of them, and almost dried up their milk. Encouraging myself, therefore, with the belief that this was nothing but the print of one of my own feet, and that I might be truly said to start at my own shadow, I began to go abroad again, and went to my country house to milk my flock: but to see with what fear I

---

[122] Psalm 27:14

[123] thoughts

[124] illusion, fantasy

went forward, how often I looked behind me, how I was ready every now and then to lay down my basket and run for my life, it would have made any one have thought I was haunted with an evil conscience, or that I had been lately most terribly frightened; and so, indeed, I had. However, I went down thus two or three days, and having seen nothing, I began to be a little bolder, and to think there was really nothing in it but my own imagination; but I could not persuade myself fully of this till I should go down to the shore again, and see this print of a foot, and measure it by my own, and see if there was any similitude or fitness, that I might be assured it was my own foot: but when I came to the place, first, it appeared evidently to me, that when I laid up my boat I could not possibly be on shore anywhere there-abouts; secondly, when I came to measure the mark with my own foot, I found my foot not so large by a great deal. Both these things filled my head with new imaginations, and gave me the vapours[125] again to the highest de-gree, so that I shook with cold like one in an ague; and I went home again, filled with the belief that some man or men had been on shore there; or, in short, that the island was inhabited, and I might be surprised before I was aware; and what course to take for my security I knew not.

Oh, what ridiculous resolutions men take when possessed with fear! It deprives them of the use of those means which reason offers for their re-lief. The first thing I proposed to myself was, to throw down my enclosures, and turn all my tame cattle wild into the woods, lest the enemy should find them, and then frequent the island in prospect of the same or the like booty: then the simple thing of digging up my two corn-fields, lest they should find such a grain there, and still be prompted to frequent the island: then to demolish my bower and tent, that they might not see any vestiges of habita-tion, and be prompted to look farther, in order to find out the persons inhab-iting.

These were the subject of the first night's cogitations after I was come home again, while the apprehensions which had so overrun my mind were fresh upon me, and my head was full of vapours. Thus, fear of danger is ten thousand times more terrifying than danger itself, when apparent to the eyes; and we find the burden of anxiety greater, by much, than the evil which we are anxious about: and what was worse than all this, I had not that relief in this trouble that from the resignation I used to practise I hoped to have. I looked, I thought, like Saul, who complained not only that the Philis-tines were upon him, but that God had forsaken him; for I did not now take due ways to compose my mind, by crying to God in my distress, and resting upon His providence, as I had done before, for my defence and deliverance; which, if I had done, I had at least been more cheerfully supported under

---

[125] nerves, heebie-jeebies

this new surprise, and perhaps carried through it with more resolution.

This confusion of my thoughts kept me awake all night; but in the morning I fell asleep; and having, by the amusement of my mind, been as it were tired, and my spirits exhausted, I slept very soundly, and waked much better composed than I had ever been before. And now I began to think sedately;[126] and, upon debate with myself, I concluded that this island (which was so exceedingly pleasant, fruitful, and no farther from the mainland than as I had seen) was not so entirely abandoned as I might imagine; that although there were no stated inhabitants who lived on the spot, yet that there might sometimes come boats off from the shore, who, either with design, or perhaps never but when they were driven by cross winds, might come to this place; that I had lived there fifteen years now and had not met with the least shadow or figure of any people yet; and that, if at any time they should be driven here, it was probable they went away again as soon as ever they could, seeing they had never thought fit to fix here upon any occasion; that the most I could suggest any danger from was from any casual accidental landing of straggling people from the main, who, as it was likely, if they were driven hither, were here against their wills, so they made no stay here, but went off again with all possible speed; seldom staying one night on shore, lest they should not have the help of the tides and daylight back again; and that, therefore, I had nothing to do but to consider of some safe retreat, in case I should see any savages land upon the spot.

Now, I began sorely to repent that I had dug my cave so large as to bring a door through again, which door, as I said, came out beyond where my fortification joined to the rock: upon maturely considering this, therefore, I resolved to draw me a second fortification, in the manner of a semicircle, at a distance from my wall, just where I had planted a double row of trees about twelve years before, of which I made mention: these trees having been planted so thick before, they wanted but few piles to be driven between them, that they might be thicker and stronger, and my wall would be soon finished. So that I had now a double wall; and my outer wall was thickened with pieces of timber, old cables, and everything I could think of, to make it strong; having in it seven little holes, about as big as I might put my arm out at. In the inside of this I thickened my wall to about ten feet thick with continually bringing earth out of my cave, and laying it at the foot of the wall, and walking upon it; and through the seven holes I contrived to plant the muskets, of which I took notice that I had got seven on shore out of the ship; these I planted like my cannon, and fitted them into frames, that held them like a carriage, so that I could fire all the seven guns in two minutes' time; this wall I was many a weary month in finishing, and yet never thought

---

[126] calmly

myself safe till it was done.

When this was done I stuck all the ground without my wall, for a great length every way, as full with stakes or sticks of the osier-like wood, which I found so apt to grow, as they could well stand; insomuch that I believe I might set in near twenty thousand of them, leaving a pretty large space between them and my wall, that I might have room to see an enemy, and they might have no shelter from the young trees, if they attempted to approach my outer wall.

Thus in two years' time I had a thick grove; and in five or six years' time I had a wood before my dwelling, growing so monstrously thick and strong that it was indeed perfectly impassable: and no men, of what kind soever, could ever imagine that there was anything beyond it, much less a habitation. As for the way which I proposed to myself to go in and out (for I left no avenue), it was by setting two ladders, one to a part of the rock which was low, and then broke in, and left room to place another ladder upon that; so when the two ladders were taken down no man living could come down to me without doing himself mischief; and if they had come down, they were still on the outside of my outer wall.

Thus I took all the measures human prudence could suggest for my own preservation; and it will be seen at length that they were not altogether without just reason; though I foresaw nothing at that time more than my mere fear suggested to me.

CHAPTER XII: A CAVE RETREAT

While this was doing, I was not altogether careless of my other affairs; for I had a great concern upon me for my little herd of goats: they were not only a ready supply to me on every occasion, and began to be sufficient for me, without the expense of powder and shot, but also without the fatigue of hunting after the wild ones; and I was loath to lose the advantage of them, and to have them all to nurse up over again.

For this purpose, after long consideration, I could think of but two ways to preserve them: one was, to find another convenient place to dig a cave underground, and to drive them into it every night; and the other was to enclose two or three little bits of land, remote from one another, and as much concealed as I could, where I might keep about half-a-dozen young goats in each place; so that if any disaster happened to the flock in general,

I might be able to raise them again with little trouble and time: and this though it would require a good deal of time and labour, I thought was the most rational design.

Accordingly, I spent some time to find out the most retired parts of the island; and I pitched upon one, which was as private, indeed, as my heart could wish: it was a little damp piece of ground in the middle of the hollow and thick woods, where, as is observed, I almost lost myself once before, endeavouring to come back that way from the eastern part of the island. Here I found a clear piece of land, near three acres, so surrounded with woods that it was almost an enclosure by nature; at least, it did not want near so much labour to make it so as the other piece of ground I had worked so hard at.

I immediately went to work with this piece of ground; and in less than a month's time I had so fenced it round that my flock, or herd, call it which you please, which were not so wild now as at first they might be supposed to be, were well enough secured in it: so, without any further delay, I removed ten young she-goats and two he-goats to this piece, and when they were there I continued to perfect the fence till I had made it as secure as the other; which, however, I did at more leisure, and it took me up more time by a great deal. All this labour I was at the expense of, purely from my apprehensions on account of the print of a man's foot; for as yet I had never seen any human creature come near the island; and I had now lived two years under this uneasiness, which, indeed, made my life much less comfortable than it was before, as may be well imagined by any who know what it is to live in the constant snare of the fear of man.[127] And this I must observe, with grief, too, that the discomposure of my mind had great impression also upon the religious part of my thoughts; for the dread and terror of falling into the hands of savages and cannibals lay so upon my spirits, that I seldom found myself in a due temper for application to my Maker; at least, not with the sedate calmness and resignation of soul which I was wont to do: I rather prayed to God as under great affliction and pressure of mind, surrounded with danger, and in expectation every night of being murdered and devoured before morning; and I must testify, from my experience, that a temper of peace, thankfulness, love, and affection, is much the more proper frame for prayer than that of terror and discomposure: and that under the dread of mischief impending, a man is no more fit for a comforting performance of the duty of praying to God than he is for a repentance on a sickbed; for these discomposures affect the mind, as the others do the body; and the discomposure of the mind must necessarily be as great a disability as

---

[127] "The fear of man bringeth a snare; but whoso putteth his trust in the LORD shall be safe" (Proverbs 29:25).

that of the body, and much greater; praying to God being properly an act of the mind, not of the body.

But to go on. After I had thus secured one part of my little living stock, I went about the whole island, searching for another private place to make such another deposit; when, wandering more to the west point of the island than I had ever done yet, and looking out to sea, I thought I saw a boat upon the sea, at a great distance. I had found a perspective glass[128] or two in one of the seamen's chests, which I saved out of our ship, but I had it not about me; and this was so remote that I could not tell what to make of it, though I looked at it till my eyes were not able to hold to look any longer; whether it was a boat or not I do not know, but as I descended from the hill I could see no more of it, so I gave it over; only I resolved to go no more out without a perspective glass in my pocket. When I was come down the hill to the end of the island, where, indeed, I had never been before, I was presently convinced that the seeing the print of a man's foot was not such a strange thing in the island as I imagined: and but that it was a special providence that I was cast upon the side of the island where the savages never came, I should easily have known that nothing was more frequent than for the canoes from the main, when they happened to be a little too far out at sea, to shoot over to that side of the island for harbour: likewise, as they often met and fought in their canoes, the victors, having taken any prisoners, would bring them over to this shore, where, according to their dreadful customs, being all cannibals, they would kill and eat them; of which hereafter.

When I was come down the hill to the shore, as I said above, being the SW. point of the island, I was perfectly confounded and amazed; nor is it possible for me to express the horror of my mind at seeing the shore spread with skulls, hands, feet, and other bones of human bodies; and particularly I observed a place where there had been a fire made, and a circle dug in the earth, like a cockpit, where I supposed the savage wretches had sat down to their human feastings upon the bodies of their fellow-creatures.

I was so astonished with the sight of these things, that I entertained no notions of any danger to myself from it for a long while: all my apprehensions were buried in the thoughts of such a pitch of inhuman, hellish brutality, and the horror of the degeneracy of human nature, which, though I had heard of it often, yet I never had so near a view of before; in short, I turned away my face from the horrid spectacle; my stomach grew sick, and I was just at the point of fainting, when nature discharged the disorder from my stomach; and having vomited with uncommon violence, I was a little relieved, but could not bear to stay in the place a moment; so I got up the hill again with all the speed I could, and walked on towards my own habita-

---

[128] telescope

tion.

When I came a little out of that part of the island I stood still awhile, as amazed, and then, recovering myself, I looked up with the utmost affection of my soul, and, with a flood of tears in my eyes, gave God thanks, that had cast my first lot in a part of the world where I was distinguished from such dreadful creatures as these; and that, though I had esteemed my present condition very miserable, had yet given me so many comforts in it that I had still more to give thanks for than to complain of: and this, above all, that I had, even in this miserable condition, been comforted with the knowledge of Himself, and the hope of His blessing: which was a felicity more than sufficiently equivalent to all the misery which I had suffered, or could suffer.

In this frame of thankfulness I went home to my castle, and began to be much easier now, as to the safety of my circumstances, than ever I was before: for I observed that these wretches never came to this island in search of what they could get; perhaps not seeking, not wanting, or not expecting anything here; and having often, no doubt, been up the covered, woody part of it without finding anything to their purpose. I knew I had been here now almost eighteen years, and never saw the least footsteps of human creature there before; and I might be eighteen years more as entirely concealed as I was now, if I did not discover myself to them, which I had no manner of occasion to do; it being my only business to keep myself entirely concealed where I was, unless I found a better sort of creatures than cannibals to make myself known to. Yet I entertained such an abhorrence of the savage wretches that I have been speaking of, and of the wretched, inhuman custom of their devouring and eating one another up, that I continued pensive and sad, and kept close within my own circle for almost two years after this: when I say my own circle, I mean by it my three plantations—viz. my castle, my country seat (which I called my bower), and my enclosure in the woods: nor did I look after this for any other use than an enclosure for my goats; for the aversion which nature gave me to these hellish wretches was such, that I was as fearful of seeing them as of seeing the devil himself. I did not so much as go to look after my boat all this time, but began rather to think of making another; for I could not think of ever making any more attempts to bring the other boat round the island to me, lest I should meet with some of these creatures at sea; in which case, if I had happened to have fallen into their hands, I knew what would have been my lot.

Time, however, and the satisfaction I had that I was in no danger of being discovered by these people, began to wear off my uneasiness about them; and I began to live just in the same composed manner as before, only with this difference, that I used more caution, and kept my eyes more about me than I did before, lest I should happen to be seen by any of them; and particularly, I was more cautious of firing my gun, lest any of them, being on the island, should happen to hear it. It was, therefore, a very good providence to me that I had furnished myself with a tame breed of goats, and that I had no need to hunt any more about the woods, or shoot at them; and if I did catch any of them after this, it was by traps and snares, as I had done before; so that for two years after this I believe I never fired my gun once off, though I never went out without it; and what was more, as I had saved three pistols out of the ship, I always carried them out with me, or at least two of them, sticking them in my goat-skin belt. I also furbished up one of the great cutlasses that I had out of the ship, and made me a belt to hang it on also; so that I was now a most formidable fellow to look at when I went abroad, if you add to the former description of myself the particular of two pistols, and a broadsword hanging at my side in a belt, but without a scabbard.

Things going on thus, as I have said, for some time, I seemed, excepting these cautions, to be reduced to my former calm, sedate way of living. All these things tended to show me more and more how far my condition was from being miserable, compared to some others; nay, to many other particulars of life which it might have pleased God to have made my lot. It put me upon reflecting how little repining there would be among mankind at any condition of life if people would rather compare their condition with those that were worse, in order to be thankful, than be always comparing them with those which are better, to assist their murmurings and complainings.

As in my present condition there were not really many things which I wanted, so indeed I thought that the frights I had been in about these savage wretches, and the concern I had been in for my own preservation, had taken off the edge of my invention, for my own conveniences; and I had dropped a good design, which I had once bent my thoughts upon, and that was to try if I could not make some of my barley into malt, and then try to brew myself some beer. This was really a whimsical thought, and I reproved myself often for the simplicity of it: for I presently saw there would be the want of several things necessary to the making my beer that it would be impossible for me to supply; as, first, casks to preserve it in, which was a thing that, as I have observed already, I could never compass: no, though I spent not only many days, but weeks, nay months, in attempting it, but to no purpose. In the next place, I had no hopes to make it keep, no yeast to make it work, no copper or kettle to make it boil; and yet with all these things wanting, I verily believe, had not the frights and terrors I was in about the savages intervened, I had undertaken it, and perhaps brought it to pass too; for I seldom gave anything over without accomplishing it, when once I had it in my head to began it. But my invention now ran quite another way; for night and day I could think of nothing but how I might destroy some of the monsters in their cruel, bloody entertainment, and if possible save the victim they should bring hither to destroy. It would take up a larger volume than this whole work is intended to be to set down all the contrivances I hatched, or rather brooded upon, in my thoughts, for the destroying these creatures, or at least frightening them so as to prevent their coming hither any more: but all this was abortive; nothing could be possible to take effect, unless I was to be there to do it myself: and what could one man do among them, when perhaps there might be twenty or thirty of them together with their darts, or their bows and arrows, with which they could shoot as true to a mark as I could with my gun?

Sometimes I thought if digging a hole under the place where they made their fire, and putting in five or six pounds of gunpowder, which, when they kindled their fire, would consequently take fire, and blow up all that was near it: but as, in the first place, I should be unwilling to waste so much powder upon them, my store being now within the quantity of one barrel, so neither could I be sure of its going off at any certain time, when it might surprise them; and, at best, that it would do little more than just blow the fire about their ears and fright them, but not sufficient to make them forsake the place: so I laid it aside; and then proposed that I would place myself in ambush in some convenient place, with my three guns all double-loaded, and in the middle of their bloody ceremony let fly at them, when I should be sure to kill or wound perhaps two or three at every shot; and then falling in upon them with my three pistols and my sword, I made no doubt but that, if there were twenty, I should kill them all. This fancy pleased my thoughts for some weeks, and I was so full of it that I often dreamed of it, and, sometimes, that I was just going to let fly at them in my sleep. I went so far with it in my imagination that I employed myself several days to find out proper places to put myself in ambuscade,[129] as I said, to watch for them, and I went frequently to the place itself, which was now grown more familiar to me; but while my mind was thus filled with thoughts of revenge and a bloody putting twenty or thirty of them to the sword, as I may call it, the horror I had at the place, and at the signals of the barbarous wretches devouring one another, abetted[130] my malice. Well, at length I found a place in the side of the hill where I was satisfied I might securely wait till I saw any of their boats coming; and might then, even before they would be ready to come on shore, convey myself unseen into some thickets of trees, in one of which there was a hollow large enough to conceal me entirely; and there I might sit and observe all their bloody doings, and take my full aim at their heads, when they were so close together as that it would be next to impos-

---

[129] ambush
[130] aided, encouraged

sible that I should miss my shot, or that I could fail wounding three or four of them at the first shot. In this place, then, I resolved to fulfil my design; and accordingly I prepared two muskets and my ordinary fowling-piece. The two muskets I loaded with a brace of slugs each, and four or five smaller bullets, about the size of pistol bullets; and the fowling-piece I loaded with near a handful of swan-shot of the largest size; I also loaded my pistols with about four bullets each; and, in this posture, well provided with ammunition for a second and third charge, I prepared myself for my expedition.

After I had thus laid the scheme of my design, and in my imagination put it in practice, I continually made my tour every morning to the top of the hill, which was from my castle, as I called it, about three miles or more, to see if I could observe any boats upon the sea, coming near the island, or standing over towards it; but I began to tire of this hard duty, after I had for two or three months constantly kept my watch, but came always back without any discovery; there having not, in all that time, been the least appearance, not only on or near the shore, but on the whole ocean, so far as my eye or glass could reach every way.

As long as I kept my daily tour to the hill, to look out, so long also I kept up the vigour of my design, and my spirits seemed to be all the while in a suitable frame for so outrageous an execution as the killing twenty or thirty naked savages, for an offence which I had not at all entered into any discussion of in my thoughts, any farther than my passions were at first fired by the horror I conceived at the unnatural custom of the people of that country, who, it seems, had been suffered by Providence, in His wise disposition of the world, to have no other guide than that of their own abominable and vitiated passions; and consequently were left, and perhaps had been so for some ages, to act such horrid things, and receive such dreadful customs, as nothing but nature, entirely abandoned by Heaven, and actuated by some hellish degeneracy, could have run them into. But now, when, as I have said, I began to be weary of the fruitless excursion which I had made so long and so far every morning in vain, so my opinion of the action itself began to alter; and I began, with cooler and calmer thoughts, to consider what I was going to engage in; what authority or call I had to pretend to be judge and executioner upon these men as criminals, whom Heaven had thought fit for so many ages to suffer unpunished to go on, and to be as it were the executioners of His judgments one upon another; how far these people were offenders against me, and what right I had to engage in the quarrel of that blood which they shed promiscuously upon one another. I debated this very often with myself thus: How do I know what God Himself judges in this particular case? It is certain these people do not commit this as a crime; it is not against their own consciences reproving, or their light reproaching them; they do not know it to be an offence, and then commit it in defiance of divine justice, as we do in almost all the sins we commit. They think it no more a crime to kill a captive taken in war than we do to kill an ox; or to eat human flesh than we do to eat mutton."

When I considered this a little, it followed necessarily that I was certainly in the wrong; that these people were not murderers, in the sense that I had before condemned them in my thoughts, any more than those Christians were murderers who often put to death the prisoners taken in battle; or more frequently, upon many occasions, put whole troops of men to the sword, without giving quarter, though they threw down their arms and submitted. In the next place, it occurred to me that although the usage they gave one another was thus brutish and inhuman, yet it was really nothing to me: these people had done me no injury: that if they attempted, or I saw it necessary, for my immediate preservation, to fall upon them, something might be said for it: but that I was yet out of their power, and they really had no knowledge of me, and consequently no design upon me; and therefore it could not be just for me to fall upon them; that this would justify the conduct of the Spaniards in all their barbarities practised in America, where they destroyed millions of these people; who, however they were idolators and barbarians, and had several bloody and barbarous rites in their customs, such as sacrificing human bodies to their idols, were yet, as to the Spaniards, very innocent people; and that the rooting them out of the country is spoken of with the utmost abhorrence and detestation by even the Spaniards themselves at this time, and by all other Christian nations of Europe, as a mere butchery, a bloody and unnatural piece of cruelty, unjustifiable either to God or man; and for which the very name of a Spaniard is reckoned to be frightful and terrible, to all people of humanity or of Christian compassion; as if the kingdom of Spain were particularly eminent for the produce of a race of men who were without principles of tenderness, or the common bowels of pity to the miserable, which is reckoned to be a mark of generous temper in the mind.

These considerations really put me to a pause, and to a kind of a full stop; and I began by little and little to be off my design, and to conclude I had taken wrong measures in my resolution to attack the savages; and that it was not my business to meddle with them, unless they first attacked me; and this it was my business, if possible, to prevent: but that, if I were discovered and attacked by them, I knew my duty. On the other hand, I argued with myself that this really was the way not to deliver myself, but entirely to ruin and destroy myself; for unless I was sure to kill every one that not only should be on shore at that time, but that should ever come on shore afterwards, if but one of them escaped to tell their country-people what had happened, they would come over again by thousands to revenge the death of their fellows, and I should only bring upon myself a certain destruction, which, at present, I had no manner of occasion for. Upon the whole, I concluded that I ought, neither in principle nor in policy, one way or other, to concern myself in this affair: that my business was, by all possible means to conceal myself from them, and not to leave the least sign for them to guess by that there were any living creatures upon the island—I mean of human shape. Religion joined in with this prudential resolution; and I was convinced now, many ways, that I was perfectly out of my duty when I was laying all my bloody schemes for the destruction of innocent creatures—I mean innocent as to me. As to the crimes they were guilty of towards one another, I had nothing to do with them; they were national, and I ought to leave them to the justice of God, who is the Governor of nations, and knows how, by national punishments, to make a just retribution for national offences, and to bring public judgments upon those who offend in a public manner, by such ways as best please Him. This appeared so clear to me now, that nothing was a greater satisfaction to me than that I had not been suffered to do a thing which I now saw so much reason to believe would have been no less a sin than that of wilful murder if I had committed it; and I gave most humble thanks on my knees to God, that He had thus delivered me from blood-guiltiness; beseeching Him to grant me the protection of His providence, that I might not fall into the hands of the barbarians, or that I might not lay my hands upon them, unless I had a more clear call from Heaven to do it, in defence of my own life.

In this disposition I continued for near a year after this; and so far was I from desiring an occasion for falling upon these wretches, that in all that time I never once went up the hill to see whether there were any of them in sight, or to know whether any of them had been on shore there or not, that I might not be tempted to renew any of my contrivances against them, or be provoked by any advantage that might present itself to fall upon them; only this I did: I went and removed my boat, which I had on the other side of the island, and carried it down to the east end of the whole island, where I ran it into a little cove, which I found under some high rocks, and where I knew, by reason of the currents, the savages durst not, at least would not, come with their boats upon any account whatever. With my boat I carried away everything that I had left there belonging to her, though not necessary for the bare going thither—viz. a mast and sail which I had made for her, and a thing like an anchor, but which, indeed, could not be called either anchor or grapnel; however, it was the best I could make of its kind: all these I removed, that there might not be the least shadow for discovery, or appearance of any boat, or of any human habitation upon the island. Besides this, I kept myself, as I said, more retired than ever, and seldom went from my cell except upon my constant employment, to milk my she-goats, and manage my little flock in the wood, which, as it was quite on the other part of the island, was out of danger; for certain, it is that these savage people, who sometimes haunted this island, never came with any thoughts of finding anything here, and consequently never wandered off from the coast, and I doubt not but they might have been several times on shore after my apprehensions of them had made me cautious, as well as before. Indeed, I looked back with some horror upon the thoughts of what my condition would have been if I had chopped upon them and been discovered before that; when, naked and unarmed, except with one gun, and that loaded often only with small shot, I walked everywhere, peeping and peering about the island, to see what I could get; what a surprise should I have been in if, when I discovered the print of a man's foot, I had, instead of that, seen fifteen or twenty savages, and found them pursuing me, and by the swiftness of their running no possibility of my escaping them! The thoughts of this sometimes sank my very soul within me, and distressed my mind so much that I could not soon recover it, to think what I should have done, and how I should not only have been unable to resist them, but even should not have had presence of mind enough to do what I might have done; much less what now, after so much consideration and preparation, I might be able to do. Indeed, after serious thinking of these things, I would be melancholy, and sometimes it would last a great while; but I resolved it all at last into thankfulness to that Providence which had delivered me from so many unseen dangers, and had kept me from those mischiefs which I could have no way been the agent in delivering myself from, because I had not the least notion of any such thing depending, or the least supposition of its being possible. This renewed a contemplation which often had come into my thoughts in former times, when first I began to see the merciful dispositions of Heaven, in the dangers we run through in this life; how wonderfully we are delivered when we know nothing of it; how, when we are in a quandary as we call it, a doubt or hesitation whether to go this way or that way, a secret hint shall direct us this way, when we intended to go that way: nay, when sense, our own inclination, and perhaps business has called us to go the other way, yet a strange impression upon the mind, from we know not what springs, and by we know not what power, shall overrule us to go this way; and it shall afterwards appear that had we gone that way, which we should have gone, and even to our imagination ought to have gone, we should have been ruined and lost. Upon these and many like reflections I afterwards made it a certain rule with me, that whenever I found those secret hints or pressings of mind to doing or not doing anything that presented, or going this way or that way, I never failed to obey the secret dictate; though I knew no other reason for it than such a pressure or such a hint hung upon my mind. I could give many examples of the success of this conduct in the course of my life, but more especially in the latter part of my inhabiting this unhappy island; besides many occasions which it is very likely I might have taken notice of, if I had seen with the same eyes then that I see with now. But it is never too late to be wise; and I cannot but advise all considering men, whose lives are attended with such extraordinary incidents as mine, or even though not so extraordinary, not to slight such secret intimations of Providence, let them come from what invisible intelligence they will. That I shall not discuss, and perhaps cannot account for; but certainly they are a proof of the converse of spirits, and a secret communication between those embodied and those unembodied, and such a proof as can never be withstood; of which I shall have occasion to give some remarkable instances in the remainder of my solitary residence in this dismal place.

I believe the reader of this will not think it strange if I confess that these anxieties, these constant dangers I lived in, and the concern that was now upon me, put an end to all invention, and to all the contrivances that I had laid for my future accommodations and conveniences. I had the care of my safety more now upon my hands than that of my food. I cared not to drive a nail, or chop a stick of wood now, for fear the noise I might make should be heard: much less would I fire a gun for the same reason: and above all I was intolerably uneasy at making any fire, lest the smoke, which is visible at a great distance in the day, should betray me. For this reason, I removed that part of my business which required fire, such as burning of pots and pipes, &c., into my new apartment in the woods; where, after I had been some time, I found, to my unspeakable consolation, a mere natural cave in the earth, which went in a vast way, and where, I daresay, no savage, had he been at the mouth of it, would be so hardy as to venture in; nor, indeed, would any man else, but one who, like me, wanted nothing so much as a safe retreat.

The mouth of this hollow was at the bottom of a great rock, where, by mere accident (I would say, if I did not see abundant reason to ascribe all such things now to Providence), I was cutting down some thick branches of trees to make charcoal; and before I go on I must observe the reason of my making this charcoal, which was this—I was afraid of making a smoke about my habitation, as I said before; and yet I could not live there without baking my bread, cooking my meat, &c.; so I contrived to burn some wood here, as I had seen done in England, under turf, till it became chark or dry coal: and then putting the fire out, I preserved the coal to carry home, and perform the other services for which fire was wanting, without danger of smoke. But this is by-the-bye. While I was cutting down some wood here, I perceived that, behind a very thick branch of low brushwood or underwood, there was a kind of hollow place: I was curious to look in it; and getting with difficulty into the mouth of it, I found it was pretty large, that is to say, sufficient for me to stand upright in it, and perhaps another with me: but I must confess to you that I made more haste out than I did in, when looking farther into the place, and which was perfectly dark, I saw two broad shining eyes of some creature, whether devil or man I knew not, which twinkled like two stars; the dim light from the cave's mouth shining directly in, and making the reflection. However, after some pause I recovered myself, and began to call myself a thousand fools, and to think that he that was afraid to see the devil was not fit to live twenty years in an island all alone; and that I might well think there was nothing in this cave that was more frightful than myself. Upon this, plucking up my courage, I took up a firebrand, and in I rushed again, with the stick flaming in my hand: I had not gone three steps in before I was almost as frightened as before; for I heard a very loud sigh, like that of a man in some pain, and it was followed by a broken noise, as of words half expressed, and then a deep sigh again. I stepped back, and was indeed struck with such a surprise that it put me into a cold sweat, and if I had had a hat on my head, I will not answer for it that my hair might not have lifted it off. But still plucking up my spirits as well as I could, and encouraging myself a little with considering that the power and presence of God was everywhere, and was able to protect me, I stepped forward again, and by the light of the firebrand, holding it up a little over my head, I saw lying on the ground a monstrous, frightful old he-goat, just making his will, as we say, and gasping for life, and, dying, indeed, of mere old age. I stirred him a little to see if I could get him out, and he essayed to get up, but was not able to raise himself; and I thought with myself he might even lie there—for if he had frightened me, so he would certainly fright any of the savages, if any of them should be so hardy as to come in there while he had any life in him.

I was now recovered from my surprise, and began to look round me, when I found the cave was but very small—that is to say, it might be about twelve feet over, but in no manner of shape, neither round nor square, no hands having ever been employed in making it but those of mere Nature. I observed also that there was a place at the farther side of it that went in further, but was so low that it required me to creep upon my hands and knees to go into it, and whither it went I knew not; so, having no candle, I gave it over for that time, but resolved to go again the next day provided with candles and a tinder-box, which I had made of the lock of one of the muskets, with some wildfire in the pan.

Accordingly, the next day I came provided with six large candles of my own making (for I made very good candles now of goat's tallow, but was hard set for candle-wick, using sometimes rags or rope-yarn, and sometimes the dried rind of a weed like nettles); and going into this low place I was obliged to creep upon all-fours as I have said, almost ten yards—which, by the way, I thought was a venture bold enough, considering that I knew not how far it might go, nor what was beyond it. When I had got through the strait, I found the roof rose higher up, I believe near twenty feet; but never was such a glorious sight seen in the island, I daresay, as it was to look round the sides and roof of this vault or cave—the wall reflected a hundred thousand lights to me from my two candles. What it was in the rock—whether diamonds or any other precious stones, or gold which I rather supposed it to be—I knew not. The place I was in was a most delightful cavity, or grotto, though perfectly dark; the floor was dry and level, and had a sort of a small loose gravel upon it, so that there was no nauseous or venomous creature to be seen, neither was there any damp or wet on the sides or roof. The only difficulty in it was the entrance—which, however, as it was a place of security, and such a retreat as I wanted; I thought was a convenience; so that I was really rejoiced at the discovery, and resolved, without any delay, to bring some of those things which I was most anxious about to this place: particularly, I resolved to bring hither my magazine of powder, and all my spare arms—viz. two fowling-pieces—for I had three in all—and three muskets—for of them I had eight in all; so I kept in my castle only five, which stood ready mounted like pieces of cannon on my outmost fence, and were ready also to take out upon any expedition. Upon this occasion of removing my ammunition I happened to open the barrel of powder which I took up out of the sea, and which had been wet, and I found that the water had penetrated about three or four inches into the powder on every side, which caking and growing hard, had preserved the inside like a kernel in the shell, so that I had near sixty pounds of very good powder in the centre of the cask. This was a very agreeable discovery to me at that time; so I carried all away thither, never keeping above two or three pounds of powder with me in my castle, for fear of a surprise of any kind; I also carried thither all the lead I had left for bullets.

I fancied myself now like one of the ancient giants who were said to live in caves and holes in the rocks, where none could come at them; for I persuaded myself, while I was here, that if five hundred savages were to hunt me, they could never find me out—or if they did, they would not venture to attack me here. The old goat whom I found expiring died in the mouth of the cave the next day after I made this discovery; and I found it much easier to dig a great hole there, and throw him in and cover him with earth, than to drag him out; so I interred him there, to prevent offence to my nose.

Questions for Review:

1. What sights does Robinson Crusoe say anyone would laugh to see?

2. What does Robinson Crusoe do about his boat situation? Explain how he strengthens his food situation.

3.   What sight terrifies Robinson Crusoe? What thoughts then frighten him? How is he comforted at first?

4.   What does he decide about the sight when he sees it again? List the steps he takes to protect himself.

5.   What does Robinson Crusoe decide to do about his goats? What new, terrifying sight does he encounter, and what does he do about it? Explain the conflict he has as to what to do.

6.   How do Robinson Crusoe's plans change? What does he encounter that assists him?

CHAPTER XIII: WRECK OF A SPANISH SHIP

I was now in the twenty-third year of my residence in this island, and was so naturalised to the place and the manner of living, that, could I but have enjoyed the certainty that no savages would come to the place to disturb me, I could have been content to have capitulated for spending the rest of my time there, even to the last moment, till I had laid me down and died, like the old goat in the cave. I had also arrived to some little diversions and amusements, which made the time pass a great deal more pleasantly with me than it did before—first, I had taught my Poll, as I noted before, to speak; and he did it so familiarly, and talked so articulately and plain, that it was very pleasant to me; and he lived with me no less than six-and-twenty years. How long he might have lived afterwards I know not, though I know they have a notion in the Brazils that they live a hundred years. My dog was a pleasant and loving companion to me for no less than sixteen years of my time, and then died of mere old age. As for my cats, they multiplied, as I have observed, to that degree that I was obliged to shoot several of them at first, to keep them from devouring me and all I had; but at length, when the two old ones I brought with me were gone, and after some time continually driving them from me, and letting them have no provision with me, they all ran wild into the woods, except two or three favourites, which I kept tame, and whose young, when they had any, I always drowned; and these were part of my family. Besides these I always kept two or three household kids about me, whom I taught to feed out of my hand; and I had two more parrots, which talked pretty well, and would all call "Robin Crusoe," but none like my first; nor, indeed, did I take the pains with any of them that I had done with him. I had also several tame sea-fowls, whose name I knew not, that I caught upon the shore, and cut their wings; and the little stakes which I had planted before my castle-wall being now grown up to a good thick grove, these fowls all lived among these low trees, and bred there, which was very agreeable to me; so that, as I said above, I began to be very well contented with the life I led, if I could have been secured from the dread of the savages. But it was otherwise directed; and it may not be amiss for all people who shall meet with my story to make this just observation from it: How frequently, in the course of our lives, the evil which in itself we seek most to shun, and which, when we are fallen into, is the most dreadful to us, is oftentimes the very means or door of our deliverance, by which alone we can be raised again from the affliction we are fallen into. I could give many examples of this in the course of my unac-countable life; but in nothing was it more particularly remarkable than in the circumstances of my last years of solitary residence in this island.

It was now the month of December, as I said above, in my twenty-third year; and this, being the southern solstice (for winter I cannot call it), was the particular time of my harvest, and required me to be pretty much abroad in the fields, when, going out early in the morning, even before it was thorough daylight, I was surprised with seeing a light of some fire upon the shore, at a distance from me of about two miles, toward that part of the island where I had observed some savages had been, as before, and not on the other side; but, to my great affliction, it was on my side of the island.

I was indeed terribly surprised at the sight, and stopped short within my grove, not daring to go out, lest I might be surprised; and yet I had no more peace within, from the apprehensions I had that if these savages, in rambling over the island, should find my corn standing or cut, or any of my works or improvements, they would immediately conclude that there were people in the place, and would then never rest till they had found me out. In this extremity I went back directly to my castle, pulled up the ladder after me, and made all things without look as wild and natural as I could.

Then I prepared myself within, putting myself in a posture of defence. I loaded all my cannon, as I called them—that is to say, my muskets, which were mounted upon my new fortification—and all my pistols, and resolved to defend myself to the last gasp—not forgetting seriously to commend myself to the Divine protection, and earnestly to pray to God to deliver me out of the hands of the barbarians. I continued in this posture about two hours, and began to be impatient for intelligence abroad, for I had no spies to send out. After sitting a while longer, and musing what I should do in this case, I was not able to bear sitting in ignorance longer; so setting up my ladder to the side of the hill, where there was a flat place, as I observed before, and then pulling the ladder after me, I set it up again and mounted the top of the hill, and pulling out my perspective glass, which I had taken on purpose, I laid me down flat on my belly on the ground, and began to look for the place. I presently found there were no less than nine naked savages sitting round a small fire they had made, not to warm them, for they had no need of that, the weather being extremely hot, but, as I supposed, to dress some of their barbarous diet of human flesh which they had brought with them, whether alive or dead I could not tell.

They had two canoes with them, which they had hauled up upon the shore; and as it was then ebb of tide, they seemed to me to wait for the return of the flood to go away again. It is not easy to imagine what confusion this sight put me into, especially seeing them come on my side of the island, and so near to me; but when I considered their coming must be always with the current of the ebb, I began afterwards to be more sedate in my mind, being satisfied that I might go abroad with safety all the time of the flood of tide, if they were not on shore before; and having made this observation, I went abroad about my harvest work with the more composure.

As I expected, so it proved; for as soon as the tide made to the westward I saw them all take boat and row (or paddle as we call it) away. I should have observed, that for an hour or more before they went off they were dancing, and I could easily discern their postures and gestures by my glass. I could not perceive, by my nicest[131] observation, but that they were stark naked, and had not the least covering upon them; but whether they were men or women I could not distinguish.

As soon as I saw them shipped and gone, I took two guns upon my shoulders, and two pistols in my girdle, and my great sword by my side without a scabbard, and with all the speed I was able to make went away to the hill where I had discovered the first appearance of all; and as soon as I get thither, which was not in less than two hours (for I could not go quickly, being so loaded with arms as I was), I perceived there had been three canoes more of the savages at that place; and looking out farther, I saw they were all at sea together, making over for the main. This was a dreadful sight to me, especially as, going down to the shore, I could see the marks of horror which the dismal work they had been about had left behind it—viz. the blood, the bones, and part of the flesh of human bodies eaten and devoured by those wretches with merriment and sport. I was so filled with indignation at the sight, that I now began to premeditate the destruction of the next that

---

[131] most precise

I saw there, let them be whom or how many soever. It seemed evident to me that the visits which they made thus to this island were not very frequent, for it was above fifteen months before any more of them came on shore there again—that is to say, I neither saw them nor any footsteps or signals of them in all that time; for as to the rainy seasons, then they are sure not to come abroad, at least not so far. Yet all this while I lived uncomfortably, by reason of the constant apprehensions of their coming upon me by surprise: from whence I observe, that the expectation of evil is more bitter than the suffering, especially if there is no room to shake off that expectation or those apprehensions.

During all this time I was in a murdering humour, and spent most of my hours, which should have been better employed, in contriving how to cir-cumvent and fall upon them the very next time I should see them—espe-cially if they should be divided, as they were the last time, into two parties; nor did I consider at all that if I killed one party—suppose ten or a dozen—I was still the next day, or week, or month, to kill another, and so another, even ad infinitum,[132] till I should be, at length, no less a murderer than they were in being man-eaters—and perhaps much more so. I spent my days now in great perplexity and anxiety of mind, expecting that I should one day or other fall, into the hands of these merciless creatures; and if I did at any time venture abroad, it was not without looking around me with the greatest care and caution imaginable. And now I found, to my great comfort, how happy it was that I had provided a tame flock or herd of goats, for I durst not upon any account fire my gun, especially near that side of the island where they usually came, lest I should alarm the savages; and if they had fled from me now, I was sure to have them come again with perhaps two or three hundred canoes with them in a few days, and then I knew what to expect. However, I wore out a year and three months more before I ever saw any more of the savages, and then I found them again, as I shall soon observe. It is true they might have been there once or twice; but either they made no stay, or at least I did not see them; but in the month of May, as near as I could calculate, and in my four-and-twentieth year, I had a very strange encounter with them; of which in its place.

The perturbation[133] of my mind during this fifteen or sixteen months' interval was very great; I slept unquietly, dreamed always frightful dreams, and often started[134] out of my sleep in the night. In the day great troubles overwhelmed my mind; and in the night I dreamed often of killing the sav-ages and of the reasons why I might justify doing it.

But to waive all this for a while. It was in the middle of May, on the six-

---

[132] Latin for "to the point of infinity" or forever
[133] uneasiness, worry
[134] awakened with a jump

teenth day, I think, as well as my poor wooden calendar would reckon, for I marked all upon the post still; I say, it was on the sixteenth of May that it blew a very great storm of wind all day, with a great deal of lightning and thunder, and; a very foul night it was after it. I knew not what was the particular occasion of it, but as I was reading in the Bible, and taken up with very serious thoughts about my present condition, I was surprised with the noise of a gun, as I thought, fired at sea. This was, to be sure, a surprise quite of a different nature from any I had met with before; for the notions this put into my thoughts were quite of another kind. I started up in the greatest haste imaginable; and, in a trice,[135] clapped my ladder to the middle place of the rock, and pulled it after me; and mounting it the second time, got to the top of the hill the very moment that a flash of fire bid me listen for a second gun, which, accordingly, in about half a minute I heard; and by the sound, knew that it was from that part of the sea where I was driven down the current in my boat. I immediately considered that this must be some ship in distress, and that they had some comrade, or some other ship in company, and fired these for signals of distress, and to obtain help. I had the presence of mind at that minute to think, that though I could not help them, it might be that they might help me; so I brought together all the dry wood I could get at hand, and making a good handsome pile, I set it on fire upon the hill. The wood was dry, and blazed freely; and, though the wind blew very hard, yet it burned fairly out; so that I was certain, if there was any such thing as a ship, they must needs see it. And no doubt they did; for as soon as ever my fire blazed up, I heard another gun, and after that several others, all from the same quarter. I plied my fire all night long, till daybreak: and when it was broad day, and the air cleared up, I saw something at a great distance at sea, full east of the island, whether a sail or a hull I could not distinguish—no, not with my glass: the distance was so great, and the weather still something hazy also; at least, it was so out at sea.

I looked frequently at it all that day, and soon perceived that it did not move; so I presently concluded that it was a ship at anchor; and being eager, you may be sure, to be satisfied, I took my gun in my hand, and ran towards the south side of the island to the rocks where I had formerly been carried away by the current; and getting up there, the weather by this time being perfectly clear, I could plainly see, to my great sorrow, the wreck of a ship, cast away in the night upon those concealed rocks which I found when I was out in my boat; and which rocks, as they checked the violence of the stream, and made a kind of counter-stream, or eddy, were the occasion of my recovering from the most desperate, hopeless condition that ever I had been in in all my life. Thus, what is one man's safety is another man's

---

[135] instant, moment

destruction; for it seems these men, whoever they were, being out of their knowledge, and the rocks being wholly under water, had been driven upon them in the night, the wind blowing hard at ENE. Had they seen the island, as I must necessarily suppose they did not, they must, as I thought, have endeavoured to have saved themselves on shore by the help of their boat; but their firing off guns for help, especially when they saw, as I imagined, my fire, filled me with many thoughts. First, I imagined that upon seeing my light they might have put themselves into their boat, and endeavoured to make the shore: but that the sea running very high, they might have been cast away. Other times I imagined that they might have lost their boat before, as might be the case many ways; particularly by the breaking of the sea upon their ship, which many times obliged men to stave, or take in pieces, their boat, and sometimes to throw it overboard with their own hands. Other times I imagined they had some other ship or ships in company, who, upon the signals of distress they made, had taken them up, and carried them off. Other times I fancied they were all gone off to sea in their boat, and being hurried away by the current that I had been formerly in, were carried out into the great ocean, where there was nothing but misery and perishing: and that, perhaps, they might by this time think of starving, and of being in a condition to eat one another. As all these were but conjectures at best, so, in the condition I was in, I could do no more than look on upon the misery of the poor men, and pity them; which had still this good effect upon my side, that it gave me more and more cause to give thanks to God, who had so happily and comfortably provided for me in my desolate condition; and that of two ships' companies, who were now cast away upon this part of the world, not one life should be spared but mine. I learned here again to observe, that it is very rare that the providence of God casts us into any condition so low, or any misery so great, but we may see something or other to be thankful for, and may see others in worse circumstances than our own. Such certainly was the case of these men, of whom I could not so much as see room to suppose any were saved; nothing could make it rational so much as to wish or expect that they did not all perish there, except the possibility only of their being taken up by another ship in company; and this was but mere possibility indeed, for I saw not the least sign or appearance of any such thing. I cannot explain, by any possible energy of words, what a strange longing I felt in my soul upon this sight, breaking out sometimes thus: "Oh that there had been but one or two, nay, or but one soul saved out of this ship, to have escaped to me, that I might but have had one companion, one fellow-creature, to have spoken to me and to have conversed with!" In all the time of my solitary life I never felt so earnest, so strong a desire after the society of my fellow-creatures, or so deep a regret at the want of it.

There are some secret springs in the affections which, when they are set a-going by some object in view, or, though not in view, yet rendered present to the mind by the power of imagination, that motion carries out the soul, by its impetuosity, to such violent, eager embracings of the object, that the absence of it is insupportable. Such were these earnest wishings that but one man had been saved. I believe I repeated the words, "Oh that it had been but one!" a thousand times; and my desires were so moved by it, that when I spoke the words my hands would clinch together, and my fingers would press the palms of my hands, so that if I had had any soft thing in my hand I should have crushed it involuntarily; and the teeth in my head would strike together, and set against one another so strong, that for some time I could not part them again. Let the naturalists[136] explain these things, and the reason and manner of them. All I can do is to describe the fact, which was even surprising to me when I found it, though I knew not from whence it proceeded; it was doubtless the effect of ardent wishes, and of strong ideas formed in my mind, realising the comfort which the conversation of one of my fellow-Christians would have been to me. But it was not to be; either their fate or mine, or both, forbade it; for, till the last year of my being on this island, I never knew whether any were saved out of that ship or no; and had only the affliction, some days after, to see the corpse of a drowned boy come on shore at the end of the island which was next the shipwreck. He had no clothes on but a seaman's waistcoat, a pair of open-kneed linen drawers, and a blue linen shirt; but nothing to direct me so much as to guess what nation he was of. He had nothing in his pockets but two pieces of eight and a tobacco pipe—the last was to me of ten times more value than the first.

It was now calm, and I had a great mind to venture out in my boat to this wreck, not doubting but I might find something on board that might be useful to me. But that did not altogether press me so much as the possibility that there might be yet some living creature on board, whose life I might not only save, but might, by saving that life, comfort my own to the last degree; and this thought clung so to my heart that I could not be quiet night or day, but I must venture out in my boat on board this wreck; and committing the rest to God's providence, I thought the impression was so strong upon my mind that it could not be resisted—that it must come from some invisible direction, and that I should be wanting to myself if I did not go.

Under the power of this impression, I hastened back to my castle, prepared everything for my voyage, took a quantity of bread, a great pot of fresh water, a compass to steer by, a bottle of rum (for I had still a great deal of that left), and a basket of raisins; and thus, loading myself with every-

---

[136] scientists

thing necessary. I went down to my boat, got the water out of her, got her afloat, loaded all my cargo in her, and then went home again for more. My second cargo was a great bag of rice, the umbrella to set up over my head for a shade, another large pot of water, and about two dozen of small loaves, or barley cakes, more than before, with a bottle of goat's milk and a cheese; all which with great labour and sweat I carried to my boat; and praying to God to direct my voyage, I put out, and rowing or paddling the canoe along the shore, came at last to the utmost point of the island on the north-east side. And now I was to launch out into the ocean, and either to venture or not to venture. I looked on the rapid currents which ran constantly on both sides of the island at a distance, and which were very terrible to me from the remembrance of the hazard I had been in before, and my heart began to fail me; for I foresaw that if I was driven into either of those currents, I should be carried a great way out to sea, and perhaps out of my reach or sight of the island again; and that then, as my boat was but small, if any little gale of wind should rise, I should be inevitably lost.

These thoughts so oppressed my mind that I began to give over my enterprise; and having hauled my boat into a little creek on the shore, I stepped out, and sat down upon a rising bit of ground, very pensive and anxious, between fear and desire, about my voyage; when, as I was musing, I could perceive that the tide was turned, and the flood come on; upon which my going was impracticable for so many hours. Upon this, presently it occurred to me that I should go up to the highest piece of ground I could find, and observe, if I could, how the sets of the tide or currents lay when the flood came in, that I might judge whether, if I was driven one way out, I might not expect to be driven another way home, with the same rapidity of the currents. This thought was no sooner in my head than I cast my eye upon a little hill which sufficiently overlooked the sea both ways, and from whence I had a clear view of the currents or sets of the tide, and which way I was to guide myself in my return. Here I found, that as the current of ebb set out close by the south point of the island, so the current of the flood set in close by the shore of the north side; and that I had nothing to do but to keep to the north side of the island in my return, and I should do well enough.

Encouraged by this observation, I resolved the next morning to set out with the first of the tide; and reposing myself for the night in my canoe, under the watch-coat I mentioned, I launched out. I first made a little out to sea, full north, till I began to feel the benefit of the current, which set eastward, and which carried me at a great rate; and yet did not so hurry me as the current on the south side had done before, so as to take from me all government of the boat; but having a strong steerage with my paddle, I went at a great rate directly for the wreck, and in less than two hours I came up to it. It was a dismal sight to look at; the ship, which by its building was

Spanish, stuck fast, jammed in between two rocks. All the stern and quarter of her were beaten to pieces by the sea; and as her forecastle, which stuck in the rocks, had run on with great violence, her mainmast and foremast were brought by the board—that is to say, broken short off; but her bowsprit was sound, and the head and bow appeared firm. When I came close to her, a dog appeared upon her, who, seeing me coming, yelped and cried; and as soon as I called him, jumped into the sea to come to me. I took him into the boat, but found him almost dead with hunger and thirst. I gave him a cake of my bread, and he devoured it like a ravenous wolf that had been starving a fortnight in the snow; I then gave the poor creature some fresh water, with which, if I would have let him, he would have burst himself. After this I went on board; but the first sight I met with was two men drowned in the cook-room, or forecastle of the ship, with their arms fast about one another. I concluded, as is indeed probable, that when the ship struck, it being in a storm, the sea broke so high and so continually over her, that the men were not able to bear it, and were strangled with the constant rushing in of the water, as much as if they had been under water. Besides the dog, there was nothing left in the ship that had life; nor any goods, that I could see, but what were spoiled by the water. There were some casks of liquor, whether wine or brandy I knew not, which lay lower in the hold, and which, the water being ebbed out, I could see; but they were too big to meddle with. I saw several chests, which I believe belonged to some of the seamen; and I got two of them into the boat, without examining what was in them. Had the stern of the ship been fixed, and the forepart broken off, I am persuaded I might have made a good voyage; for by what I found in those two chests I had room to suppose the ship had a great deal of wealth on board; and, if I may guess from the course she steered, she must have been bound from Buenos Ayres, or the Rio de la Plata, in the south part of America, beyond the Brazils to the Havannah, in the Gulf of Mexico, and so perhaps to Spain. She had, no doubt, a great treasure in her, but of no use, at that time, to anybody; and what became of the crew I then knew not.

I found, besides these chests, a little cask full of liquor, of about twenty gallons, which I got into my boat with much difficulty. There were several muskets in the cabin, and a great powder-horn, with about four pounds of powder in it; as for the muskets, I had no occasion for them, so I left them, but took the powder-horn. I took a fire-shovel and tongs, which I wanted extremely, as also two little brass kettles, a copper pot to make chocolate, and a gridiron; and with this cargo, and the dog, I came away, the tide beginning to make home again—and the same evening, about an hour within night, I reached the island again, weary and fatigued to the last degree. I reposed that night in the boat and in the morning I resolved to harbour what I had got in my new cave, and not carry it home to my castle. After refreshing myself, I got all my cargo on shore, and began to examine the particulars. The cask of liquor I found to be a kind of rum, but not such as we had at the Brazils; and, in a word, not at all good; but when I came to open the chests, I found several things of great use to me—for example, I found in one a fine case of bottles, of an extraordinary kind, and filled with cordial waters, fine and very good; the bottles held about three pints each, and were tipped with silver. I found two pots of very good succades, or sweet-meats,[137] so fastened also on the top that the salt-water had not hurt them; and two more of the same, which the water had spoiled. I found some very good shirts, which were very welcome to me; and about a dozen and a half of white linen handkerchiefs and coloured neckcloths; the former were also very welcome, being exceedingly refreshing to wipe my face in a hot day. Besides this, when I came to the till in the chest, I found there three great bags of pieces of eight, which held about eleven hundred pieces in all; and in one of them, wrapped up in a paper, six doubloons of gold, and some small bars or wedges of gold; I suppose they might all weigh near a pound. In the other chest were some clothes, but of little value; but, by the circumstances, it must have belonged to the gunner's mate; though there was no powder in it, except two pounds of fine glazed powder, in three flasks, kept, I suppose, for charging their fowling-pieces on occasion. Upon the whole, I got very little by this voyage that was of any use to me; for, as to the money, I had no manner of occasion for it; it was to me as the dirt under my feet, and I would have given it all for three or four pair of English shoes and stockings, which were things I greatly wanted, but had had none on my feet for many years. I had, indeed, got two pair of shoes now, which I took off the feet of two drowned men whom I saw in the wreck, and I found two pair more in one of the chests, which were very welcome to me; but they were not like our English shoes, either for ease or service, being rather what we call pumps than shoes. I found in this seaman's chest about fifty pieces of eight, in rials, but no gold: I supposed this belonged to a poorer man than the other, which seemed to belong to some officer. Well, however, I lugged this money home to my cave, and laid it up, as I had done that before which I had brought from our own ship; but it was a great pity, as I said, that the other part of this ship had not come to my share: for I am satisfied I might have loaded my canoe several times over with money; and, thought I, if I ever escape to England, it might lie here safe enough till I come again and fetch it.

---

[137] candy

Questions for Review:

1. How long has Robinson Crusoe been on the island? How would you describe his life?

2. Explain this remark by Robinson Crusoe: "How frequently, in the course of our lives, the evil which in itself we seek most to shun, and which, when we are fallen into, is the most dreadful to us, is oftentimes the very means or door of our deliverance, by which alone we can be raised again from the affliction we are fallen into."

3. What does Robinson Crusoe see one day? What repulsive sight does he then encounter? What does he do in response to this?

4. What does he hear one day, and how does he respond? Explain his wish on having heard the sound.

5. What does he find upon sailing out to inspect?

CHAPTER XIV: A DREAM REALISED

Having now brought all my things on shore and secured them, I went back to my boat, and rowed or paddled her along the shore to her old harbour, where I laid her up, and made the best of my way to my old habitation, where I found everything safe and quiet. I began now to repose myself, live after my old fashion, and take care of my family affairs; and for a while I lived easy enough, only that I was more vigilant than I used to be, looked out oftener, and did not go abroad so much; and if at any time I did stir with any freedom, it was always to the east part of the island, where I was pretty well satisfied the savages never came, and where I could go without so many precautions, and such a load of arms and ammunition as I always carried with me if I went the other way. I lived in this condition near two years more; but my unlucky head, that was always to let me know it was born to make my body miserable, was all these two years filled with projects and designs how, if it were possible, I might get away from this island: for sometimes I was for making another voyage to the wreck, though my reason told me that there was nothing left there worth the hazard of my voyage; sometimes for a ramble one way, sometimes another—and I believe verily, if I had had the boat that I went from Sallee in, I should have ventured to sea, bound anywhere, I knew not whither. I have been, in all my circumstances, a memento to those who are touched with the general plague of mankind, whence, for aught I know, one half of their miseries flow: I mean that of not being satisfied with the station wherein God and Nature hath placed them—for, not to look back upon my primitive condition, and the excellent advice of my father, the opposition to which was, as I may call it, my original sin, my subsequent mistakes of the same kind had been the means of my coming into this miserable condition; for had that Providence which so happily seated me at the Brazils as a planter blessed me with confined desires, and I could have been contented to have gone on gradually, I might have been by this time—I mean in the time of my being in this island—one of the most considerable planters in the Brazils—nay, I am persuaded, that by the improvements I had made in that little time I lived there, and the increase I should probably have made if I had remained, I might have been worth a hundred thousand moidores—and what business had I to leave a settled fortune, a well-stocked plantation, improving and increasing, to turn supercargo to Guinea to fetch negroes, when patience and time would have so increased our stock at home, that we could have bought them at our own door from those whose business it was to fetch them? And though it had cost us something more, yet the difference of that price was by no means worth saving at so great a hazard. But as this is usually the fate of young heads, so reflection upon the folly of it is as commonly the exercise of more years, or of the dear-bought experience of time—so it was with me now; and yet so deep had the mistake taken root in my temper, that I could not satisfy myself in my station, but was continually poring upon the means and possibility of my escape from this place; and that I may, with greater pleasure to the reader, bring on the remaining part of my story, it may not be improper to give some account of my first conceptions on the subject of this foolish scheme for my escape, and how, and upon what foundation, I acted.

I am now to be supposed retired into my castle, after my late voyage to the wreck, my frigate laid up and secured under water, as usual, and my condition restored to what it was before: I had more wealth, indeed, than I had before, but was not at all the richer; for I had no more use for it than the Indians of Peru had before the Spaniards came there.

It was one of the nights in the rainy season in March, the four-and-twentieth year of my first setting foot in this island of solitude. I was lying in my bed or hammock, awake, very well in health, had no pain, no distemper, no uneasiness of body, nor any uneasiness of mind more than ordinary, but could by no means close my eyes, that is, so as to sleep; no, not a wink all night long, otherwise than as follows: It is impossible to set down the innumerable crowd of thoughts that whirled through that great thoroughfare of the brain, the memory, in this night's time. I ran over the whole history of my life in miniature, or by abridgment, as I may call it, to my coming to this island, and also of that part of my life since I came to this island. In my reflections upon the state of my case since I came on shore on this island, I was comparing the happy posture of my affairs in the first years of my habitation here, with the life of anxiety, fear, and care which I had lived in ever since I had seen the print of a foot in the sand. Not that I did not believe the savages had frequented the island even all the while, and might have been several hundreds of them at times on shore there; but I had never known it, and was incapable of any apprehensions about it; my satisfaction was perfect, though my danger was the same, and I was as happy in not knowing my danger as if I had never really been exposed to it. This furnished my thoughts with many very profitable reflections, and particularly this one: How infinitely good that Providence is, which has provided, in its government of mankind, such narrow bounds to his sight and knowledge of things; and though he walks in the midst of so many thousand dangers, the sight of which, if discovered to him, would distract his mind and sink his spirits, he is kept serene and calm, by having the events of things hid from his eyes, and knowing nothing of the dangers which surround him.

After these thoughts had for some time entertained me, I came to reflect seriously upon the real danger I had been in for so many years in this very island, and how I had walked about in the greatest security, and with all possible tranquillity, even when perhaps nothing but the brow of a hill, a great tree, or the casual approach of night, had been between me and the worst kind of destruction—viz. that of falling into the hands of cannibals and savages, who would have seized on me with the same view as I would on a goat or turtle; and have thought it no more crime to kill and devour me than I did of a pigeon or a curlew. I would unjustly slander myself if I should say I was not sincerely thankful to my great Preserver, to whose singular protection I acknowledged, with great humanity, all these unknown deliverances were due, and without which I must inevitably have fallen into their merciless hands.

When these thoughts were over, my head was for some time taken up in considering the nature of these wretched creatures, I mean the savages, and how it came to pass in the world that the wise Governor of all things should give up any of His creatures to such inhumanity—nay, to something so much below even brutality itself—as to devour its own kind: but as this ended in some (at that time) fruitless speculations, it occurred to me to inquire what part of the world these wretches lived in? how far off the coast was from whence they came? what they ventured over so far from home for? what kind of boats they had? and why I might not order myself and my business so that I might be able to go over thither, as they were to come to me?

I never so much as troubled myself to consider what I should do with myself when I went thither; what would become of me if I fell into the hands of these savages; or how I should escape them if they attacked me; no, nor so much as how it was possible for me to reach the coast, and not to be attacked by some or other of them, without any possibility of delivering myself: and if I should not fall into their hands, what I should do for provision, or whither I should bend my course: none of these thoughts, I say, so much as came in my way; but my mind was wholly bent upon the notion of my passing over in my boat to the mainland. I looked upon my present condition as the most miserable that could possibly be; that I was not able to throw myself into anything but death, that could be called worse; and if I reached the shore of the main I might perhaps meet with relief, or I might coast along, as I did on the African shore, till I came to some inhabited country, and where I might find some relief; and after all, perhaps I might fall in with some Christian ship that might take me in: and if the worst came to the worst, I could but die, which would put an end to all these miseries at once. Pray note, all this was the fruit of a disturbed mind, an impatient temper, made desperate, as it were, by the long continuance of my troubles, and the disappointments I had met in the wreck I had been on board of, and where I had been so near obtaining what I so earnestly longed for—somebody to speak to, and to learn some knowledge from them of the place where I was, and of the probable means of my deliverance. I was agitated wholly by these thoughts; all my calm of mind, in my resignation to Providence, and waiting the issue of the dispositions of Heaven, seemed to be suspended; and I had as it were no power to turn my thoughts to anything but to the project of a voyage to the main, which came upon me with such force, and such an impetuosity of desire, that it was not to be resisted.

When this had agitated my thoughts for two hours or more, with such violence that it set my very blood into a ferment, and my pulse beat as if I had been in a fever, merely with the extraordinary fervour of my mind about it, Nature—as if I had been fatigued and exhausted with the very thoughts of it—threw me into a sound sleep. One would have thought I should have dreamed of it, but I did not, nor of anything relating to it, but I dreamed that as I was going out in the morning as usual from my castle, I saw upon the shore two canoes and eleven savages coming to land, and that they brought with them another savage whom they were going to kill in order to eat him; when, on a sudden, the savage that they were going to kill jumped away, and ran for his life; and I thought in my sleep that he came running into my little thick grove before my fortification, to hide himself; and that I seeing him alone, and not perceiving that the others sought him that way, showed myself to him, and smiling upon him, encouraged him: that he kneeled down to me, seeming to pray me to assist him; upon which I showed him my ladder, made him go up, and carried him into my cave, and he became my servant; and that as soon as I had got this man, I said to myself, "Now I may certainly venture to the mainland, for this fellow will serve me as a pilot, and will tell me what to do, and whither to go for provisions, and whither not to go for fear of being devoured; what places to venture into, and what to shun." I waked with this thought; and was under such inexpressible impressions of joy at the prospect of my escape in my dream, that the disappointments which I felt upon coming to myself, and finding that it was no more than a dream, were equally extravagant the other way, and threw me into a very great dejection of spirits.

Upon this, however, I made this conclusion: that my only way to go about to attempt an escape was, to endeavour to get a savage into my possession: and, if possible, it should be one of their prisoners, whom they had condemned to be eaten, and should bring hither to kill. But these thoughts still were attended with this difficulty: that it was impossible to effect this without attacking a whole caravan of them, and killing them all; and this was not only a very desperate attempt, and might miscarry, but, on the other hand, I had greatly scrupled the lawfulness of it to myself; and my heart trembled at the thoughts of shedding so much blood, though it was for my deliverance. I need not repeat the arguments which occurred to me against this, they being the same mentioned before; but though I had other reasons to offer now—viz. that those men were enemies to my life, and would devour me if they could; that it was self-preservation, in the highest degree, to deliver myself from this death of a life, and was acting in my own defence as much as if they were actually assaulting me, and the like; I say though these things argued for it, yet the thoughts of shedding human blood for my deliverance were very terrible to me, and such as I could by no means reconcile myself to for a great while. However, at last, after many secret disputes with myself, and after great perplexities about it (for all these arguments, one way and another, struggled in my head a long time), the eager prevailing desire of deliverance at length mastered all the rest; and I resolved, if possible, to get one of these savages into my hands, cost what it would. My next thing was to contrive how to do it, and this, indeed, was very difficult to resolve on; but as I could pitch upon no probable means for it, so I resolved to put myself upon the watch, to see them when they came on shore, and leave the rest to the event; taking such measures as the opportunity should present, let what would be.

With these resolutions in my thoughts, I set myself upon the scout as often as possible, and indeed so often that I was heartily tired of it; for it was above a year and a half that I waited; and for great part of that time went out to the west end, and to the south-west corner of the island almost every day, to look for canoes, but none appeared. This was very discouraging, and began to trouble me much, though I cannot say that it did in this case (as it had done some time before) wear off the edge of my desire to the thing; but the longer it seemed to be delayed, the more eager I was for it: in a word, I was not at first so careful to shun the sight of these savages, and avoid being seen by them, as I was now eager to be upon them. Besides, I fancied myself able to manage one, nay, two or three savages, if I had them, so as to make them entirely slaves to me, to do whatever I should direct them, and to prevent their being able at any time to do me any hurt. It was a great while that I pleased myself with this affair; but nothing still presented itself; all my fancies and schemes came to nothing, for no savages came near me for a great while.

About a year and a half after I entertained these notions (and by long musing had, as it were, resolved them all into nothing, for want of an occasion to put them into execution), I was surprised one morning by seeing no less than five canoes all on shore together on my side the island, and the people who belonged to them all landed and out of my sight. The number of them broke all my measures; for seeing so many, and knowing that they always came four or six, or sometimes more in a boat, I could not tell what to think of it, or how to take my measures to attack twenty or thirty men single-handed; so lay still in my castle, perplexed and discomforted. However, I put myself into the same position for an attack that I had formerly provided, and was just ready for action, if anything had presented. Having waited a good while, listening to hear if they made any noise, at length, being very impatient, I set my guns at the foot of my ladder, and clambered up to the top of the hill, by my two stages, as usual; standing so, however, that my head did not appear above the hill, so that they could not perceive me by any means. Here I observed, by the help of my perspective glass, that they were no less than thirty in number; that they had a fire kindled, and that they had meat dressed. How they had cooked it I knew not, or what it was; but they were all dancing, in I know not how many barbarous gestures and figures, their own way, round the fire.

While I was thus looking on them, I perceived, by my perspective, two miserable wretches dragged from the boats, where, it seems, they were laid by, and were now brought out for the slaughter. I perceived one of them immediately fall; being knocked down, I suppose, with a club or wooden sword, for that was their way; and two or three others were at work immediately, cutting him open for their cookery, while the other victim was left standing by himself, till they should be ready for him. In that very moment this poor wretch, seeing himself a little at liberty and unbound, Nature inspired him with hopes of life, and he started away from them, and ran with incredible swiftness along the sands, directly towards me; I mean towards that part of the coast where my habitation was. I was dreadfully frightened, I must acknowledge, when I perceived him run my way; and especially when, as I thought, I saw him pursued by the whole body: and now I expected that part of my dream was coming to pass, and that he would certainly take shelter in my grove; but I could not depend, by any means, upon my dream, that the other savages would not pursue him thither and find him there. However, I kept my station, and my spirits began to recover when I found that there was not above three men that followed him; and still more was I encouraged, when I found that he outstripped them exceedingly in running, and gained ground on them; so that, if he could but hold out for half-an-hour, I saw easily he would fairly get away from them all.

There was between them and my castle the creek, which I mentioned often in the first part of my story, where I landed my cargoes out of the ship; and this I saw plainly he must necessarily swim over, or the poor wretch would be taken there; but when the savage escaping came thither, he made nothing of it, though the tide was then up; but plunging in, swam through in about thirty strokes, or thereabouts, landed, and ran with exceeding strength and swiftness. When the three persons came to the creek, I found that two of them could swim, but the third could not, and that, standing on the other side, he looked at the others, but went no farther, and soon after went softly back again; which, as it happened, was very well for him in the end. I observed that the two who swam were yet more than twice as strong swimming over the creek as the fellow was that fled from them. It came very warmly upon my thoughts, and indeed irresistibly, that now was the time to get me a servant, and, perhaps, a companion or assistant; and that I was plainly called by Providence to save this poor creature's life. I immediately ran down the ladders with all possible expedition, fetched my two guns, for they were both at the foot of the ladders, as I observed before, and getting up again with the same haste to the top of the hill, I crossed towards the sea; and having a very short cut, and all down hill, placed myself in the way between the pursuers and the pursued, hallowing aloud to him that fled, who, looking back, was at first perhaps as much frightened at me as at them; but I beckoned with my hand to him to come back; and, in the meantime, I slowly advanced towards the two that followed; then rushing at once upon the foremost, I knocked him down with the stock of my piece. I was loath to fire, because I would not have the rest hear; though, at that distance, it would not have been easily heard, and being out of sight of the smoke, too, they would not have known what to make of it. Having knocked this fellow down, the other who pursued him stopped, as if he had been frightened, and I advanced towards him: but as I came nearer, I perceived presently he had a bow and arrow, and was fitting it to shoot at me: so I was then obliged to shoot at him first, which I did, and killed him at the first shot. The poor savage who fled, but had stopped, though he saw both his enemies fallen and killed, as he thought, yet was so frightened with the fire and noise of my piece that he stood stock still, and neither came forward nor went backward, though he seemed rather inclined still to fly than to come on. I hallooed again to him, and made signs to come forward, which he easily understood, and came a little way; then stopped again, and then a little farther, and stopped again; and I could then perceive that he stood trembling, as if he had been taken prisoner, and had just been to be killed, as his two enemies were. I beckoned to him again to come to me, and gave him all the signs of encouragement that I could think of; and he came nearer and nearer, kneeling down every ten or twelve steps, in token of acknowledgment for saving his life. I smiled at him, and looked pleasantly, and beckoned to him to come still nearer; at length he came close to me; and then he kneeled down again, kissed the ground, and laid his head upon the ground, and taking me by the foot, set my foot upon his head; this, it seems, was in token of swearing to be my slave for ever. I took him up and made much of him, and encouraged him all I could. But there was more work to do yet; for I perceived the savage whom I had knocked down was not killed, but stunned with the blow, and began to come to himself: so I pointed to him, and showed him the savage, that he was not dead; upon this he spoke some words to me, and though I could not understand them, yet I thought they were pleasant to hear; for they were the first sound of a man's voice that I had heard, my own excepted, for above twenty-five years. But there was no time for such reflections now; the savage who was knocked down recovered himself so far as to sit up upon the ground, and I perceived that my savage began to be afraid; but when I saw that, I presented my other piece at the man, as if I would shoot him: upon this my savage, for so I call him now, made a motion to me to lend him my sword, which hung naked in a belt by my side, which I did. He no sooner had it, but he runs to his enemy, and at one blow cut off his head so cleverly, no executioner in Germany could have done it sooner or better; which I thought very strange for one who, I had reason to believe, never saw a sword in his life before, except their own wooden swords: however, it seems, as I learned afterwards, they make their wooden swords so sharp, so heavy, and the wood is so hard, that they will even cut off heads with them, ay, and arms, and that at one blow, too. When he had done this, he comes laughing to me in sign of triumph, and brought me the sword again, and with abundance of gestures which I did not understand, laid it down, with the head of the savage that he had killed, just before me. But that which astonished him most was to know how I killed the other Indian so far off; so, pointing to him, he made signs to me to let him go to him; and I bade him go, as well as I could. When he came to him, he stood like one amazed, looking at him, turning him first on one side, then on the other; looked at the wound the bullet had made, which it seems was just in his breast, where it had made a hole, and no great quantity of blood had followed; but he had bled inwardly, for he was quite dead. He took up his bow and arrows, and came back; so I turned to go away, and beckoned him to follow me, making signs to him that more might come after them. Upon this he made signs to me that he should bury them with sand, that they might not be seen by the rest, if they followed; and so I made signs to him again to do so. He fell to work; and in an instant he had scraped a hole in the sand with his hands big enough to bury the first in, and then dragged him into it, and covered him; and did so by the other also; I believe he had him buried them both in a quarter of an hour. Then, calling away, I carried him, not to my castle, but quite away to my cave, on the farther part of the island: so I did not let my dream come to pass in that part, that he came into my grove for shelter. Here I gave him bread and a bunch of raisins to eat, and a draught of water, which I found he was indeed in great distress for, from his running: and having refreshed him, I made signs for him to go and lie down to sleep, showing him a place where I had laid some rice-straw, and a blanket upon it, which I used to sleep upon myself sometimes; so the poor creature lay down, and went to sleep.

He was a comely, handsome fellow, perfectly well made, with straight, strong limbs, not too large; tall, and well-shaped; and, as I reckon, about twenty-six years of age. He had a very good countenance, not a fierce and surly aspect, but seemed to have something very manly in his face; and yet he had all the sweetness and softness of a European in his countenance, too, especially when he smiled. His hair was long and black, not curled like wool; his forehead very high and large; and a great vivacity and sparkling sharpness in his eyes. The colour of his skin was not quite black, but very tawny; and yet not an ugly, yellow, nauseous tawny, as the Brazilians and Virginians, and other natives of America are, but of a bright kind of a dun olive-colour, that had in it something very agreeable, though not very easy to describe. His face was round and plump; his nose small, not flat, like the negroes; a very good mouth, thin lips, and his fine teeth well set, and as white as ivory.

After he had slumbered, rather than slept, about half-an-hour, he awoke again, and came out of the cave to me: for I had been milking my goats which I had in the enclosure just by: when he espied me he came running to me, laying himself down again upon the ground, with all the possible signs of an humble, thankful disposition, making a great many antic gestures to show it. At last he lays his head flat upon the ground, close to my foot, and sets my other foot upon his head, as he had done before; and after this made all the signs to me of subjection, servitude, and submission imaginable, to let me know how he would serve me so long as he lived. I understood him in many things, and let him know I was very well pleased with him. In a little time I began to speak to him; and teach him to speak to me: and first, I let him know his name should be Friday, which was the day I saved his life: I called him so for the memory of the time. I likewise taught him to say Master; and then let him know that was to be my name: I likewise taught him to say Yes and No and to know the meaning of them. I gave him some milk in an earthen pot, and let him see me drink it before him, and sop my bread in it; and gave him a cake of bread to do the

like, which he quickly complied with, and made signs that it was very good for him. I kept there with him all that night; but as soon as it was day I beckoned to him to come with me, and let him know I would give him some clothes; at which he seemed very glad, for he was stark naked. As we went by the place where he had buried the two men, he pointed exactly to the place, and showed me the marks that he had made to find them again, making signs to me that we should dig them up again and eat them. At this I appeared very angry, expressed my abhorrence of it, made as if I would vomit at the thoughts of it, and beckoned with my hand to him to come away, which he did immediately, with great submission. I then led him up to the top of the hill, to see if his enemies were gone; and pulling out my glass I looked, and saw plainly the place where they had been, but no appearance of them or their canoes; so that it was plain they were gone, and had left their two comrades behind them, without any search after them.

But I was not content with this discovery; but having now more courage, and consequently more curiosity, I took my man Friday with me, giving him the sword in his hand, with the bow and arrows at his back, which I found he could use very dexterously, making him carry one gun for me, and I two for myself; and away we marched to the place where these creatures had been; for I had a mind now to get some further intelligence of them. When I came to the place my very blood ran chill in my veins, and my heart sunk within me, at the horror of the spectacle; indeed, it was a dreadful sight, at least it was so to me, though Friday made nothing of it. The place was covered with human bones, the ground dyed with their blood, and great pieces of flesh left here and there, half-eaten, mangled, and scorched; and, in short, all the tokens of the triumphant feast they had been making there, after a victory over their enemies. I saw three skulls, five hands, and the bones of three or four legs and feet, and abundance of other parts of the bodies; and Friday, by his signs, made me understand that they brought over four prisoners to feast upon; that three of them were eaten up, and that he, pointing to himself, was the fourth; that there had been a great battle between them and their next king, of whose subjects, it seems, he had been one, and that they had taken a great number of prisoners; all which were carried to several places by those who had taken them in the fight, in order to feast upon them, as was done here by these wretches upon those they brought hither.

I caused Friday to gather all the skulls, bones, flesh, and whatever remained, and lay them together in a heap, and make a great fire upon it, and burn them all to ashes. I found Friday had still a hankering stomach after some of the flesh, and was still a cannibal in his nature; but I showed so much abhorrence at the very thoughts of it, and at the least appearance of it, that he durst not discover it: for I had, by some means, let him know that I would kill him if he offered it.

When he had done this, we came back to our castle; and there I fell to work for my man Friday; and first of all, I gave him a pair of linen drawers, which I had out of the poor gunner's chest I mentioned, which I found in the wreck, and which, with a little alteration, fitted him very well; and then I made him a jerkin of goat's skin, as well as my skill would allow (for I was now grown a tolerably good tailor); and I gave him a cap which I made of hare's skin, very convenient, and fashionable enough; and thus he was clothed, for the present, tolerably well, and was mighty well pleased to see himself almost as well clothed as his master. It is true he went awkwardly in these clothes at first: wearing the drawers was very awkward to him, and the sleeves of the waist-coat galled his shoulders and the inside of his arms; but a little easing them where he complained they hurt him, and using himself to them, he took to them at length very well.

The next day, after I came home to my hutch with him, I began to consider where I should lodge him: and that I might do well for him and yet be perfectly easy myself, I made a little tent for him in the vacant place between my two fortifications, in the inside of the last, and in the outside of the first. As there was a door or entrance there into my cave, I made a formal framed door-case, and a door to it, of boards, and set it up in the passage, a little within the entrance; and, causing the door to open in the inside, I barred it up in the night, taking in my ladders, too; so that Friday could no way come at me in the inside of my innermost wall, without making so much noise in getting over that it must needs awaken me; for my first wall had now a complete roof over it of long poles, covering all my tent, and leaning up to the side of the hill; which was again laid across with smaller sticks, instead of laths, and then thatched over a great thickness with the rice-straw, which was strong, like reeds; and at the hole or place which was left to go in or out by the ladder I had placed a kind of trap-door, which, if it had been attempted on the outside, would not have opened at all, but would have fallen down and made a great noise—as to weapons, I took them all into my side every night. But I needed none of all this precaution; for never man had a more faithful, loving, sincere servant than Friday was to me: without passions, sullenness, or designs, perfectly obliged and engaged; his very affections were tied to me, like those of a child to a father; and I daresay he would have sacrificed his life to save mine upon any occasion whatsoever—the many testimonies he gave me of this put it out of doubt, and soon convinced me that I needed to use no precautions for my safety on his account.

This frequently gave me occasion to observe, and that with wonder, that however it had pleased God in His providence, and in the government of the works of His hands, to take from so great a part of the world of His creatures the best uses to which their faculties and the powers of their souls are adapted, yet that He has bestowed upon them the same powers, the same reason, the same affections, the same sentiments of kindness and obligation, the same passions and resentments of wrongs, the same sense of gratitude, sincerity, fidelity, and all the capacities of doing good and receiving good that He has given to us; and that when He pleases to offer them occasions of exerting these, they are as ready, nay, more ready, to apply them to the right uses for which they were bestowed than we are. This made me very melancholy sometimes, in reflecting, as the several occasions presented, how mean a use we make of all these, even though we have these powers enlightened by the great lamp of instruction, the Spirit of God, and by the knowledge of His word added to our understanding; and why it has pleased God to hide the like saving knowledge from so many millions of souls, who, if I might judge by this poor savage, would make a much better use of it than we did. From hence I sometimes was led too far, to invade the sovereignty of Providence, and, as it were, arraign the justice of so arbitrary a disposition of things, that should hide that sight from some, and reveal it to others, and yet expect a like duty from both; but I shut it up, and checked my thoughts with this conclusion: first, that we did not know by what light and law these should be condemned; but that as God was necessarily, and by the nature of His being, infinitely holy and just, so it could not be, but if these creatures were all sentenced to absence from Himself, it was on account of sinning against that light which, as the Scripture says, was a law to themselves, and by such rules as their consciences would acknowledge to be just, though the foundation was not discovered to us;[138] and secondly, that still as we all are the clay in the hand of the potter, no vessel could say to him, "Why hast thou formed me thus?"

But to return to my new companion. I was greatly delighted with him, and made it my business to teach him everything that was proper to make him useful, handy, and helpful; but especially to make him speak, and understand me when I spoke; and he was the aptest scholar that ever was; and particularly was so merry, so constantly diligent, and so pleased when he could but understand me, or make me understand him, that it was very pleasant for me to talk to him. Now my life began to be so easy that I began to say to myself that could I but have been safe from more savages, I cared not if I was never to remove from the place where I lived.

Questions for Review:

1. List several thoughts that preoccupy Robinson Crusoe's mind. What troubles him? What does he purpose to do?

2. Describe the scene a year and a half later.

3. Describe Friday.

4. What precautions does Robinson Crusoe take at first? Why does he soon drop them?

5. Explain Robinson Crusoe's thoughts about Friday, in comparison to many others in "Christian" nations. What things does he teach him?

---

[138] See Romans 2:12-16.

CHAPTER XV: FRIDAY'S EDUCATION

After I had been two or three days returned to my castle, I thought that, in order to bring Friday off from his horrid way of feeding, and from the relish of a cannibal's stomach, I ought to let him taste other flesh; so I took him out with me one morning to the woods. I went, indeed, intending to kill a kid out of my own flock; and bring it home and dress it; but as I was going I saw a she-goat lying down in the shade, and two young kids sitting by her. I catched hold of Friday. "Hold," said I, "stand still;" and made signs to him not to stir: immediately I presented my piece, shot, and killed one of the kids. The poor creature, who had at a distance, indeed, seen me kill the savage, his enemy, but did not know, nor could imagine how it was done, was sensibly surprised, trembled, and shook, and looked so amazed that I thought he would have sunk down. He did not see the kid I shot at, or perceive I had killed it, but ripped up his waistcoat to feel whether he was not wounded; and, as I found presently, thought I was resolved to kill him: for he came and kneeled down to me, and embracing my knees, said a great many things I did not understand; but I could easily see the meaning was to pray me not to kill him.

I soon found a way to convince him that I would do him no harm; and taking him up by the hand, laughed at him, and pointing to the kid which I had killed, beckoned to him to run and fetch it, which he did: and while he was wondering, and looking to see how the creature was killed, I loaded my gun again. By-and-by I saw a great fowl, like a hawk, sitting upon a tree within shot; so, to let Friday understand a little what I would do, I called him to me again, pointed at the fowl, which was indeed a parrot, though I thought it had been a hawk; I say, pointing to the parrot, and to my gun, and to the ground under the parrot, to let him see I would make it fall, I made him understand that I would shoot and kill that bird; accordingly, I fired, and bade him look, and immediately he saw the parrot fall. He stood like one frightened again, notwithstanding all I had said to him; and I found he was the more amazed, because he did not see me put anything into the gun, but thought that there must be some wonderful fund of death and destruction in that thing, able to kill man, beast, bird, or anything near or far off; and the astonishment this created in him was such as could not wear off for a long time; and I believe, if I would have let him, he would have worshipped me and my gun. As for the gun itself, he would not so much as touch it for several days after; but he would speak to it and talk to it, as if it had answered him, when he was by himself; which, as I afterwards learned of him, was to desire it not to kill him. Well, after his astonishment was a little over at this, I pointed to him to run and fetch the bird I had shot, which he did, but stayed some time; for the parrot, not being quite dead, had fluttered away a good distance from the place where she fell: however, he found her, took her up, and brought her to me; and as I had perceived his ignorance about the gun before, I took this advantage to charge the gun again, and not to let him see me do it, that I might be ready for any other mark that might present; but nothing more offered at that time: so I brought home the kid, and the same evening I took the skin off, and cut it out as well as I could; and having a pot fit for that purpose, I boiled or stewed some of the flesh, and made some very good broth. After I had begun to eat some I gave some to my man, who seemed very glad of it, and liked it very well; but that which was strangest to him was to see me eat salt with it. He made a sign to me that the salt was not good to eat; and putting a little into his own mouth, he seemed to nauseate it, and would spit and sputter at it, washing his mouth with fresh water after it: on the other hand, I took some meat into my mouth without salt, and I pretended to spit and sputter for want of salt, as much as he had done at the salt; but it would not do; he would never care for salt with meat or in his broth; at least, not for a great while, and then but a very little.

Having thus fed him with boiled meat and broth, I was resolved to feast him the next day by roasting a piece of the kid: this I did by hanging it before the fire on a string, as I had seen many people do in England, setting two poles up, one on each side of the fire, and one across the top, and tying the string to the cross stick, letting the meat turn continually. This Friday admired very much; but when he came to taste the flesh, he took so many ways to tell me how well he liked it, that I could not but understand him: and at last he told me, as well as he could, he would never eat man's flesh any more, which I was very glad to hear.

The next day I set him to work beating some corn out, and sifting it in the manner I used to do, as I observed before; and he soon understood how to do it as well as I, especially after he had seen what the meaning of it was, and that it was to make bread of; for after that I let him see me make my bread, and bake it too; and in a little time Friday was able to do all the work for me as well as I could do it myself.

I began now to consider, that having two mouths to feed instead of one, I must provide more ground for my harvest, and plant a larger quantity of corn than I used to do; so I marked out a larger piece of land, and began the fence in the same manner as before, in which Friday worked not only very willingly and very hard, but did it very cheerfully: and I told him what it was for; that it was for corn to make more bread, because he was now with me, and that I might have enough for him and myself too. He appeared very sensible of that part, and let me know that he thought I had much more labour upon me on his account than I had for myself; and that he would work the harder for me if I would tell him what to do.

This was the pleasantest year of all the life I led in this place. Friday began to talk pretty well, and understand the names of almost everything I had occasion to call for, and of every place I had to send him to, and talked a great deal to me; so that, in short, I began now to have some use for my tongue again, which, indeed, I had very little occasion for before. Besides the pleasure of talking to him, I had a singular satisfaction in the fellow himself: his simple, unfeigned honesty appeared to me more and more every day, and I began really to love the creature; and on his side I believe he loved me more than it was possible for him ever to love anything before.

I had a mind once to try if he had any inclination for his own country again; and having taught him English so well that he could answer me almost any question, I asked him whether the nation that he belonged to never conquered in battle? At which he smiled, and said—"Yes, yes, we always fight the better;" that is, he meant always get the better in fight; and so we began the following discourse:—

Master.—You always fight the better; how came you to be taken prisoner, then, Friday?

Friday.—My nation beat much for all that.

Master.—How beat? If your nation beat them, how came you to be taken?

Friday.—They more many than my nation, in the place where me was; they take one, two, three, and me: my nation over-beat them in the yonder place, where me no was; there my nation take one, two, great thousand.

Master.—But why did not your side recover you from the hands of your enemies, then?

Friday.—They run, one, two, three, and me, and make go in the canoe; my nation have no canoe that time.

Master.—Well, Friday, and what does your nation do with the men they take? Do they carry them away and eat them, as these did?

Friday.—Yes, my nation eat mans too; eat all up.

Master.—Where do they carry them?

Friday.—Go to other place, where they think.

Master.—Do they come hither?

Friday.—Yes, yes, they come hither; come other else place.

Master.—Have you been here with them?

Friday.—Yes, I have been here (points to the NW. side of the island, which, it seems, was their side).

By this I understood that my man Friday had formerly been among the savages who used to come on shore on the farther part of the island, on the same man-eating occasions he was now brought for; and some time after, when I took the courage to carry him to that side, being the same I formerly mentioned, he presently knew the place, and told me he was there once, when they ate up twenty men, two women, and one child; he could not tell twenty in English, but he numbered them by laying so many stones in a row, and pointing to me to tell them over.

I have told this passage, because it introduces what follows: that after this discourse I had with him, I asked him how far it was from our island to the shore, and whether the canoes were not often lost. He told me there was no danger, no canoes ever lost: but that after a little way out to sea, there was a current and wind, always one way in the morning, the other in the afternoon. This I understood to be no more than the sets of the tide, as going out or coming in; but I afterwards understood it was occasioned by the great draft and reflux of the mighty river Orinoco, in the mouth or gulf of which river, as I found afterwards, our island lay; and that this land, which I perceived to be W. and NW., was the great island Trinidad, on the north point of the mouth of the river. I asked Friday a thousand questions about the country, the inhabitants, the sea, the coast, and what nations were near; he told me all he knew with the greatest openness imaginable. I asked him the names of the several nations of his sort of people, but could get no other name than Caribs; from whence I easily understood that these were the Caribbees, which our maps place on the part of America which reaches from the mouth of the river Orinoco to Guiana, and onwards to St. Martha. He told me that up a great way beyond the moon, that was beyond the setting of the moon, which must be west from their country, there dwelt white bearded men, like me, and pointed to my great whiskers, which I mentioned before; and that they had killed much mans, that was his word: by all which I understood he meant the Spaniards, whose cruelties in America had been spread over the whole country, and were remembered by all the nations from father to son.

I inquired if he could tell me how I might go from this island, and get among those white men. He told me, "Yes, yes, you may go in two canoe." I could not understand what he meant, or make him describe to me what he meant by two canoe, till at last, with great difficulty, I found he meant it must be in a large boat, as big as two canoes. This part of Friday's discourse I began to relish very well; and from this time I entertained some hopes that, one time or other, I might find an opportunity to make my escape from this place, and that this poor savage might be a means to help me.

During the long time that Friday had now been with me, and that he began to speak to me, and understand me, I was not wanting to lay a foundation of religious knowledge in his mind; particularly I asked him one time, who made him. The creature did not understand me at all, but thought I had asked who was his father—but I took it up by another handle, and asked him who made the sea, the ground we walked on, and the hills and woods. He told me, "It was one Benamuckee, that lived beyond all;" he could describe nothing of this great person, but that he was very old, "much older," he said, "than the sea or land, than the moon or the stars." I asked him then, if this old person had made all things, why did not all things worship him? He looked very grave, and, with a perfect look of innocence, said, "All things say O to him." I asked him if the people who die in his country went away anywhere? He said, "Yes; they all went to Benamuckee." Then I asked him whether those they eat up went thither too. He said, "Yes."

From these things, I began to instruct him in the knowledge of the true God; I told him that the great Maker of all things lived up there, pointing up towards heaven; that He governed the world by the same power and providence by which He made it; that He was omnipotent, and could do everything for us, give everything to us, take everything from us; and thus, by degrees, I opened his eyes. He listened with great attention, and received with pleasure the notion of Jesus Christ being sent to redeem us; and of the manner of making our prayers to God, and His being able to hear us, even in heaven. He told me one day, that if our God could hear us, up beyond the sun, he must needs be a greater God than their Benamuckee, who lived but a little way off, and yet could not hear till they went up to the great mountains where he dwelt to speak to them. I asked him if ever he went thither to speak to him. He said, "No; they never went that were young men; none went thither but the old men," whom he called their Oowokakee; that is, as I made him explain to me, their religious, or clergy; and that they went to say O (so he called saying prayers), and then came back and told them what Benamuckee said. By this I observed, that there is priestcraft even among the most blinded, ignorant pagans in the world; and the policy of making a secret of religion, in order to preserve the veneration of the people to the clergy, not only to be found in the Roman, but, perhaps, among all religions in the world, even among the most brutish and barbarous savages.

I endeavoured to clear up this fraud to my man Friday; and told him that the pretence of their old men going up to the mountains to say O to their god Benamuckee was a cheat; and their bringing word from thence what he said was much more so; that if they met with any answer, or spake with any one there, it must be with an evil spirit; and then I entered into a long discourse with him about the devil, the origin of him, his rebellion against God, his enmity to man, the reason of it, his setting himself up in the dark parts of the world to be worshipped instead of God, and as God, and the many stratagems he made use of to delude mankind to their ruin; how he had a secret access to our passions and to our affections, and to adapt his snares to our inclinations, so as to cause us even to be our own tempters, and run upon our destruction by our own choice.

I found it was not so easy to imprint right notions in his mind about the devil as it was about the being of a God. Nature assisted all my arguments to evidence to him even the necessity of a great First Cause, an overruling, governing Power, a secret directing Providence, and of the equity and justice of paying homage to Him that made us, and the like; but there appeared nothing of this kind in the notion of an evil spirit, of his origin, his being, his nature, and above all, of his inclination to do evil, and to draw us in to do so too; and the poor creature puzzled me once in such a manner, by a question merely natural and innocent, that I scarce knew what to say to him. I had been talking a great deal to him of the power of God, His omnipotence, His aversion to sin, His being a consuming fire to the workers of iniquity; how, as He had made us all, He could destroy us and all the world in a moment; and he listened with great seriousness to me all the while. After this I had been telling him how the devil was God's enemy in the hearts of men, and used all his malice and skill to defeat the good designs of Providence, and to ruin the kingdom of Christ in the world, and the like. "Well," says Friday, "but you say God is so strong, so great; is He not much strong, much might as the devil?" "Yes, yes," says I, "Friday; God is stronger than the devil—God is above the devil, and therefore we pray to God to tread him down under our feet,[139] and enable us to resist his temptations and quench his fiery darts."[140] "But," says he again, "if God much stronger, much might as the wicked devil, why God no kill the devil, so make him no

---

[139] "And the God of peace shall bruise Satan under your feet shortly" (Romans 16:20).

[140] "Wherefore take unto you the whole armour of God, that ye may be able to withstand in the evil day, and having done all, to stand. Stand therefore, having your loins girt about with truth, and having on the breastplate of righteousness; And your feet shod with the preparation of the gospel of peace; Above all, taking the shield of faith, wherewith ye shall be able to quench all the fiery darts of the wicked" (Ephesians 6:13-16).

more do wicked?" I was strangely surprised at this question; and, after all, though I was now an old man, yet I was but a young doctor, and ill qualified for a casuist or a solver of difficulties; and at first I could not tell what to say; so I pretended not to hear him, and asked him what he said; but he was too earnest for an answer to forget his question, so that he repeated it in the very same broken words as above. By this time I had recovered myself a little, and I said, "God will at last punish him severely; he is reserved for the judgment, and is to be cast into the bottomless pit, to dwell with everlasting fire."[141] This did not satisfy Friday; but he returns upon me, repeating my words, "'Reserve at last!' me no understand—but why not kill the devil now; not kill great ago?" "You may as well ask me," said I, "why God does not kill you or me, when we do wicked things here that offend Him—we are preserved to repent and be pardoned." He mused some time on this. "Well, well," says he, mighty affectionately, "that well—so you, I, devil, all wicked, all preserve, repent, God pardon all." Here I was run down again by him to the last degree; and it was a testimony to me, how the mere notions of nature, though they will guide reasonable creatures to the knowledge of a God, and of a worship or homage due to the supreme being of God, as the consequence of our nature, yet nothing but divine revelation can form the knowledge of Jesus Christ, and of redemption purchased for us; of a Mediator of the new covenant, and of an Intercessor at the footstool of God's throne; I say, nothing but a revelation from Heaven can form these in the soul; and that, therefore, the gospel of our Lord and Saviour Jesus Christ, I mean the Word of God, and the Spirit of God, promised for the guide and sanctifier of His people, are the absolutely necessary instructors of the souls of men in the saving knowledge of God and the means of salvation.

I therefore diverted the present discourse between me and my man, rising up hastily, as upon some sudden occasion of going out; then sending him for something a good way off, I seriously prayed to God that He would enable me to instruct savingly this poor savage; assisting, by His Spirit, the heart of the poor ignorant creature to receive the light of the knowledge of God in Christ, reconciling him to Himself, and would guide me so to speak to him from the Word of God that his conscience might be convinced, his eyes opened, and his soul saved. When he came again to me, I entered into a long discourse with him upon the subject of the redemption of man by the Saviour of the world, and of the doctrine of the gospel preached from Heaven, viz. of repentance towards God, and faith in our blessed Lord Jesus. I then explained to him as well as I could why our blessed Redeemer took not on Him the nature of angels but the seed of Abraham; and how, for

---

[141] See 2 Peter 2:4 and Matthew 25:40-41.

that reason, the fallen angels had no share in the redemption; that He came only to the lost sheep of the house of Israel, and the like.

I had, God knows, more sincerity than knowledge in all the methods I took for this poor creature's instruction, and must acknowledge, what I believe all that act upon the same principle will find, that in laying things open to him, I really informed and instructed myself in many things that either I did not know or had not fully considered before, but which occurred naturally to my mind upon searching into them, for the information of this poor savage; and I had more affection in my inquiry after things upon this occasion than ever I felt before: so that, whether this poor wild wretch was better for me or no, I had great reason to be thankful that ever he came to me; my grief sat lighter, upon me; my habitation grew comfortable to me beyond measure: and when I reflected that in this solitary life which I have been confined to, I had not only been moved to look up to heaven myself, and to seek the Hand that had brought me here, but was now to be made an instrument, under Providence, to save the life, and, for aught I knew, the soul of a poor savage, and bring him to the true knowledge of religion and of the Christian doctrine, that he might know Christ Jesus, in whom is life eternal; I say, when I reflected upon all these things, a secret joy ran through every part of My soul, and I frequently rejoiced that ever I was brought to this place, which I had so often thought the most dreadful of all afflictions that could possibly have befallen me.

I continued in this thankful frame all the remainder of my time; and the conversation which employed the hours between Friday and me was such as made the three years which we lived there together perfectly and completely happy, if any such thing as complete happiness can be formed in a sublunary state. This savage was now a good Christian, a much better than I; though I have reason to hope, and bless God for it, that we were equally penitent, and comforted, restored penitents. We had here the Word of God to read, and no farther off from His Spirit to instruct than if we had been in England. I always applied myself, in reading the Scripture, to let him know, as well as I could, the meaning of what I read; and he again, by his serious inquiries and questionings, made me, as I said before, a much better scholar in the Scripture knowledge than I should ever have been by my own mere private reading. Another thing I cannot refrain from observing here also, from experience in this retired part of my life, viz. how infinite and inexpressible a blessing it is that the knowledge of God, and of the doctrine of salvation by Christ Jesus, is so plainly laid down in the Word of God, so easy to be received and understood, that, as the bare reading the Scripture made me capable of understanding enough of my duty to carry me directly on to the great work of sincere repentance for my sins, and laying hold of a Saviour for life and salvation, to a stated reformation in practice, and obedience to all God's commands, and this without any teacher or instructor, I mean human; so the same plain instruction sufficiently served to the enlightening this savage creature, and bringing him to be such a Christian as I have known few equal to him in my life.

As to all the disputes, wrangling, strife, and contention which have happened in the world about religion, whether niceties in doctrines or schemes of church government, they were all perfectly useless to us, and, for aught I can yet see, they have been so to the rest of the world. We had the sure guide to heaven, viz. the Word of God; and we had, blessed be God, comfortable views of the Spirit of God teaching and instructing by His word, leading us into all truth, and making us both willing and obedient to the instruction of His word. And I cannot see the least use that the greatest knowledge of the disputed points of religion, which have made such confusion in the world, would have been to us, if we could have obtained it. But I must go on with the historical part of things, and take every part in its order.

After Friday and I became more intimately acquainted, and that he could understand almost all I said to him, and speak pretty fluently, though in broken English, to me, I acquainted him with my own history, or at least so much of it as related to my coming to this place: how I had lived there, and how long; I let him into the mystery, for such it was to him, of gunpowder and bullet, and taught him how to shoot. I gave him a knife, which he was wonderfully delighted with; and I made him a belt, with a frog[142] hanging to it, such as in England we wear hangers in; and in the frog, instead of a hanger, I gave him a hatchet, which was not only as good a weapon in some cases, but much more useful upon other occasions.

I described to him the country of Europe, particularly England, which I came from; how we lived, how we worshipped God, how we behaved to one another, and how we traded in ships to all parts of the world. I gave him an account of the wreck which I had been on board of, and showed him, as near as I could, the place where she lay; but she was all beaten in pieces before, and gone. I showed him the ruins of our boat, which we lost when we escaped, and which I could not stir with my whole strength then; but was now fallen almost all to pieces. Upon seeing this boat, Friday stood, musing a great while, and said nothing. I asked him what it was he studied upon. At last says he, "Me see such boat like come to place at my nation." I did not understand him a good while; but at last, when I had examined further into it, I understood by him that a boat, such as that had been, came on shore upon the country where he lived: that is, as he explained it, was driven thither by stress of weather. I presently imagined that some European

---

[142] a leather or cloth loop used to attach a sword

ship must have been cast away upon their coast, and the boat might get loose and drive ashore; but was so dull that I never once thought of men making their escape from a wreck thither, much less whence they might come: so I only inquired after a description of the boat.

Friday described the boat to me well enough; but brought me better to understand him when he added with some warmth, "We save the white mans from drown." Then I presently asked if there were any white mans, as he called them, in the boat. "Yes," he said; "the boat full of white mans." I asked him how many. He told upon his fingers seventeen. I asked him then what became of them. He told me, "They live, they dwell at my nation."

This put new thoughts into my head; for I presently imagined that these might be the men belonging to the ship that was cast away in the sight of my island, as I now called it; and who, after the ship was struck on the rock, and they saw her inevitably lost, had saved themselves in their boat, and were landed upon that wild shore among the savages. Upon this I inquired of him more critically what was become of them. He assured me they lived still there; that they had been there about four years; that the savages left them alone, and gave them victuals to live on. I asked him how it came to pass they did not kill them and eat them. He said, "No, they make brother with them;" that is, as I understood him, a truce; and then he added, "They no eat mans but when make the war fight;" that is to say, they never eat any men but such as come to fight with them and are taken in battle.

It was after this some considerable time, that being upon the top of the hill at the east side of the island, from whence, as I have said, I had, in a clear day, discovered the main or continent of America, Friday, the weather being very serene, looks very earnestly towards the mainland, and, in a kind of surprise, falls a jumping and dancing, and calls out to me, for I was at some distance from him. I asked him what was the matter. "Oh, joy!" says he; "Oh, glad! there see my country, there my nation!" I observed an extraordinary sense of pleasure appeared in his face, and his eyes sparkled, and his countenance discovered a strange eagerness, as if he had a mind to be in his own country again. This observation of mine put a great many thoughts into me, which made me at first not so easy about my new man Friday as I was before; and I made no doubt but that, if Friday could get back to his own nation again, he would not only forget all his religion but all his obligation to me, and would be forward enough to give his countrymen an account of me, and come back, perhaps with a hundred or two of them, and make a feast upon me, at which he might be as merry as he used to be with those of his enemies when they were taken in war. But I wronged the poor honest creature very much, for which I was very sorry afterwards. However, as my jealousy increased, and held some weeks, I was a little more circumspect,[143] and not so familiar and kind to him as before: in which I was certainly wrong too; the honest, grateful creature having no thought about it but what consisted with the best principles, both as a religious Christian and as a grateful friend, as appeared afterwards to my full satisfaction.

While my jealousy of him lasted, you may be sure I was every day pumping him to see if he would discover any of the new thoughts which I suspected were in him; but I found everything he said was so honest and so innocent, that I could find nothing to nourish my suspicion; and in spite of all my uneasiness, he made me at last entirely his own again; nor did he in the least perceive that I was uneasy, and therefore I could not suspect him of deceit.

One day, walking up the same hill, but the weather being hazy at sea, so that we could not see the continent, I called to him, and said, "Friday, do not you wish yourself in your own country, your own nation?" "Yes," he said, "I be much O glad to be at my own nation." "What would you do there?" said I. "Would you turn wild again, eat men's flesh again, and be a savage as you were before?" He looked full of concern, and shaking his head, said, "No, no, Friday tell them to live good; tell them to pray God; tell them to eat corn-bread, cattle flesh, milk; no eat man again." "Why, then," said I to him, "they will kill you." He looked grave at that, and then said, "No, no, they no kill me, they willing love learn." He meant by this, they would be willing to learn. He added, they learned much of the bearded mans that came in the boat. Then I asked him if he would go back to them. He smiled at that, and told me that he could not swim so far. I told him I would make a canoe for him. He told me he would go if I would go with him. "I go!" says I; "why, they will eat me if I come there." "No, no," says he, "me make they no eat you; me make they much love you." He meant, he would tell them how I had killed his enemies, and saved his life, and so he would make them love me. Then he told me, as well as he could, how kind they were to seventeen white men, or bearded men, as he called them who came on shore there in distress.

From this time, I confess, I had a mind to venture over, and see if I could possibly join with those bearded men, who I made no doubt were Spaniards and Portuguese; not doubting but, if I could, we might find some method to escape from thence, being upon the continent, and a good company together, better than I could from an island forty miles off the shore, alone and without help. So, after some days, I took Friday to work again by way of discourse, and told him I would give him a boat to go back to his own nation; and, accordingly, I carried him to my frigate, which lay on the other side of the island, and having cleared it of water (for I always kept it sunk

---

[143] wary, cautious

in water), I brought it out, showed it him, and we both went into it. I found he was a most dexterous fellow at managing it, and would make it go almost as swift again as I could. So when he was in, I said to him, "Well, now, Friday, shall we go to your nation?" He looked very dull at my saying so; which it seems was because he thought the boat was too small to go so far. I then told him I had a bigger; so the next day I went to the place where the first boat lay which I had made, but which I could not get into the water. He said that was big enough; but then, as I had taken no care of it, and it had lain two or three and twenty years there, the sun had so split and dried it, that it was rotten. Friday told me such a boat would do very well, and would carry "much enough vittle, drink, bread;" this was his way of talking.

Questions for Review:

1.   Describe what Robinson Crusoe teaches Friday. What happens when he shows Friday what his gun can do?

2.   What makes this year the "pleasantest year" of all?

3.   What does Friday tell about his past? What does Robinson Crusoe ask him?

4.   What does Robinson Crusoe learn about Friday's notions of God? How does Robinson Crusoe instruct him? What comment about "priestcraft" does he make? (Compare this to 1 Timothy 2:5-6, 1 Peter 2:9, and Hebrews 8.) How does Friday's conversion help Robinson Crusoe?

5.   Robinson Crusoe remarks how plain the gospel is. How does the Bible confirm this?

6.   What else does Robinson Crusoe teach Friday? What exciting information does he learn from Friday about his homeland?

7.   Why is Friday overjoyed one day? How does Robinson Crusoe react? What plans do they make?

CHAPTER XVI: RESCUE OF PRISONERS FROM CANNIBALS

Upon the whole, I was by this time so fixed upon my design of going over with him to the continent that I told him we would go and make one as big as that, and he should go home in it. He answered not one word, but looked very grave and sad. I asked him what was the matter with him. He asked me again, "Why you angry mad with Friday?—what me done?" I asked him what he meant. I told him I was not angry with him at all. "No angry!" says he, repeating the words several times; "why send Friday home away to my nation?" "Why," says I, "Friday, did not you say you wished you were there?" "Yes, yes," says he, "wish we both there; no wish Friday there, no master there." In a word, he would not think of going there without me. "I go there, Friday?" says I; "what shall I do there?" He turned very quick upon me at this. "You do great deal much good," says he; "you teach wild mans be good, sober, tame mans; you tell them know God, pray God, and live new life." "Alas, Friday!" says I, "thou knowest not what thou sayest; I am but an ignorant man myself." "Yes, yes," says he, "you teachee me good, you teachee them good." "No, no, Friday," says I, "you shall go without me; leave me here to live by myself, as I did before." He looked confused again at that word; and running to one of the hatchets which he used to wear, he takes it up hastily, and gives it to me. "What must I do with this?" says I to him. "You take kill Friday," says he. "What must kill you for?" said I again. He returns very quick—"What you send Friday away for? Take kill Friday, no send Friday away." This he spoke so earnestly that I saw tears stand in his eyes. In a word, I so plainly discovered the utmost affection in him to me, and a firm resolution in him, that I told him then and often after, that I would never send him away from me if he was willing to stay with me.

Upon the whole, as I found by all his discourse a settled affection to me, and that nothing could part him from me, so I found all the foundation of his desire to go to his own country was laid in his ardent affection to the people, and his hopes of my doing them good; a thing which, as I had no notion of myself, so I had not the least thought or intention, or desire of undertaking it. But still I found a strong inclination to attempting my escape, founded on the supposition gathered from the discourse, that there were seventeen bearded men there; and therefore, without any more delay, I went to work with Frday to find out a great tree proper to fell, and make a large periagua, or canoe, to undertake the voyage. There were trees enough in the island to have built a little fleet, not of periaguas or canoes, but even of good, large vessels; but the main thing I looked at was, to get one so near the water that we might launch it when it was made, to avoid the mistake I committed at first. At last Friday pitched upon a tree; for I found he knew much better than I what kind of wood was fittest for it; nor can I tell to this day what wood to call the tree we cut down, except that it was very like the tree we call fustic, or between that and the Nicaragua wood, for it was much of the same colour and smell. Friday wished to burn the hollow or cavity of this tree out, to make it for a boat, but I showed him how to cut it with tools; which, after I had showed him how to use, he did very handily; and in about a month's hard labour we finished it and made it very handsome; especially when, with our axes, which I showed him how to handle, we cut and hewed the outside into the true shape of a boat. After this, however, it cost us near a fortnight's time to get her along, as it were inch by inch, upon great rollers into the water; but when she was in, she would have carried twenty men with great ease.

When she was in the water, though she was so big, it amazed me to see with what dexterity and how swift my man Friday could manage her, turn her, and paddle her along. So I asked him if he would, and if we might venture over in her. "Yes," he said, "we venture over in her very well, though great blow wind." However I had a further design that he knew nothing of, and that was, to make a mast and a sail, and to fit her with an anchor and cable. As to a mast, that was easy enough to get; so I pitched upon a straight young cedar-tree, which I found near the place, and which there were great plenty of in the island, and I set Friday to work to cut it down, and gave him directions how to shape and order it. But as to the sail, that was my particular care. I knew I had old sails, or rather pieces of old sails, enough; but as I had had them now six-and-twenty years by me, and had not been very careful to preserve them, not imagining that I should ever have this kind of use for them, I did not doubt but they were all rotten; and, indeed, most of them were so. However, I found two pieces which appeared pretty good, and with these I went to work; and with a great deal of pains, and awkward stitching, you may be sure, for want of needles, I at length made a three-cornered ugly thing, like what we call in England a shoulder-of-mutton sail, to go with a boom at bottom, and a little short sprit at the top, such as usually our ships' long-boats sail with, and such as I best knew how to manage, as it was such a one as I had to the boat in which I made my escape from Barbary, as related in the first part of my story.

I was near two months performing this last work, viz. rigging and fitting my masts and sails; for I finished them very complete, making a small stay, and a sail, or foresail, to it, to assist if we should turn to windward; and, what was more than all, I fixed a rudder to the stern of her to steer with. I was but a bungling shipwright, yet as I knew the usefulness and even necessity of such a thing, I applied myself with so much pains to do it, that at last I brought it to pass; though, considering the many dull contrivances I had for it that failed, I think it cost me almost as much labour as making the boat.

After all this was done, I had my man Friday to teach as to what belonged to the navigation of my boat; though he knew very well how to paddle a canoe, he knew nothing of what belonged to a sail and a rudder; and was the most amazed when he saw me work the boat to and again in the sea by the rudder, and how the sail jibed, and filled this way or that way as the course we sailed changed; I say when he saw this he stood like one astonished and amazed. However, with a little use, I made all these things familiar to him, and he became an expert sailor, except that of the compass I could make him understand very little. On the other hand, as there was very little cloudy weather, and seldom or never any fogs in those parts, there was the less occasion for a compass, seeing the stars were always to be seen by night, and the shore by day, except in the rainy seasons, and then nobody cared to stir abroad either by land or sea.

I was now entered on the seven-and-twentieth year of my captivity in this place; though the three last years that I had this creature with me ought rather to be left out of the account, my habitation being quite of another kind than in all the rest of the time. I kept the anniversary of my landing here with the same thankfulness to God for His mercies as at first: and if I had such cause of acknowledgment at first, I had much more so now, having such additional testimonies of the care of Providence over me, and the great hopes I had of being effectually and speedily delivered; for I had an invincible impression upon my thoughts that my deliverance was at hand, and that I should not be another year in this place. I went on, however, with my husbandry; digging, planting, and fencing as usual. I gathered and cured my grapes, and did every necessary thing as before.

The rainy season was in the meantime upon me, when I kept more within doors than at other times. We had stowed our new vessel as secure as we could, bringing her up into the creek, where, as I said in the beginning, I landed my rafts from the ship; and hauling her up to the shore at high-water mark, I made my man Friday dig a little dock, just big enough to hold her, and just deep enough to give her water enough to float in; and then, when the tide was out, we made a strong dam across the end of it, to keep the water out; and so she lay, dry as to the tide from the sea: and to keep the rain off we laid a great many boughs of trees, so thick that she was as well thatched as a house; and thus we waited for the months of November and December, in which I designed to make my adventure.

When the settled season began to come in, as the thought of my design returned with the fair weather, I was preparing daily for the voyage. And the first thing I did was to lay by a certain quantity of provisions, being the stores for our voyage; and intended in a week or a fortnight's time to open the dock, and launch out our boat. I was busy one morning upon something of this kind, when I called to Friday, and bid him to go to the sea-shore and see if he could find a turtle or a tortoise, a thing which we generally got once a week, for the sake of the eggs as well as the flesh. Friday had not been long gone when he came running back, and flew over my outer wall or fence, like one that felt not the ground or the steps he set his foot on; and before I had time to speak to him he cries out to me, "O master! O master! O sorrow! O bad!"—"What's the matter, Friday?" says I. "O yonder there," says he, "one, two, three canoes; one, two, three!" By this way of speaking I concluded there were six; but on inquiry I found there were but three. "Well, Friday," says I, "do not be frightened." So I heartened him up as well as I could. However, I saw the poor fellow was most terribly scared, for nothing ran in his head but that they were come to look for him, and would cut him in pieces and eat him; and the poor fellow trembled so that I scarcely knew what to do with him. I comforted him as well as I could, and told him I was in as much danger as he, and that they would eat me as well as him. "But," says I, "Friday, we must resolve to fight them. Can you fight, Friday?" "Me shoot," says he, "but there come many great number." "No matter for that," said I again; "our guns will fright them that we do not kill." So I asked him whether, if I resolved to defend him, he would defend me, and stand by me, and do just as I bid him. He said, "Me die when you bid die, master." So I went and fetched a good dram of rum and gave him; for I had been so good a husband of my rum that I had a great deal left. When we had drunk it, I made him take the two fowling-pieces, which we always carried, and loaded them with large swan-shot, as big as small pistol-bullets. Then I took four muskets, and loaded them with two slugs and five small bullets each; and my two pistols I loaded with a brace of bullets each. I hung my great sword, as usual, naked by my side, and gave Friday his hatchet. When I had thus prepared myself, I took my perspective glass, and went up to the side of the hill, to see what I could discover; and I found quickly by my glass that there were one-and-twenty savages, three prisoners, and three canoes; and that their whole business seemed to be the triumphant banquet upon these three human bodies: a barbarous feast, indeed! but nothing more than, as I had observed, was usual with them. I observed also that they had landed, not where they had done when Friday made his escape, but nearer to my creek, where the shore was low, and where a thick wood came almost close down to the sea. This, with the abhorrence of the inhuman errand these wretches came about, filled me with such indignation that I came down again to Friday, and told him I was resolved to go down to them and kill them all; and asked him if he would stand by me. He had now got over his fright, and his spirits being a little raised with the dram I had given him, he was very cheerful, and told me, as before, he would die when I bid die.

In this fit of fury I divided the arms which I had charged, as before, between us; I gave Friday one pistol to stick in his girdle, and three guns upon his shoulder, and I took one pistol and the other three guns myself; and in this posture we marched out. I took a small bottle of rum in my pocket, and gave Friday a large bag with more powder and bullets; and as to orders, I charged him to keep close behind me, and not to stir, or shoot, or do anything till I bid him, and in the meantime not to speak a word. In this posture I fetched a compass to my right hand of near a mile, as well to get over the creek as to get into the wood, so that I could come within shot of them before I should be discovered, which I had seen by my glass it was easy to do.

While I was making this march, my former thoughts returning, I began to abate my resolution: I do not mean that I entertained any fear of their number, for as they were naked, unarmed wretches, it is certain I was superior to them—nay, though I had been alone. But it occurred to my thoughts, what call, what occasion, much less what necessity I was in to go and dip my hands in blood, to attack people who had neither done or intended me any wrong? Who, as to me, were innocent, and whose barbarous customs were their own disaster, being in them a token, indeed, of God's having left them, with the other nations of that part of the world, to such stupidity, and to such inhuman courses, but did not call me to take upon me to be a judge of their actions, much less an executioner of His justice—that whenever He thought fit He would take the cause into His own hands, and by national vengeance punish them as a people for national crimes, but that, in the meantime, it was none of my business—that it was true Friday might justify it, because he was a declared enemy and in a state of war with those very particular people, and it was lawful for him to attack them—but I could not say the same with regard to myself. These things were so warmly pressed upon my thoughts all the way as I went, that I resolved I would only go and place myself near them that I might observe their barbarous feast, and that I would act then as God should direct; but that unless something offered that was more a call to me than yet I knew of, I would not meddle with them.

With this resolution I entered the wood, and, with all possible wariness and silence, Friday following close at my heels, I marched till I came to the skirts of the wood on the side which was next to them, only that one corner of the wood lay between me and them. Here I called softly to Friday, and showing him a great tree which was just at the corner of the wood, I bade him go to the tree, and bring me word if he could see there plainly what they were doing. He did so, and came immediately back to me, and told me they might be plainly viewed there—that they were all about their fire, eating the flesh of one of their prisoners, and that another lay bound upon the sand a little from them, whom he said they would kill next; and this fired the very soul within me. He told me it was not one of their nation, but one of the bearded men he had told me of, that came to their country in the boat. I was filled with horror at the very naming of the white bearded man; and going to the tree, I saw plainly by my glass a white man, who lay upon the beach of the sea with his hands and his feet tied with flags, or things like rushes, and that he was an European, and had clothes on.

There was another tree and a little thicket beyond it, about fifty yards nearer to them than the place where I was, which, by going a little way about, I saw I might come at undiscovered, and that then I should be within half a shot of them; so I withheld my passion, though I was indeed enraged to the highest degree; and going back about twenty paces, I got behind some bushes, which held all the way till I came to the other tree, and then came to a little rising ground, which gave me a full view of them at the distance of about eighty yards.

I had now not a moment to lose, for nineteen of the dreadful wretches sat upon the ground, all close huddled together, and had just sent the other two to butcher the poor Christian, and bring him perhaps limb by limb to their fire, and they were stooping down to untie the bands at his feet. I turned to Friday. "Now, Friday," said I, "do as I bid thee." Friday said he would. "Then, Friday," says I, "do exactly as you see me do; fail in nothing." So I set down one of the muskets and the fowling-piece upon the ground, and Friday did the like by his, and with the other musket I took my aim at the savages, bidding him to do the like; then asking him if he was ready, he said, "Yes." "Then fire at them," said I; and at the same moment I fired also.

Friday took his aim so much better than I, that on the side that he shot he killed two of them, and wounded three more; and on my side I killed one, and wounded two. They were, you may be sure, in a dreadful consternation: and all of them that were not hurt jumped upon their feet, but did not immediately know which way to run, or which way to look, for they knew not from whence their destruction came. Friday kept his eyes close upon me, that, as I had bid him, he might observe what I did; so, as soon as the first shot was made, I threw down the piece, and took up the fowling-piece, and

Friday did the like; he saw me cock and present; he did the same again. "Are you ready, Friday?" said I. "Yes," says he. "Let fly, then," says I, "in the name of God!" and with that I fired again among the amazed wretches, and so did Friday; and as our pieces were now loaded with what I call swan-shot, or small pistol-bullets, we found only two drop; but so many were wounded that they ran about yelling and screaming like mad creatures, all bloody, and most of them miserably wounded; whereof three more fell quickly after, though not quite dead.

"Now, Friday," says I, laying down the discharged pieces, and taking up the musket which was yet loaded, "follow me," which he did with a great deal of courage; upon which I rushed out of the wood and showed myself, and Friday close at my foot. As soon as I perceived they saw me, I shouted as loud as I could, and bade Friday do so too, and running as fast as I could, which, by the way, was not very fast, being loaded with arms as I was, I made directly towards the poor victim, who was, as I said, lying upon the beach or shore, between the place where they sat and the sea. The two butchers who were just going to work with him had left him at the surprise of our first fire, and fled in a terrible fright to the seaside, and had jumped into a canoe, and three more of the rest made the same way. I turned to Friday, and bade him step forwards and fire at them; he understood me immediately, and running about forty yards, to be nearer them, he shot at them; and I thought he had killed them all, for I saw them all fall of a heap into the boat, though I saw two of them up again quickly; however, he killed two of them, and wounded the third, so that he lay down in the bottom of the boat as if he had been dead.

While my man Friday fired at them, I pulled out my knife and cut the flags that bound the poor victim; and loosing his hands and feet, I lifted him up, and asked him in the Portuguese tongue what he was. He answered in Latin, Christianus; but was so weak and faint that he could scarce stand or speak. I took my bottle out of my pocket and gave it him, making signs that he should drink, which he did; and I gave him a piece of bread, which he ate. Then I asked him what countryman he was: and he said, Espagniole; and being a little recovered, let me know, by all the signs he could possibly make, how much he was in my debt for his deliverance. "Seignior," said I, with as much Spanish as I could make up, "we will talk afterwards, but we must fight now: if you have any strength left, take this pistol and sword, and lay about you." He took them very thankfully; and no sooner had he the arms in his hands, but, as if they had put new vigour into him, he flew upon his murderers like a fury, and had cut two of them in pieces in an instant; for the truth is, as the whole was a surprise to them, so the poor creatures were so much frightened with the noise of our pieces that they fell down for mere amazement and fear, and had no more power to attempt their own escape than their flesh had to resist our shot; and that was the case of those five that Friday shot at in the boat; for as three of them fell with the hurt they received, so the other two fell with the fright.

I kept my piece in my hand still without firing, being willing to keep my charge ready, because I had given the Spaniard my pistol and sword: so I called to Friday, and bade him run up to the tree from whence we first fired, and fetch the arms which lay there that had been discharged, which he did with great swiftness; and then giving him my musket, I sat down myself to load all the rest again, and bade them come to me when they wanted. While I was loading these pieces, there happened a fierce engagement between the Spaniard and one of the savages, who made at him with one of their great wooden swords, the weapon that was to have killed him before, if I had not prevented it. The Spaniard, who was as bold and brave as could be imagined, though weak, had fought the Indian a good while, and had cut two great wounds on his head; but the savage being a stout, lusty fellow, closing in with him, had thrown him down, being faint, and was wringing my sword out of his hand; when the Spaniard, though undermost, wisely quitting the sword, drew the pistol from his girdle, shot the savage through the body, and killed him upon the spot, before I, who was running to help him, could come near him.

Friday, being now left to his liberty, pursued the flying wretches, with no weapon in his hand but his hatchet: and with that he despatched those three who as I said before, were wounded at first, and fallen, and all the rest he could come up with: and the Spaniard coming to me for a gun, I gave him one of the fowling-pieces, with which he pursued two of the savages, and wounded them both; but as he was not able to run, they both got from him into the wood, where Friday pursued them, and killed one of them, but the other was too nimble for him; and though he was wounded, yet had plunged himself into the sea, and swam with all his might off to those two who were left in the canoe; which three in the canoe, with one wounded, that we knew not whether he died or no, were all that escaped our hands of one-and-twenty. The account of the whole is as follows: Three killed at our first shot from the tree; two killed at the next shot; two killed by Friday in the boat; two killed by Friday of those at first wounded; one killed by Friday in the wood; three killed by the Spaniard; four killed, being found dropped here and there, of the wounds, or killed by Friday in his chase of them; four escaped in the boat, whereof one wounded, if not dead—twenty-one in all.

Those that were in the canoe worked hard to get out of gun-shot, and though Friday made two or three shots at them, I did not find that he hit any of them. Friday would fain have had me take one of their canoes, and pursue them; and indeed I was very anxious about their escape, lest, carrying the news home to their people, they should come back perhaps with two or three hundred of the canoes and devour us by mere multitude; so I consented to pursue them by sea, and running to one of their canoes, I jumped in and bade Friday follow me: but when I was in the canoe I was surprised to find another poor creature lie there, bound hand and foot, as the Spaniard was, for the slaughter, and almost dead with fear, not knowing what was the matter; for he had not been able to look up over the side of the boat, he was tied so hard neck and heels, and had been tied so long that he had really but little life in him.

I immediately cut the twisted flags or rushes which they had bound him with, and would have helped him up; but he could not stand or speak, but groaned most piteously, believing, it seems, still, that he was only unbound in order to be killed. When Friday came to him I bade him speak to him, and tell him of his deliverance; and pulling out my bottle, made him give the poor wretch a dram, which, with the news of his being delivered, revived him, and he sat up in the boat. But when Friday came to hear him speak, and look in his face, it would have moved any one to tears to have seen how Friday kissed him, embraced him, hugged him, cried, laughed, hallooed, jumped about, danced, sang; then cried again, wrung his hands, beat his own face and head; and then sang and jumped about again like a distracted creature. It was a good while before I could make him speak to me or tell me what was the matter; but when he came a little to himself he told me that it was his father.

It is not easy for me to express how it moved me to see what ecstasy and filial affection had worked in this poor savage at the sight of his father, and of his being delivered from death; nor indeed can I describe half the extravagances of his affection after this: for he went into the boat and out of the boat a great many times: when he went in to him he would sit down by him, open his breast, and hold his father's head close to his bosom for many minutes together, to nourish it; then he took his arms and ankles, which were numbed and stiff with the binding, and chafed and rubbed them with his hands; and I, perceiving what the case was, gave him some rum out of my bottle to rub them with, which did them a great deal of good.

This affair put an end to our pursuit of the canoe with the other savages, who were now almost out of sight; and it was happy for us that we did not, for it blew so hard within two hours after, and before they could be got a quarter of their way, and continued blowing so hard all night, and that from the north-west, which was against them, that I could not suppose their boat could live, or that they ever reached their own coast.

But to return to Friday; he was so busy about his father that I could not find in my heart to take him off for some time; but after I thought he could leave him a little, I called him to me, and he came jumping and laughing, and pleased to the highest extreme: then I asked him if he had given his father any bread. He shook his head, and said, "None; ugly dog eat all up self." I then gave him a cake of bread out of a little pouch I carried on purpose; I also gave him a dram for himself; but he would not taste it, but carried it to his father. I had in my pocket two or three bunches of raisins, so I gave him a handful of them for his father. He had no sooner given his father these raisins but I saw him come out of the boat, and run away as if he had been bewitched, for he was the swiftest fellow on his feet that ever I saw: I say, he ran at such a rate that he was out of sight, as it were, in an instant; and though I called, and hallooed out too after him, it was all one— away he went; and in a quarter of an hour I saw him come back again, though not so fast as he went; and as he came nearer I found his pace slacker, because he had something in his hand. When he came up to me I found he had been quite home for an earthen jug or pot, to bring his father some fresh water, and that he had got two more cakes or loaves of bread: the bread he gave me, but the water he carried to his father; however, as I was very thirsty too, I took a little of it. The water revived his father more than all the rum or spirits I had given him, for he was fainting with thirst.

When his father had drunk, I called to him to know if there was any water left. He said, "Yes"; and I bade him give it to the poor Spaniard, who was in as much want of it as his father; and I sent one of the cakes that Friday brought to the Spaniard too, who was indeed very weak, and was reposing himself upon a green place under the shade of a tree; and whose limbs were also very stiff, and very much swelled with the rude[144] bandage he had been tied with. When I saw that upon Friday's coming to him with the water he sat up and drank, and took the bread and began to eat, I went to him and gave him a handful of raisins. He looked up in my face with all the tokens of gratitude and thankfulness that could appear in any countenance; but was so weak, notwithstanding he had so exerted himself in the fight, that he could not stand up upon his feet—he tried to do it two or three times, but was really not able, his ankles were so swelled and so painful to him; so I bade him sit still, and caused Friday to rub his ankles, and bathe them with rum, as he had done his father's.

I observed the poor affectionate creature, every two minutes, or perhaps less, all the while he was here, turn his head about to see if his father was in the same place and posture as he left him sitting; and at last he found he was not to be seen; at which he started up, and, without speaking a word, flew with that swiftness to him that one could scarce perceive his feet to touch the ground as he went; but when he came, he only found he had laid himself down to ease his limbs, so Friday came back to me presently; and then I spoke to the Spaniard to let Friday help him up if he could, and lead him to

[144] crude, primitive

the boat, and then he should carry him to our dwelling, where I would take care of him. But Friday, a lusty, strong fellow, took the Spaniard upon his back, and carried him away to the boat, and set him down softly upon the side or gunnel of the canoe, with his feet in the inside of it; and then lifting him quite in, he set him close to his father; and presently stepping out again, launched the boat off, and paddled it along the shore faster than I could walk, though the wind blew pretty hard too; so he brought them both safe into our creek, and leaving them in the boat, ran away to fetch the other canoe. As he passed me I spoke to him, and asked him whither he went. He told me, "Go fetch more boat;" so away he went like the wind, for sure never man or horse ran like him; and he had the other canoe in the creek almost as soon as I got to it by land; so he wafted me over, and then went to help our new guests out of the boat, which he did; but they were neither of them able to walk; so that poor Friday knew not what to do.

To remedy this, I went to work in my thought, and calling to Friday to bid them sit down on the bank while he came to me, I soon made a kind of hand-barrow to lay them on, and Friday and I carried them both up together upon it between us.

But when we got them to the outside of our wall, or fortification, we were at a worse loss than before, for it was impossible to get them over, and I was resolved not to break it down; so I set to work again, and Friday and I, in about two hours' time, made a very handsome tent, covered with old sails, and above that with boughs of trees, being in the space without our outward fence and between that and the grove of young wood which I had planted; and here we made them two beds of such things as I had—viz. of good rice-straw, with blankets laid upon it to lie on, and another to cover them, on each bed.

My island was now peopled, and I thought myself very rich in subjects; and it was a merry reflection, which I frequently made, how like a king I looked. First of all, the whole country was my own property, so that I had an undoubted right of dominion. Secondly, my people were perfectly subjected—I was absolutely lord and lawgiver—they all owed their lives to me, and were ready to lay down their lives, if there had been occasion for it, for me. It was remarkable, too, I had but three subjects, and they were of three different religions—my man Friday was a Protestant, his father was a Pagan and a cannibal, and the Spaniard was a Papist.[145] However, I allowed liberty of conscience throughout my dominions. But this is by the way.

As soon as I had secured my two weak, rescued prisoners, and given them shelter, and a place to rest them upon, I began to think of making some provision for them; and the first thing I did, I ordered Friday to take a year-

---

[145] Roman Catholic (a "Papist" is someone who follows the Pope)

ling goat, betwixt a kid and a goat, out of my particular flock, to be killed; when I cut off the hinder-quarter, and chopping it into small pieces, I set Friday to work to boiling and stewing, and made them a very good dish, I assure you, of flesh and broth; and as I cooked it without doors, for I made no fire within my inner wall, so I carried it all into the new tent, and having set a table there for them, I sat down, and ate my own dinner also with them, and, as well as I could, cheered them and encouraged them. Friday was my interpreter, especially to his father, and, indeed, to the Spaniard too; for the Spaniard spoke the language of the savages pretty well.

After we had dined, or rather supped, I ordered Friday to take one of the canoes, and go and fetch our muskets and other firearms, which, for want of time, we had left upon the place of battle; and the next day I ordered him to go and bury the dead bodies of the savages, which lay open to the sun, and would presently be offensive. I also ordered him to bury the horrid remains of their barbarous feast, which I could not think of doing myself; nay, I could not bear to see them if I went that way; all which he punctually performed, and effaced[146] the very appearance of the savages being there; so that when I went again, I could scarce know where it was, otherwise than by the corner of the wood pointing to the place.

I then began to enter into a little conversation with my two new subjects; and, first, I set Friday to inquire of his father what he thought of the escape of the savages in that canoe, and whether we might expect a return of them, with a power too great for us to resist. His first opinion was, that the savages in the boat never could live out the storm which blew that night they went off, but must of necessity be drowned, or driven south to those other shores, where they were as sure to be devoured as they were to be drowned if they were cast away; but, as to what they would do if they came safe on shore, he said he knew not; but it was his opinion that they were so dreadfully frightened with the manner of their being attacked, the noise, and the fire, that he believed they would tell the people they were all killed by thunder and lightning, not by the hand of man; and that the two which appeared— viz. Friday and I—were two heavenly spirits, or furies, come down to destroy them, and not men with weapons. This, he said, he knew; because he heard them all cry out so, in their language, one to another; for it was impossible for them to conceive that a man could dart fire, and speak thunder, and kill at a distance, without lifting up the hand, as was done now: and this old savage was in the right; for, as I understood since, by other hands, the savages never attempted to go over to the island afterwards, they were so terrified with the accounts given by those four men (for it seems they did escape the sea), that they believed whoever went to that enchanted

---

[146] erased

island would be destroyed with fire from the gods. This, however, I knew not; and therefore was under continual apprehensions for a good while, and kept always upon my guard, with all my army: for, as there were now four of us, I would have ventured upon a hundred of them, fairly in the open field, at any time.

CHAPTER XVII: VISIT OF MUTINEERS

In a little time, however, no more canoes appearing, the fear of their coming wore off; and I began to take my former thoughts of a voyage to the main into consideration; being likewise assured by Friday's father that I might depend upon good usage from their nation, on his account, if I would go. But my thoughts were a little suspended when I had a serious discourse with the Spaniard, and when I understood that there were sixteen more of his countrymen and Portuguese, who having been cast away and made their escape to that side, lived there at peace, indeed, with the savages, but were very sore put to it for necessaries, and, indeed, for life. I asked him all the particulars of their voyage, and found they were a Spanish ship, bound from the Rio de la Plata to the Havanna, being directed to leave their loading there, which was chiefly hides and silver, and to bring back what European goods they could meet with there; that they had five Portuguese seamen on board, whom they took out of another wreck; that five of their own men were drowned when first the ship was lost, and that these escaped through infinite dangers and hazards, and arrived, almost starved, on the cannibal coast, where they expected to have been devoured every moment. He told me they had some arms with them, but they were perfectly useless, for that they had neither powder nor ball, the washing of the sea having spoiled all their powder but a little, which they used at their first landing to provide themselves with some food.

I asked him what he thought would become of them there, and if they had formed any design of making their escape. He said they had many consultations about it; but that having neither vessel nor tools to build one, nor provisions of any kind, their councils always ended in tears and despair. I asked him how he thought they would receive a proposal from me, which might tend towards an escape; and whether, if they were all here, it might not be done. I told him with freedom, I feared mostly their treachery and ill-usage of me, if I put my life in their hands; for that gratitude was no inherent virtue in the nature of man, nor did men always square their dealings by the obligations they had received so much as they did by the advantages they expected. I told him it would be very hard that I should be made the instrument of their deliverance, and that they should afterwards make me their prisoner in New Spain, where an Englishman was certain to be made a sacrifice, what necessity or what accident soever brought him thither; and that I had rather be delivered up to the savages, and be devoured alive, than fall into the merciless claws of the priests, and be carried into the Inquisition.[147] I added that, otherwise, I was persuaded, if they were all here, we might, with so many hands, build a barque large enough to carry us all away, either to the Brazils southward, or to the islands or Spanish coast northward; but that if, in requital, they should, when I had put weapons into their hands, carry me by force among their own people, I might be ill-used for my kindness to them, and make my case worse than it was before.

He answered, with a great deal of candour and ingenuousness, that their condition was so miserable, and that they were so sensible of it, that he believed they would abhor the thought of using any man unkindly that should contribute to their deliverance; and that, if I pleased, he would go to them with the old man, and discourse with them about it, and return again and bring me their answer; that he would make conditions with them upon their solemn oath, that they should be absolutely under my direction as their commander and captain; and they should swear upon the holy sacraments and gospel to be true to me, and go to such Christian country as I should agree to, and no other; and to be directed wholly and absolutely by my orders till they were landed safely in such country as I intended, and that he would bring a contract from them, under their hands, for that purpose. Then he told me he would first swear to me himself that he would never stir from me as long as he lived till I gave him orders; and that he would take my side to the last drop of his blood, if there should happen the least breach of faith among his countrymen. He told me they were all of them very civil, honest men, and they were under the greatest distress imaginable, having neither weapons nor clothes, nor any food, but at the mercy and discretion of the savages; out of all hopes of ever returning to their own country; and that he was sure, if I would undertake their relief, they would live and die by me.

Upon these assurances, I resolved to venture to relieve them, if possible, and to send the old savage and this Spaniard over to them to treat. But when

---

[147] During the Inquisition, non-Roman Catholics were jailed, tortured, and killed for refusing to adhere to the beliefs of the Roman Church.

we had got all things in readiness to go, the Spaniard himself started an objection, which had so much prudence in it on one hand, and so much sincerity on the other hand, that I could not but be very well satisfied in it; and, by his advice, put off the deliverance of his comrades for at least half a year. The case was thus: he had been with us now about a month, during which time I had let him see in what manner I had provided, with the assistance of Providence, for my support; and he saw evidently what stock of corn and rice I had laid up; which, though it was more than sufficient for myself, yet it was not sufficient, without good husbandry, for my family, now it was increased to four; but much less would it be sufficient if his countrymen, who were, as he said, sixteen, still alive, should come over; and least of all would it be sufficient to victual our vessel, if we should build one, for a voyage to any of the Christian colonies of America; so he told me he thought it would be more advisable to let him and the other two dig and cultivate some more land, as much as I could spare seed to sow, and that we should wait another harvest, that we might have a supply of corn for his countrymen, when they should come; for want might be a temptation to them to disagree, or not to think themselves delivered, otherwise than out of one difficulty into another. "You know," says he, "the children of Israel, though they rejoiced at first for their being delivered out of Egypt, yet rebelled even against God Himself, that delivered them, when they came to want bread in the wilderness."

His caution was so seasonable, and his advice so good, that I could not but be very well pleased with his proposal, as well as I was satisfied with his fidelity;[148] so we fell to digging, all four of us, as well as the wooden tools we were furnished with permitted; and in about a month's time, by the end of which it was seed-time, we had got as much land cured and trimmed up as we sowed two-and-twenty bushels of barley on, and sixteen jars of rice, which was, in short, all the seed we had to spare: indeed, we left ourselves barely sufficient, for our own food for the six months that we had to expect our crop; that is to say reckoning from the time we set our seed aside for sowing; for it is not to be supposed it is six months in the ground in that country.

Having now society enough, and our numbers being sufficient to put us out of fear of the savages, if they had come, unless their number had been very great, we went freely all over the island, whenever we found occasion; and as we had our escape or deliverance upon our thoughts, it was impossible, at least for me, to have the means of it out of mine. For this purpose I marked out several trees, which I thought fit for our work, and I set Friday and his father to cut them down; and then I caused the Spaniard, to whom I

---

[148] faithfulness

imparted my thoughts on that affair, to oversee and direct their work. I showed them with what indefatigable[149] pains I had hewed a large tree into single planks, and I caused them to do the like, till they made about a dozen large planks, of good oak, near two feet broad, thirty-five feet long, and from two inches to four inches thick: what prodigious labour it took up any one may imagine.

At the same time I contrived to increase my little flock of tame goats as much as I could; and for this purpose I made Friday and the Spaniard go out one day, and myself with Friday the next day (for we took our turns), and by this means we got about twenty young kids to breed up with the rest; for whenever we shot the dam, we saved the kids, and added them to our flock. But above all, the season for curing the grapes coming on, I caused such a prodigious quantity to be hung up in the sun, that, I believe, had we been at Alicant,[150] where the raisins of the sun are cured, we could have filled sixty or eighty barrels; and these, with our bread, formed a great part of our food—very good living too, I assure you, for they are exceedingly nourishing.

It was now harvest, and our crop in good order: it was not the most plentiful increase I had seen in the island, but, however, it was enough to answer our end; for from twenty-two bushels of barley we brought in and thrashed out above two hundred and twenty bushels; and the like in proportion of the rice; which was store enough for our food to the next harvest, though all the sixteen Spaniards had been on shore with me; or, if we had been ready for a voyage, it would very plentifully have victualled our ship to have carried us to any part of the world; that is to say, any part of America. When we had thus housed and secured our magazine of corn, we fell to work to make more wicker-ware, viz. great baskets, in which we kept it; and the Spaniard was very handy and dexterous at this part, and often blamed me that I did not make some things for defence of this kind of work; but I saw no need of it.

And now, having a full supply of food for all the guests I expected, I gave the Spaniard leave to go over to the main, to see what he could do with those he had left behind him there. I gave him a strict charge not to bring any man who would not first swear in the presence of himself and the old savage that he would in no way injure, fight with, or attack the person he should find in the island, who was so kind as to send for them in order to their deliverance; but that they would stand by him and defend him against all such attempts, and wherever they went would be entirely under and subjected to his command; and that this should be put in writing, and signed in their

---

[149] dogged, untiring
[150] a Spanish province famous for its wine production

hands. How they were to have done this, when I knew they had neither pen nor ink, was a question which we never asked. Under these instructions, the Spaniard and the old savage, the father of Friday, went away in one of the canoes which they might be said to have come in, or rather were brought in, when they came as prisoners to be devoured by the savages. I gave each of them a musket, with a firelock on it, and about eight charges of powder and ball, charging them to be very good husbands of both, and not to use either of them but upon urgent occasions.

This was a cheerful work, being the first measures used by me in view of my deliverance for now twenty-seven years and some days. I gave them provisions of bread and of dried grapes, sufficient for themselves for many days, and sufficient for all the Spaniards—for about eight days' time; and wishing them a good voyage, I saw them go, agreeing with them about a signal they should hang out at their return, by which I should know them again when they came back, at a distance, before they came on shore. They went away with a fair gale on the day that the moon was at full, by my account in the month of October; but as for an exact reckoning of days, after I had once lost it I could never recover it again; nor had I kept even the number of years so punctually as to be sure I was right; though, as it proved when I afterwards examined my account, I found I had kept a true reckoning of years.

It was no less than eight days I had waited for them, when a strange and unforeseen accident intervened, of which the like has not, perhaps, been heard of in history. I was fast asleep in my hutch one morning, when my man Friday came running in to me, and called aloud, "Master, master, they are come, they are come!" I jumped up, and regardless of danger I went, as soon as I could get my clothes on, through my little grove, which, by the way, was by this time grown to be a very thick wood; I say, regardless of danger I went without my arms, which was not my custom to do; but I was surprised when, turning my eyes to the sea, I presently saw a boat at about a league and a half distance, standing in for the shore, with a shoulder-of-mutton sail, as they call it, and the wind blowing pretty fair to bring them in: also I observed, presently, that they did not come from that side which the shore lay on, but from the southernmost end of the island. Upon this I called Friday in, and bade him lie close, for these were not the people we looked for, and that we might not know yet whether they were friends or enemies. In the next place I went in to fetch my perspective glass to see what I could make of them; and having taken the ladder out, I climbed up to the top of the hill, as I used to do when I was apprehensive of anything, and to take my view the plainer without being discovered. I had scarce set my foot upon the hill when my eye plainly discovered a ship lying at anchor, at about two leagues and a half distance from me, SSE., but not above a league and a half from the shore. By my observation it appeared plainly to be an English ship, and the boat appeared to be an English long-boat.

I cannot express the confusion I was in, though the joy of seeing a ship, and one that I had reason to believe was manned by my own countrymen, and consequently friends, was such as I cannot describe; but yet I had some secret doubts hung about me—I cannot tell from whence they came—bidding me keep upon my guard. In the first place, it occurred to me to consider what business an English ship could have in that part of the world, since it was not the way to or from any part of the world where the English had any traffic; and I knew there had been no storms to drive them in there in distress; and that if they were really English it was most probable that they were here upon no good design; and that I had better continue as I was than fall into the hands of thieves and murderers.

Let no man despise the secret hints and notices of danger which sometimes are given him when he may think there is no possibility of its being real. That such hints and notices are given us I believe few that have made any observation of things can deny; that they are certain discoveries of an invisible world, and a converse of spirits, we cannot doubt; and if the tendency of them seems to be to warn us of danger, why should we not suppose they are from some friendly agent (whether supreme, or inferior and subordinate, is not the question), and that they are given for our good?

The present question abundantly confirms me in the justice of this reasoning; for had I not been made cautious by this secret admonition, come it from whence it will, I had been done inevitably, and in a far worse condition than before, as you will see presently. I had not kept myself long in this posture till I saw the boat draw near the shore, as if they looked for a creek to thrust in at, for the convenience of landing; however, as they did not come quite far enough, they did not see the little inlet where I formerly landed my rafts, but ran their boat on shore upon the beach, at about half a mile from me, which was very happy for me; for otherwise they would have landed just at my door, as I may say, and would soon have beaten me out of my castle, and perhaps have plundered me of all I had. When they were on shore I was fully satisfied they were Englishmen, at least most of them; one or two I thought were Dutch, but it did not prove so; there were in all eleven men, whereof three of them I found were unarmed and, as I thought, bound; and when the first four or five of them were jumped on shore, they took those three out of the boat as prisoners: one of the three I could perceive using the most passionate gestures of entreaty, affliction, and despair, even to a kind of extravagance; the other two, I could perceive, lifted up their hands sometimes, and appeared concerned indeed, but not to such a degree as the first. I was perfectly confounded at the sight, and knew not what the meaning of it should be. Friday called out to me in English, as well as he could, "O master! you see English mans eat prisoner as well as savage mans." "Why, Friday," says I, "do you think they are going to eat them, then?" "Yes," says Friday, "they will eat them." "No no," says I, "Friday; I am afraid they will murder them, indeed; but you may be sure they will not eat them."

All this while I had no thought of what the matter really was, but stood trembling with the horror of the sight, expecting every moment when the three prisoners should be killed; nay, once I saw one of the villains lift up his arm with a great cutlass, as the seamen call it, or sword, to strike one of the poor men; and I expected to see him fall every moment; at which all the blood in my body seemed to run chill in my veins. I wished heartily now for the Spaniard, and the savage that had gone with him, or that I had any way to have come undiscovered within shot of them, that I might have secured the three men, for I saw no firearms they had among them; but it fell out to my mind another way. After I had observed the outrageous usage of the three men by the insolent seamen, I observed the fellows run scattering about the island, as if they wanted to see the country. I observed that the three other men had liberty to go also where they pleased; but they sat down all three upon the ground, very pensive, and looked like men in despair. This put me in mind of the first time when I came on shore, and began to look about me; how I gave myself over for lost; how wildly I looked round me; what dreadful apprehensions I had; and how I lodged in the tree all night for fear of being devoured by wild beasts. As I knew nothing that night of the supply I was to receive by the providential driving of the ship nearer the land by the storms and tide, by which I have since been so long nourished and supported; so these three poor desolate men knew nothing how certain of deliverance and supply they were, how near it was to them, and how effectually and really they were in a condition of safety, at the same time that they thought themselves lost and their case desperate. So little do we see before us in the world, and so much reason have we to depend cheerfully upon the great Maker of the world, that He does not leave His creatures so absolutely destitute, but that in the worst circumstances they have always something to be thankful for, and sometimes are nearer deliverance than they imagine; nay, are even brought to their deliverance by the means by which they seem to be brought to their destruction.

It was just at high-water when these people came on shore; and while they rambled about to see what kind of a place they were in, they had carelessly stayed till the tide was spent, and the water was ebbed considerably away, leaving their boat aground. They had left two men in the boat, who, as I found afterwards, having drunk a little too much brandy, fell asleep; however, one of them waking a little sooner than the other and finding the boat too fast aground for him to stir it, hallooed out for the rest, who were straggling about: upon which they all soon came to the boat: but it was past all their strength to launch her, the boat being very heavy, and the shore on that side being a soft oozy sand, almost like a quicksand. In this condition, like true seamen, who are, perhaps, the least of all mankind given to fore-thought, they gave it over, and away they strolled about the country again; and I heard one of them say aloud to another, calling them off from the boat, "Why, let her alone, Jack, can't you? she'll float next tide;" by which I was fully confirmed in the main inquiry of what countrymen they were. All this while I kept myself very close, not once daring to stir out of my castle any farther than to my place of observation near the top of the hill: and very glad I was to think how well it was fortified. I knew it was no less than ten hours before the boat could float again, and by that time it would be dark, and I might be at more liberty to see their motions, and to hear their discourse, if they had any. In the meantime I fitted myself up for a battle as before, though with more caution, knowing I had to do with another kind of enemy than I had at first. I ordered Friday also, whom I had made an excellent marksman with his gun, to load himself with arms. I took myself two fowling-pieces, and I gave him three muskets. My figure, indeed, was very fierce; I had my formidable goat-skin coat on, with the great cap I have mentioned, a naked sword by my side, two pistols in my belt, and a gun upon each shoulder.

It was my design, as I said above, not to have made any attempt till it was dark; but about two o'clock, being the heat of the day, I found that they were all gone straggling into the woods, and, as I thought, laid down to sleep. The three poor distressed men, too anxious for their condition to get any sleep, had, however, sat down under the shelter of a great tree, at about a quarter of a mile from me, and, as I thought, out of sight of any of the rest. Upon this I resolved to discover myself to them, and learn something of their condition; immediately I marched as above, my man Friday at a good distance behind me, as formidable for his arms as I, but not making quite so staring a spectre-like figure as I did. I came as near them undiscovered as I could, and then, before any of them saw me, I called aloud to them in Span-ish, "What are ye, gentlemen?" They started up at the noise, but were ten times more confounded when they saw me, and the uncouth figure that I made. They made no answer at all, but I thought I perceived them just going to fly from me, when I spoke to them in English. "Gentlemen," said I, "do not be surprised at me; perhaps you may have a friend near when you did not expect it." "He must be sent directly from heaven then," said one of them very gravely to me, and pulling off his hat at the same time to me; "for our condition is past the help of man." "All help is from heaven, sir," said I, "but can you put a stranger in the way to help you? for you seem to be in some great distress. I saw you when you landed; and when you seemed to make application to the brutes that came with you, I saw one of them lift up his sword to kill you."

The poor man, with tears running down his face, and trembling, looking like one astonished, returned, "Am I talking to God or man? Is it a real man or an angel?" "Be in no fear about that, sir," said I; "if God had sent an angel to relieve you, he would have come better clothed, and armed after another manner than you see me; pray lay aside your fears; I am a man, an Englishman, and disposed to assist you; you see I have one servant only; we have arms and ammunition; tell us freely, can we serve you? What is your case?" "Our case, sir," said he, "is too long to tell you while our murderers are so near us; but, in short, sir, I was commander of that ship—my men have mutinied against me; they have been hardly prevailed on not to murder me, and, at last, have set me on shore in this desolate place, with these two men with me—one my mate, the other a passenger—where we expected to perish, believing the place to be uninhabited, and know not yet what to think of it." "Where are these brutes, your enemies?" said I; "do you know where they are gone? There they lie, sir," said he, pointing to a thicket of trees; "my heart trembles for fear they have seen us and heard you speak; if they have, they will certainly murder us all." "Have they any firearms?" said I. He answered, "They had only two pieces, one of which they left in the boat." "Well, then," said I, "leave the rest to me; I see they are all asleep; it is an easy thing to kill them all; but shall we rather take them prisoners?" He told me there were two desperate villains among them that it was scarce safe to show any mercy to; but if they were secured, he believed all the rest would return to their duty. I asked him which they were. He told me he could not at that distance distinguish them, but he would obey my orders in anything I would direct. "Well," says I, "let us retreat out of their view or hearing, lest they awake, and we will resolve further." So they willingly went back with me, till the woods covered us from them.

"Look you, sir," said I, "if I venture upon your deliverance, are you willing to make two conditions with me?" He anticipated my proposals by telling me that both he and the ship, if recovered, should be wholly directed and commanded by me in everything; and if the ship was not recovered, he would live and die with me in what part of the world soever I would send him; and the two other men said the same. "Well," says I, "my conditions are but two; first, that while you stay in this island with me, you will not pretend to any authority here; and if I put arms in your hands, you will, upon all occasions, give them up to me, and do no prejudice to me or mine upon this island, and in the meantime be governed by my orders; secondly, that if the ship is or may be recovered, you will carry me and my man to England passage free."

He gave me all the assurances that the invention or faith of man could devise that he would comply with these most reasonable demands, and besides would owe his life to me, and acknowledge it upon all occasions as long as he lived. "Well, then," said I, "here are three muskets for you, with powder and ball; tell me next what you think is proper to be done." He showed all the testimonies of his gratitude that he was able, but offered to be wholly guided by me. I told him I thought it was very hard venturing anything; but the best method I could think of was to fire on them at once as they lay, and if any were not killed at the first volley, and offered to submit, we might save them, and so put it wholly upon God's providence to direct the shot. He said, very modestly, that he was loath to kill them if he could help it; but that those two were incorrigible villains, and had been the authors of all the mutiny in the ship, and if they escaped, we should be undone still, for they would go on board and bring the whole ship's company, and destroy us all. "Well, then," says I, "necessity legitimates my advice, for it is the only way to save our lives." However, seeing him still cautious of shedding blood, I told him they should go themselves, and manage as they found convenient.

In the middle of this discourse we heard some of them awake, and soon after we saw two of them on their feet. I asked him if either of them were the heads of the mutiny? He said, "No." "Well, then," said I, "you may let them escape; and Providence seems to have awakened them on purpose to save themselves. Now," says I, "if the rest escape you, it is your fault." Animated with this, he took the musket I had given him in his hand, and a pistol in his belt, and his two comrades with him, with each a piece in his hand; the two men who were with him going first made some noise, at which one of the seamen who was awake turned about, and seeing them coming, cried out to the rest; but was too late then, for the moment he cried out they fired—I mean the two men, the captain wisely reserving his own piece. They had so well aimed their shot at the men they knew, that one of them was killed on the spot, and the other very much wounded; but not being dead, he started up on his feet, and called eagerly for help to the other; but the captain stepping to him, told him it was too late to cry for help, he should call upon God to forgive his villainy, and with that word knocked him down with the stock of his musket, so that he never spoke more; there were three more in the company, and one of them was slightly wounded. By this time I was come; and when they saw their danger, and that it was in vain to resist, they begged for mercy. The captain told them he would spare their lives if they would give him an assurance of their abhorrence of the treachery they had been guilty of, and would swear to be faithful to him in recovering the ship, and afterwards in carrying her back to Jamaica, from whence they came. They gave him all the protestations of their sincerity that could be desired; and he was willing to believe them, and spare their lives, which I was not against, only that I obliged him to keep them bound hand and foot while they were on the island.

While this was doing, I sent Friday with the captain's mate to the boat with orders to secure her, and bring away the oars and sails, which they did; and by-and-by three straggling men, that were (happily for them) parted from the rest, came back upon hearing the guns fired; and seeing the captain, who was before their prisoner, now their conqueror, they submitted to be bound also; and so our victory was complete.

It now remained that the captain and I should inquire into one another's circumstances. I began first, and told him my whole history, which he heard with an attention even to amazement—and particularly at the wonderful manner of my being furnished with provisions and ammunition; and, indeed, as my story is a whole collection of wonders, it affected him deeply. But when he reflected from thence upon himself, and how I seemed to have been preserved there on purpose to save his life, the tears ran down his face, and he could not speak a word more. After this communication was at an end, I carried him and his two men into my apartment, leading them in just where I came out, viz. at the top of the house, where I refreshed them with such provisions as I had, and showed them all the contrivances I had made during my long, long inhabiting that place.

All I showed them, all I said to them, was perfectly amazing; but above all, the captain admired my fortification, and how perfectly I had concealed my retreat with a grove of trees, which having been now planted nearly twenty years, and the trees growing much faster than in England, was become a little wood, so thick that it was impassable in any part of it but at that one side where I had reserved my little winding passage into it. I told him this was my castle and my residence, but that I had a seat in the country, as most princes have, whither I could retreat upon occasion, and I would show him that too another time; but at present our business was to consider how to recover the ship. He agreed with me as to that, but told me he was perfectly at a loss what measures to take, for that there were still six-and-twenty hands on board, who, having entered into a cursed conspiracy, by which they had all forfeited their lives to the law, would be hardened in it now by desperation, and would carry it on, knowing that if they were subdued they would be brought to the gallows as soon as they came to England, or to any of the English colonies, and that, therefore, there would be no attacking them with so small a number as we were.

I mused for some time on what he had said, and found it was a very rational conclusion, and that therefore something was to be resolved on speedily, as well to draw the men on board into some snare for their surprise as to prevent their landing upon us, and destroying us. Upon this, it presently occurred to me that in a little while the ship's crew, wondering what was become of their comrades and of the boat, would certainly come on shore in their other boat to look for them, and that then, perhaps, they might come armed, and be too strong for us: this he allowed to be rational. Upon this, I told him the first thing we had to do was to stave the boat which lay upon the beach, so that they might not carry her of, and taking everything out of her, leave her so far useless as not to be fit to swim. Accordingly, we went on board, took the arms which were left on board out of her, and whatever else we found there—which was a bottle of brandy, and another of rum, a few biscuit-cakes, a horn of powder, and a great lump of sugar in a piece of canvas (the sugar was five or six pounds): all which was very welcome to me, especially the brandy and sugar, of which I had had none left for many years.

When we had carried all these things on shore (the oars, mast, sail, and rudder of the boat were carried away before), we knocked a great hole in her bottom, that if they had come strong enough to master us, yet they could not carry off the boat. Indeed, it was not much in my thoughts that we could be able to recover the ship; but my view was, that if they went away without the boat, I did not much question to make her again fit to carry as to the Leeward Islands, and call upon our friends the Spaniards in my way, for I had them still in my thoughts.

Questions for Review:

1. Sum up the discussion between Robinson Crusoe and Friday regarding sailing to Friday's home. How do they prepare to do so?

2. Describe the danger Friday encounters, and what ensues.

3. What surprise does Friday discover? Why is it so meaningful?

4. What do Robinson Crusoe and Friday do for the victims of the cannibals? What does Robinson Crusoe send Friday to do at the battle?

5. What do they find out about the possibility of being attacked again?

6. What does Robinson Crusoe find out from the Spaniard? What vow does he extract from him?

7. What sensible idea does the Spaniard have? How do they make this happen? Where does Robinson Crusoe send him, and with what instructions?

8. What news does Friday bring? Why is Robinson Crusoe cautious? ($\rightarrow$)

9. What do the prisoners think of Robinson Crusoe at first? Describe what he does for them, and what he finds out from them, and how they respond.

10. Describe the conversation Robinson Crusoe has with the captain. What do they plan?

CHAPTER XVIII: THE SHIP RECOVERED

While we were thus preparing our designs, and had first, by main strength, heaved the boat upon the beach, so high that the tide would not float her off at high-water mark, and besides, had broke a hole in her bottom too big to be quickly stopped, and were set down musing what we should do, we heard the ship fire a gun, and make a waft with her ensign as a signal for the boat to come on board—but no boat stirred; and they fired several times, making other signals for the boat. At last, when all their signals and firing proved fruitless, and they found the boat did not stir, we saw them, by the help of my glasses, hoist another boat out and row towards the shore; and we found, as they approached, that there were no less than ten men in her, and that they had firearms with them.

As the ship lay almost two leagues from the shore, we had a full view of them as they came, and a plain sight even of their faces; because the tide having set them a little to the east of the other boat, they rowed up under shore, to come to the same place where the other had landed, and where the boat lay; by this means, I say, we had a full view of them, and the captain knew the persons and characters of all the men in the boat, of whom, he said, there were three very honest fellows, who, he was sure, were led into this conspiracy by the rest, being overpowered and frightened; but that as for the boatswain, who it seems was the chief officer among them, and all the rest, they were as outrageous as any of the ship's crew, and were no doubt made desperate in their new enterprise; and terribly apprehensive he was that they would be too powerful for us. I smiled at him, and told him that men in our circumstances were past the operation of fear; that seeing almost every condition that could be was better than that which we were supposed to be in, we ought to expect that the consequence, whether death or life, would be sure to be a deliverance. I asked him what he thought of the circumstances of my life, and whether a deliverance were not worth venturing for? "And where, sir," said I, "is your belief of my being preserved here on purpose to save your life, which elevated you a little while ago? For my part," said I, "there seems to be but one thing amiss in all the prospect of it." "What is that?" says he. "Why," said I, "it is, that as you say there are three or four honest fellows among them which should be spared, had they been all of the wicked part of the crew I should have thought God's providence had singled them out to deliver them into your hands; for depend upon it, every man that comes ashore is our own, and shall die or live as they behave to us." As I spoke this with a raised voice and cheerful countenance, I found it greatly encouraged him; so we set vigorously to our business.

We had, upon the first appearance of the boat's coming from the ship, considered of separating our prisoners; and we had, indeed, secured them effectually. Two of them, of whom the captain was less assured than ordinary, I sent with Friday, and one of the three delivered men, to my cave, where they were remote enough, and out of danger of being heard or discovered, or of finding their way out of the woods if they could have delivered themselves. Here they left them bound, but gave them provisions; and promised them, if they continued there quietly, to give them their liberty in a day or two; but that if they attempted their escape they should be put to death without mercy. They promised faithfully to bear their confinement with patience, and were very thankful that they had such good usage as to have provisions and light left them; for Friday gave them candles (such as we made ourselves) for their comfort; and they did not know but that he stood sentinel[151] over them at the entrance.

The other prisoners had better usage; two of them were kept pinioned, indeed, because the captain was not able to trust them; but the other two were taken into my service, upon the captain's recommendation, and upon their solemnly engaging to live and die with us; so with them and the three honest men we were seven men, well armed; and I made no doubt we should be able to deal well enough with the ten that were coming, considering that the captain had said there were three or four honest men among them also. As soon as they got to the place where their other boat lay, they ran their boat into the beach and came all on shore, hauling the boat up after them, which I was glad to see, for I was afraid they would rather have left the boat at an anchor some distance from the shore, with some hands in her to guard her, and so we should not be able to seize the boat. Being on shore, the first thing they did, they ran all to their other boat; and it was easy to see they

---

[151] guard

were under a great surprise to find her stripped, as above, of all that was in her, and a great hole in her bottom. After they had mused a while upon this, they set up two or three great shouts, hallooing with all their might, to try if they could make their companions hear; but all was to no purpose. Then they came all close in a ring, and fired a volley of their small arms, which indeed we heard, and the echoes made the woods ring. But it was all one; those in the cave, we were sure, could not hear; and those in our keeping, though they heard it well enough, yet durst give no answer to them. They were so astonished at the surprise of this, that, as they told us afterwards, they resolved to go all on board again to their ship, and let them know that the men were all murdered, and the long-boat staved; accordingly, they immediately launched their boat again, and got all of them on board.

The captain was terribly amazed, and even confounded, at this, believing they would go on board the ship again and set sail, giving their comrades over for lost, and so he should still lose the ship, which he was in hopes we should have recovered; but he was quickly as much frightened the other way.

They had not been long put off with the boat, when we perceived them all coming on shore again; but with this new measure in their conduct, which it seems they consulted together upon, viz. to leave three men in the boat, and the rest to go on shore, and go up into the country to look for their fellows. This was a great disappointment to us, for now we were at a loss what to do, as our seizing those seven men on shore would be no advantage to us if we let the boat escape; because they would row away to the ship, and then the rest of them would be sure to weigh and set sail, and so our recovering the ship would be lost. However, we had no remedy but to wait and see what the issue of things might present. The seven men came on shore, and the three who remained in the boat put her off to a good distance from the shore, and came to an anchor to wait for them; so that it was impossible for us to come at them in the boat. Those that came on shore kept close together, marching towards the top of the little hill under which my habitation lay; and we could see them plainly, though they could not perceive us. We should have been very glad if they would have come nearer us, so that we might have fired at them, or that they would have gone farther off, that we might come abroad. But when they were come to the brow of the hill where they could see a great way into the valleys and woods, which lay towards the north-east part, and where the island lay lowest, they shouted and hallooed till they were weary; and not caring, it seems, to venture far from the shore, nor far from one another, they sat down together under a tree to consider it. Had they thought fit to have gone to sleep there, as the other part of them had done, they had done the job for us; but they were too full of apprehensions of danger to venture to go to sleep, though they could not tell what the danger was they had to fear.

The captain made a very just proposal to me upon this consultation of theirs, viz. that perhaps they would all fire a volley again, to endeavour to make their fellows hear, and that we should all sally upon them just at the juncture when their pieces were all discharged, and they would certainly yield, and we should have them without bloodshed. I liked this proposal, provided it was done while we were near enough to come up to them before they could load their pieces again. But this event did not happen; and we lay still a long time, very irresolute what course to take. At length I told them there would be nothing done, in my opinion, till night; and then, if they did not return to the boat, perhaps we might find a way to get between them and the shore, and so might use some stratagem with them in the boat to get them on shore. We waited a great while, though very impatient for their removing; and were very uneasy when, after long consultation, we saw them all start up and march down towards the sea; it seems they had such dreadful apprehensions of the danger of the place that they resolved to go on board the ship again, give their companions over for lost, and so go on with their intended voyage with the ship.

As soon as I perceived them go towards the shore, I imagined it to be as it really was that they had given over their search, and were going back again; and the captain, as soon as I told him my thoughts, was ready to sink at the apprehensions of it; but I presently thought of a stratagem to fetch them back again, and which answered my end to a tittle. I ordered Friday and the captain's mate to go over the little creek westward, towards the place where the savages came on shore, when Friday was rescued, and so soon as they came to a little rising round, at about half a mile distant, I bid them halloo out, as loud as they could, and wait till they found the seamen heard them; that as soon as ever they heard the seamen answer them, they should return it again; and then, keeping out of sight, take a round, always answering when the others hallooed, to draw them as far into the island and among the woods as possible, and then wheel about again to me by such ways as I directed them.

They were just going into the boat when Friday and the mate hallooed; and they presently heard them, and answering, ran along the shore westward, towards the voice they heard, when they were stopped by the creek, where the water being up, they could not get over, and called for the boat to come up and set them over; as, indeed, I expected. When they had set themselves over, I observed that the boat being gone a good way into the creek, and, as it were, in a harbour within the land, they took one of the three men out of her, to go along with them, and left only two in the boat, having fastened her to the stump of a little tree on the shore. This was what I wished for; and immediately leaving Friday and the captain's mate to their business, I took the rest with me; and, crossing the creek out of their sight, we surprised the two men before they were aware—one of them lying on the shore, and the other being in the boat. The fellow on shore was between sleeping and waking, and going to start up; the captain, who was foremost, ran in upon him, and knocked him down; and then called out to him in the boat to yield, or he was a dead man. They needed very few arguments to persuade a single man to yield, when he saw five men upon him and his comrade knocked down: besides, this was, it seems, one of the three who were not so hearty in the mutiny as the rest of the crew, and therefore was easily persuaded not only to yield, but afterwards to join very sincerely with us. In the meantime, Friday and the captain's mate so well managed their business with the rest that they drew them, by hallooing and answering, from one hill to another, and from one wood to another, till they not only heartily tired them, but left them where they were, very sure they could not reach back to the boat before it was dark; and, indeed, they were heartily tired themselves also, by the time they came back to us.

We had nothing now to do but to watch for them in the dark, and to fall upon them, so as to make sure work with them. It was several hours after Friday came back to me before they came back to their boat; and we could hear the foremost of them, long before they came quite up, calling to those behind to come along; and could also hear them answer, and complain how lame and tired they were, and not able to come any faster: which was very welcome news to us. At length they came up to the boat: but it is impossible to express their confusion when they found the boat fast aground in the creek, the tide ebbed out, and their two men gone. We could hear them call one to another in a most lamentable manner, telling one another they were got into an enchanted island; that either there were inhabitants in it, and they should all be murdered, or else there were devils and spirits in it, and they should be all carried away and devoured. They hallooed again, and called their two comrades by their names a great many times; but no answer. After some time we could see them, by the little light there was, run about, wringing their hands like men in despair, and sometimes they would go and sit down in the boat to rest themselves: then come ashore again, and walk about again, and so the same thing over again. My men would fain have had me give them leave to fall upon them at once in the dark; but I was willing to take them at some advantage, so as to spare them, and kill as few of them as I could; and especially I was unwilling to hazard the killing of any of our men, knowing the others were very well armed. I resolved to wait, to see if they did not separate; and therefore, to make sure of them, I drew my ambuscade nearer, and ordered Friday and the captain to creep upon their hands and feet, as close to the ground as they could, that they might not be discovered, and get as near them as they could possibly before they offered to fire.

They had not been long in that posture when the boatswain, who was the principal ringleader of the mutiny, and had now shown himself the most dejected and dispirited of all the rest, came walking towards them, with two more of the crew; the captain was so eager at having this principal rogue so much in his power, that he could hardly have patience to let him come so near as to be sure of him, for they only heard his tongue before: but when they came nearer, the captain and Friday, starting up on their feet, let fly at them. The boatswain was killed upon the spot: the next man was shot in the body, and fell just by him, though he did not die till an hour or two after; and the third ran for it. At the noise of the fire I immediately advanced with my whole army, which was now eight men, viz. myself, generalissimo;[152] Friday, my lieutenant-general; the captain and his two men, and the three prisoners of war whom we had trusted with arms. We came upon them, indeed, in the dark, so that they could not see our number; and I made the man they had left in the boat, who was now one of us, to call them by name, to try if I could bring them to a parley,[153] and so perhaps might reduce them to terms; which fell out just as we desired: for indeed it was easy to think, as their condition then was, they would be very willing to capitulate. So he calls out as loud as he could to one of them, "Tom Smith! Tom Smith!" Tom Smith answered immediately, "Is that Robinson?" for it seems he knew the voice. The other answered, "Ay, ay; for God's sake, Tom Smith, throw down your arms and yield, or you are all dead men this moment." "Who must we yield to? Where are they?" says Smith again. "Here they are," says he; "here's our captain and fifty men with him, have been hunting you these two hours; the boatswain is killed; Will Fry is wounded, and I am a prisoner; and if you do not yield you are all lost." "Will they give us quarter, then?" says Tom Smith, "and we will yield." "I'll go and ask, if you promise to yield," said Robinson: so he asked the captain, and the captain himself then calls out, "You, Smith, you know my voice; if you lay down your arms immediately and submit, you shall have your lives, all but Will Atkins."

Upon this Will Atkins cried out, "Captain, give me quarter; what have I done? They have all been as bad as I!" Which, by the way, was not true; for it seems this Will Atkins was the first man that laid hold of the captain when they first mutinied, and used him barbarously in tying his hands and giving him injurious language. However, the captain told him he must lay down his arms at discretion, and trust to the governor's mercy: by which he meant me, for they all called me governor. In a word, they all laid down their arms

[152] supreme commander
[153] negotiation, meeting

and begged their lives; and I sent the man that had parleyed with them, and two more, who bound them all; and then my great army of fifty men, which, with those three, were in all but eight, came up and seized upon them, and upon their boat; only that I kept myself and one more out of sight for reasons of state.

Our next work was to repair the boat, and think of seizing the ship: and as for the captain, now he had leisure to parley with them, he expostulated with them upon the villainy of their practices with him, and upon the further wickedness of their design, and how certainly it must bring them to misery and distress in the end, and perhaps to the gallows. They all appeared very penitent,[154] and begged hard for their lives. As for that, he told them they were not his prisoners, but the commander's of the island; that they thought they had set him on shore in a barren, uninhabited island; but it had pleased God so to direct them that it was inhabited, and that the governor was an Englishman; that he might hang them all there, if he pleased; but as he had given them all quarter, he supposed he would send them to England, to be dealt with there as justice required, except Atkins, whom he was commanded by the governor to advise to prepare for death, for that he would be hanged in the morning.

Though this was all but a fiction of his own, yet it had its desired effect; Atkins fell upon his knees to beg the captain to intercede with the governor for his life; and all the rest begged of him, for God's sake, that they might not be sent to England.

It now occurred to me that the time of our deliverance was come, and that it would be a most easy thing to bring these fellows in to be hearty in getting possession of the ship; so I retired in the dark from them, that they might not see what kind of a governor they had, and called the captain to me; when I called, at a good distance, one of the men was ordered to speak again, and say to the captain, "Captain, the commander calls for you;" and presently the captain replied, "Tell his excellency I am just coming." This more perfectly amazed them, and they all believed that the commander was just by, with his fifty men. Upon the captain coming to me, I told him my project for seizing the ship, which he liked wonderfully well, and resolved to put it in execution the next morning. But, in order to execute it with more art, and to be secure of success, I told him we must divide the prisoners, and that he should go and take Atkins, and two more of the worst of them, and send them pinioned to the cave where the others lay. This was committed to Friday and the two men who came on shore with the captain. They conveyed them to the cave as to a prison: and it was, indeed, a dismal place, especially to men in their condition. The others I ordered to my bower, as I

---

[154] sorry, remorseful

called it, of which I have given a full description: and as it was fenced in, and they pinioned, the place was secure enough, considering they were upon their behaviour.

To these in the morning I sent the captain, who was to enter into a parley with them; in a word, to try them, and tell me whether he thought they might be trusted or not to go on board and surprise the ship. He talked to them of the injury done him, of the condition they were brought to, and that though the governor had given them quarter for their lives as to the present action, yet that if they were sent to England they would all be hanged in chains; but that if they would join in so just an attempt as to recover the ship, he would have the governor's engagement for their pardon.

Any one may guess how readily such a proposal would be accepted by men in their condition; they fell down on their knees to the captain, and promised, with the deepest imprecations,[155] that they would be faithful to him to the last drop, and that they should owe their lives to him, and would go with him all over the world; that they would own him as a father to them as long as they lived. "Well," says the captain, "I must go and tell the governor what you say, and see what I can do to bring him to consent to it." So he brought me an account of the temper he found them in, and that he verily believed they would be faithful. However, that we might be very secure, I told him he should go back again and choose out those five, and tell them, that they might see he did not want men, that he would take out those five to be his assistants, and that the governor would keep the other two, and the three that were sent prisoners to the castle (my cave), as hostages for the fidelity of those five; and that if they proved unfaithful in the execution, the five hostages should be hanged in chains alive on the shore. This looked severe, and convinced them that the governor was in earnest; however, they had no way left them but to accept it; and it was now the business of the prisoners, as much as of the captain, to persuade the other five to do their duty.

Our strength was now thus ordered for the expedition: first, the captain, his mate, and passenger; second, the two prisoners of the first gang, to whom, having their character from the captain, I had given their liberty, and trusted them with arms; third, the other two that I had kept till now in my bower, pinioned, but on the captain's motion had now released; fourth, these five released at last; so that there were twelve in all, besides five we kept prisoners in the cave for hostages.

I asked the captain if he was willing to venture with these hands on board the ship; but as for me and my man Friday, I did not think it was proper for us to stir, having seven men left behind; and it was employment

---

[155] oaths

enough for us to keep them asunder, and supply them with victuals. As to the five in the cave, I resolved to keep them fast, but Friday went in twice a day to them, to supply them with necessaries; and I made the other two carry provisions to a certain distance, where Friday was to take them.

When I showed myself to the two hostages, it was with the captain, who told them I was the person the governor had ordered to look after them; and that it was the governor's pleasure they should not stir anywhere but by my direction; that if they did, they would be fetched into the castle, and be laid in irons: so that as we never suffered them to see me as governor, I now appeared as another person, and spoke of the governor, the garrison, the castle, and the like, upon all occasions.

The captain now had no difficulty before him, but to furnish his two boats, stop the breach[156] of one, and man them. He made his passenger captain of one, with four of the men; and himself, his mate, and five more, went in the other; and they contrived their business very well, for they came up to the ship about midnight. As soon as they came within call of the ship, he made Robinson hail them, and tell them they had brought off the men and the boat, but that it was a long time before they had found them, and the like, holding them in a chat till they came to the ship's side; when the captain and the mate entering first with their arms, immediately knocked down the second mate and carpenter with the butt-end of their muskets, being very faithfully seconded by their men; they secured all the rest that were upon the main and quarter decks, and began to fasten the hatches, to keep them down that were below; when the other boat and their men, entering at the forechains, secured the forecastle of the ship, and the scuttle which went down into the cook-room, making three men they found there prisoners. When this was done, and all safe upon deck, the captain ordered the mate, with three men, to break into the round-house, where the new rebel captain lay, who, having taken the alarm, had got up, and with two men and a boy had got firearms in their hands; and when the mate, with a crow, split open the door, the new captain and his men fired boldly among them, and wounded the mate with a musket ball, which broke his arm, and wounded two more of the men, but killed nobody. The mate, calling for help, rushed, however, into the round-house, wounded as he was, and, with his pistol, shot the new captain through the head, the bullet entering at his mouth, and came out again behind one of his ears, so that he never spoke a word more: upon which the rest yielded, and the ship was taken effectually, without any more lives lost.

As soon as the ship was thus secured, the captain ordered seven guns to be fired, which was the signal agreed upon with me to give me notice of his

---

[156] hole (in the bottom of the boat)

success, which, you may be sure, I was very glad to hear, having sat watching upon the shore for it till near two o'clock in the morning. Having thus heard the signal plainly, I laid me down; and it having been a day of great fatigue to me, I slept very sound, till I was surprised with the noise of a gun; and presently starting up, I heard a man call me by the name of "Governor! Governor!" and presently I knew the captain's voice; when, climbing up to the top of the hill, there he stood, and, pointing to the ship, he embraced me in his arms, "My dear friend and deliverer," says he, "there's your ship; for she is all yours, and so are we, and all that belong to her." I cast my eyes to the ship, and there she rode, within little more than half a mile of the shore; for they had weighed her anchor as soon as they were masters of her, and, the weather being fair, had brought her to an anchor just against the mouth of the little creek; and the tide being up, the captain had brought the pinnace in near the place where I had first landed my rafts, and so landed just at my door. I was at first ready to sink down with the surprise; for I saw my deliverance, indeed, visibly put into my hands, all things easy, and a large ship just ready to carry me away whither I pleased to go. At first, for some time, I was not able to answer him one word; but as he had taken me in his arms I held fast by him, or I should have fallen to the ground. He perceived the surprise, and immediately pulled a bottle out of his pocket and gave me a dram of cordial, which he had brought on purpose for me. After I had drunk it, I sat down upon the ground; and though it brought me to myself, yet it was a good while before I could speak a word to him. All this time the poor man was in as great an ecstasy as I, only not under any surprise as I was; and he said a thousand kind and tender things to me, to compose and bring me to myself; but such was the flood of joy in my breast, that it put all my spirits into confusion: at last it broke out into tears, and in a little while after I recovered my speech; I then took my turn, and embraced him as my deliverer, and we rejoiced together. I told him I looked upon him as a man sent by Heaven to deliver me, and that the whole transaction seemed to be a chain of wonders; that such things as these were the testimonies we had of a secret hand of Providence governing the world, and an evidence that the eye of an infinite Power could search into the remotest corner of the world, and send help to the miserable whenever He pleased. I forgot not to lift up my heart in thankfulness to Heaven; and what heart could forbear to bless Him, who had not only in a miraculous manner provided for me in such a wilderness, and in such a desolate condition, but from whom every deliverance must always be acknowledged to proceed.

When we had talked a while, the captain told me he had brought me some little refreshment, such as the ship afforded, and such as the wretches that had been so long his masters had not plundered him of. Upon this, he called aloud to the boat, and bade his men bring the things ashore that were for the governor; and, indeed, it was a present as if I had been one that was not to be carried away with them, but as if I had been to dwell upon the island still. First, he had brought me a case of bottles full of excellent cordial waters, six large bottles of Madeira wine (the bottles held two quarts each), two pounds of excellent good tobacco, twelve good pieces of the ship's beef, and six pieces of pork, with a bag of peas, and about a hundred-weight of biscuit; he also brought me a box of sugar, a box of flour, a bag full of lemons, and two bottles of lime-juice, and abundance of other things. But besides these, and what was a thousand times more useful to me, he brought me six new clean shirts, six very good neckcloths, two pair of gloves, one pair of shoes, a hat, and one pair of stockings, with a very good suit of clothes of his own, which had been worn but very little: in a word, he clothed me from head to foot. It was a very kind and agreeable present, as any one may imagine, to one in my circumstances, but never was anything in the world of that kind so unpleasant, awkward, and uneasy as it was to me to wear such clothes at first.

After these ceremonies were past, and after all his good things were brought into my little apartment, we began to consult what was to be done with the prisoners we had; for it was worth considering whether we might venture to take them with us or no, especially two of them, whom he knew to be incorrigible[157] and refractory[158] to the last degree; and the captain said he knew they were such rogues that there was no obliging them, and if he did carry them away, it must be in irons, as malefactors, to be delivered over to justice at the first English colony he could come to; and I found that the captain himself was very anxious about it. Upon this, I told him that, if he desired it, I would undertake to bring the two men he spoke of to make it their own request that he should leave them upon the island. "I should be very glad of that," says the captain, "with all my heart." "Well," says I, "I will send for them up and talk with them for you." So I caused Friday and the two hostages, for they were now discharged, their comrades having performed their promise; I say, I caused them to go to the cave, and bring up the five men, pinioned as they were, to the bower, and keep them there till I came. After some time, I came thither dressed in my new habit; and now I was called governor again. Being all met, and the captain with me, I caused the men to be brought before me, and I told them I had got a full account of their villainous behaviour to the captain, and how they had run away with the ship, and were preparing to commit further robberies, but that Providence had ensnared them in their own ways, and that they were fallen

---

[157] hopelessly evil
[158] rebellious

into the pit which they had dug for others.[159] I let them know that by my direction the ship had been seized; that she lay now in the road; and they might see by-and-by that their new captain had received the reward of his villainy, and that they would see him hanging at the yard-arm; that, as to them, I wanted to know what they had to say why I should not execute them as pirates taken in the fact, as by my commission they could not doubt but I had authority so to do. One of them answered in the name of the rest, that they had nothing to say but this, that when they were taken the captain promised them their lives, and they humbly implored my mercy. But I told them I knew not what mercy to show them; for as for myself, I had resolved to quit the island with all my men, and had taken passage with the captain to go to England; and as for the captain, he could not carry them to England other than as prisoners in irons, to be tried for mutiny and running away with the ship; the consequence of which, they must needs know, would be the gallows; so that I could not tell what was best for them, unless they had a mind to take their fate in the island. If they desired that, as I had liberty to leave the island, I had some inclination to give them their lives, if they thought they could shift on shore. They seemed very thankful for it, and said they would much rather venture to stay there than be carried to England to be hanged. So I left it on that issue.

However, the captain seemed to make some difficulty of it, as if he durst not leave them there. Upon this I seemed a little angry with the captain, and told him that they were my prisoners, not his; and that seeing I had offered them so much favour, I would be as good as my word; and that if he did not think fit to consent to it I would set them at liberty, as I found them: and if he did not like it he might take them again if he could catch them. Upon this they appeared very thankful, and I accordingly set them at liberty, and bade them retire into the woods, to the place whence they came, and I would leave them some firearms, some ammunition, and some directions how they should live very well if they thought fit. Upon this I prepared to go on board the ship; but told the captain I would stay that night to prepare my things, and desired him to go on board in the meantime, and keep all right in the ship, and send the boat on shore next day for me; ordering him, at all events, to cause the new captain, who was killed, to be hanged at the yard-arm, that these men might see him.

When the captain was gone I sent for the men up to me to my apartment, and entered seriously into discourse with them on their circumstances. I told them I thought they had made a right choice; that if the captain had carried them away they would certainly be hanged. I showed them the new captain

---

[159] "He that diggeth a pit shall fall into it; and whoso breaketh an hedge [wall], a serpent shall bite him" (Ecclesiastes 10:8). Ouch.

hanging at the yard-arm of the ship, and told them they had nothing less to expect.

When they had all declared their willingness to stay, I then told them I would let them into the story of my living there, and put them into the way of making it easy to them. Accordingly, I gave them the whole history of the place, and of my coming to it; showed them my fortifications, the way I made my bread, planted my corn, cured my grapes; and, in a word, all that was necessary to make them easy. I told them the story also of the seventeen Spaniards that were to be expected, for whom I left a letter, and made them promise to treat them in common with themselves. Here it may be noted that the captain, who had ink on board, was greatly surprised that I never hit upon a way of making ink of charcoal and water, or of something else, as I had done things much more difficult.

I left them my firearms—viz. five muskets, three fowling-pieces, and three swords. I had above a barrel and a half of powder left; for after the first year or two I used but little, and wasted none. I gave them a description of the way I managed the goats, and directions to milk and fatten them, and to make both butter and cheese. In a word, I gave them every part of my own story; and told them I should prevail with the captain to leave them two barrels of gunpowder more, and some garden-seeds, which I told them I would have been very glad of. Also, I gave them the bag of peas which the captain had brought me to eat, and bade them be sure to sow and increase them.

Questions for Review:

1. How do Robinson Crusoe and his men capture the mutineers?

2. What is ironic and humorous about the men calling Robinson Crusoe "governor"? How does he overcome the ship?

3. How does Robinson Crusoe react when he realizes he can sail away? Describe the captain's generosity, and which gift is most precious.

4. Sum up the deal Robinson Crusoe offers the mutineers. How does he generously help them?

CHAPTER XIX: RETURN TO ENGLAND

Having done all this I left them the next day, and went on board the ship. We prepared immediately to sail, but did not weigh[160] that night. The next morning early, two of the five men came swimming to the ship's side, and making the most lamentable complaint of the other three, begged to be taken into the ship for God's sake, for they should be murdered, and begged the captain to take them on board, though he hanged them immediately. Upon this the captain pretended to have no power without me; but after some difficulty, and after their solemn promises of amendment, they were taken on board, and were, some time after, soundly whipped and pickled;[161] after which they proved very honest and quiet fellows.

Some time after this, the boat was ordered on shore, the tide being up, with the things promised to the men; to which the captain, at my intercession, caused their chests and clothes to be added, which they took, and were very thankful for. I also encouraged them, by telling them that if it lay in my power to send any vessel to take them in, I would not forget them.

When I took leave of this island, I carried on board, for relics, the great goat-skin cap I had made, my umbrella, and one of my parrots; also, I forgot not to take the money I formerly mentioned, which had lain by me so long useless that it was grown rusty or tarnished, and could hardly pass for silver till it had been a little rubbed and handled, as also the money I found in the wreck of the Spanish ship. And thus I left the island, the 19th of December, as I found by the ship's account, in the year 1686, after I had been upon it eight-and-twenty years, two months, and nineteen days; being delivered from this second captivity the same day of the month that I first made my escape in the long-boat from among the Moors of Sallee. In this vessel, after a long voyage, I arrived in England the 11th of June, in the year 1687, having been thirty-five years absent.

When I came to England I was as perfect a stranger to all the world as if I had never been known there. My benefactor and faithful steward, whom I had left my money in trust with, was alive, but had had great misfortunes in

---

[160] pull up the anchor
[161] had vinegar or salt rubbed into their whipped backs to increase the pain of a whipping

the world; was become a widow the second time, and very low in the world. I made her very easy as to what she owed me, assuring her I would give her no trouble; but, on the contrary, in gratitude for her former care and faithfulness to me, I relieved her as my little stock would afford; which at that time would, indeed, allow me to do but little for her; but I assured her I would never forget her former kindness to me; nor did I forget her when I had sufficient to help her, as shall be observed in its proper place. I went down afterwards into Yorkshire; but my father was dead, and my mother and all the family extinct, except that I found two sisters, and two of the children of one of my brothers; and as I had been long ago given over for dead, there had been no provision made for me; so that, in a word, I found nothing to relieve or assist me; and that the little money I had would not do much for me as to settling in the world.

I met with one piece of gratitude indeed, which I did not expect; and this was, that the master of the ship, whom I had so happily delivered, and by the same means saved the ship and cargo, having given a very handsome account to the owners of the manner how I had saved the lives of the men and the ship, they invited me to meet them and some other merchants concerned, and all together made me a very handsome compliment upon the subject, and a present of almost £200 sterling.

But after making several reflections upon the circumstances of my life, and how little way this would go towards settling me in the world, I resolved to go to Lisbon, and see if I might not come at some information of the state of my plantation in the Brazils, and of what was become of my partner, who, I had reason to suppose, had some years past given me over for dead. With this view I took shipping for Lisbon, where I arrived in April following, my man Friday accompanying me very honestly in all these ramblings, and proving a most faithful servant upon all occasions. When I came to Lisbon, I found out, by inquiry, and to my particular satisfaction, my old friend, the captain of the ship who first took me up at sea off the shore of Africa. He was now grown old, and had left off going to sea, having put his son, who was far from a young man, into his ship, and who still used the Brazil trade. The old man did not know me, and indeed I hardly knew him. But I soon brought him to my remembrance, and as soon brought myself to his remembrance, when I told him who I was.

After some passionate expressions of the old acquaintance between us, I inquired, you may be sure, after my plantation and my partner. The old man told me he had not been in the Brazils for about nine years; but that he could assure me that when he came away my partner was living, but the trustees whom I had joined with him to take cognisance of my part were both dead: that, however, he believed I would have a very good account of the improvement of the plantation; for that, upon the general belief of my being cast away and drowned, my trustees had given in the account of the produce of my part of the plantation to the procurator-fiscal, who had appropriated it, in case I never came to claim it, one-third to the king, and two-thirds to the monastery of St. Augustine, to be expended for the benefit of the poor, and for the conversion of the Indians to the Catholic faith: but that, if I appeared, or any one for me, to claim the inheritance, it would be restored; only that the improvement, or annual production, being distributed to charitable uses, could not be restored: but he assured me that the steward of the king's revenue from lands, and the providore, or steward of the monastery, had taken great care all along that the incumbent, that is to say my partner, gave every year a faithful account of the produce, of which they had duly received my moiety.[162] I asked him if he knew to what height of improvement he had brought the plantation, and whether he thought it might be worth looking after; or whether, on my going thither, I should meet with any obstruction to my possessing my just right in the moiety. He told me he could not tell exactly to what degree the plantation was improved; but this he knew, that my partner was grown exceeding rich upon the enjoying his part of it; and that, to the best of his remembrance, he had heard that the king's third of my part, which was, it seems, granted away to some other monastery or religious house, amounted to above two hundred moidores a year: that as to my being restored to a quiet possession of it, there was no question to be made of that, my partner being alive to witness my title, and my name being also enrolled in the register of the country; also he told me that the survivors of my two trustees were very fair, honest people, and very wealthy; and he believed I would not only have their assistance for putting me in possession, but would find a very considerable sum of money in their hands for my account, being the produce of the farm while their fathers held the trust, and before it was given up, as above; which, as he remembered, was for about twelve years.

I showed myself a little concerned and uneasy at this account, and inquired of the old captain how it came to pass that the trustees should thus dispose of my effects, when he knew that I had made my will, and had made him, the Portuguese captain, my universal heir, &c.

He told me that was true; but that as there was no proof of my being dead, he could not act as executor until some certain account should come of my death; and, besides, he was not willing to intermeddle with a thing so remote: that it was true he had registered my will, and put in his claim; and could he have given any account of my being dead or alive, he would have acted by procuration, and taken possession of the ingenio (so they call the sugar-house), and have given his son, who was now at the Brazils, orders

---

[162] share, portion

to do it. "But," says the old man, "I have one piece of news to tell you, which perhaps may not be so acceptable to you as the rest; and that is, believing you were lost, and all the world believing so also, your partner and trustees did offer to account with me, in your name, for the first six or eight years' profits, which I received. There being at that time great disbursements for increasing the works, building an ingenio, and buying slaves, it did not amount to near so much as afterwards it produced; however," says the old man, "I shall give you a true account of what I have received in all, and how I have disposed of it."

After a few days' further conference with this ancient friend, he brought me an account of the first six years' income of my plantation, signed by my partner and the merchant-trustees, being always delivered in goods, viz. tobacco in roll, and sugar in chests, besides rum, molasses, &c., which is the consequence of a sugar-work; and I found by this account, that every year the income considerably increased; but, as above, the disbursements being large, the sum at first was small: however, the old man let me see that he was debtor to me four hundred and seventy moidores of gold, besides sixty chests of sugar and fifteen double rolls of tobacco, which were lost in his ship; he having been shipwrecked coming home to Lisbon, about eleven years after my having the place. The good man then began to complain of his misfortunes, and how he had been obliged to make use of my money to recover his losses, and buy him a share in a new ship. "However, my old friend," says he, "you shall not want a supply in your necessity; and as soon as my son returns you shall be fully satisfied." Upon this he pulls out an old pouch, and gives me one hundred and sixty Portugal moidores in gold; and giving the writings of his title to the ship, which his son was gone to the Brazils in, of which he was quarter-part owner, and his son another, he puts them both into my hands for security of the rest.

I was too much moved with the honesty and kindness of the poor man to be able to bear this; and remembering what he had done for me, how he had taken me up at sea, and how generously he had used me on all occasions, and particularly how sincere a friend he was now to me, I could hardly refrain weeping at what he had said to me; therefore I asked him if his circumstances admitted him to spare so much money at that time, and if it would not straiten him? He told me he could not say but it might straiten him a little; but, however, it was my money, and I might want[163] it more than he.

Everything the good man said was full of affection, and I could hardly refrain from tears while he spoke; in short, I took one hundred of the moidores, and called for a pen and ink to give him a receipt for them: then I returned him the rest, and told him if ever I had possession of the plantation

---

[163] need, lack

I would return the other to him also (as, indeed, I afterwards did); and that as to the bill of sale of his part in his son's ship, I would not take it by any means; but that if I wanted the money, I found he was honest enough to pay me; and if I did not, but came to receive what he gave me reason to expect, I would never have a penny more from him.

When this was past, the old man asked me if he should put me into a method to make my claim to my plantation. I told him I thought to go over to it myself. He said I might do so if I pleased, but that if I did not, there were ways enough to secure my right, and immediately to appropriate the profits to my use: and as there were ships in the river of Lisbon just ready to go away to Brazil, he made me enter my name in a public register, with his affidavit, affirming, upon oath, that I was alive, and that I was the same person who took up the land for the planting the said plantation at first. His being regularly attested by a notary, and a procuration affixed, he directed me to send it, with a letter of his writing, to a merchant of his acquaintance at the place; and then proposed my staying with him till an account came of the return.

Never was anything more honourable than the proceedings upon this procuration; for in less than seven months I received a large packet from the survivors of my trustees, the merchants, for whose account I went to sea, in which were the following, particular letters and papers enclosed:—

First, there was the account-current of the produce of my farm or plantation, from the year when their fathers had balanced with my old Portugal captain, being for six years; the balance appeared to be one thousand one hundred and seventy-four moidores in my favour.

Secondly, there was the account of four years more, while they kept the effects in their hands, before the government claimed the administration, as being the effects of a person not to be found, which they called civil death; and the balance of this, the value of the plantation increasing, amounted to nineteen thousand four hundred and forty-six crusadoes, being about three thousand two hundred and forty moidores.

Thirdly, there was the Prior of St. Augustine's account, who had received the profits for above fourteen years; but not being able to account for what was disposed of by the hospital, very honestly declared he had eight hundred and seventy-two moidores not distributed, which he acknowledged to my account: as to the king's part, that refunded nothing.

There was a letter of my partner's, congratulating me very affectionately upon my being alive, giving me an account how the estate was improved, and what it produced a year; with the particulars of the number of squares, or acres that it contained, how planted, how many slaves there were upon it: and making two-and-twenty crosses for blessings, told me he had said so many Ave Marias[164] to thank the Blessed Virgin that I was alive; inviting me very passionately to come over and take possession of my own, and in the meantime to give him orders to whom he should deliver my effects if I did not come myself; concluding with a hearty tender of his friendship, and that of his family; and sent me as a present seven fine leopards' skins, which he had, it seems, received from Africa, by some other ship that he had sent thither, and which, it seems, had made a better voyage than I. He sent me also five chests of excellent sweetmeats, and a hundred pieces of gold un-coined, not quite so large as moidores. By the same fleet my two merchant-trustees shipped me one thousand two hundred chests of sugar, eight hundred rolls of tobacco, and the rest of the whole account in gold.

I might well say now, indeed, that the latter end of Job was better than the beginning.[165] It is impossible to express the flutterings of my very heart when I found all my wealth about me; for as the Brazil ships come all in fleets, the same ships which brought my letters brought my goods: and the effects were safe in the river before the letters came to my hand. In a word, I turned pale, and grew sick; and, had not the old man run and fetched me a cordial, I believe the sudden surprise of joy had overset nature, and I had died upon the spot: nay, after that I continued very ill, and was so some hours, till a physician being sent for, and something of the real cause of my illness being known, he ordered me to be let blood; after which I had relief, and grew well: but I verily believe, if I had not been eased by a vent given in that manner to the spirits, I should have died.

I was now master, all on a sudden, of above five thousand pounds sterling in money, and had an estate, as I might well call it, in the Brazils, of above a thousand pounds a year, as sure as an estate of lands in England: and, in a word, I was in a condition which I scarce knew how to understand, or how to compose myself for the enjoyment of it. The first thing I did was to recompense[166] my original benefactor, my good old captain, who had been first charitable to me in my distress, kind to me in my beginning, and honest to me at the end. I showed him all that was sent to me; I told him that, next to the providence of Heaven, which disposed all things, it was owing to him; and that it now lay on me to reward him, which I would do a hundred-fold: so I first returned to him the hundred moidores I had received of him; then I sent for a notary, and caused him to draw up a general release or dis-charge from the four hundred and seventy moidores, which he had ac-knowledged he owed me, in the fullest and firmest manner possible. After which I caused a procuration to be drawn, empowering him to be the re-ceiver of the annual profits of my plantation: and appointing my partner to

---

[164] Latin for "Hail, Mary" (prayers to Mary offered by Roman Catholics)
[165] See Job 42:12.
[166] reward, repay

account with him, and make the returns, by the usual fleets, to him in my name; and by a clause in the end, made a grant of one hundred moidores a year to him during his life, out of the effects, and fifty moidores a year to his son after him, for his life: and thus I requited my old man.

I had now to consider which way to steer my course next, and what to do with the estate that Providence had thus put into my hands; and, indeed, I had more care upon my head now than I had in my state of life in the island where I wanted nothing but what I had, and had nothing but what I wanted; whereas I had now a great charge upon me, and my business was how to secure it. I had not a cave now to hide my money in, or a place where it might lie without lock or key, till it grew mouldy and tarnished before anybody would meddle with it; on the contrary, I knew not where to put it, or whom to trust with it. My old patron, the captain, indeed, was honest, and that was the only refuge I had. In the next place, my interest in the Brazils seemed to summon me thither; but now I could not tell how to think of going thither till I had settled my affairs, and left my effects in some safe hands behind me. At first I thought of my old friend the widow, who I knew was honest, and would be just to me; but then she was in years, and but poor, and, for aught I knew, might be in debt: so that, in a word, I had no way but to go back to England myself and take my effects with me.

It was some months, however, before I resolved upon this; and, therefore, as I had rewarded the old captain fully, and to his satisfaction, who had been my former benefactor, so I began to think of the poor widow, whose husband had been my first benefactor, and she, while it was in her power, my faithful steward and instructor. So, the first thing I did, I got a merchant in Lisbon to write to his correspondent in London, not only to pay a bill, but to go find her out, and carry her, in money, a hundred pounds from me, and to talk with her, and comfort her in her poverty, by telling her she should, if I lived, have a further supply: at the same time I sent my two sisters in the country a hundred pounds each, they being, though not in want, yet not in very good circumstances; one having been married and left a widow; and the other having a husband not so kind to her as he should be. But among all my relations or acquaintances I could not yet pitch upon one to whom I durst[167] commit the gross of my stock, that I might go away to the Brazils, and leave things safe behind me; and this greatly perplexed me.

I had once a mind to have gone to the Brazils and have settled myself there, for I was, as it were, naturalised to the place; but I had some little scruple in my mind about religion, which insensibly drew me back. However, it was not religion that kept me from going there for the present; and as I had made no scruple of being openly of the religion of the country all

---

[167] dared

the while I was among them, so neither did I yet; only that, now and then, having of late thought more of it than formerly, when I began to think of living and dying among them, I began to regret having professed myself a Papist, and thought it might not be the best religion to die with.

But, as I have said, this was not the main thing that kept me from going to the Brazils, but that really I did not know with whom to leave my effects behind me; so I resolved at last to go to England, where, if I arrived, I concluded that I should make some acquaintance, or find some relations, that would be faithful to me; and, accordingly, I prepared to go to England with all my wealth.

In order to prepare things for my going home, I first (the Brazil fleet being just going away) resolved to give answers suitable to the just and faithful account of things I had from thence; and, first, to the Prior of St. Augustine I wrote a letter full of thanks for his just dealings, and the offer of the eight hundred and seventy-two moidores which were undisposed of, which I desired might be given, five hundred to the monastery, and three hundred and seventy-two to the poor, as the prior should direct; desiring the good padre's prayers for me, and the like. I wrote next a letter of thanks to my two trustees, with all the acknowledgment that so much justice and honesty called for: as for sending them any present, they were far above having any occasion of it. Lastly, I wrote to my partner, acknowledging his industry in the improving the plantation, and his integrity in increasing the stock of the works; giving him instructions for his future government of my part, according to the powers I had left with my old patron, to whom I desired him to send whatever became due to me, till he should hear from me more particularly; assuring him that it was my intention not only to come to him, but to settle myself there for the remainder of my life. To this I added a very handsome present of some Italian silks for his wife and two daughters, for such the captain's son informed me he had; with two pieces of fine English broadcloth, the best I could get in Lisbon, five pieces of black baize, and some Flanders lace of a good value.

Having thus settled my affairs, sold my cargo, and turned all my effects into good bills of exchange, my next difficulty was which way to go to England: I had been accustomed enough to the sea, and yet I had a strange aversion to go to England by the sea at that time, and yet I could give no reason for it, yet the difficulty increased upon me so much, that though I had once shipped my baggage in order to go, yet I altered my mind, and that not once but two or three times.

It is true I had been very unfortunate by sea, and this might be one of the reasons; but let no man slight the strong impulses of his own thoughts in cases of such moment: two of the ships which I had singled out to go in, I mean more particularly singled out than any other, having put my things on board one of them, and in the other having agreed with the captain; I say two of these ships miscarried. One was taken by the Algerines, and the other was lost on the Start, near Torbay, and all the people drowned except three; so that in either of those vessels I had been made miserable.

Having been thus harassed in my thoughts, my old pilot, to whom I communicated everything, pressed me earnestly not to go by sea, but either to go by land to the Groyne, and cross over the Bay of Biscay to Rochelle, from whence it was but an easy and safe journey by land to Paris, and so to Calais and Dover; or to go up to Madrid, and so all the way by land through France. In a word, I was so prepossessed against my going by sea at all, except from Calais to Dover, that I resolved to travel all the way by land; which, as I was not in haste, and did not value the charge, was by much the pleasanter way: and to make it more so, my old captain brought an English gentleman, the son of a merchant in Lisbon, who was willing to travel with me; after which we picked up two more English merchants also, and two young Portuguese gentlemen, the last going to Paris only; so that in all there were six of us and five servants; the two merchants and the two Portuguese, contenting themselves with one servant between two, to save the charge; and as for me, I got an English sailor to travel with me as a servant, besides my man Friday, who was too much a stranger to be capable of supplying the place of a servant on the road.

In this manner I set out from Lisbon; and our company being very well mounted and armed, we made a little troop, whereof they did me the honour to call me captain, as well because I was the oldest man, as because I had two servants, and, indeed, was the origin of the whole journey.

As I have troubled you with none of my sea journals, so I shall trouble you now with none of my land journals; but some adventures that happened to us in this tedious and difficult journey I must not omit.

When we came to Madrid, we, being all of us strangers to Spain, were willing to stay some time to see the court of Spain, and what was worth observing; but it being the latter part of the summer, we hastened away, and set out from Madrid about the middle of October; but when we came to the edge of Navarre, we were alarmed, at several towns on the way, with an account that so much snow was falling on the French side of the mountains, that several travellers were obliged to come back to Pampeluna, after having attempted at an extreme hazard to pass on.

When we came to Pampeluna itself, we found it so indeed; and to me, that had been always used to a hot climate, and to countries where I could scarce bear any clothes on, the cold was insufferable; nor, indeed, was it more painful than surprising to come but ten days before out of Old Castile, where the weather was not only warm but very hot, and immediately to feel a wind from the Pyrenean Mountains so very keen, so severely cold, as to be intolerable and to endanger benumbing and perishing of our fingers and toes.

Poor Friday was really frightened when he saw the mountains all covered with snow, and felt cold weather, which he had never seen or felt before in his life. To mend the matter, when we came to Pampeluna it continued snowing with so much violence and so long, that the people said winter was come before its time; and the roads, which were difficult before, were now quite impassable; for, in a word, the snow lay in some places too thick for us to travel, and being not hard frozen, as is the case in the northern countries, there was no going without being in danger of being buried alive every step. We stayed no less than twenty days at Pampeluna; when (seeing the winter coming on, and no likelihood of its being better, for it was the severest winter all over Europe that had been known in the memory of man) I proposed that we should go away to Fontarabia, and there take shipping for Bordeaux, which was a very little voyage. But, while I was considering this, there came in four French gentlemen, who, having been stopped on the French side of the passes, as we were on the Spanish, had found out a guide, who, traversing the country near the head of Languedoc, had brought them over the mountains by such ways that they were not much incommoded[168] with the snow; for where they met with snow in any quantity, they said it was frozen hard enough to bear them and their horses. We sent for this guide, who told us he would undertake to carry us the same way, with no hazard from the snow, provided we were armed sufficiently to protect ourselves from wild beasts; for, he said, in these great snows it was frequent for some wolves to show themselves at the foot of the mountains, being made ravenous for want of food, the ground being covered with snow. We told him we were well enough prepared for such creatures as they were, if he would insure us from a kind of two-legged wolves, which we were told we were in most danger from, especially on the French side of the mountains. He satisfied us that there was no danger of that kind in the way that we were to go; so we readily agreed to follow him, as did also twelve other gentlemen with their servants, some French, some Spanish, who, as I said, had attempted to go, and were obliged to come back again.

Accordingly, we set out from Pampeluna with our guide on the 15th of November; and indeed I was surprised when, instead of going forward, he came directly back with us on the same road that we came from Madrid, about twenty miles; when, having passed two rivers, and come into the plain country, we found ourselves in a warm climate again, where the country was pleasant, and no snow to be seen; but, on a sudden, turning to his left, he approached the mountains another way; and though it is true the hills and

---

[168] inconvenienced

precipices looked dreadful, yet he made so many tours, such meanders, and led us by such winding ways, that we insensibly passed the height of the mountains without being much encumbered with the snow; and all on a sudden he showed us the pleasant and fruitful provinces of Languedoc and Gascony, all green and flourishing, though at a great distance, and we had some rough way to pass still.

We were a little uneasy, however, when we found it snowed one whole day and a night so fast that we could not travel; but he bid us be easy; we should soon be past it all: we found, indeed, that we began to descend every day, and to come more north than before; and so, depending upon our guide, we went on.

It was about two hours before night when, our guide being something before us, and not just in sight, out rushed three monstrous wolves, and after them a bear, from a hollow way adjoining to a thick wood; two of the wolves made at the guide, and had he been far before us, he would have been devoured before we could have helped him; one of them fastened upon his horse, and the other attacked the man with such violence, that he had not time, or presence of mind enough, to draw his pistol, but hallooed and cried out to us most lustily. My man Friday being next me, I bade him ride up and see what was the matter. As soon as Friday came in sight of the man, he hallooed out as loud as the other, "O master! O master!" but like a bold fellow, rode directly up to the poor man, and with his pistol shot the wolf in the head that attacked him.

It was happy for the poor man that it was my man Friday; for, having been used to such creatures in his country, he had no fear upon him, but went close up to him and shot him; whereas, any other of us would have fired at a farther distance, and have perhaps either missed the wolf or endangered shooting the man.

But it was enough to have terrified a bolder man than I; and, indeed, it alarmed all our company, when, with the noise of Friday's pistol, we heard on both sides the most dismal howling of wolves; and the noise, redoubled by the echo of the mountains, appeared to us as if there had been a prodigious number of them; and perhaps there was not such a few as that we had no cause of apprehension: however, as Friday had killed this wolf, the other that had fastened upon the horse left him immediately, and fled, without doing him any damage, having happily fastened upon his head, where the bosses of the bridle had stuck in his teeth. But the man was most hurt; for the raging creature had bit him twice, once in the arm, and the other time a little above his knee; and though he had made some defence, he was just tumbling down by the disorder of his horse, when Friday came up and shot the wolf.

It is easy to suppose that at the noise of Friday's pistol we all mended our pace, and rode up as fast as the way, which was very difficult, would give us leave, to see what was the matter. As soon as we came clear of the trees, which blinded us before, we saw clearly what had been the case, and how Friday had disengaged the poor guide, though we did not presently discern what kind of creature it was he had killed.

Questions for Review:

1. Describe the ship's sailing, and what Robinson Crusoe takes with him.

2. What does Robinson Crusoe find in England and Lisbon?

3. What does he find out regarding his plantations?

4. Explain how he prepares to return to England. Why does he hesitate several times? How does this hesitation benefit him?

5. What happens on his land travels?

CHAPTER XX: FIGHT BETWEEN FRIDAY AND A BEAR

But never was a fight managed so hardily, and in such a surprising manner as that which followed between Friday and the bear, which gave us all, though at first we were surprised and afraid for him, the greatest diversion imaginable. As the bear is a heavy, clumsy creature, and does not gallop as the wolf does, who is swift and light, so he has two particular qualities, which generally are the rule of his actions; first, as to men, who are not his proper prey (he does not usually attempt them, except they first attack him, unless he be excessively hungry, which it is probable might now be the case, the ground being covered with snow), if you do not meddle with him, he will not meddle with you; but then you must take care to be very civil to him, and give him the road, for he is a very nice gentleman; he will not go a step out of his way for a prince; nay, if you are really afraid, your best way is to look another way and keep going on; for sometimes if you stop, and stand still, and look steadfastly at him, he takes it for an affront;[169] but if you throw or toss anything at him, though it were but a bit of stick as big as your finger, he thinks himself abused, and sets all other business aside to pursue his revenge, and will have satisfaction in point of honour—that is his first quality: the next is, if he be once affronted, he will never leave you, night or day, till he has his revenge, but follows at a good round rate till he overtakes you.

My man Friday had delivered our guide, and when we came up to him he was helping him off his horse, for the man was both hurt and frightened, when on a sudden we espied the bear come out of the wood; and a monstrous one it was, the biggest by far that ever I saw. We were all a little surprised when we saw him; but when Friday saw him, it was easy to see joy and courage in the fellow's countenance. "O! O! O!" says Friday, three times, pointing to him; "O master, you give me te leave, me shakee te hand with him; me makee you good laugh."

I was surprised to see the fellow so well pleased. "You fool," says I, "he will eat you up."—"Eatee me up! eatee me up!" says Friday, twice over again; "me eatee him up; me makee you good laugh; you all stay here, me show you good laugh." So down he sits, and gets off his boots in a moment, and puts on a pair of pumps (as we call the flat shoes they wear, and which he had in his pocket), gives my other servant his horse, and with his gun away he flew, swift like the wind.

The bear was walking softly on, and offered to meddle with nobody, till Friday coming pretty near, calls to him, as if the bear could understand him. "Hark ye, hark ye," says Friday, "me speakee with you." We followed at a distance, for now being down on the Gascony side of the mountains, we were entered a vast forest, where the country was plain and pretty open, though it had many trees in it scattered here and there. Friday, who had, as we say, the heels of the bear, came up with him quickly, and took up a great stone, and threw it at him, and hit him just on the head, but did him no more harm than if he had thrown it against a wall; but it answered Friday's end, for the rogue was so void of fear that he did it purely to make the bear follow him, and show us some laugh as he called it. As soon as the bear felt the blow, and saw him, he turns about and comes after him, taking very long strides, and shuffling on at a strange rate, so as would have put a horse to a middling gallop; away reins Friday, and takes his course as if he ran towards us for help; so we all resolved to fire at once upon the bear, and deliver my man; though I was angry at him for bringing the bear back upon us, when he was going about his own business another way; and especially I was angry that he had turned the bear upon us, and then ran away; and I called

[169] offense, insult

out, "You dog! Is this your making us laugh? Come away, and take your horse, that we may shoot the creature." He heard me, and cried out, "No shoot, no shoot; stand still, and you get much laugh:" and as the nimble creature ran two feet for the bear's one, he turned on a sudden on one side of us, and seeing a great oak-tree fit for his purpose, he beckoned to us to follow; and doubling his pace, he got nimbly up the tree, laying his gun down upon the ground, at about five or six yards from the bottom of the tree. The bear soon came to the tree, and we followed at a distance: the first thing he did he stopped at the gun, smelt at it, but let it lie, and up he scrambles into the tree, climbing like a cat, though so monstrous heavy. I was amazed at the folly, as I thought it, of my man, and could not for my life see anything to laugh at, till seeing the bear get up the tree, we all rode near to him.

When we came to the tree, there was Friday got out to the small end of a large branch, and the bear got about half-way to him. As soon as the bear got out to that part where the limb of the tree was weaker, "Ha!" says he to us, "now you see me teachee the bear dance:" so he began jumping and shaking the bough, at which the bear began to totter, but stood still, and began to look behind him, to see how he should get back; then, indeed, we did laugh heartily. But Friday had not done with him by a great deal; when seeing him stand still, he called out to him again, as if he had supposed the bear could speak English, "What, you come no farther? pray you come farther;" so he left jumping and shaking the tree; and the bear, just as if he understood what he said, did come a little farther; then he began jumping again, and the bear stopped again. We thought now was a good time to knock him in the head, and called to Friday to stand still and we should shoot the bear: but he cried out earnestly, "Oh, pray! Oh, pray! no shoot, me shoot by and then:" he would have said by-and-by. However, to shorten the story, Friday danced so much, and the bear stood so ticklish, that we had laughing enough, but still could not imagine what the fellow would do: for first we thought he depended upon shaking the bear off; and we found the bear was too cunning for that too; for he would not go out far enough to be thrown down, but clung fast with his great broad claws and feet, so that we could not imagine what would be the end of it, and what the jest would be at last. But Friday put us out of doubt quickly: for seeing the bear cling fast to the bough, and that he would not be persuaded to come any farther, "Well, well," says Friday, "you no come farther, me go; you no come to me, me come to you;" and upon this he went out to the smaller end, where it would bend with his weight, and gently let himself down by it, sliding down the bough till he came near enough to jump down on his feet, and away he ran to his gun, took it up, and stood still. "Well," said I to him, "Friday, what will you do now? Why don't you shoot him?" "No shoot," says Friday, "no yet; me shoot now, me no kill; me stay, give you one more laugh:" and, indeed, so he did; for when the bear saw his enemy gone, he came back from the bough, where he stood, but did it very cautiously, looking behind him every step, and coming backward till he got into the body of the tree, then, with the same hinder end foremost, he came down the tree, grasping it with his claws, and moving one foot at a time, very leisurely. At this juncture, and just before he could set his hind foot on the ground, Friday stepped up close to him, clapped the muzzle of his piece into his ear, and shot him dead. Then the rogue turned about to see if we did not laugh; and when he saw we were pleased by our looks, he began to laugh very loud. "So we kill bear in my country," says Friday. "So you kill them?" says I; "why, you have no guns."—"No," says he, "no gun, but shoot great much long arrow." This was a good diversion to us; but we were still in a wild place, and our guide very much hurt, and what to do we hardly knew; the howling of wolves ran much in my head; and, indeed, except the noise I once heard on the shore of Africa, of which I have said something already, I never heard anything that filled me with so much horror.

These things, and the approach of night, called us off, or else, as Friday would have had us, we should certainly have taken the skin of this monstrous creature off, which was worth saving; but we had near three leagues to go, and our guide hastened us; so we left him, and went forward on our journey.

The ground was still covered with snow, though not so deep and dangerous as on the mountains; and the ravenous creatures, as we heard afterwards, were come down into the forest and plain country, pressed by hunger, to seek for food, and had done a great deal of mischief in the villages, where they surprised the country people, killed a great many of their sheep and horses, and some people too. We had one dangerous place to pass, and our guide told us if there were more wolves in the country we should find them there; and this was a small plain, surrounded with woods on every side, and a long, narrow defile, or lane, which we were to pass to get through the wood, and then we should come to the village where we were to lodge. It was within half-an-hour of sunset when we entered the wood, and a little after sunset when we came into the plain: we met with nothing in the first wood, except that in a little plain within the wood, which was not above two furlongs over, we saw five great wolves cross the road, full speed, one after another, as if they had been in chase of some prey, and had it in view; they took no notice of us, and were gone out of sight in a few moments. Upon this, our guide, who, by the way, was but a fainthearted fellow, bid us keep in a ready posture, for he believed there were more wolves a-coming. We kept our arms ready, and our eyes about us; but we saw no more wolves till we came through that wood, which was near half a league, and entered the plain. As soon as we came into the plain, we had occasion enough to look about us. The first object we met with was a dead horse; that is to say, a poor horse which the wolves had killed, and at least a dozen of them at work, we could not say eating him, but picking his bones rather; for they had eaten up all the flesh before. We did not think fit to disturb them at their feast, neither did they take much notice of us. Friday would have let fly at them, but I would not suffer him by any means; for I found we were like to have more business upon our hands than we were aware of. We had not gone half over the plain when we began to hear the wolves howl in the wood on our left in a frightful manner, and presently after we saw about a hundred coming on directly towards us, all in a body, and most of them in a line, as regularly as an army drawn up by experienced officers. I scarce knew in what manner to receive them, but found to draw ourselves in a close line was the only way; so we formed in a moment; but that we might not have too much interval, I ordered that only every other man should fire, and that the others, who had not fired, should stand ready to give them a second volley immediately, if they continued to advance upon us; and then that those that had fired at first should not pretend to load their fusees again, but stand ready, every one with a pistol, for we were all armed with a fusee and a pair of pistols each man; so we were, by this method, able to fire six volleys, half of us at a time; however, at present we had no necessity; for upon firing the first volley, the enemy made a full stop, being terrified as well with the noise as with the fire. Four of them being shot in the head, dropped; several others were wounded, and went bleeding off, as we could see by the snow. I found they stopped, but did not immediately retreat; whereupon, remembering that I had been told that the fiercest creatures were terrified at the voice of a man, I caused all the company to halloo as loud as they could; and I found the notion not altogether mistaken; for upon our shout they began to retire and turn about. I then ordered a second volley to be fired in their rear, which put them to the gallop, and away they went to the woods. This gave us leisure to charge our pieces again; and that we might lose no time, we kept going; but we had but little more than loaded our fusees, and put ourselves in readiness, when we heard a terrible noise in the same wood on our left, only that it was farther onward, the same way we were to go.

The night was coming on, and the light began to be dusky, which made it worse on our side; but the noise increasing, we could easily perceive that it was the howling and yelling of those hellish creatures; and on a sudden we perceived three troops of wolves, one on our left, one behind us, and one in our front, so that we seemed to be surrounded with them: however, as they did not fall upon us, we kept our way forward, as fast as we could make our horses go, which, the way being very rough, was only a good hard trot. In this manner, we came in view of the entrance of a wood, through which we were to pass, at the farther side of the plain; but we were greatly surprised, when coming nearer the lane or pass, we saw a confused number of wolves standing just at the entrance. On a sudden, at another opening of the wood, we heard the noise of a gun, and looking that way, out rushed a horse, with a saddle and a bridle on him, flying like the wind, and sixteen or seventeen wolves after him, full speed: the horse had the advantage of them; but as we supposed that he could not hold it at that rate, we doubted not but they would get up with him at last: no question but they did.

But here we had a most horrible sight; for riding up to the entrance where the horse came out, we found the carcasses of another horse and of two men, devoured by the ravenous creatures; and one of the men was no doubt the same whom we heard fire the gun, for there lay a gun just by him fired off; but as to the man, his head and the upper part of his body was eaten up. This filled us with horror, and we knew not what course to take; but the creatures resolved us soon, for they gathered about us presently, in hopes of prey; and I verily believe there were three hundred of them. It happened, very much to our advantage, that at the entrance into the wood, but a little way from it, there lay some large timber-trees, which had been cut down the summer before, and I suppose lay there for carriage. I drew my little troop in among those trees, and placing ourselves in a line behind one long tree, I advised them all to alight, and keeping that tree before us for a breastwork, to stand in a triangle, or three fronts, enclosing our horses in the centre. We did so, and it was well we did; for never was a more furious charge than the creatures made upon us in this place. They came on with a growling kind of noise, and mounted the piece of timber, which, as I said, was our breastwork, as if they were only rushing upon their prey; and this fury of theirs, it seems, was principally occasioned by their seeing our horses behind us. I ordered our men to fire as before, every other man; and they took their aim so sure that they killed several of the wolves at the first volley; but there was a necessity to keep a continual firing, for they came on like devils, those behind pushing on those before.

When we had fired a second volley of our fusees, we thought they stopped a little, and I hoped they would have gone off, but it was but a moment, for others came forward again; so we fired two volleys of our pistols; and I believe in these four firings we had killed seventeen or eighteen of them, and lamed twice as many, yet they came on again. I was loth to spend our shot too hastily; so I called my servant, not my man Friday, for he was better employed, for, with the greatest dexterity imaginable, he had charged my fusee and his own while we were engaged—but, as I said, I called my other man, and giving him a horn of powder, I had him lay a train all along the piece of timber, and let it be a large train. He did so, and had but just time to get away, when the wolves came up to it, and some got upon it, when I, snapping an unchanged pistol close to the powder, set it on fire; those that were upon the timber were scorched with it, and six or seven of them fell; or rather jumped in among us with the force and fright of the fire; we despatched these in an instant, and the rest were so frightened with the light, which the night—for it was now very near dark—made more terrible that they drew back a little; upon which I ordered our last pistols to be fired off in one volley, and after that we gave a shout; upon this the wolves turned tail, and we sallied immediately upon near twenty lame ones that we found struggling on the ground, and fell to cutting them with our swords, which answered our expectation, for the crying and howling they made was better understood by their fellows; so that they all fled and left us.

We had, first and last, killed about threescore[170] of them, and had it been daylight we had killed many more. The field of battle being thus cleared, we made forward again, for we had still near a league to go. We heard the ravenous creatures howl and yell in the woods as we went several times, and sometimes we fancied we saw some of them; but the snow dazzling our eyes, we were not certain. In about an hour more we came to the town where we were to lodge, which we found in a terrible fright and all in arms; for, it seems, the night before the wolves and some bears had broken into the village, and put them in such terror that they were obliged to keep guard night and day, but especially in the night, to preserve their cattle, and indeed their people.

The next morning our guide was so ill, and his limbs swelled so much with the rankling of his two wounds, that he could go no farther; so we were obliged to take a new guide here, and go to Toulouse, where we found a warm climate, a fruitful, pleasant country, and no snow, no wolves, nor anything like them; but when we told our story at Toulouse, they told us it was nothing but what was ordinary in the great forest at the foot of the mountains, especially when the snow lay on the ground; but they inquired much what kind of guide we had got who would venture to bring us that way in such a severe season, and told us it was surprising we were not all devoured. When we told them how we placed ourselves and the horses in the middle, they blamed us exceedingly, and told us it was fifty to one but we had been all destroyed, for it was the sight of the horses which made the wolves so furious, seeing their prey, and that at other times they are really afraid of a gun; but being excessively hungry, and raging on that account, the eagerness to come at the horses had made them senseless of danger, and that if we had not by the continual fire, and at last by the stratagem of the train of powder, mastered them, it had been great odds but that we had been

---

[170] A *score* is 20, so three times 20, or 60.

torn to pieces; whereas, had we been content to have sat still on horse-back, and fired as horsemen, they would not have taken the horses so much for their own, when men were on their backs, as otherwise; and withal, they told us that at last, if we had stood altogether, and left our horses, they would have been so eager to have devoured them, that we might have come off safe, especially having our firearms in our hands, being so many in number. For my part, I was never so sensible of danger in my life; for, seeing above three hundred devils come roaring and open-mouthed to devour us, and having nothing to shelter us or retreat to, I gave myself over for lost; and, as it was, I believe I shall never care to cross those mountains again: I think I would much rather go a thousand leagues by sea, though I was sure to meet with a storm once a-week.

I have nothing uncommon to take notice of in my passage through France—nothing but what other travellers have given an account of with much more advantage than I can. I travelled from Toulouse to Paris, and without any considerable stay came to Calais, and landed safe at Dover the 14th of January, after having had a severe cold season to travel in.

I was now come to the centre of my travels, and had in a little time all my new-discovered estate safe about me, the bills of exchange which I brought with me having been currently paid.

My principal guide and privy-counsellor was my good ancient widow, who, in gratitude for the money I had sent her, thought no pains too much nor care too great to employ for me; and I trusted her so entirely that I was perfectly easy as to the security of my effects; and, indeed, I was very happy from the beginning, and now to the end, in the unspotted integrity of this good gentlewoman.

And now, having resolved to dispose of my plantation in the Brazils, I wrote to my old friend at Lisbon, who, having offered it to the two merchants, the survivors of my trustees, who lived in the Brazils, they accepted the offer, and remitted thirty-three thousand pieces of eight to a correspondent of theirs at Lisbon to pay for it.

In return, I signed the instrument of sale in the form which they sent from Lisbon, and sent it to my old man, who sent me the bills of exchange for thirty-two thousand eight hundred pieces of eight for the estate, reserving the payment of one hundred moidores a year to him (the old man) during his life, and fifty moidores afterwards to his son for his life, which I had promised them, and which the plantation was to make good as a rent-charge. And thus I have given the first part of a life of fortune and adventure—a life of Providence's chequer-work, and of a variety which the world will seldom be able to show the like of; beginning foolishly, but closing much more happily than any part of it ever gave me leave so much as to hope for.

Any one would think that in this state of complicated good fortune I was past running any more hazards—and so, indeed, I had been, if other circumstances had concurred; but I was inured to a wandering life, had no family, nor many relations; nor, however rich, had I contracted fresh acquaintance; and though I had sold my estate in the Brazils, yet I could not keep that country out of my head, and had a great mind to be upon the wing again; especially I could not resist the strong inclination I had to see my island, and to know if the poor Spaniards were in being there. My true friend, the widow, earnestly dissuaded me from it, and so far prevailed with me, that for almost seven years she prevented my running abroad, during which time I took my two nephews, the children of one of my brothers, into my care; the eldest, having something of his own, I bred up as a gentleman, and gave him a settlement of some addition to his estate after my decease. The other I placed with the captain of a ship; and after five years, finding him a sensible, bold, enterprising young fellow, I put him into a good ship, and sent him to sea; and this young fellow afterwards drew me in, as old as I was, to further adventures myself.

In the meantime, I in part settled myself here; for, first of all, I married, and that not either to my disadvantage or dissatisfaction, and had three children, two sons and one daughter; but my wife dying, and my nephew coming home with good success from a voyage to Spain, my inclination to go abroad, and his importunity, prevailed, and engaged me to go in his ship as a private trader to the East Indies; this was in the year 1694.

In this voyage I visited my new colony in the island, saw my successors the Spaniards, had the old story of their lives and of the villains I left there; how at first they insulted the poor Spaniards, how they afterwards agreed, disagreed, united, separated, and how at last the Spaniards were obliged to use violence with them; how they were subjected to the Spaniards, how honestly the Spaniards used them—a history, if it were entered into, as full of variety and wonderful accidents as my own part—particularly, also, as to their battles with the Caribbeans, who landed several times upon the island, and as to the improvement they made upon the island itself, and how five of them made an attempt upon the mainland, and brought away eleven men and five women prisoners, by which, at my coming, I found about twenty young children on the island.

Here I stayed about twenty days, left them supplies of all necessary things, and particularly of arms, powder, shot, clothes, tools, and two workmen, which I had brought from England with me, viz. a carpenter and a smith.

Besides this, I shared the lands into parts with them, reserved to myself the property of the whole, but gave them such parts respectively as they agreed on; and having settled all things with them, and engaged them not to leave the place, I left them there.

From thence I touched at the Brazils, from whence I sent a bark,[171] which I bought there, with more people to the island; and in it, besides other supplies, I sent seven women, being such as I found proper for service, or for wives to such as would take them. As to the Englishmen, I promised to send them some women from England, with a good cargo of necessaries, if they would apply themselves to planting—which I afterwards could not perform. The fellows proved very honest and diligent after they were mastered and had their properties set apart for them. I sent them, also, from the Brazils, five cows, three of them being big with calf, some sheep, and some hogs, which when I came again were considerably increased.

But all these things, with an account how three hundred Caribbees came and invaded them, and ruined their plantations, and how they fought with that whole number twice, and were at first defeated, and one of them killed; but at last, a storm destroying their enemies' canoes, they famished or destroyed almost all the rest, and renewed and recovered the possession of their plantation, and still lived upon the island.

All these things, with some very surprising incidents in some new adventures of my own, for ten years more, I shall give a farther account of in the Second Part of my Story.

Questions for Review:

1. Describe Friday's encounter with the bear and the group's battle with wolves.

2. What do the locals tell the traveling group about the wolves?

3. Sum up the story's conclusion.

---

[171] ship

For Additional Thought:

1. What do you believe would have happened to Robinson Crusoe, spiritually, had he not been shipwrecked on the deserted island? Do you agree with him that God might have sent him there to drive him toward salvation?

2. How does reading the Bible affect Robinson Crusoe? What lessons about Bible reading does he offer?

3. Robinson Crusoe remarks, "How frequently, in the course of our lives, the evil which in itself we seek most to shun, and which, when we are fallen into, is the most dreadful to us, is oftentimes the very means or door of our deliverance, by which alone we can be raised again from the affliction we are fallen into." Can you name something that has happened to you that shows the truth of this statement?

4. Robinson Crusoe rejoices at how "the doctrine of salvation by Christ Jesus is so plainly laid down in the word of God, so easy to be... understood." How simple is the gospel? Write down these verses, look them up, and write down what they teach and what they reveal about simplicity:

    *   Mark 10:13-15

    *   John 3:14-18

    *   Acts 8:36-37

    *   Acts 10:42-43

    *   Acts 16:27-31

    *   Romans 4:3-5

    *   1 Corinthians 15:3-4

    *   1 Timothy 2:5-6

    *   2 Timothy 3:14-15

THE TRAGEDY OF JULIUS CAESAR

BY

WILLIAM SHAKESPEARE

Introduction

The essentials on the historical Julius Caesar are these: He lived from 100-44 BC and climbed the military and political ladder, advancing from soldier to tribune to governor of Farther Spain. He formed a three-man political coalition ("The First Triumvirate) with Pompey the Great and Marcus Licinius Crassus in 60 BC, gaining fame for victories in the Gallic Wars, in what is now France and Belgium. (Julius Caesar also wrote a history of these events, *Commentaries on the Gallic War*, often still translated today by Latin students.)

Fearing his increased power and ambitions for more, in 50 BC the Roman Senate ordered Julius Caesar to return to Rome without his army; he refused, crossing the Rubicon River (between Gaul and Italy) and touching off the Roman Civil War. His resulting appointment as dictator of Rome led to his assassination on March 15, 44 BC, and another civil war to determine control of the Roman Empire.

William Shakespeare is thought to have written the play *Julius Caesar* in 1599, basing much of his plot on a book known as *Lives* by Plutarch, a Greek historian. *Julius Caesar* is written almost completely in *iambic pentameter*, a poetic meter with ten syllables and five beats per line, with the accent on the second, fourth, sixth, eighth, and tenth syllables. For example (accented syllables in bold), here are two lines from *Julius Caesar*:

*"When **Cae**sar **says,** "Do **this**," it **is** per**form'd**."*

and

*"**Bru**tus, I **do** ob**serve** you **now** of **late**."*

Julius Caesar contains some of Shakespeare's most famous speeches and memorable lines. Suggestion: Write down or highlight any phrases you think are particularly interesting or notable. Other suggestions:

- *Julius Caesar* was written as a *play*, so as you read it, imagine actors performing it!

- In a notebook, make a list of major characters, and jot down thoughts you have about each one at the end of each scene.

- Carefully read the notes on the bottom of the pages of *Julius Caesar*, which I have included to make cultural references, unclear phrases, and more archaic terms familiar.

- At the end of each act, jot down your impressions on what message or messages you believe Shakespeare is trying to impart to the reader.

Enjoy *Julius Caesar*!

DRAMATIS PERSONAE

JULIUS CAESAR

OCTAVIUS CAESAR MARCUS ANTONIUS M. AEMIL. LEPIDUS	Triumvirs after his death
CICERO PUBLIUS POPILIUS LENA	Senators
MARCUS BRUTUS CASSIUS CASCA TREBONIUS LIGARIUS DECIUS BRUTUS METELLUS CIMBER CINNA	Conspirators against Caesar
FLAVIUS MARULLUS	Tribunes
ARTEMIDORUS	A Sophist of Cnidos

A Soothsayer

CINNA	A poet

Another Poet

LUCILIUS
TITINIUS
MESSALA
Young CATO
VOLUMNIUS

Friends to Brutus
and Cassius

VARRO
CLITUS
CLAUDIUS
STRATO
LUCIUS
DARDANIUS

Servants to Brutus

PINDARUS

Servant to Cassius

The Ghost of Caesar

Senators, Citizens, Soldiers,
Commoners, Messengers,
and Servants

CALPURNIA

Wife to Caesar

PORTIA

Wife to Brutus

SCENE: ROME: SARDIS, AND THE PLAINS OF PHILIPPI.

ACT I.

SCENE I. ROME. A STREET.

[Enter Flavius, Marullus, and a Throng of Citizens.]

FLAVIUS.
Hence! home, you idle creatures, get you home!
Is this a holiday? What! know you not,
Being mechanical,[1] you ought not walk
Upon a labouring day without the sign
Of your profession? Speak, what trade art thou?

FIRST CITIZEN.
Why, sir, a carpenter.

MARULLUS.
Where is thy leather apron and thy rule?
What dost thou with thy best apparel on?
You, sir; what trade are you?

SECOND CITIZEN.
Truly, sir, in respect of a fine workman, I am but, as you would say, a cobbler.

MARULLUS.
But what trade art thou? Answer me directly.

SECOND CITIZEN.
A trade, sir, that, I hope, I may use with a safe conscience, which is indeed, sir, a mender of bad soles.

MARULLUS.
What trade, thou knave?[2] Thou naughty knave, what trade?

---

[1] belonging to the craftsman class
[2] deceitful scoundrel

SECOND CITIZEN.
Nay, I beseech you, sir, be not out with me;[3] yet, if you be out, sir, I can
mend you.

MARULLUS.
What mean'st thou by that? Mend me, thou saucy fellow!

SECOND CITIZEN.
Why, sir, cobble you.

FLAVIUS.
Thou art a cobbler, art thou?

SECOND CITIZEN.
Truly, Sir, all that I live by is with the awl; I meddle with no tradesman's
matters, nor women's matters, but with awl.[4] I am indeed, sir, a surgeon to
old shoes; when they are in great danger, I recover them. As proper men
as ever trod upon neat's-leather have gone upon my handiwork.

FLAVIUS.
But wherefore art not in thy shop today?
Why dost thou lead these men about the streets?

SECOND CITIZEN.
Truly, sir, to wear out their shoes to get myself into more work. But
indeed, sir, we make holiday to see Caesar and to rejoice in his triumph.

MARULLUS.
Wherefore rejoice? What conquest brings he home?
What tributaries follow him to Rome,
To grace in captive bonds his chariot wheels?
You blocks, you stones, you worse than senseless things!
O you hard hearts, you cruel men of Rome,
Knew you not Pompey?[5] Many a time and oft
Have you climb'd up to walls and battlements,
To towers and windows, yea, to chimney tops,
Your infants in your arms, and there have sat

---

[3] "Be not out with me" means "Don't be angry with me."
[4] Here the cobbler is making a few puns using the words *all* and *awl* (a tool he uses to punch holes while making or repairing shoes).
[5] Gnaeus Pompeius Magnus (106-48 B.C.) was, with Marcus Licinius Crassus and (Gaius) Julius Caesar, a member of the First Triumvirate, a military-political trio which dominated for several years. Julius Caesar and Pompey had a falling out (as power seekers tend to do), becoming enemies, and Pompey was later murdered in Egypt.

The livelong day with patient expectation
To see great Pompey pass the streets of Rome.
And when you saw his chariot but appear,
Have you not made an universal shout
That Tiber[6] trembled underneath her banks
To hear the replication of your sounds
Made in her concave shores?
And do you now put on your best attire?
And do you now cull out a holiday?
And do you now strew flowers in his way
That comes in triumph over Pompey's blood?[7]
Be gone!
Run to your houses, fall upon your knees,
Pray to the gods to intermit the plague
That needs must light on this ingratitude.

FLAVIUS.
Go, go, good countrymen, and, for this fault,
Assemble all the poor men of your sort,
Draw them to Tiber banks, and weep your tears
Into the channel, till the lowest stream
Do kiss the most exalted shores of all.

[Exeunt[8] CITIZENS.]

See whether their basest metal be not moved;
They vanish tongue-tied in their guiltiness.
Go you down that way towards the Capitol;
This way will I. Disrobe the images,
If you do find them deck'd with ceremonies.

MARULLUS.
May we do so?
You know it is the feast of Lupercal.[9]

FLAVIUS.
It is no matter; let no images

---

[6] The Tiber is a 252-mile long river.

[7] Pompey's sons

[8] Latin for "they leave"; this indicates that the players referred to leave the stage during the play.

[9] Lupercalia was a feast observed in Rome in mid-February. (Lupercus is the Roman "god" of shepherds.) Observance of the feast was supposed to keep evil spirits at bay and increase fertility in both animals and humans.

Be hung with Caesar's trophies. I'll about
And drive away the vulgar[10] from the streets;
So do you too, where you perceive them thick.
These growing feathers pluck'd from Caesar's wing
Will make him fly an ordinary pitch,[11]
Who else would soar above the view of men,
And keep us all in servile[12] fearfulness.

[Exeunt.]

Questions for Review:

1. How do the tribunes and commoners view Julius Caesar's return differently?

2. What else happens to suggest the groups are discordant?

3. Why does Marullus rebuke the workmen, and what does this say about the character of "mobs"?

4. What is the double meaning of the cobbler's words when he says he is a "mender of bad soles"?

5. How does Flavius plan to "pluck feathers from Julius Caesar's wing"?

SCENE II. THE SAME. A PUBLIC PLACE.

[Enter, in procession, with music, Caesar; Antony, for the course;
Calpurnia, Portia, Decius, Cicero, Brutus, Cassius, and Casca; a great
crowd following, among them a Soothsayer.]

CAESAR.
Calpurnia,—

CASCA.
Peace, ho! Caesar speaks.

[Music ceases.]

---

[10] Commoners. The Latin *vulgaris* means "common people." The word *vulgar* in the English language, until recently, meant "low-class" or "common," which differed from how the word is almost always used today (as a synonym for "offensive" or "crude").
[11] height
[12] like a slave

CAESAR.
Calpurnia,—

CALPURNIA.
Here, my lord.

CAESAR.
Stand you directly in Antonius' way,
When he doth run his course.—Antonius,—

ANTONY.
Caesar, my lord?

CAESAR.
Forget not in your speed, Antonius,
To touch Calpurnia; for our elders say,
The barren, touched in this holy chase,
Shake off their sterile curse.

ANTONY.
I shall remember.
When Caesar says, "Do this," it is perform'd.

CAESAR.
Set on; and leave no ceremony out.

[Music.]

SOOTHSAYER.
Caesar!

CAESAR.
Ha! Who calls?

CASCA.
Bid every noise be still. Peace yet again!

[Music ceases.]

CAESAR.
Who is it in the press[13] that calls on me?

---

[13] The "press" is the crowd. The word *press* is used several times to refer to a crowd around Jesus. (See Mark 2:4, Mark 5:27-30, Luke 8:19, and Luke 19:3. In Luke 8:40-48, Jesus asks a question while in the middle of the press, similar to Julius Caesar.)

I hear a tongue, shriller than all the music,
Cry "Caesar"! Speak, Caesar is turn'd to hear.

SOOTHSAYER.
Beware the Ides of March.[14]

CAESAR.
What man is that?

BRUTUS.
A soothsayer bids you beware the Ides of March.

CAESAR.
Set him before me; let me see his face.

CASSIUS.
Fellow, come from the throng; look upon Caesar.

CAESAR.
What say'st thou to me now? Speak once again.

SOOTHSAYER.
Beware the Ides of March.

CAESAR.
He is a dreamer; let us leave him. Pass.

[Sennet.[15] Exeunt all but BRUTUS and CASSIUS.]

CASSIUS.
Will you go see the order of the course?

BRUTUS.
Not I.

CASSIUS.
I pray you, do.

BRUTUS.
I am not gamesome;[16] I do lack some part
Of that quick spirit that is in Antony.
Let me not hinder, Cassius, your desires;
I'll leave you.

---

[14] March 15th
[15] a blast from a trumpet/trumpets that announces someone important is arriving or leaving
[16] sporting, playful

CASSIUS.

Brutus, I do observe you now of late:
I have not from your eyes that gentleness
And show of love as I was wont[17] to have:
You bear too stubborn and too strange a hand
Over your friend that loves you.

BRUTUS.

Cassius,
Be not deceived: if I have veil'd my look,
I turn the trouble of my countenance[18]
Merely[19] upon myself. Vexed I am
Of late with passions of some difference,
Conceptions only proper to myself,
Which give some soil perhaps to my behaviors;
But let not therefore my good friends be grieved—
Among which number, Cassius, be you one—
Nor construe any further my neglect,
Than that poor Brutus, with himself at war,
Forgets the shows of love to other men.

CASSIUS.

Then, Brutus, I have much mistook your passion;
By means whereof this breast of mine hath buried
Thoughts of great value, worthy cogitations.[20]
Tell me, good Brutus, can you see your face?

BRUTUS.

No, Cassius, for the eye sees not itself
But by reflection, by some other thing.

CASSIUS.

'Tis just:
And it is very much lamented, Brutus,
That you have no such mirrors as will turn
Your hidden worthiness into your eye,
That you might see your shadow. I have heard
Where many of the best respect in Rome,
Except immortal Caesar! speaking of Brutus,

---

[17] accustomed, used
[18] face
[19] only, totally
[20] reflective thoughts, meditations

And groaning underneath this age's yoke,
Have wish'd that noble Brutus had his eyes.

BRUTUS.
Into what dangers would you lead me, Cassius,
That you would have me seek into myself
For that which is not in me?

CASSIUS.
Therefore, good Brutus, be prepared to hear;
And since you know you cannot see yourself
So well as by reflection, I, your glass,
Will modestly discover to yourself
That of yourself which you yet know not of.
And be not jealous on me, gentle Brutus;
Were I a common laugher, or did use
To stale[21] with ordinary oaths my love
To every new protester; if you know
That I do fawn[22] on men, and hug them hard
And after scandal them; or if you know
That I profess myself, in banqueting,
To all the rout, then hold me dangerous.

[Flourish and shout.]

BRUTUS.
What means this shouting? I do fear the people
Choose Caesar for their king.

CASSIUS.
Ay, do you fear it?
Then must I think you would not have it so.

BRUTUS.
I would not, Cassius; yet I love him well,
But wherefore do you hold me here so long?
What is it that you would impart to me?
If it be aught[23] toward the general good,
Set honor in one eye and death i' the other
And I will look on both indifferently;

---

[21] "use to stale": use over and over until they got tiresome, or stale
[22] flatter
[23] anything

For let the gods so speed me as I love
The name of honor more than I fear death.

CASSIUS.
I know that virtue to be in you, Brutus,
As well as I do know your outward favor.
Well, honor is the subject of my story.
I cannot tell what you and other men
Think of this life; but, for my single self,
I had as lief[24] not be as live to be
In awe of such a thing as I myself.
I was born free as Caesar; so were you:
We both have fed as well; and we can both
Endure the winter's cold as well as he:
For once, upon a raw and gusty day,
The troubled Tiber chafing with her shores,
Caesar said to me, "Darest thou, Cassius, now
Leap in with me into this angry flood
And swim to yonder point?" Upon the word,
Accoutred[25] as I was, I plunged in,
And bade him follow: so indeed he did.
The torrent roar'd, and we did buffet it
With lusty sinews, throwing it aside
And stemming it with hearts of controversy;[26]
But ere we could arrive the point proposed,
Caesar cried, "Help me, Cassius, or I sink!"
I, as Aeneas, our great ancestor,
Did from the flames of Troy upon his shoulder
The old Anchises bear, so from the waves of Tiber
Did I the tired Caesar: and this man
Is now become a god; and Cassius is
A wretched creature, and must bend his body,
If Caesar carelessly but nod on him.
He had a fever when he was in Spain;
And when the fit[27] was on him I did mark
How he did shake: 'tis true, this god did shake:

---

[24] willing
[25] weighed down with clothes or other items (which makes swimming more difficult)
[26] "hearts of controversy": minds bent on competing against the other man
[27] an epileptic fit

His coward lips did from their color fly;[28]
And that same eye whose bend doth awe the world
Did lose his luster. I did hear him groan:
Ay, and that tongue of his that bade the Romans
Mark him, and write his speeches in their books,
Alas, it cried, "Give me some drink, Titinius,"
As a sick girl. Ye gods, it doth amaze me,
A man of such a feeble temper should
So get the start of the majestic world,
And bear the palm alone.

[Shout. Flourish.]

BRUTUS.
Another general shout!
I do believe that these applauses are
For some new honors that are heap'd on Caesar.

CASSIUS.
Why, man, he doth bestride the narrow world
Like a Colossus;[29] and we petty men
Walk under his huge legs and peep about
To find ourselves dishonorable graves.
Men at some time are masters of their fates:
The fault, dear Brutus, is not in our stars,
But in ourselves,that we are underlings.
"Brutus" and "Caesar": what should be in that "Caesar"?
Why should that name be sounded more than yours?
Write them together, yours is as fair a name;
Sound them, it doth become the mouth as well;
Weigh them, it is as heavy; conjure with them,
"Brutus" will start a spirit as soon as "Caesar."
Now, in the names of all the gods at once,
Upon what meat doth this our Caesar feed
That he is grown so great? Age, thou art shamed!
Rome, thou hast lost the breed of noble bloods!
When went there by an age since the great flood,

---

[28] That is, his lips became pale. Cassius here is comparing Julius Caesar's "coward lips" to a soldier in a battle who, in fear, runs from his "color" (battle flag).
[29] That is, Julius Caesar stands astride the world like the Colossus of Rhodes, a 100-foot tall statue that in ancient times stood on a harbor in the Greek city (and island) named Rhodes. The Colossus of Rhodes was referred to as one of the "Seven Wonders of the Ancient World" (and incidentally, it inspired the appearance of the Statue of Liberty).

But it was famed with more than with one man?
When could they say, till now, that talk'd of Rome,
That her wide walls encompass'd but one man?
Now is it Rome indeed, and room enough,
When there is in it but one only man.
O, you and I have heard our fathers say
There was a Brutus[30] once that would have brook'd[31]
Th' eternal devil to keep his state in Rome,
As easily as a king!

BRUTUS.

That you do love me, I am nothing jealous;
What you would work me to, I have some aim:
How I have thought of this, and of these times,
I shall recount hereafter; for this present,
I would not, so with love I might entreat[32] you,
Be any further moved. What you have said,
I will consider; what you have to say,
I will with patience hear; and find a time
Both meet[33] to hear and answer such high things.
Till then, my noble friend, chew upon this:
Brutus had rather be a villager
Than to repute himself a son of Rome
Under these hard conditions as this time
Is like to lay upon us.

CASSIUS.

I am glad that my weak words
Have struck but thus much show of fire from Brutus.

BRUTUS.

The games are done, and Caesar is returning.

CASSIUS.

As they pass by, pluck Casca by the sleeve;

---

[30] Here Cassius refers to the founder of the Roman Republic, Lucius Junus Brutus.

[31] tolerated

[32] beg, plead with

[33] "Meet" here means "appropriate," "proper," or "acceptable." The word *meet* first occurs in the English translation of the Bible in Genesis 2:18, when God says about Adam, "*It is* not good that man should be alone; I will make him an help **meet** for him." (See also, for example, Luke 15:32, Philippians 1:17, and Timothy 2:21.)

And he will, after his sour fashion, tell you
What hath proceeded worthy note today.

[Re-enter Caesar and his Train.]

BRUTUS.
I will do so.—But, look you, Cassius,
The angry spot doth glow on Caesar's brow,
And all the rest look like a chidden train:[34]
Calpurnia's cheek is pale; and Cicero
Looks with such ferret and such fiery eyes
As we have seen him in the Capitol,
Being cross'd in conference by some senators.

CASSIUS.
Casca will tell us what the matter is.

CAESAR.
Antonius,—

ANTONY.
Caesar?

CAESAR.
Let me have men about me that are fat;
Sleek-headed men, and such as sleep o' nights:
Yond Cassius has a lean and hungry look;
He thinks too much: such men are dangerous.

ANTONY.
Fear him not, Caesar; he's not dangerous;
He is a noble Roman and well given.

CAESAR.
Would he were fatter! But I fear him not:
Yet, if my name were liable to fear,
I do not know the man I should avoid
So soon as that spare Cassius. He reads much;
He is a great observer, and he looks
Quite through the deeds of men: he loves no plays,
As thou dost, Antony; he hears no music:
Seldom he smiles; and smiles in such a sort
As if he mock'd himself and scorn'd his spirit

---

[34] an entourage of assistants that has been rebuked or reproached ("chidden")

That could be moved to smile at any thing.
Such men as he be never at heart's ease
Whiles they behold a greater than themselves;
And therefore are they very dangerous.
I rather tell thee what is to be fear'd
Than what I fear, for always I am Caesar.
Come on my right hand, for this ear is deaf,
And tell me truly what thou think'st of him.

[Exeunt Caesar and his Train. Casca stays.]

CASCA.
You pull'd me by the cloak; would you speak with me?

BRUTUS.
Ay, Casca, tell us what hath chanced today,
That Caesar looks so sad.

CASCA.
Why, you were with him, were you not?

BRUTUS.
I should not then ask Casca what had chanced.

CASCA.
Why, there was a crown offer'd him; and being offer'd him, he put it by with the back of his hand, thus; and then the people fell a-shouting.

BRUTUS.
What was the second noise for?

CASCA.
Why, for that too.

CASSIUS.
They shouted thrice: what was the last cry for?

CASCA.
Why, for that too.

BRUTUS.
Was the crown offer'd him thrice?

CASCA.
Ay, marry,[35] was't, and he put it by thrice, every time gentler than other; and at every putting-by mine honest neighbors shouted.

CASSIUS.
Who offer'd him the crown?

CASCA.
Why, Antony.

BRUTUS.
Tell us the manner of it, gentle Casca.

CASCA.
I can as well be hang'd, as tell the manner of it: it was mere foolery; I did not mark it. I saw Mark Antony offer him a crown;—yet 'twas not a crown neither, 'twas one of these coronets;—and, as I told you, he put it by once: but, for all that, to my thinking, he would fain[36] have had it. Then he offered it to him again: then he put it by again: but, to my thinking, he was very loath to lay his fingers off it. And then he offered it the third time; he put it the third time by; and still, as he refused it, the rabblement shouted, and clapp'd their chopt[37] hands, and threw up their sweaty night-caps, and uttered such a deal of stinking breath because Caesar refused the crown, that it had almost choked Caesar, for he swooned and fell down at it: and for mine own part, I durst not laugh for fear of opening my lips and receiving the bad air.

CASSIUS.
But, soft! I pray you. What, did Caesar swoon?

CASCA.
He fell down in the market-place, and foam'd at mouth, and was speechless.

BRUTUS.
'Tis very like: he hath the falling-sickness.[38]

CASSIUS.
No, Caesar hath it not; but you, and I,
And honest Casca, we have the falling-sickness.

---

[35] The word *marry* here means "Indeed!" or "Truly!" or "That's right!"
[36] gladly
[37] chapped
[38] epilepsy

CASCA.

I know not what you mean by that; but I am sure Caesar fell down. If the tag-rag people did not clap him and hiss him, according as he pleased and displeased them, as they use to do the players in the theatre, I am no true man.

BRUTUS.

What said he when he came unto himself?

CASCA.

Marry, before he fell down, when he perceived the common herd was glad he refused the crown, he pluck'd me ope his doublet,[39] and offered them his throat to cut: an I had been a man of any occupation, if I would not have taken him at a word, I would I might go to hell among the rogues:— and so he fell. When he came to himself again, he said, if he had done or said any thing amiss, he desired their worships to think it was his infirmity. Three or four wenches[40] where I stood cried, "Alas, good soul!" and forgave him with all their hearts. But there's no heed to be taken of them: if Caesar had stabb'd their mothers, they would have done no less.

BRUTUS.

And, after that he came, thus sad away?

CASCA.

Ay.

CASSIUS.

Did Cicero say any thing?

CASCA.

Ay, he spoke Greek.

CASSIUS.

To what effect?

CASCA.

Nay, an I tell you that, I'll ne'er look you i' the face again: but those that understood him smiled at one another and shook their heads; but for mine own part, it was Greek to me. I could tell you more news too: Marullus and Flavius, for pulling scarfs off Caesar's images, are put to silence. Fare you well. There was more foolery yet, if could remember it.

---

[39] "pluck'd me ope his doublet": asked me to open his garment
[40] women

CASSIUS.
Will you sup with me tonight, Casca?

CASCA.
No, I am promised forth.[41]

CASSIUS.
Will you dine with me tomorrow?

CASCA.
Ay, if I be alive, and your mind hold,[42] and your dinner worth the eating.

CASSIUS.
Good; I will expect you.

CASCA.
Do so; farewell both.

[Exit CASCA.]

BRUTUS.
What a blunt fellow is this grown to be!
He was quick mettle[43] when he went to school.

CASSIUS.
So is he now in execution
Of any bold or noble enterprise,
However he puts on this tardy form.
This rudeness is a sauce to his good wit,
Which gives men stomach to digest his words
With better appetite.

BRUTUS.
And so it is. For this time I will leave you:
Tomorrow, if you please to speak with me,
I will come home to you; or, if you will,
Come home to me, and I will wait for you.

CASSIUS.
I will do so: till then, think of the world.—

[Exit Brutus.]

---

[41] "I am promised forth" means "I have already made a previous commitment."
[42] "if your mind hold": if Cassius doesn't change his mind about inviting Casca
[43] "quick mettle": gutsy, courageous

Well, Brutus, thou art noble; yet, I see,
Thy honorable metal may be wrought,
From that it is disposed: therefore 'tis meet
That noble minds keep ever with their likes;
For who so firm that cannot be seduced?
Caesar doth bear me hard,[44] but he loves Brutus;
If I were Brutus now and he were Cassius,
He should not humor me. I will this night,
In several hands, in at his windows throw,
As if they came from several citizens,
Writings all tending to the great opinion
That Rome holds of his name; wherein obscurely
Caesar's ambition shall be glanced at:
And after this let Caesar seat him sure;
For we will shake him, or worse days endure.   *[Exit.]*

Questions for Review:

1.   How does Julius Caesar react to the warning of the sooth-sayer?

2.   Cassius says he has heard many Romans wish that "noble Brutus had his eyes." What does he mean?

3.   What kind of man is Brutus? What does Cassius notice about him? What does Brutus say when Cassius points this out?

4.   Why does Brutus fear the shouts of the people? What does Cassius think of the idea that Julius Caesar is godlike?

5.   What does Julius Caesar think about Cassius, and how does this contrast with the "fat, sleek-headed men" he keeps around him?

6.   How does Julius Caesar view himself? What is ironic about his telling Antony to come around to his good ear so he can hear Antony?

7.   Why do the Roman people shout three times? How does Julius Caesar's manner change each time he refuses the crown?

8.   Why does Julius Caesar "fall down"? What does Cassius mean when he says, "we have the falling sickness"?

9.   What kind of character is Casca? What do Brutus and Cassius plan?

---

[44] "bear me hard": holds a grudge against me

SCENE III. THE SAME. A STREET.

[Thunder and lightning. Enter, from opposite sides, CASCA, with his sword drawn, and CICERO.]

CICERO.
Good even, Casca: brought you Caesar home?
Why are you breathless, and why stare you so?

CASCA.
Are not you moved, when all the sway of earth
Shakes like a thing unfirm? O Cicero,
I have seen tempests, when the scolding winds
Have rived[45] the knotty oaks; and I have seen
Th' ambitious ocean swell and rage and foam,
To be exalted with the threatening clouds:
But never till tonight, never till now,
Did I go through a tempest dropping fire.
Either there is a civil strife in heaven,
Or else the world too saucy with the gods,
Incenses them to send destruction.

CICERO.
Why, saw you anything more wonderful?

CASCA.
A common slave—you'd know him well by sight—
Held up his left hand, which did flame and burn
Like twenty torches join'd, and yet his hand
Not sensible of fire remain'd unscorch'd.
Besides,—I ha' not since put up my sword,—
Against the Capitol I met a lion,
Who glared upon me, and went surly by,
Without annoying me: and there were drawn
Upon a heap a hundred ghastly women,
Transformed with their fear; who swore they saw
Men, all in fire, walk up and down the streets.
And yesterday the bird of night[46] did sit
Even at noonday upon the marketplace,
Howling and shrieking. When these prodigies[47]

---

[45] split
[46] an owl
[47] natural phenomena acting as omens

Do so conjointly meet, let not men say
"These are their reasons; they are natural";
For I believe they are portentous[48] things
Unto the climate that they point upon.

CICERO.
Indeed, it is a strange-disposed time.
But men may construe things after their fashion,
Clean from the purpose of the things themselves.
Comes Caesar to the Capitol tomorrow?

CASCA.
He doth, for he did bid Antonius
Send word to you he would be there to-morrow.

CICERO.
Good then, Casca: this disturbed sky
Is not to walk in.

CASCA.
Farewell, Cicero.

[Exit Cicero.]

[Enter Cassius.]

CASSIUS.
Who's there?

CASCA.
A Roman.

CASSIUS.
Casca, by your voice.

CASCA.
Your ear is good. Cassius, what night is this!

CASSIUS.
A very pleasing night to honest men.

CASCA.
Who ever knew the heavens menace so?

---

[48] important, signficant

CASSIUS.
Those that have known the earth so full of faults.
For my part, I have walk'd about the streets,
Submitting me unto the perilous night;
And, thus unbraced, Casca, as you see,
Have bared my bosom to the thunder-stone;
And when the cross blue lightning seem'd to open
The breast of heaven, I did present myself
Even in the aim and very flash of it.

CASCA.
But wherefore[49] did you so much tempt the Heavens?
It is the part of men to fear and tremble,
When the most mighty gods by tokens send
Such dreadful heralds to astonish us.

CASSIUS.
You are dull, Casca; and those sparks of life
That should be in a Roman you do want,[50]
Or else you use not. You look pale and gaze,
And put on fear and cast yourself in wonder,
To see the strange impatience of the Heavens:
But if you would consider the true cause
Why all these fires, why all these gliding ghosts,
Why birds and beasts, from quality and kind;
Why old men, fools, and children calculate;—
Why all these things change from their ordinance,
Their natures, and preformed faculties
To monstrous quality;—why, you shall find
That Heaven hath infused them with these spirits,
To make them instruments of fear and warning
Unto some monstrous state. Now could I, Casca,
Name to thee a man most like this dreadful night;
That thunders, lightens, opens graves, and roars,
As doth the lion in the Capitol;
A man no mightier than thyself or me
In personal action; yet prodigious grown,
And fearful, as these strange eruptions are.

---

[49] why
[50] lack

CASCA.

'Tis Caesar that you mean; is it not, Cassius?

CASSIUS.

Let it be who it is: for Romans now
Have thews[51] and limbs like to their ancestors;
But, woe the while! our fathers' minds are dead,
And we are govern'd with our mothers' spirits;
Our yoke and sufferance show us womanish.

CASCA.

Indeed they say the senators to-morrow
Mean to establish Caesar as a king;
And he shall wear his crown by sea and land,
In every place save here in Italy.

CASSIUS.

I know where I will wear this dagger then;
Cassius from bondage will deliver Cassius:
Therein, ye gods, you make the weak most strong;
Therein, ye gods, you tyrants do defeat:
Nor stony tower, nor walls of beaten brass,
Nor airless dungeon, nor strong links of iron
Can be retentive to the strength of spirit;
But life, being weary of these worldly bars,
Never lacks power to dismiss itself.
If I know this, know all the world besides,
That part of tyranny that I do bear
I can shake off at pleasure.

[Thunders still.]

CASCA.

So can I:
So every bondman in his own hand bears
The power to cancel his captivity.[52]

CASSIUS.

And why should Caesar be a tyrant then?
Poor man! I know he would not be a wolf,
But that he sees the Romans are but sheep:

---

[51] muscles, sinews
[52] that is, a sword

He were no lion, were not Romans hinds.[53]
Those that with haste will make a mighty fire
Begin it with weak straws: what trash is Rome,
What rubbish, and what offal,[54] when it serves
For the base matter to illuminate
So vile a thing as Caesar! But, O grief,
Where hast thou led me? I perhaps speak this
Before a willing bondman: then I know
My answer must be made; but I am arm'd,
And dangers are to me indifferent.

CASCA.
You speak to Casca; and to such a man
That is no fleering tell-tale. Hold, my hand:
Be factious for redress of all these griefs;[55]
And I will set this foot of mine as far
As who goes farthest.

CASSIUS.
There's a bargain made.
Now know you, Casca, I have moved already
Some certain of the noblest-minded Romans
To undergo with me an enterprise
Of honorable-dangerous consequence;
And I do know by this, they stay for me
In Pompey's Porch: for now, this fearful night,
There is no stir or walking in the streets;
And the complexion of the element
Is favor'd like the work we have in hand,
Most bloody, fiery, and most terrible.

CASCA.
Stand close awhile, for here comes one in haste.

CASSIUS.
'Tis Cinna; I do know him by his gait;[56]
He is a friend.—

---

[53] deer
[54] the unused, thrown-out parts of a butchered animal
[55] "Be factious for redress of all these griefs": Create a group ("faction") to do something about the tyranny of Julius Caesar.
[56] way of walking

[Enter Cinna.]

Cinna, where haste you so?

CINNA.
To find out you. Who's that? Metellus Cimber?

CASSIUS.
No, it is Casca, one incorporate
To our attempts. Am I not stay'd for, Cinna?

CINNA.
I am glad on't. What a fearful night is this!
There's two or three of us have seen strange sights.

CASSIUS.
Am I not stay'd for? tell me.

CINNA.
Yes,
You are. O Cassius, if you could but win
The noble Brutus to our party,—

CASSIUS.
Be you content. Good Cinna, take this paper,
And look you lay it in the praetor's[57] chair,
Where Brutus may but find it; and throw this
In at his window; set this up with wax
Upon old Brutus' statue: all this done,
Repair to Pompey's Porch, where you shall find us.
Is Decius Brutus and Trebonius there?

CINNA.
All but Metellus Cimber, and he's gone
To seek you at your house. Well, I will hie[58]
And so bestow these papers as you bade me.

CASSIUS.
That done, repair to Pompey's theatre.—

[Exit Cinna.]

---

[57] a high-ranking government official
[58] hurry

Come, Casca, you and I will yet, ere day,
See Brutus at his house: three parts of him
Is ours already; and the man entire,
Upon the next encounter, yields him ours.

CASCA.

O, he sits high in all the people's hearts!
And that which would appear offense in us,
His countenance, like richest alchemy,[59]
Will change to virtue and to worthiness.

CASSIUS.

Him, and his worth, and our great need of him,
You have right well conceited. Let us go,
For it is after midnight; and, ere day,
We will awake him, and be sure of him.

[Exeunt.]

Questions for Review:

1. Describe the conversation between Cicero and Casca, the omens, weather, etc.

2. Cassius compares Julius Caesar to what animal? Why?

3. What does Cassius mean when he says, "Our fathers' minds are dead"?

4. Why does the conspiracy so desperately want Brutus?

---

[59] The word *alchemy* here refers attempts by some scientists to turn less valuable metals into gold. Cassius is saying that a conspiracy against Julius Caesar, which would look offensive ("less valuable") to many Romans, would have a look of "virtue" or "worthiness" (or valuable as gold) if the well-respected Brutus participates.

ACT II.

SCENE I. ROME.
THE ORCHARD OF BRUTUS.

[Enter Brutus.]

BRUTUS.
What, Lucius, ho!—
I cannot, by the progress of the stars,
Give guess how near to day.—Lucius, I say!—
I would it were my fault to sleep so soundly.—
When, Lucius, when! Awake, I say! What, Lucius!

[Enter Lucius.]

LUCIUS.
Call'd you, my lord?

BRUTUS.
Get me a taper[60] in my study, Lucius:
When it is lighted, come and call me here.

LUCIUS.
I will, my lord.

[Exit.]

BRUTUS.
It must be by his death: and, for my part,
I know no personal cause to spurn at him,
But for the general.[61] He would be crown'd:
How that might change his nature, there's the question:
It is the bright day that brings forth the adder;
And that craves wary walking. Crown him?—that:
And then, I grant, we put a sting in him,
That at his will he may do danger with.
Th' abuse of greatness is, when it disjoins
Remorse from power; and, to speak truth of Caesar,
I have not known when his affections sway'd
More than his reason. But 'tis a common proof,

---

[60] candle
[61] "for the general": for the general good of Rome

That lowliness is young ambition's ladder,
Whereto the climber-upward turns his face;
But, when he once attains the upmost round,
He then unto the ladder turns his back,
Looks in the clouds, scorning the base degrees
By which he did ascend: so Caesar may;
Then, lest he may, prevent. And, since the quarrel
Will bear no color for the thing he is,
Fashion it thus,—that what he is, augmented,
Would run to these and these extremities:
And therefore think him as a serpent's egg
Which hatch'd, would, as his kind grow mischievous;
And kill him in the shell.[62]

[Re-enter Lucius.]

LUCIUS.
The taper burneth in your closet, sir.
Searching the window for a flint I found
This paper thus seal'd up, and I am sure
It did not lie there when I went to bed.

BRUTUS.
Get you to bed again; it is not day.
Is not tomorrow, boy, the Ides of March?

LUCIUS.
I know not, sir.

BRUTUS.
Look in the calendar, and bring me word.

LUCIUS.
I will, sir.

[Exit.]

---

[62] "And since the quarrel...And kill him in the shell" means that Brutus doesn't think he can make a convincing argument for plotting against Julius Caesar as he is *now*...but he *can* make the case that he must be done away with on the grounds that he might become more of a tyrant.

BRUTUS.
The exhalations,[63] whizzing in the air
Give so much light that I may read by them.—

[Opens the letter and reads.]

> "Brutus, thou sleep'st: awake and see thyself.
> Shall Rome, &c. Speak, strike, redress—!
> Brutus, thou sleep'st: awake!—"

Such instigations have been often dropp'd
Where I have took them up.
"Shall Rome, & c." Thus must I piece it out:
Shall Rome stand under one man's awe? What, Rome?
My ancestors did from the streets of Rome
The Tarquin[64] drive, when he was call'd a king.—
"Speak, strike, redress!"—Am I entreated, then,
To speak and strike? O Rome, I make thee promise,
If the redress will follow, thou receivest
Thy full petition at the hand of Brutus!

[Re-enter Lucius.]

LUCIUS.
Sir, March is wasted fifteen days.

[Knocking within.]

BRUTUS.
'Tis good. Go to the gate, somebody knocks.—

[Exit Lucius.]

Since Cassius first did whet me against Caesar
I have not slept.
Between the acting of a dreadful thing
And the first motion, all the interim is
Like a phantasma[65] or a hideous dream:

---

[63] shooting stars, meteors
[64] Lucius Tarquinius Superbus, Rome's final king, who was overthrown in 509 B. C. His overthrow led to Rome's form of government changing from a monarchy to a republic.
[65] a weird, sometimes ghostly vision

The genius[66] and the mortal instruments[67]
Are then in council; and the state of man,
Like to a little kingdom, suffers then
The nature of an insurrection.

[Re-enter Lucius].

LUCIUS.
Sir, 'tis your brother Cassius at the door,
Who doth desire to see you.

BRUTUS.
Is he alone?

LUCIUS.
No, sir, there are more with him.

BRUTUS.
Do you know them?

LUCIUS.
No, sir, their hats are pluck'd about their ears,
And half their faces buried in their cloaks,
That by no means I may discover them
By any mark of favor.

BRUTUS.
Let 'em enter.—

[Exit Lucius.]

They are the faction.—O conspiracy,
Shamest thou to show thy dangerous brow by night,
When evils are most free? O, then, by day
Where wilt thou find a cavern dark enough
To mask thy monstrous visage?[68] Seek none, conspiracy;
Hide it in smiles and affability:[69]
For if thou path, thy native semblance on,[70]

---

[66] a person's soul
[67] "mortal instruments": the tools of a human (a "mortal"), such as the mind and determination and desire, that he uses to act
[68] face, expression
[69] friendliness
[70] "if thou path, thy native semblance on": if you continue with your faces appearing grim (as would be expected when planning such a serious and severe act)

Not Erebus[71] itself were dim enough
To hide thee from prevention.

[Enter Cassius, Casca, Decius, Cinna, Metellus Cimber, and Trebonius.]

CASSIUS.
I think we are too bold upon your rest:
Good morrow, Brutus; do we trouble you?

BRUTUS.
I have been up this hour, awake all night.
Know I these men that come along with you?

CASSIUS.
Yes, every man of them; and no man here
But honors you; and every one doth wish
You had but that opinion of yourself
Which every noble Roman bears of you.
This is Trebonius.

BRUTUS.
He is welcome hither.

CASSIUS.
This Decius Brutus.

BRUTUS.
He is welcome too.

CASSIUS.
This, Casca; this, Cinna; and this, Metellus Cimber.

BRUTUS.
They are all welcome.——
What watchful cares do interpose themselves
Betwixt your eyes and night?

CASSIUS.
Shall I entreat a word?

[BRUTUS and CASSIUS whisper apart.]

DECIUS.
Here lies the east: doth not the day break here?

---

[71] Greek "god" representing darkness

CASCA.
No.

CINNA.
O, pardon, sir, it doth, and yon grey lines
That fret the clouds are messengers of day.

CASCA.
You shall confess that you are both deceived.
Here, as I point my sword, the Sun arises;
Which is a great way growing on the South,
Weighing the youthful season of the year.
Some two months hence, up higher toward the North
He first presents his fire; and the high East
Stands, as the Capitol, directly here.

BRUTUS.
Give me your hands all over, one by one.

CASSIUS.
And let us swear our resolution.

BRUTUS.
No, not an oath: if not the face of men,
The sufferance of our souls, the time's abuse—
If these be motives weak, break off betimes,[72]
And every man hence to his idle bed;
So let high-sighted tyranny range on,
Till each man drop by lottery. But if these,
As I am sure they do, bear fire enough
To kindle cowards, and to steel with valour
The melting spirits of women; then, countrymen,
What need we any spur but our own cause
To prick us to redress? what other bond
Than secret Romans, that have spoke the word,
And will not palter?[73] and what other oath
Than honesty to honesty engaged,
That this shall be, or we will fall for it?
Swear priests, and cowards, and men cautelous,[74]

---

[72] *Betimes* means "early." (See for example Genesis 26:31 and Proverbs 13:24.)
[73] waver, hesitate to make a decision
[74] deceptive, tricky

Old feeble carrions,[75] and such suffering souls
That welcome wrongs; unto bad causes swear
Such creatures as men doubt: but do not stain
The even virtue of our enterprise,
Nor th' insuppressive mettle of our spirits,
To think that or our cause or our performance
Did need an oath; when every drop of blood
That every Roman bears, and nobly bears,
Is guilty of a several bastardy,
If he do break the smallest particle
Of any promise that hath pass'd from him.

CASSIUS.
But what of Cicero? Shall we sound him?
I think he will stand very strong with us.

CASCA.
Let us not leave him out.

CINNA.
No, by no means.

METELLUS.
O, let us have him! for his silver hairs
Will purchase us a good opinion,
And buy men's voices to commend our deeds:
It shall be said, his judgment ruled our hands;
Our youths and wildness shall no whit appear,
But all be buried in his gravity.

BRUTUS.
O, name him not! let us not break with him;
For he will never follow any thing
That other men begin.

CASSIUS.
Then leave him out.

CASCA.
Indeed, he is not fit.

DECIUS.
Shall no man else be touch'd but only Caesar?

---

[75] dead bodies

CASSIUS.

Decius, well urged.—I think it is not meet,
Mark Antony, so well beloved of Caesar,
Should outlive Caesar: we shall find of him
A shrewd contriver; and you know his means,
If he improve them, may well stretch so far
As to annoy us all: which to prevent,
Let Antony and Caesar fall together.

BRUTUS.

Our course will seem too bloody, Caius Cassius,
To cut the head off, and then hack the limbs,
Like wrath in death, and envy afterwards;
For Antony is but a limb of Caesar.
Let us be sacrificers, but not butchers, Caius.
We all stand up against the spirit of Caesar;
And in the spirit of men there is no blood:
O, that we then could come by Caesar's spirit,
And not dismember Caesar! But, alas,
Caesar must bleed for it! And, gentle friends,
Let's kill him boldly, but not wrathfully;
Let's carve him as a dish fit for the gods,
Not hew him as a carcass fit for hounds;
And let our hearts, as subtle masters do,
Stir up their servants to an act of rage,
And after seem to chide 'em. This shall mark
Our purpose necessary, and not envious;
Which so appearing to the common eyes,
We shall be call'd purgers, not murderers.
And for Mark Antony, think not of him;
For he can do no more than Caesar's arm
When Caesar's head is off.

CASSIUS.

Yet I do fear him;
For in th' ingrafted love he bears to Caesar—

BRUTUS.

Alas, good Cassius, do not think of him:
If he love Caesar, all that he can do
Is to himself,—take thought and die for Caesar.
And that were much he should; for he is given
To sports, to wildness, and much company.

338

TREBONIUS.
There is no fear in him; let him not die;
For he will live, and laugh at this hereafter.

[Clock strikes.]

BRUTUS.
Peace! count the clock.

CASSIUS.
The clock hath stricken three.

TREBONIUS.
'Tis time to part.

CASSIUS.
But it is doubtful yet
Whether Caesar will come forth today or no;
For he is superstitious grown of late,
Quite from the main opinion he held once
Of fantasy, of dreams, and ceremonies.[76]
It may be these apparent prodigies,
The unaccustom'd terror of this night,
And the persuasion of his augurers[77]
May hold him from the Capitol to-day.

DECIUS.
Never fear that: if he be so resolved,
I can o'ersway him, for he loves to hear
That unicorns may be betray'd with trees,
And bears with glasses, elephants with holes,
Lions with toils, and men with flatterers:
But when I tell him he hates flatterers,
He says he does, being then most flattered.
Let me work;
For I can give his humor the true bent,
And I will bring him to the Capitol.

CASSIUS.
Nay, we will all of us be there to fetch him.

---

[76] signs, visions
[77] fortuneteller, interpreter of signs or omens

BRUTUS.
By the eighth hour: is that the uttermost?[78]

CINNA.
Be that the uttermost; and fail not then.

METELLUS.
Caius Ligarius doth bear Caesar hard,
Who rated him for speaking well of Pompey:
I wonder none of you have thought of him.

BRUTUS.
Now, good Metellus, go along by him:
He loves me well, and I have given him reason;
Send him but hither, and I'll fashion him.

CASSIUS.
The morning comes upon 's. We'll leave you, Brutus;—
And, friends, disperse yourselves, but all remember
What you have said, and show yourselves true Romans.

BRUTUS.
Good gentlemen, look fresh and merrily;
Let not our looks put on our purposes,
But bear it as our Roman actors do,
With untired spirits and formal constancy:
And so, good morrow to you every one.—

[Exeunt all but Brutus.]

Boy! Lucius!—Fast asleep? It is no matter;
Enjoy the honey-heavy dew of slumber:
Thou hast no figures nor no fantasies,
Which busy care draws in the brains of men;
Therefore thou sleep'st so sound.

[Enter Portia.]

PORTIA.
Brutus, my lord!

BRUTUS.
Portia, what mean you? wherefore rise you now?

[78] latest

It is not for your health thus to commit
Your weak condition to the raw-cold morning.

PORTIA.
Nor for yours neither. You've ungently, Brutus,
Stole from[79] my bed: and yesternight, at supper,
You suddenly arose, and walk'd about,
Musing and sighing, with your arms across;
And, when I ask'd you what the matter was,
You stared upon me with ungentle looks:
I urged you further; then you scratch'd your head,
And too impatiently stamp'd with your foot:
Yet I insisted, yet you answer'd not;
But, with an angry wafture of your hand,
Gave sign for me to leave you. So I did;
Fearing to strengthen that impatience
Which seem'd too much enkindled; and withal[80]
Hoping it was but an effect of humour,[81]
Which sometime hath his hour with every man.
It will not let you eat, nor talk, nor sleep;
And, could it work so much upon your shape
As it hath much prevail'd on your condition,
I should not know you, Brutus. Dear my lord,
Make me acquainted with your cause of grief.

BRUTUS.
I am not well in health, and that is all.

PORTIA.
Brutus is wise, and, were he not in health,
He would embrace the means to come by it.

BRUTUS.
Why, so I do. Good Portia, go to bed.

PORTIA.
Is Brutus sick? and is it physical[82]
To walk unbraced and suck up the humours

---

[79] silently left
[80] with that
[81] "effect of humour": the result of a (bad) mood
[82] healthful

Of the dank[83] morning? What, is Brutus sick,
And will he steal out of his wholesome bed
To dare the vile contagion of the night,
And tempt the rheumy and unpurged air
To add unto his sickness? No, my Brutus;
You have some sick offense within your mind,
Which, by the right and virtue of my place,
I ought to know of: and, upon my knees,
I charge you, by my once commended beauty,
By all your vows of love, and that great vow
Which did incorporate and make us one,
That you unfold to me, yourself, your half,
Why you are heavy, and what men to-night
Have had resort to you; for here have been
Some six or seven, who did hide their faces
Even from darkness.

BRUTUS.
Kneel not, gentle Portia.

PORTIA.
I should not need, if you were gentle Brutus.
Within the bond of marriage, tell me, Brutus,
Is it excepted I should know no secrets
That appertain to you? Am I yourself
But, as it were, in sort or limitation,—
To keep with you at meals, comfort your bed,
And talk to you sometimes? Dwell I but in the suburbs
Of your good pleasure? If it be no more,
Portia is Brutus' harlot, not his wife.

BRUTUS.
You are my true and honorable wife;
As dear to me as are the ruddy drops
That visit my sad heart.

PORTIA.
If this were true, then should I know this secret.
I grant I am a woman; but withal
A woman that Lord Brutus took to wife:
I grant I am a woman; but withal

---

[83] chilly, damp

A woman well reputed, Cato's[84] daughter.
Think you I am no stronger than my sex,
Being so father'd and so husbanded?
Tell me your counsels, I will not disclose 'em.
I have made strong proof of my constancy,
Giving myself a voluntary wound
Here in the thigh: can I bear that with patience
And not my husband's secrets?

BRUTUS.
O ye gods,
Render me worthy of this noble wife!

[Knocking within.]

Hark, hark, one knocks: Portia, go in awhile;
And by and by thy bosom shall partake
The secrets of my heart:
All my engagements I will construe to thee,
All the charactery of my sad brows.
Leave me with haste.

[Exit Portia.]

—Lucius, who's that knocks?

[Re-enter Lucius with Ligarius.]

LUCIUS.
Here is a sick man that would speak with you.

BRUTUS.
Caius Ligarius, that Metellus spake of.—
Boy, stand aside.—Caius Ligarius,—how?

LIGARIUS.
Vouchsafe good-morrow from a feeble tongue.

BRUTUS.
O, what a time have you chose out, brave Caius,
To wear a kerchief! Would you were not sick!

---

[84] Portia's father Cato is Marcus Porcius Cato Uticensis (95-46 B. C.), who was also known as "Cato the Younger." He was known for his self-denial, toughness, and integrity, and here Portia is telling Brutus that even though she is of the "gentler sex," she comes from tough stock and can be counted on to help him.

LIGARIUS.
I am not sick, if Brutus have in hand
Any exploit worthy the name of honour.

BRUTUS.
Such an exploit have I in hand, Ligarius,
Had you a healthful ear to hear of it.

LIGARIUS.
By all the gods that Romans bow before,
I here discard my sickness. Soul of Rome!
Brave son, derived from honorable loins!
Thou, like an exorcist, hast conjured up
My mortified spirit. Now bid me run,
And I will strive with things impossible;
Yea, get the better of them. What's to do?

BRUTUS.
A piece of work that will make sick men whole.

LIGARIUS.
But are not some whole that we must make sick?

BRUTUS.
That must we also. What it is, my Caius,
I shall unfold to thee, as we are going,
To whom it must be done.

LIGARIUS.
Set on your foot;
And with a heart new-fired I follow you,
To do I know not what: but it sufficeth
That Brutus leads me on.

BRUTUS.
Follow me then.

[Exeunt.]

Questions for Review:

1. Describe the struggle in Brutus's mind. What does Brutus think will happen if Julius Caesar is crowned? How does this analogy compare to Genesis 3?

2. How does Brutus want to hide the intentions of the conspiracy? Why doesn't he want the conspirators to swear an oath?

3. Describe the two contrasting views of Cassius and Brutus over whether to kill Marc Antony with Julius Caesar.

4. What is funny about Decius's remark about flattery?

5. Summarize Brutus's and Portia's conversation.

6. Look up the phrase "crossing the Rubicon" and write a brief explanation of what it means.

SCENE II. A ROOM IN CAESAR'S PALACE.

[Thunder and lightning. Enter Caesar, in his nightgown.]

CAESAR.
Nor heaven nor earth have been at peace tonight:
Thrice hath Calpurnia in her sleep cried out,
"Help, ho! They murder Caesar!"—Who's within?

[Enter a Servant.]

SERVANT.
My lord?

CAESAR.
Go bid the priests do present sacrifice,
And bring me their opinions of success.

SERVANT.
I will, my lord.

[Exit.]

[Enter Calpurnia.]

CALPURNIA.
What mean you, Caesar? Think you to walk forth?
You shall not stir out of your house to-day.

CAESAR.
Caesar shall forth: the things that threaten me

Ne'er look but on my back; when they shall see
The face of Caesar, they are vanished.

CALPURNIA.
Caesar, I never stood on ceremonies,
Yet now they fright me. There is one within,
Besides the things that we have heard and seen,
Recounts most horrid sights seen by the watch.
A lioness hath whelped[85] in the streets;
And graves have yawn'd, and yielded up their dead;
Fierce fiery warriors fight upon the clouds,
In ranks and squadrons and right form of war,
Which drizzled blood upon the Capitol;
The noise of battle hurtled in the air,
Horses did neigh, and dying men did groan;
And ghosts did shriek and squeal about the streets.
O Caesar,these things are beyond all use,
And I do fear them!

CAESAR.
What can be avoided
Whose end is purposed by the mighty gods?
Yet Caesar shall go forth; for these predictions
Are to the world in general as to Caesar.

CALPURNIA.
When beggars die, there are no comets seen;
The heavens themselves blaze forth the death of princes.

CAESAR.
Cowards die many times before their deaths;
The valiant never taste of death but once.
Of all the wonders that I yet have heard,
It seems to me most strange that men should fear;
Seeing that death, a necessary end,
Will come when it will come.—
[Re-enter Servant.]

What say the augurers?

SERVANT.
They would not have you to stir forth to-day.

---

[85] given birth

346

Plucking the entrails of an offering forth,
They could not find a heart within the beast.

CAESAR.
The gods do this in shame of cowardice:
Caesar should be a beast without a heart,
If he should stay at home today for fear.
No, Caesar shall not: danger knows full well
That Caesar is more dangerous than he:
We are two lions litter'd in one day,
And I the elder and more terrible;
And Caesar shall go forth.

CALPURNIA.
Alas, my lord,
Your wisdom is consumed in confidence!
Do not go forth to-day: call it my fear
That keeps you in the house, and not your own.
We'll send Mark Antony to the Senate-house,
And he shall say you are not well to-day:
Let me, upon my knee, prevail in this.

CAESAR.
Mark Antony shall say I am not well,
And, for thy humor, I will stay at home.

[Enter Decius.]

Here's Decius Brutus, he shall tell them so.

DECIUS.
Caesar, all hail! Good morrow, worthy Caesar:
I come to fetch you to the Senate-house.

CAESAR.
And you are come in very happy time
To bear my greeting to the Senators,
And tell them that I will not come to-day.
Cannot, is false; and that I dare not, falser:
I will not come to-day. Tell them so, Decius.

CALPURNIA.
Say he is sick.

CAESAR.

Shall Caesar send a lie?
Have I in conquest stretch'd mine arm so far,
To be afeard to tell grey-beards the truth?—
Decius, go tell them Caesar will not come.

DECIUS.

Most mighty Caesar, let me know some cause,
Lest I be laugh'd at when I tell them so.

CAESAR.

The cause is in my will; I will not come:
That is enough to satisfy the Senate.
But, for your private satisfaction,
Because I love you, I will let you know:
Calpurnia here, my wife, stays me at home:
She dreamt to-night she saw my statue,
Which, like a fountain with an hundred spouts,
Did run pure blood; and many lusty Romans
Came smiling and did bathe their hands in it:
And these does she apply for warnings and portents
And evils imminent; and on her knee
Hath begg'd that I will stay at home to-day.

DECIUS.

This dream is all amiss interpreted:
It was a vision fair and fortunate.
Your statue spouting blood in many pipes,
In which so many smiling Romans bathed,
Signifies that from you great Rome shall suck
Reviving blood; and that great men shall press
For tinctures, stains, relics, and cognizance.[86]
This by Calpurnia's dream is signified.

CAESAR.

And this way have you well expounded it.

DECIUS.

I have, when you have heard what I can say;
And know it now: The Senate have concluded

---

[86] "press for tinctures, stains, relics, and cognizance": crowd around to get souvenirs of your blood for themselves (a modern comparison might be screaming teenaged girls who try to get a lock of hair from a movie star or rock star)

To give this day a crown to mighty Caesar.
If you shall send them word you will not come,
Their minds may change. Besides, it were a mock
Apt to be render'd,[87] for someone to say
"Break up the Senate till another time,
When Caesar's wife shall meet with better dreams."
If Caesar hide himself, shall they not whisper
"Lo, Caesar is afraid"?
Pardon me, Caesar; for my dear dear love
To your proceeding bids me tell you this;
And reason to my love is liable.[88]

CAESAR.
How foolish do your fears seem now, Calpurnia!
I am ashamed I did yield to them.
Give me my robe, for I will go.

[Enter Publius, Brutus, Ligarius, Metellus, Casca, Trebonius, and Cinna.]

And look where Publius is come to fetch me.

PUBLIUS.
Good morrow, Caesar.

CAESAR.
Welcome, Publius.—
What, Brutus, are you stirr'd so early too?—
Good morrow, Casca.—Caius Ligarius,
Caesar was ne'er so much your enemy
As that same ague which hath made you lean.—[89]
What is't o'clock?

BRUTUS.
Caesar, 'tis strucken eight.

CAESAR.
I thank you for your pains and courtesy.

[Enter Antony.]

---

[87] "a mock apt to be render'd": a likely way people will mock Julius Caesar's decision to stay home
[88] of secondary importance
[89] "ague...lean": sickness that made you appear thin

See! Antony, that revels long o'nights,
Is notwithstanding up.—Good morrow, Antony.

ANTONY.
So to most noble Caesar.

CAESAR.
Bid them prepare within:
I am to blame to be thus waited for.—
Now, Cinna;—now, Metellus;—what, Trebonius!
I have an hour's talk in store for you:
Remember that you call on me to-day;
Be near me, that I may remember you.

TREBONIUS.
Caesar, I will. *[Aside.]* and so near will I be,
That your best friends shall wish I had been further.

CAESAR.
Good friends, go in, and taste some wine with me;
And we, like friends, will straightway go together.

BRUTUS.
[Aside.] That every like is not the same, O Caesar,
The heart of Brutus yearns to think upon!

[Exeunt.]

Questions for Review:

1. Why does Calpurnia want Julius Caesar to stay home?

2. How does the augurers' interpretation of the "beast without a heart" differ from Julius Caesar's interpretation?

3. List several ways in which Caesar shows his arrogance.

4. Interpret this saying of Julius Caesar: "Cowards die many times before their deaths; the valiant never taste of death but once."

5. What does Decius say to Julius Caesar to save the conspirators' plans?

SCENE III. A STREET NEAR THE CAPITOL.

[Enter Artemidorus, reading paper.]

ARTEMIDORUS.
"Caesar, beware of Brutus; take heed of Cassius; come not near Casca; have an eye to Cinna; trust not Trebonius; mark well Metellus Cimber; Decius Brutus loves thee not; thou hast wrong'd Caius Ligarius. There is but one mind in all these men, and it is bent against Caesar. If thou be'st not immortal, look about you: security gives way to conspiracy. The mighty gods defend thee! Thy lover,[90] Artemidorus."

Here will I stand till Caesar pass along,
And as a suitor will I give him this.
My heart laments that virtue cannot live
Out of the teeth of emulation.[91]
If thou read this, O Caesar, thou mayest live;
If not, the Fates with traitors do contrive.

[Exit.]

SCENE IV. ANOTHER PART OF THE SAME STREET, BEFORE THE HOUSE OF BRUTUS.

[Enter Portia and Lucius.]

PORTIA.
I pr'ythee, boy, run to the Senate-house;
Stay not to answer me, but get thee gone.
Why dost thou stay?

LUCIUS.
To know my errand, madam.

PORTIA.
I would have had thee there, and here again,
Ere I can tell thee what thou shouldst do there.—
[Aside.] O constancy, be strong upon my side!
Set a huge mountain 'tween my heart and tongue!

---

[90] close friend
[91] rivalry, jealousy

I have a man's mind, but a woman's might.
How hard it is for women to keep counsel!—
Art thou here yet?

LUCIUS.
Madam, what should I do?
Run to the Capitol, and nothing else?
And so return to you, and nothing else?

PORTIA.
Yes, bring me word, boy, if thy lord look well,
For he went sickly forth: and take good note
What Caesar doth, what suitors press to him.
Hark, boy! what noise is that?

LUCIUS.
I hear none, madam.

PORTIA.
Pr'ythee, listen well:
I heard a bustling rumour, like a fray,
And the wind brings it from the Capitol.

LUCIUS.
Sooth,[92] madam, I hear nothing.

[Enter Artemidorus.]

PORTIA.
Come hither, fellow:
Which way hast thou been?

ARTEMIDORUS.
At mine own house, good lady.

PORTIA.
What is't o'clock?

ARTEMIDORUS.
About the ninth hour, lady.

PORTIA.
Is Caesar yet gone to the Capitol?

---

[92] truly

ARTEMIDORUS.
Madam, not yet: I go to take my stand
To see him pass on to the Capitol.

PORTIA.
Thou hast some suit to Caesar, hast thou not?

ARTEMIDORUS.
That I have, lady: if it will please Caesar
To be so good to Caesar as to hear me,
I shall beseech him to befriend himself.

PORTIA.
Why, know'st thou any harm's intended towards him?

ARTEMIDORUS.
None that I know will be, much that I fear may chance.
Good morrow to you.—Here the street is narrow:
The throng that follows Caesar at the heels,
Of Senators, of Praetors, common suitors,
Will crowd a feeble man almost to death:
I'll get me to a place more void, and there
Speak to great Caesar as he comes along.

[Exit.]

PORTIA.
I must go in.—*[Aside.]* Ah me, how weak a thing
The heart of woman is!—O Brutus,
The heavens speed thee in thine enterprise!—
Sure, the boy heard me.—Brutus hath a suit
That Caesar will not grant.—O, I grow faint.—
Run, Lucius, and commend me to my lord;
Say I am merry: come to me again,
And bring me word what he doth say to thee. *[Exeunt.]*

Questions for Review:

1. Why does Artemidorus write to Julius Caesar? Explain the meaning of his words "My heart laments that virtue cannot live out of the teeth of emulation."

2. How can we tell that Portia is flustered in this scene? What does she want her servant boy to do?

3. What is ironic about Portia's plea, "O Brutus, the heavens speed thee in thine enterprise"?

ACT III.

SCENE I. ROME. BEFORE THE CAPITOL; THE SENATE SITTING.

[A crowd of people in the street leading to the Capitol, among them Artemidorus and the Soothsayer. Flourish. Enter Caesar, Brutus, Cassius, Casca, Decius, Metellus, Trebonius, Cinna, Antony, Lepidus, Popilius, Publius, and others.]

CAESAR.
The Ides of March are come.

SOOTHSAYER.
Ay, Caesar; but not gone.

ARTEMIDORUS.
Hail, Caesar! read this schedule.

DECIUS.
Trebonius doth desire you to o'er-read,
At your best leisure, this his humble suit.

ARTEMIDORUS.
O Caesar, read mine first; for mine's a suit
That touches Caesar nearer: read it, great Caesar.

CAESAR.
What touches us ourself shall be last served.

ARTEMIDORUS.
Delay not, Caesar; read it instantly.

CAESAR.
What, is the fellow mad?

PUBLIUS.
Sirrah,[93] give place.

CASSIUS.
What, urge you your petitions in the street?
Come to the Capitol.

[Caesar enters the Capitol, the rest following. All the Senators rise.]

POPILIUS.
I wish your enterprise to-day may thrive.

CASSIUS.
What enterprise, Popilius?

POPILIUS.
Fare you well. *[Advances to Caesar.]*

BRUTUS.
What said Popilius Lena?

CASSIUS.
He wish'd to-day our enterprise might thrive.
I fear our purpose is discovered.

BRUTUS.
Look, how he makes to Caesar: mark him.

CASSIUS.
Casca, be sudden, for we fear prevention.—
Brutus, what shall be done? If this be known,
Cassius or Caesar never shall turn back,
For I will slay myself.

BRUTUS.
Cassius, be constant:
Popilius Lena speaks not of our purposes;
For, look, he smiles, and Caesar doth not change.

CASSIUS.
Trebonius knows his time, for, look you, Brutus,
He draws Mark Antony out of the way.
[Exeunt Antony and Trebonius. Caesar and the Senators take their seats.]

---

[93] an insulting way to address a male

DECIUS.
Where is Metellus Cimber? Let him go,
And presently prefer his suit to Caesar.

BRUTUS.
He is address'd; press near and second him.

CINNA.
Casca, you are the first that rears your hand.

CASCA.
Are we all ready?

CAESAR.
What is now amiss
That Caesar and his Senate must redress?

METELLUS.
Most high, most mighty, and most puissant[94] Caesar,
Metellus Cimber throws before thy seat
An humble heart.

[Kneeling.]

CAESAR.
I must prevent thee, Cimber.
These couchings[95] and these lowly courtesies
Might fire the blood of ordinary men,
And turn pre-ordinance and first decree
Into the law of children. Be not fond,
To think that Caesar bears such rebel blood
That will be thaw'd from the true quality
With that which melteth fools; I mean, sweet words,
Low-crooked curtsies, and base spaniel-fawning.
Thy brother by decree is banished:
If thou dost bend, and pray, and fawn for him,
I spurn thee like a cur[96] out of my way.

METELLUS.
Caesar, thou dost me wrong.

---

[94] mighty, powerful
[95] manners (specifically, bowing to Julius Caesar)
[96] "spurn thee like a cur": kick you aside like a worthless dog

CAESAR.
Caesar did never wrong but with just cause,
Nor without cause will he be satisfied.

METELLUS.
Is there no voice more worthy than my own,
To sound more sweetly in great Caesar's ear
For the repealing of my banish'd brother?

BRUTUS.
I kiss thy hand, but not in flattery, Caesar;
Desiring thee that Publius Cimber may
Have an immediate freedom of repeal.

CAESAR.
What, Brutus?

CASSIUS.
Pardon, Caesar; Caesar, pardon:
As low as to thy foot doth Cassius fall,
To beg enfranchisement for Publius Cimber.

CAESAR.
I could be well moved, if I were as you;
If I could pray to move, prayers would move me:
But I am constant as the northern star,
Of whose true-fix'd and resting quality
There is no fellow in the firmament.[97]
The skies are painted with unnumber'd sparks,
They are all fire, and every one doth shine;
But there's but one in all doth hold his place:
So in the world; 'tis furnish'd well with men,
And men are flesh and blood, and apprehensive;[98]
Yet in the number I do know but one
That unassailable[99] holds on his rank,
Unshaked of motion: and that I am he,
Let me a little show it, even in this,—
That I was constant Cimber should be banish'd,
And constant do remain to keep him so.

---

[97] skies, space
[98] quick to learn, observant
[99] unbeatable, unable to be challenged

CINNA.
O Caesar,—

CAESAR.
Hence! wilt thou lift up Olympus?

DECIUS.
Great Caesar,—

CAESAR.
Doth not Brutus bootless[100] kneel?

CASCA.
Speak, hands, for me!

[Casca stabs Caesar in the neck. Caesar catches hold of his arm. He is then stabbed by several other Conspirators, and at last by Marcus Brutus.]

CAESAR.
Et tu, Brute?— Then fall, Caesar!

[Dies. The Senators and People retire in confusion.]

CINNA.
Liberty! Freedom! Tyranny is dead!—
Run hence, proclaim, cry it about the streets.

CASSIUS.
Some to the common pulpits and cry out,
"Liberty, freedom, and enfranchisement!"

BRUTUS.
People and Senators, be not affrighted;
Fly not; stand still; ambition's debt is paid.

CASCA.
Go to the pulpit, Brutus.

DECIUS.
And Cassius too.

BRUTUS.
Where's Publius?

---

[100] in vain

CINNA.
Here, quite confounded with this mutiny.

METELLUS.
Stand fast together, lest some friend of Caesar's
Should chance—

BRUTUS.
Talk not of standing.—Publius, good cheer!
There is no harm intended to your person,
Nor to no Roman else: so tell them, Publius.

CASSIUS.
And leave us, Publius; lest that the people
Rushing on us, should do your age some mischief.

BRUTUS.
Do so;—and let no man abide this deed
But we the doers.

[Re-enter Trebonius.]

CASSIUS.
Where's Antony?

TREBONIUS.
Fled to his house amazed.
Men, wives, and children stare, cry out, and run,
As it were doomsday.

BRUTUS.
Fates, we will know your pleasures:
That we shall die, we know; 'tis but the time
And drawing days out, that men stand upon.

CASCA.
Why, he that cuts off twenty years of life
Cuts off so many years of fearing death.

BRUTUS.
Grant that, and then is death a benefit:
So are we Caesar's friends, that have abridged[101]
His time of fearing death.—Stoop, Romans, stoop,

---

[101] shortened

And let us bathe our hands in Caesar's blood
Up to the elbows, and besmear our swords:
Then walk we forth, even to the market-place,
And waving our red weapons o'er our heads,
Let's all cry, "Peace, freedom, and liberty!"

CASSIUS.
Stoop then, and wash. How many ages hence
Shall this our lofty scene be acted o'er
In States unborn and accents yet unknown![102]

BRUTUS.
How many times shall Caesar bleed in sport,
That now on Pompey's basis lies along
No worthier than the dust!

CASSIUS.
So oft as that shall be,
So often shall the knot of us be call'd
The men that gave their country liberty.

DECIUS.
What, shall we forth?

CASSIUS.
Ay, every man away:
Brutus shall lead; and we will grace his heels
With the most boldest and best hearts of Rome.

BRUTUS.
Soft, who comes here?

[Enter a Servant.]

A friend of Antony's.

SERVANT.
Thus, Brutus, did my master bid me kneel;
Thus did Mark Antony bid me fall down;
And, being prostrate, thus he bade me say:
Brutus is noble, wise, valiant, and honest;
Caesar was mighty, bold, royal, and loving;
Say I love Brutus and I honor him;

---

[102] "Stoop then...accents yet unknown": Get Shakespeare's little joke here?

Say I fear'd Caesar, honour'd him, and loved him.
If Brutus will vouchsafe that Antony
May safely come to him, and be resolved
How Caesar hath deserved to lie in death,
Mark Antony shall not love Caesar dead
So well as Brutus living; but will follow
The fortunes and affairs of noble Brutus
Thorough the hazards of this untrod state
With all true faith. So says my master Antony.

BRUTUS.

Thy master is a wise and valiant Roman;
I never thought him worse.
Tell him, so please him come unto this place,
He shall be satisfied and, by my honour,
Depart untouch'd.

SERVANT.

I'll fetch him presently.

[Exit.]

BRUTUS.

I know that we shall have him well to friend.

CASSIUS.

I wish we may: but yet have I a mind
That fears him much; and my misgiving still
Falls shrewdly to the purpose.

BRUTUS.

But here comes Antony.—

[Re-enter Antony.]

Welcome, Mark Antony.

ANTONY.

O mighty Caesar! Dost thou lie so low?
Are all thy conquests, glories, triumphs, spoils,
Shrunk to this little measure? Fare thee well.—
I know not, gentlemen, what you intend,
Who else must be let blood, who else is rank:
If I myself, there is no hour so fit

As Caesar's death-hour, nor no instrument
Of half that worth as those your swords, made rich
With the most noble blood of all this world.
I do beseech ye, if you bear me hard,
Now, whilst your purpled hands do reek and smoke,
Fulfill your pleasure. Live a thousand years,
I shall not find myself so apt to die:
No place will please me so, no means of death,
As here by Caesar, and by you cut off,
The choice and master spirits of this age.

BRUTUS.
O Antony, beg not your death of us!
Though now we must appear bloody and cruel,
As, by our hands and this our present act
You see we do; yet see you but our hands
And this the bleeding business they have done:
Our hearts you see not; they are pitiful;[103]
And pity to the general wrong of Rome—
As fire drives out fire, so pity pity—
Hath done this deed on Caesar. For your part,
To you our swords have leaden points, Mark Antony;
Our arms in strength of amity, and our hearts
Of brothers' temper, do receive you in
With all kind love, good thoughts, and reverence.

CASSIUS.
Your voice shall be as strong as any man's
In the disposing of new dignities.[104]

BRUTUS.
Only be patient till we have appeased
The multitude, beside themselves with fear,
And then we will deliver you the cause
Why I, that did love Caesar when I struck him,
Have thus proceeded.

---

[103] "Pitiful" means "full of pity" or tenderhearted. Example: In 1 Peter 3:8-9, Peter exhorts
Christians this way: "*[B]e ye* all of one mind, having compassion one of another, love as
brethren, be **pitiful**, *be* courteous: not rendering evil for evil, or railing for railing: but con-
trariwise blessing; knowing that ye are thereunto called, that ye should inherit a blessing."
[104] handing out to various men positions in the new government

ANTONY.
I doubt not of your wisdom.
Let each man render me his bloody hand:
First, Marcus Brutus, will I shake with you;—
Next, Caius Cassius, do I take your hand;—
Now, Decius Brutus, yours;—now yours, Metellus;—
Yours, Cinna;—and, my valiant Casca, yours;—
Though last, not least in love, yours, good Trebonius.
Gentlemen all—alas, what shall I say?
My credit now stands on such slippery ground,
That one of two bad ways you must conceit me,
Either a coward or a flatterer.—
That I did love thee, Caesar, O, 'tis true:
If then thy spirit look upon us now,
Shall it not grieve thee dearer than thy death
To see thy Antony making his peace,
Shaking the bloody fingers of thy foes,—
Most noble!—in the presence of thy corse?[105]
Had I as many eyes as thou hast wounds,
Weeping as fast as they stream forth thy blood,
It would become me better than to close
In terms of friendship with thine enemies.
Pardon me, Julius! Here wast thou bay'd, brave hart;[106]
Here didst thou fall; and here thy hunters stand,
Sign'd in thy spoil, and crimson'd in thy death.—
O world, thou wast the forest to this hart;
And this, indeed, O world, the heart of thee.—
How like a deer strucken by many princes,
Dost thou here lie!

CASSIUS.
Mark Antony,—

ANTONY.
Pardon me, Caius Cassius:
The enemies of Caesar shall say this;
Then, in a friend, it is cold modesty.

CASSIUS.
I blame you not for praising Caesar so;

---

[105] corpse
[106] deer

But what compact mean you to have with us?
Will you be prick'd in number of our friends,
Or shall we on, and not depend on you?

ANTONY.
Therefore I took your hands; but was indeed
Sway'd from the point, by looking down on Caesar.
Friends am I with you all, and love you all,
Upon this hope, that you shall give me reasons
Why and wherein Caesar was dangerous.

BRUTUS.
Or else were this a savage spectacle:
Our reasons are so full of good regard
That were you, Antony, the son of Caesar,
You should be satisfied.

ANTONY.
That's all I seek:
And am moreover suitor that I may
Produce his body to the market-place;
And in the pulpit, as becomes a friend,
Speak in the order of his funeral.

BRUTUS.
You shall, Mark Antony.

CASSIUS.
Brutus, a word with you.
[Aside to Brutus.] You know not what you do; do not consent
That Antony speak in his funeral:
Know you how much the people may be moved
By that which he will utter?

BRUTUS.
[Aside to Cassius.] By your pardon:
I will myself into the pulpit first,
And show the reason of our Caesar's death:
What Antony shall speak, I will protest
He speaks by leave and by permission;
And that we are contented Caesar shall
Have all true rights and lawful ceremonies.
It shall advantage more than do us wrong.

CASSIUS.
[Aside to Brutus.] I know not what may fall; I like it not.

BRUTUS.
Mark Antony, here, take you Caesar's body.
You shall not in your funeral speech blame us,
But speak all good you can devise of Caesar;
And say you do't by our permission;
Else shall you not have any hand at all
About his funeral: and you shall speak
In the same pulpit whereto I am going,
After my speech is ended.

ANTONY.
Be it so;
I do desire no more.

BRUTUS.
Prepare the body, then, and follow us.

[Exeunt all but Antony.]

ANTONY.
O, pardon me, thou bleeding piece of earth,
That I am meek and gentle with these butchers!
Thou art the ruins of the noblest man
That ever lived in the tide of times.
Woe to the hand that shed this costly blood!
Over thy wounds now do I prophesy,—
Which, like dumb mouths do ope their ruby lips
To beg the voice and utterance of my tongue,—
A curse shall light upon the limbs of men;
Domestic fury and fierce civil strife
Shall cumber[107] all the parts of Italy;
Blood and destruction shall be so in use,
And dreadful objects so familiar,
That mothers shall but smile when they behold
Their infants quarter'd with the hands of war;
All pity choked with custom of fell deeds:
And Caesar's spirit, ranging for revenge,
With Atë[108] by his side come hot from Hell,

[107] weigh down, burden
[108] Greek "goddess" of confusion and ruin

Shall in these confines with a monarch's voice
Cry "Havoc!" and let slip the dogs of war,
That this foul deed shall smell above the earth
With carrion men, groaning for burial.—

[Enter a Servant].

You serve Octavius Caesar, do you not?

SERVANT.
I do, Mark Antony.

ANTONY.
Caesar did write for him to come to Rome.

SERVANT.
He did receive his letters, and is coming;
And bid me say to you by word of mouth,—
[Seeing the body.] O Caesar!—

ANTONY.
Thy heart is big, get thee apart and weep.
Passion, I see, is catching; for mine eyes,
Seeing those beads of sorrow stand in thine,
Began to water. Is thy master coming?

SERVANT.
He lies tonight within seven leagues of Rome.

ANTONY.
Post back with speed, and tell him what hath chanced.
Here is a mourning Rome, a dangerous Rome,
No Rome of safety for Octavius yet;
Hie hence, and tell him so. Yet stay awhile;
Thou shalt not back till I have borne this corse
Into the market-place: there shall I try,
In my oration, how the people take
The cruel issue of these bloody men;
According to the which thou shalt discourse
To young Octavius of the state of things.
Lend me your hand.
[Exeunt with Caesar's body.]

Questions for Review:

1. How does Julius Caesar's arrogance cost him? Describe the way he compares himself to "the northern star."

2. Why do you think Julius Caesar says, "Et tu, Brute?"?

3. How do the conspirators react after their deed is done? Do you think bathing their hands the way they do is a smart move?

4. What does Antony's servant ask of Brutus after the murder of Julius Caesar? How do Brutus and Cassius still differ on their opinion of Antony? How does Brutus explain the conspirators' murder of Julius Caesar to Antony?

5. Why is Cassius worried about allowing Antony to speak at Julius Caesar's funeral? What restrictions are put on him?

SCENE II. THE SAME. THE FORUM.

[Enter Brutus and Cassius, with a throng of Citizens.]

CITIZENS.
We will be satisfied; let us be satisfied.

BRUTUS.
Then follow me, and give me audience, friends.—
Cassius, go you into the other street
And part the numbers.—
Those that will hear me speak, let 'em stay here;
Those that will follow Cassius, go with him;
And public reasons shall be rendered
Of Caesar's death.

FIRST CITIZEN.
I will hear Brutus speak.

SECOND CITIZEN.
I will hear Cassius; and compare their reasons,
When severally we hear them rendered.

[Exit Cassius, with some of the Citizens. Brutus goes into the rostrum.]

THIRD CITIZEN.
The noble Brutus is ascended: silence!

BRUTUS.
Be patient till the last. Romans, countrymen, and lovers! Hear me for my cause; and be silent, that you may hear: believe me for mine honour, and have respect to mine honour, that you may believe: censure me in your wisdom; and awake your senses, that you may the better judge. If there be any in this assembly, any dear friend of Caesar's, to him I say that Brutus' love to Caesar was no less than his. If then that friend demand why Brutus rose against Caesar, this is my answer,—Not that I loved Caesar less, but that I loved Rome more. Had you rather Caesar were living, and die all slaves, than that Caesar were dead, to live all freemen? As Caesar loved me, I weep for him; as he was fortunate, I rejoice at it; as he was valiant, I honour him; but, as he was ambitious, I slew him. There is tears for his love; joy for his fortune; honour for his valour; and death for his ambition. Who is here so base that would be a bondman? If any, speak; for him have I offended. Who is here so rude that would not be a Roman? If any, speak; for him have I offended. Who is here so vile that will not love his country? If any, speak; for him have I offended. I pause for a reply.

CITIZENS.
None, Brutus, none.

BRUTUS.
Then none have I offended. I have done no more to Caesar than you shall do to Brutus. The question of his death is enroll'd in the Capitol, his glory not extenuated,[109] wherein he was worthy, nor his offenses enforced, for which he suffered death.

[Enter Antony and others, with Caesar's body.]

Here comes his body, mourned by Mark Antony, who, though he had no hand in his death, shall receive the benefit of his dying, a place in the commonwealth; as which of you shall not? With this I depart—that, as I slew my best lover for the good of Rome, I have the same dagger for myself, when it shall please my country to need my death.

CITIZENS.
Live, Brutus! live, live!

---

[109] lessened, minimized

FIRST CITIZEN.
Bring him with triumph home unto his house.

SECOND CITIZEN.
Give him a statue with his ancestors.

THIRD CITIZEN.
Let him be Caesar.

FOURTH CITIZEN.
Caesar's better parts
Shall be crown'd in Brutus.

FIRST CITIZEN.
We'll bring him to his house with shouts and clamours.

BRUTUS.
My countrymen,—

SECOND CITIZEN.
Peace! silence! Brutus speaks.

FIRST CITIZEN.
Peace, ho!

BRUTUS.
Good countrymen, let me depart alone,
And, for my sake, stay here with Antony:
Do grace to Caesar's corpse, and grace his speech
Tending to Caesar's glory; which Mark Antony,
By our permission, is allow'd to make.
I do entreat you, not a man depart,
Save I alone, till Antony have spoke.

[Exit.]

FIRST CITIZEN.
Stay, ho! and let us hear Mark Antony.

THIRD CITIZEN.
Let him go up into the public chair;
We'll hear him.—Noble Antony, go up.

ANTONY.
For Brutus' sake, I am beholding to you.

[Goes up.]

FOURTH CITIZEN.
What does he say of Brutus?

THIRD CITIZEN.
He says, for Brutus' sake,
He finds himself beholding to us all.

FOURTH CITIZEN.
'Twere best he speak no harm of Brutus here.

FIRST CITIZEN.
This Caesar was a tyrant.

THIRD CITIZEN.
Nay, that's certain:
We are blest that Rome is rid of him.

SECOND CITIZEN.
Peace! let us hear what Antony can say.

ANTONY.
You gentle Romans,—

CITIZENS.
Peace, ho! let us hear him.

ANTONY.
Friends, Romans, countrymen, lend me your ears;
I come to bury Caesar, not to praise him.
The evil that men do lives after them;
The good is oft interred with their bones:
So let it be with Caesar. The noble Brutus
Hath told you Caesar was ambitious:
If it were so, it was a grievous fault;
And grievously hath Caesar answer'd it.
Here, under leave of Brutus and the rest,—
For Brutus is an honourable man;
So are they all, all honourable men,—
Come I to speak in Caesar's funeral.
He was my friend, faithful and just to me:
But Brutus says he was ambitious;
And Brutus is an honourable man.
He hath brought many captives home to Rome,

Whose ransoms did the general coffers fill:
Did this in Caesar seem ambitious?
When that the poor have cried, Caesar hath wept:
Ambition should be made of sterner stuff:
Yet Brutus says he was ambitious;
And Brutus is an honourable man.
You all did see that on the Lupercal
I thrice presented him a kingly crown,
Which he did thrice refuse: was this ambition?
Yet Brutus says he was ambitious;
And, sure, he is an honourable man.
I speak not to disprove what Brutus spoke,
But here I am to speak what I do know.
You all did love him once,—not without cause:
What cause withholds you, then, to mourn for him?—
O judgment, thou art fled to brutish beasts,
And men have lost their reason!—Bear with me;
My heart is in the coffin there with Caesar,
And I must pause till it come back to me.

FIRST CITIZEN.
Methinks there is much reason in his sayings.

SECOND CITIZEN.
If thou consider rightly of the matter,
Caesar has had great wrong.

THIRD CITIZEN.
Has he not, masters?
I fear there will a worse come in his place.

FOURTH CITIZEN.
Mark'd ye his words? He would not take the crown;
Therefore 'tis certain he was not ambitious.

FIRST CITIZEN.
If it be found so, some will dear abide it.[110]

SECOND CITIZEN.
Poor soul! his eyes are red as fire with weeping.

---

[110] "dear abide it": suffer dearly for it

THIRD CITIZEN.
There's not a nobler man in Rome than Antony.

FOURTH CITIZEN.
Now mark him; he begins again to speak.

ANTONY.
But yesterday the word of Caesar might
Have stood against the world: now lies he there,
And none so poor to do him reverence.
O masters, if I were disposed to stir
Your hearts and minds to mutiny and rage,
I should do Brutus wrong and Cassius wrong,
Who, you all know, are honourable men:
I will not do them wrong; I rather choose
To wrong the dead, to wrong myself, and you,
Than I will wrong such honourable men.
But here's a parchment with the seal of Caesar,—
I found it in his closet,—'tis his will:
Let but the commons hear this testament,—
Which, pardon me, I do not mean to read,—
And they would go and kiss dead Caesar's wounds,
And dip their napkins in his sacred blood;
Yea, beg a hair of him for memory,
And, dying, mention it within their wills,
Bequeathing it as a rich legacy
Unto their issue.

FOURTH CITIZEN.
We'll hear the will: read it, Mark Antony.

CITIZENS.
The will, the will! We will hear Caesar's will.

ANTONY.
Have patience, gentle friends, I must not read it;
It is not meet you know how Caesar loved you.
You are not wood, you are not stones, but men;
And, being men, hearing the will of Caesar,
It will inflame you, it will make you mad.
'Tis good you know not that you are his heirs;
For if you should, O, what would come of it!

FOURTH CITIZEN.
Read the will! we'll hear it, Antony;
You shall read us the will,—Caesar's will!

ANTONY.
Will you be patient? will you stay awhile?
I have o'ershot myself to tell you of it:
I fear I wrong the honorable men
Whose daggers have stabb'd Caesar; I do fear it.

FOURTH CITIZEN.
They were traitors: honourable men!

CITIZENS.
The will! The testament!

SECOND CITIZEN.
They were villains, murderers. The will! read the will!

ANTONY.
You will compel me, then, to read the will?
Then make a ring about the corpse of Caesar,
And let me show you him that made the will.
Shall I descend? and will you give me leave?

CITIZENS.
Come down.

SECOND CITIZEN.
Descend.

[He comes down.]

THIRD CITIZEN.
You shall have leave.

FOURTH CITIZEN.
A ring! stand round.

FIRST CITIZEN.
Stand from the hearse, stand from the body.

SECOND CITIZEN.
Room for Antony!—most noble Antony!

ANTONY.

Nay, press not so upon me; stand far off.

CITIZENS.

Stand back; room! bear back.

ANTONY.

If you have tears, prepare to shed them now.
You all do know this mantle: I remember
The first time ever Caesar put it on;
'Twas on a Summer's evening, in his tent,
That day he overcame the Nervii.
Look, in this place ran Cassius' dagger through:
See what a rent the envious Casca made:
Through this the well-beloved Brutus stabb'd;
And as he pluck'd his cursed steel away,
Mark how the blood of Caesar follow'd it,—
As rushing out of doors, to be resolved
If Brutus so unkindly knock'd, or no;
For Brutus, as you know, was Caesar's angel:[111]
Judge, O you gods, how dearly Caesar loved him!
This was the most unkindest cut of all;
For when the noble Caesar saw him stab,
Ingratitude, more strong than traitors' arms,
Quite vanquish'd him: then burst his mighty heart;
And, in his mantle muffling up his face,
Even at the base of Pompey's statua,
Which all the while ran blood, great Caesar fell.
O, what a fall was there, my countrymen!
Then I, and you, and all of us fell down,
Whilst bloody treason flourish'd over us.
O, now you weep; and, I perceive, you feel
The dint of pity: these are gracious drops.
Kind souls, what, weep you when you but behold
Our Caesar's vesture wounded? Look you here,
Here is himself, marr'd, as you see, with traitors.

FIRST CITIZEN.

O piteous spectacle!

---

[111] close assistant, advisor, or friend

SECOND CITIZEN.
O noble Caesar!

THIRD CITIZEN.
O woeful day!

FOURTH CITIZEN.
O traitors, villains!

FIRST CITIZEN.
O most bloody sight!

SECOND CITIZEN.
We will be revenged.

CITIZENS.
Revenge,—about,—seek,—burn,—fire,—kill,—slay,—let not a traitor live!

ANTONY.
Stay, countrymen.

FIRST CITIZEN.
Peace there! hear the noble Antony.

SECOND CITIZEN.
We'll hear him, we'll follow him, we'll die with him.

ANTONY.
Good friends, sweet friends, let me not stir you up
To such a sudden flood of mutiny.
They that have done this deed are honourable:
What private griefs they have, alas, I know not,
That made them do it; they're wise and honourable,
And will, no doubt, with reasons answer you.
I come not, friends, to steal away your hearts:
I am no orator, as Brutus is;
But, as you know me all, a plain blunt man,
That love my friend; and that they know full well
That gave me public leave to speak of him:
For I have neither wit, nor words, nor worth,
Action, nor utterance, nor the power of speech,
To stir men's blood: I only speak right on;
I tell you that which you yourselves do know;
Show you sweet Caesar's wounds, poor dumb mouths,

And bid them speak for me: but were I Brutus,
And Brutus Antony, there were an Antony
Would ruffle up your spirits, and put a tongue
In every wound of Caesar, that should move
The stones of Rome to rise and mutiny.

CITIZENS.
We'll mutiny.

FIRST CITIZEN.
We'll burn the house of Brutus.

THIRD CITIZEN.
Away, then! come, seek the conspirators.

ANTONY.
Yet hear me, countrymen; yet hear me speak.

CITIZENS.
Peace, ho! hear Antony; most noble Antony!

ANTONY.
Why, friends, you go to do you know not what.
Wherein hath Caesar thus deserved your loves?
Alas, you know not; I must tell you then:
You have forgot the will I told you of.

CITIZENS.
Most true; the will!—let's stay, and hear the will.

ANTONY.
Here is the will, and under Caesar's seal.
To every Roman citizen he gives,
To every several man, seventy-five drachmas.

SECOND CITIZEN.
Most noble Caesar!—we'll revenge his death.

THIRD CITIZEN.
O, royal Caesar!

ANTONY.
Hear me with patience.

CITIZENS.
Peace, ho!

ANTONY.
Moreover, he hath left you all his walks,
His private arbors, and new-planted orchards,
On this side Tiber: he hath left them you,
And to your heirs forever; common pleasures,
To walk abroad, and recreate yourselves.
Here was a Caesar! when comes such another?

FIRST CITIZEN.
Never, never.—Come, away, away!
We'll burn his body in the holy place,
And with the brands fire the traitors' houses.
Take up the body.

SECOND CITIZEN.
Go, fetch fire.

THIRD CITIZEN.
Pluck down benches.

FOURTH CITIZEN.
Pluck down forms, windows, any thing.

[Exeunt Citizens, with the body.]

ANTONY.
Now let it work.—Mischief, thou art afoot,
Take thou what course thou wilt!—

[Enter a Servant.]

How now, fellow?

SERVANT.
Sir, Octavius is already come to Rome.

ANTONY.
Where is he?

SERVANT.
He and Lepidus are at Caesar's house.

ANTONY.
And thither will I straight to visit him:
He comes upon a wish. Fortune is merry,
And in this mood will give us any thing.

SERVANT.
I heard 'em say Brutus and Cassius
Are rid like madmen through the gates of Rome.

ANTONY.
Belike they had some notice of the people,
How I had moved them. Bring me to Octavius.

[Exeunt.]

Questions for Review:

1. What argument does Brutus make before the crowd?

2. Does he prove that Julius Caesar was ambitious? How does the crowd receive him?

3. Summarize Antony's speech to the crowd. What phrase describing the conspirators does he repeat?

4. How does Julius Caesar's will make the crowd react?

SCENE III. THE SAME. THE STREET.

[Enter Cinna, the poet.]

CINNA.
I dreamt to-night that I did feast with Caesar,
And things unluckily charge my fantasy:
I have no will to wander forth of doors,
Yet something leads me forth.

[Enter Citizens.]

FIRST CITIZEN.
What is your name?

SECOND CITIZEN.
Whither are you going?

THIRD CITIZEN.
Where do you dwell?

FOURTH CITIZEN.
Are you a married man or a bachelor?

SECOND CITIZEN.
Answer every man directly.

FIRST CITIZEN.
Ay, and briefly.

FOURTH CITIZEN.
Ay, and wisely.

THIRD CITIZEN.
Ay, and truly; you were best.

CINNA.
What is my name? Whither am I going? Where do I dwell? Am I a married man or a bachelor? Then, to answer every man directly and briefly, wisely and truly. Wisely I say I am a bachelor.

SECOND CITIZEN.
That's as much as to say they are fools that marry; you'll bear me a bang for that, I fear.[112] Proceed; directly.

CINNA.
Directly, I am going to Caesar's funeral.

FIRST CITIZEN.
As a friend, or an enemy?

CINNA.
As a friend.

SECOND CITIZEN.
That matter is answered directly.

FOURTH CITIZEN.
For your dwelling,—briefly.

---

[112] "That's as much...bang for that" is this citizen's way of saying, "I'm going to punch you, or worse, for saying that it's foolish to marry." We can conclude, therefore, that this citizen is unhappily married.

CINNA.
Briefly, I dwell by the Capitol.

THIRD CITIZEN.
Your name, sir, truly.

CINNA.
Truly, my name is Cinna.

FIRST CITIZEN.
Tear him to pieces! he's a conspirator.

CINNA.
I am Cinna the poet, I am Cinna the poet.

FOURTH CITIZEN.
Tear him for his bad verses, tear him for his bad verses.

CINNA.
I am not Cinna the conspirator.

FOURTH CITIZEN.
It is no matter, his name's Cinna; pluck but his name out of his heart, and turn him going.

THIRD CITIZEN.
Tear him, tear him! Come; brands, ho! firebrands. To Brutus', to Cassius'; burn all. Some to Decius' house, and some to Casca's, some to Ligarius': away, go!

[Exeunt.]

ACT IV.

SCENE I. ROME. A ROOM IN ANTONY'S HOUSE.

[Antony, Octavius, and Lepidus, seated at a table.]

ANTONY.
These many then shall die; their names are prick'd.[113]

---

[113] written down on a list

OCTAVIUS.
Your brother too must die: consent you, Lepidus?

LEPIDUS.
I do consent,—

OCTAVIUS.
Prick him down, Antony.

LEPIDUS.
—Upon condition Publius shall not live,
Who is your sister's son, Mark Antony.

ANTONY.
He shall not live; look, with a spot I damn him.
But, Lepidus, go you to Caesar's house;
Fetch the will hither, and we shall determine
How to cut off some charge in legacies.

LEPIDUS.
What, shall I find you here?

OCTAVIUS.
Or here, or at the Capitol.

[Exit Lepidus.]

ANTONY.
This is a slight unmeritable man,[114]
Meet to be sent on errands: is it fit,
The three-fold world divided, he should stand
One of the three to share it?

OCTAVIUS.
So you thought him;
And took his voice who should be prick'd to die,
In our black sentence and proscription.

ANTONY.
Octavius, I have seen more days than you:
And, though we lay these honors on this man,
To ease ourselves of divers slanderous loads,

---

[114] Calling Lepidus a "slight unmeritable man" is Antony's way of saying Lepidus is a light-weight, unworthy of being an equal member of this triumvirate.

He shall but bear them as the ass bears gold,
To groan and sweat under the business,
Either led or driven, as we point the way;
And having brought our treasure where we will,
Then take we down his load and turn him off,
Like to the empty ass, to shake his ears
And graze in commons.

OCTAVIUS.
You may do your will;
But he's a tried and valiant soldier.

ANTONY.
So is my horse, Octavius; and for that
I do appoint him store of provender:[115]
It is a creature that I teach to fight,
To wind, to stop, to run directly on,
His corporal motion govern'd by my spirit.
And, in some taste, is Lepidus but so;
He must be taught, and train'd, and bid go forth:
A barren-spirited fellow; one that feeds
On objects, arts, and imitations,
Which, out of use and staled by other men,
Begin his fashion: do not talk of him
But as a property. And now, Octavius,
Listen great things. Brutus and Cassius
Are levying powers: we must straight make head;
Therefore let our alliance be combined,
Our best friends made, our means stretch'd;
And let us presently go sit in council,
How covert matters may be best disclosed,
And open perils surest answered.

OCTAVIUS.
Let us do so: for we are at the stake,
And bay'd about with many enemies;
And some that smile have in their hearts, I fear,
Millions of mischiefs.

[Exeunt.]

---

[115] "store of provender": a portion of food

SCENE II. BEFORE BRUTUS'S TENT, IN THE CAMP NEAR SARDIS.

[Drum. Enter Brutus, Lucilius, Titinius, and Soldiers; Pindarus meeting them; Lucius at some distance.]

BRUTUS.
Stand, ho!

LUCILIUS.
Give the word, ho! and stand.

BRUTUS.
What now, Lucilius! is Cassius near?

LUCILIUS.
He is at hand; and Pindarus is come
To do you salutation from his master.

[Pindarus gives a letter to Brutus.]

BRUTUS.
He greets me well.—Your master, Pindarus,
In his own change, or by ill officers,
Hath given me some worthy cause to wish
Things done, undone: but, if he be at hand,
I shall be satisfied.

PINDARUS.
I do not doubt
But that my noble master will appear
Such as he is, full of regard and honour.
BRUTUS.
He is not doubted.—A word, Lucilius:
How he received you, let me be resolved.

LUCILIUS.
With courtesy and with respect enough;
But not with such familiar instances,
Nor with such free and friendly conference,
As he hath used of old.

BRUTUS.
Thou hast described
A hot friend cooling: ever note, Lucilius,

When love begins to sicken and decay,
It useth an enforced ceremony.
There are no tricks in plain and simple faith;
But hollow men, like horses hot at hand,
Make gallant show and promise of their mettle;
But, when they should endure the bloody spur,
They fall their crests, and, like deceitful jades
Sink in the trial.[116] Comes his army on?

LUCILIUS.
They meant his night in Sard is to be quarter'd:
The greater part, the Horse in general,
Are come with Cassius.

[March within.]

BRUTUS.
Hark! he is arrived.
March gently on to meet him.

[Enter Cassius and Soldiers.]

CASSIUS.
Stand, ho!

BRUTUS.
Stand, ho! Speak the word along.

FIRST SOLDIER.
Stand!

SECOND SOLDIER.
Stand!

THIRD SOLDIER.
Stand!

CASSIUS.
Most noble brother, you have done me wrong.

---

[116] Here Brutus compares "hollow men" to old, broken-down horses who fail and whose heads droop down in defeat when the race is on.

BRUTUS.
Judge me, you gods! wrong I mine enemies?
And, if not so, how should I wrong a brother?

CASSIUS.
Brutus, this sober form of yours hides wrongs;
And when you do them—

BRUTUS.
Cassius, be content;
Speak your griefs softly, I do know you well.
Before the eyes of both our armies here,
Which should perceive nothing but love from us,
Let us not wrangle; bid them move away;
Then in my tent, Cassius, enlarge your griefs,
And I will give you audience.

CASSIUS.
Pindarus,
Bid our commanders lead their charges off
A little from this ground.

BRUTUS.
Lucilius, do you the like; and let no man
Come to our tent till we have done our conference.—
Lucius and Titinius, guard our door.

[Exeunt.]

Questions for Review:

1. What happens to Cinna the poet (not Cinna the conspirator)? What point might Shakespeare be making about average citizens or mobs?

2. Summarize the plans of the triumvirs.

3. How do Octavius and Antony view Lepidus? Explain Antony's statement, "He shall but bear them as the ass bears gold." What are Antony's plans for Lepidus?

4. What has happened between Brutus and Cassius?

5. Explain Brutus's man/horse comparison.

SCENE III. WITHIN THE TENT OF BRUTUS.

[Enter Brutus and Cassius.]

CASSIUS.
That you have wrong'd me doth appear in this:
You have condemn'd and noted Lucius Pella
For taking bribes here of the Sardians;
Whereas my letters, praying on his side
Because I knew the man, were slighted off.

BRUTUS.
You wrong'd yourself to write in such a case.

CASSIUS.
In such a time as this it is not meet
That every nice offense should bear his comment.

BRUTUS.
Let me tell you, Cassius, you yourself
Are much condemn'd to have an itching palm,
To sell and mart your offices for gold
To undeservers.[117]

CASSIUS.
I an itching palm!
You know that you are Brutus that speak this,
Or, by the gods, this speech were else your last.

BRUTUS.
The name of Cassius honors this corruption,
And chastisement doth therefore hide his head.

CASSIUS.
Chastisement!

BRUTUS.
Remember March, the Ides of March remember:
Did not great Julius bleed for justice' sake?
What villain touch'd his body, that did stab,
And not for justice? What! shall one of us,
That struck the foremost man of all this world
But for supporting robbers,—shall we now

---

[117] Here Brutus accuses Cassius of taking bribes.

Contaminate our fingers with base bribes
And sell the mighty space of our large honours
For so much trash as may be grasped thus?
I had rather be a dog, and bay the moon,
Than such a Roman.

CASSIUS.
Brutus, bay not me,
I'll not endure it: you forget yourself,
To hedge me in; I am a soldier, ay,
Older in practice, abler than yourself
To make conditions.

BRUTUS.
Go to; you are not, Cassius.

CASSIUS.
I am.

BRUTUS.
I say you are not.

CASSIUS.
Urge me no more, I shall forget myself;
Have mind upon your health, tempt me no farther.

BRUTUS.
Away, slight man!

CASSIUS.
Is't possible?

BRUTUS.
Hear me, for I will speak.
Must I give way and room to your rash choler?[118]
Shall I be frighted when a madman stares?

CASSIUS.
O gods, ye gods! must I endure all this?

BRUTUS.
All this? ay, more: fret till your proud heart break;
Go show your slaves how choleric you are,

---

[118] anger, bad temper

And make your bondmen tremble. Must I budge?
Must I observe you? Must I stand and crouch
Under your testy humour? By the gods,
You shall digest the venom of your spleen,
Though it do split you; for, from this day forth,
I'll use you for my mirth, yea, for my laughter,
When you are waspish.[119]

CASSIUS.
Is it come to this?

BRUTUS.
You say you are a better soldier:
Let it appear so; make your vaunting[120] true,
And it shall please me well: for mine own part,
I shall be glad to learn of abler men.

CASSIUS.
You wrong me every way, you wrong me, Brutus.
I said, an elder soldier, not a better:
Did I say "better"?

BRUTUS.
If you did, I care not.

CASSIUS.
When Caesar lived, he durst not thus have moved me.

BRUTUS.
Peace, peace! you durst[121] not so have tempted him.

CASSIUS.
I durst not?

BRUTUS.
No.

CASSIUS.
What, durst not tempt him?

BRUTUS.
For your life you durst not.

---

[119] touchy, irritable
[120] boasting
[121] dared

CASSIUS.
Do not presume too much upon my love;
I may do that I shall be sorry for.

BRUTUS.
You have done that you should be sorry for.
There is no terror, Cassius, in your threats,
For I am arm'd so strong in honesty,
That they pass by me as the idle wind
Which I respect not. I did send to you
For certain sums of gold, which you denied me;—
For I can raise no money by vile means:
By Heaven, I had rather coin my heart,
And drop my blood for drachmas, than to wring
From the hard hands of peasants their vile trash
By any indirection:—I did send
To you for gold to pay my legions,
Which you denied me: was that done like Cassius?
Should I have answer'd Caius Cassius so?
When Marcus Brutus grows so covetous
To lock such rascal counters from his friends,
Be ready, gods, with all your thunderbolts,
Dash him to pieces!

CASSIUS.
I denied you not.

BRUTUS.
You did.

CASSIUS.
I did not. He was but a fool
That brought my answer back. Brutus hath rived my heart:
A friend should bear his friend's infirmities,
But Brutus makes mine greater than they are.

BRUTUS.
I do not, till you practise them on me.

CASSIUS.
You love me not.

BRUTUS.
I do not like your faults.

CASSIUS.
A friendly eye could never see such faults.

BRUTUS.
A flatterer's would not, though they do appear
As huge as high Olympus.

CASSIUS.
Come, Antony and young Octavius, come,
Revenge yourselves alone on Cassius,
For Cassius is a-weary of the world;
Hated by one he loves; braved by his brother;
Check'd like a bondman; all his faults observed,
Set in a note-book, learn'd and conn'd by rote,[122]
To cast into my teeth. O, I could weep
My spirit from mine eyes!—There is my dagger,
And here my naked breast; within, a heart
Dearer than Plutus'[123] mine, richer than gold:
If that thou be'st a Roman, take it forth;
I, that denied thee gold, will give my heart:
Strike as thou didst at Caesar; for I know,
When thou didst hate him worst, thou lovedst him better
Than ever thou lovedst Cassius.

BRUTUS.
Sheathe your dagger:
Be angry when you will, it shall have scope;
Do what you will, dishonor shall be humour.
O Cassius, you are yoked with a lamb
That carries anger as the flint bears fire;
Who, much enforced, shows a hasty spark,
And straight is cold again.

CASSIUS.
Hath Cassius lived
To be but mirth and laughter to his Brutus,
When grief, and blood ill-temper'd, vexeth him?

---

[122] "Set in a note-book, learn'd and conn'd by rote": written down, obsessed over, and memorized
[123] Greek "god" of wealth

BRUTUS.
When I spoke that, I was ill-temper'd too.

CASSIUS.
Do you confess so much? Give me your hand.

BRUTUS.
And my heart too.

CASSIUS.
O Brutus,—

BRUTUS.
What's the matter?

CASSIUS.
—Have not you love enough to bear with me,
When that rash humor which my mother gave me
Makes me forgetful?

BRUTUS.
Yes, Cassius; and from henceforth,
When you are over-earnest with your Brutus,
He'll think your mother chides, and leave you so.

[Noise within.]

POET.
[Within.] Let me go in to see the generals:
There is some grudge between 'em; 'tis not meet
They be alone.

LUCILIUS.
[Within.] You shall not come to them.

POET.
[Within.] Nothing but death shall stay me.

[Enter Poet, followed by Lucilius, and Titinius.]

CASSIUS.
How now! What's the matter?

POET.
For shame, you generals! what do you mean?

Love, and be friends, as two such men should be;
For I have seen more years, I'm sure, than ye.

CASSIUS.
Ha, ha! How vilely doth this cynic rhyme!

BRUTUS.
Get you hence, sirrah; saucy fellow, hence!

CASSIUS.
Bear with him, Brutus; 'tis his fashion.

BRUTUS.
I'll know his humor when he knows his time:
What should the wars do with these jigging fools?—
Companion, hence!

CASSIUS.
Away, away, be gone!

[Exit Poet.]

BRUTUS.
Lucilius and Titinius, bid the commanders
Prepare to lodge their companies tonight.

CASSIUS.
And come yourselves and bring Messala with you
Immediately to us.
[Exeunt Lucilius and Titinius.]

BRUTUS.
Lucius, a bowl of wine!
[Exit Lucius.]

CASSIUS.
I did not think you could have been so angry.

BRUTUS.
O Cassius, I am sick of many griefs.

CASSIUS.
Of your philosophy you make no use,
If you give place to accidental evils.

BRUTUS.
No man bears sorrow better. Portia is dead.

CASSIUS.
Ha! Portia!

BRUTUS.
She is dead.

CASSIUS.
How 'scaped I killing, when I cross'd you so?—
O insupportable and touching loss!—
Upon what sickness?

BRUTUS.
Impatient of my absence,
And grief that young Octavius with Mark Antony
Have made themselves so strong;—for with her death
That tidings came;—with this she fell distract,
And, her attendants absent, swallow'd fire.[124]

CASSIUS.
And died so?

BRUTUS.
Even so.

CASSIUS.
O ye immortal gods!

[Re-enter Lucius, with wine and a taper.]

BRUTUS.
Speak no more of her.—Give me a bowl of wine.—
In this I bury all unkindness, Cassius.

[Drinks.]

CASSIUS.
My heart is thirsty for that noble pledge.
Fill, Lucius, till the wine o'erswell the cup;
I cannot drink too much of Brutus' love.

[Drinks.]

---

[124] swallowed hot coals

BRUTUS.
Come in, Titinius!—

[Exit Lucius.]

[Re-enter Titinius, with Messala.]

Welcome, good Messala.—
Now sit we close about this taper here,
And call in question our necessities.

CASSIUS.
Portia, art thou gone?

BRUTUS.
No more, I pray you.—
Messala, I have here received letters,
That young Octavius and Mark Antony
Come down upon us with a mighty power,
Bending their expedition toward Philippi.

MESSALA.
Myself have letters of the selfsame tenour.

BRUTUS.
With what addition?

MESSALA.
That by proscription and bills of outlawry
Octavius, Antony, and Lepidus
Have put to death an hundred Senators.

BRUTUS.
There in our letters do not well agree:
Mine speak of seventy Senators that died
By their proscriptions, Cicero being one.

CASSIUS.
Cicero one!

MESSALA.
Cicero is dead,
And by that order of proscription.—
Had you your letters from your wife, my lord?

BRUTUS.
No, Messala.

MESSALA.
Nor nothing in your letters writ of her?

BRUTUS.
Nothing, Messala.

MESSALA.
That, methinks, is strange.

BRUTUS.
Why ask you? hear you aught of her in yours?

MESSALA.
No, my lord.

BRUTUS.
Now, as you are a Roman, tell me true.

MESSALA.
Then like a Roman bear the truth I tell:
For certain she is dead, and by strange manner.

BRUTUS.
Why, farewell, Portia. We must die, Messala:
With meditating that she must die once,
I have the patience to endure it now.

MESSALA.
Even so great men great losses should endure.

CASSIUS.
I have as much of this in art as you,
But yet my nature could not bear it so.

BRUTUS.
Well, to our work alive. What do you think
Of marching to Philippi presently?

CASSIUS.
I do not think it good.

BRUTUS.
Your reason?

CASSIUS.
This it is:
'Tis better that the enemy seek us;:
So shall he waste his means, weary his soldiers,
Doing himself offense; whilst we, lying still,
Are full of rest, defense, and nimbleness.

BRUTUS.
Good reasons must, of force, give place to better.
The people 'twixt Philippi and this ground
Do stand but in a forced affection;
For they have grudged us contribution:
The enemy, marching along by them,
By them shall make a fuller number up,
Come on refresh'd, new-added, and encouraged;
From which advantage shall we cut him off,
If at Philippi we do face him there,
These people at our back.

CASSIUS.
Hear me, good brother.

BRUTUS.
Under your pardon. You must note besides,
That we have tried the utmost of our friends,
Our legions are brim-full, our cause is ripe:
The enemy increaseth every day;
We, at the height, are ready to decline.
There is a tide in the affairs of men
Which, taken at the flood, leads on to fortune;
Omitted, all the voyage of their life
Is bound in shallows and in miseries.
On such a full sea are we now afloat;
And we must take the current when it serves,
Or lose our ventures.

CASSIUS.
Then, with your will, go on:
We'll along ourselves, and meet them at Philippi.

BRUTUS.
The deep of night is crept upon our talk,
And nature must obey necessity;

Which we will niggard[125] with a little rest.
There is no more to say?

CASSIUS.
No more. Good night:
Early to-morrow will we rise, and hence.

BRUTUS.
Lucius!—My gown.—Farewell now, good Messala:—
Good night, Titinius:—noble, noble Cassius,
Good night, and good repose.

CASSIUS.
O my dear brother!
This was an ill beginning of the night.
Never come such division 'tween our souls!
Let it not, Brutus.

BRUTUS.
Every thing is well.

CASSIUS.
Good night, my lord.

BRUTUS.
Good night, good brother.

TITINIUS. MESSALA.
Good night, Lord Brutus.

BRUTUS.
Farewell, everyone.—

[Exeunt Cassius, Titinius, and Messala.]
[Re-enter Lucius, with the gown.]

Give me the gown. Where is thy instrument?

LUCIUS.
Here in the tent.

BRUTUS.
What, thou speak'st drowsily:

---

[125] delay, put off

Poor knave, I blame thee not, thou art o'erwatch'd.[126]
Call Claudius and some other of my men;
I'll have them sleep on cushions in my tent.

LUCIUS.
Varro and Claudius!
[Enter Varro and Claudius.]

VARRO.
Calls my lord?

BRUTUS.
I pray you, sirs, lie in my tent and sleep;
It may be I shall raise you by-and-by
On business to my brother Cassius.

VARRO.
So please you, we will stand and watch your pleasure.

BRUTUS.
I would not have it so; lie down, good sirs:
It may be I shall otherwise bethink me.—
Look, Lucius, here's the book I sought for so;
I put it in the pocket of my gown.

[Servants lie down.]

LUCIUS.
I was sure your lordship did not give it me.

BRUTUS.
Bear with me, good boy, I am much forgetful.
Canst thou hold up thy heavy eyes awhile,
And touch thy instrument a strain or two?

LUCIUS.
Ay, my lord, an't please you.

BRUTUS.
It does, my boy:
I trouble thee too much, but thou art willing.

LUCIUS.
It is my duty, sir.

---

[126] overworked, exhausted

BRUTUS.
I should not urge thy duty past thy might;
I know young bloods look for a time of rest.

LUCIUS.
I have slept, my lord, already.

BRUTUS.
It was well done; and thou shalt sleep again;
I will not hold thee long: if I do live,
I will be good to thee.—

[Lucius plays and sings till he falls asleep.]

This is a sleepy tune.—O murderous Slumber,
Lay'st thou thy leaden mace upon my boy,
That plays thee music?—Gentle knave, good night;
I will not do thee so much wrong to wake thee:
If thou dost nod, thou breakst thy instrument;
I'll take it from thee; and, good boy, good night.—
Let me see, let me see; is not the leaf turn'd down
Where I left reading? Here it is, I think.
[Enter the Ghost of Caesar.]

How ill this taper burns! Ha! who comes here?
I think it is the weakness of mine eyes
That shapes this monstrous apparition.
It comes upon me.—Art thou any thing?
Art thou some god, some angel, or some devil,
That makest my blood cold and my hair to stare?
Speak to me what thou art.

GHOST.
Thy evil spirit, Brutus.

BRUTUS.
Why comest thou?

GHOST.
To tell thee thou shalt see me at Philippi.

BRUTUS.
Well; then I shall see thee again?

GHOST.
Ay, at Philippi.

BRUTUS.
Why, I will see thee at Philippi, then.   *[Ghost vanishes.]*

Now I have taken heart, thou vanishest:
Ill spirit, I would hold more talk with thee.—
Boy! Lucius!—Varro! Claudius! Sirs, awake!—Claudius!

LUCIUS.
The strings, my lord, are false.

BRUTUS.
He thinks he still is at his instrument.—
Lucius, awake!

LUCIUS.
My lord?

BRUTUS.
Didst thou dream, Lucius, that thou so criedst out?

LUCIUS.
My lord, I do not know that I did cry.

BRUTUS.
Yes, that thou didst: didst thou see any thing?

LUCIUS.
Nothing, my lord.

BRUTUS.
Sleep again, Lucius.—Sirrah Claudius!—
[To Varro.] Fellow thou, awake!

VARRO.
My lord?

CLAUDIUS.
My lord?

BRUTUS.
Why did you so cry out, sirs, in your sleep?

VARRO. CLAUDIUS.
Did we, my lord?

BRUTUS.
Ay: saw you any thing?

VARRO.
No, my lord, I saw nothing.

CLAUDIUS.
Nor I, my lord.

BRUTUS.
Go and commend me to my brother Cassius;
Bid him set on his powers betimes before,
And we will follow.

VARRO. CLAUDIUS.
It shall be done, my lord.

[Exeunt.]

Questions for Review:

1. Describe the initial argument between Cassius and Brutus.

2. How do the two men differently view friendship?

3. What has Brutus suffered that makes him irritable and disturbed?

4. How do Brutus and Cassius disagree about Philippi? Explain what Brutus means by saying, "We, at the height, are ready to decline."

5. What spirit visits Brutus in his tent? Why do you think the spirit tells Brutus it is "*thy* evil spirit"?

6. Brutus and Cassius killed Julius Caesar to bring peace and liberty to Rome. What has it actually brought?

7. What is ironic about the scene showing Brutus' refusal to listen to advice? What does the inability to find his own book reinforce?

ACT V.

SCENE I. THE PLAINS OF PHILIPPI.

[Enter Octavius, Antony, and their Army.]

OCTAVIUS.
Now, Antony, our hopes are answered.
You said the enemy would not come down,
But keep the hills and upper regions:
It proves not so; their battles are at hand:
They mean to warn us at Philippi here,
Answering before we do demand of them.

ANTONY.
Tut, I am in their bosoms, and I know
Wherefore they do it: they could be content
To visit other places; and come down
With fearful bravery, thinking by this face
To fasten in our thoughts that they have courage;
But 'tis not so.

[Enter a Messenger.]

MESSENGER.
Prepare you, generals:
The enemy comes on in gallant show;
Their bloody sign of battle is hung out,
And something to be done immediately.

ANTONY.
Octavius, lead your battle softly on,
Upon the left hand of the even field.

OCTAVIUS.
Upon the right hand I; keep thou the left.

ANTONY.
Why do you cross me in this exigent?[127]

OCTAVIUS.
I do not cross you; but I will do so.

---

[127] important detail

[March. Drum. Enter Brutus, Cassius, and their Army; Lucilius, Titinius, Messala, and Others.]

BRUTUS.
They stand, and would have parley.

CASSIUS.
Stand fast, Titinius: we must out and talk.

OCTAVIUS.
Mark Antony, shall we give sign of battle?

ANTONY.
No, Caesar, we will answer on their charge.
Make forth; the generals would have some words.

OCTAVIUS.
Stir not until the signal.

BRUTUS.
Words before blows: is it so, countrymen?

OCTAVIUS.
Not that we love words better, as you do.

BRUTUS.
Good words are better than bad strokes, Octavius.

ANTONY.
In your bad strokes, Brutus, you give good words:
Witness the hole you made in Caesar's heart,
Crying, "Long live! Hail, Caesar!"

CASSIUS.
Antony,
The posture of your blows are yet unknown;
But for your words, they rob the Hybla bees,[128]
And leave them honeyless.

ANTONY.
Not stingless too.

BRUTUS.
O, yes, and soundless too,

---

[128] Hybla was an ancient town famous for its honey.

For you have stol'n their buzzing, Antony,
And very wisely threat before you sting.

ANTONY.
Villains, you did not so when your vile daggers
Hack'd one another in the sides of Caesar:
You show'd your teeth like apes, and fawn'd like hounds,
And bow'd like bondmen, kissing Caesar's feet;
Whilst Casca, like a cur, behind
Struck Caesar on the neck. O flatterers!

CASSIUS.
Flatterers!—Now, Brutus, thank yourself:
This tongue had not offended so to-day,
If Cassius might have ruled.

OCTAVIUS.
Come, come, the cause: if arguing makes us sweat,
The proof of it will turn to redder drops.
Look,—
I draw a sword against conspirators:
When think you that the sword goes up again?
Never, till Caesar's three and thirty wounds
Be well avenged; or till another Caesar
Have added slaughter to the sword of traitors.

BRUTUS.
Caesar, thou canst not die by traitors' hands,
Unless thou bring'st them with thee.

OCTAVIUS.
So I hope;
I was not born to die on Brutus' sword.

BRUTUS.
O, if thou wert the noblest of thy strain,
Young man, thou couldst not die more honourably.

CASSIUS.
A peevish school boy, worthless of such honour,
Join'd with a masker and a reveller!

ANTONY.
Old Cassius still!

OCTAVIUS.
Come, Antony; away!—
Defiance, traitors, hurl we in your teeth:
If you dare fight today, come to the field;
If not, when you have stomachs.

[Exeunt Octavius, Antony, and their Army.]

CASSIUS.
Why, now, blow wind, swell billow, and swim bark!
The storm is up, and all is on the hazard.

BRUTUS.
Ho, Lucilius! Hark, a word with you.

LUCILIUS.
My lord?

[Brutus and Lucilius talk apart.]

CASSIUS.
Messala,—

MESSALA.
What says my General?

CASSIUS.
Messala,
This is my birth-day; as this very day
Was Cassius born. Give me thy hand, Messala:
Be thou my witness that against my will,
As Pompey was, am I compell'd to set
Upon one battle all our liberties.
You know that I held Epicurus strong,
And his opinion: now I change my mind,
And partly credit things that do presage. [129]
Coming from Sardis, on our former ensign
Two mighty eagles fell; and there they perch'd,
Gorging and feeding from our soldiers' hands;
Who to Philippi here consorted us:
This morning are they fled away and gone;

---

[129] That is, Cassius formerly followed the teachings of Greek philosopher Epicurus, who rejected the idea of signs being given by the "gods" or superstition—but now he believes in omens, after seeing the two eagles on the battlefield.

And in their steads do ravens, crows, and kites
Fly o'er our heads and downward look on us,
As we were sickly prey: their shadows seem
A canopy most fatal, under which
Our army lies, ready to give up the ghost.

MESSALA.
Believe not so.

CASSIUS.
I but believe it partly;
For I am fresh of spirit, and resolved
To meet all perils very constantly.

BRUTUS.
Even so, Lucilius.

CASSIUS.
Now, most noble Brutus,
The gods to-day stand friendly, that we may,
Lovers in peace, lead on our days to age!
But, since th' affairs of men rest still incertain,
Let's reason with the worst that may befall.
If we do lose this battle, then is this
The very last time we shall speak together:
What are you then determined to do?

BRUTUS.
Even by the rule of that philosophy
By which I did blame Cato for the death
Which he did give himself;[130]—I know not how,
But I do find it cowardly and vile,
For fear of what might fall, so to prevent
The time of life;—arming myself with patience
To stay the providence of some high powers
That govern us below.

CASSIUS.
Then, if we lose this battle,
You are contented to be led in triumph
Thorough the streets of Rome?

---

[130] That is, suicide.

BRUTUS.
No, Cassius, no: think not, thou noble Roman,
That ever Brutus will go bound to Rome;
He bears too great a mind. But this same day
Must end that work the Ides of March begun;
And whether we shall meet again I know not.
Therefore our everlasting farewell take:
For ever, and for ever, farewell, Cassius!
If we do meet again, why, we shall smile;
If not, why, then this parting was well made.

CASSIUS.
For ever and for ever farewell, Brutus!
If we do meet again, we'll smile indeed;
If not, 'tis true this parting was well made.

BRUTUS.
Why then, lead on. O, that a man might know
The end of this day's business ere it come!
But it sufficeth that the day will end,
And then the end is known.—Come, ho! away!   *[Exeunt.]*

SCENE II. THE SAME.
THE FIELD OF BATTLE.

[Alarum. Enter Brutus and Messala.]

BRUTUS.
Ride, ride, Messala, ride, and give these bills[131]
Unto the legions on the other side:
Let them set on at once; for I perceive
But cold demeanor in Octavius' wing,
And sudden push gives them the overthrow.
Ride, ride, Messala: let them all come down.

[Exeunt.]

Questions for Review:

1. How do Octavius and Antony view the advancing army of Brutus and
    Cassius? What hints of Octavius's character do we see?

---

[131] dispatches (military instructions)

2. Interpret Antony's words: "In your bad strokes, Brutus, you give good words…"

3. Describe Brutus's view of suicide. What message does he give Messala?

SCENE III. ANOTHER PART OF THE FIELD.

[Alarum. Enter Cassius and Titinius.]

CASSIUS.
O, look, Titinius, look, the villains fly!
Myself have to mine own turn'd enemy:
This ensign here of mine was turning back;
I slew the coward, and did take it from him.

TITINIUS.
O Cassius, Brutus gave the word too early;
Who, having some advantage on Octavius,
Took it too eagerly: his soldiers fell to spoil,
Whilst we by Antony are all enclosed.
[Enter Pindarus.]

PINDARUS.
Fly further off, my lord, fly further off;
Mark Antony is in your tents, my lord:
Fly, therefore, noble Cassius, fly far off.

CASSIUS.
This hill is far enough.—Look, look, Titinius;
Are those my tents where I perceive the fire?

TITINIUS.
They are, my lord.

CASSIUS.
Titinius, if thou lovest me,
Mount thou my horse and hide thy spurs in him,
Till he have brought thee up to yonder troops
And here again; that I may rest assured
Whether yond troops are friend or enemy.

TITINIUS.
I will be here again, even with a thought.

[Exit.]

CASSIUS.
Go, Pindarus, get higher on that hill:
My sight was ever thick: regard Titinius,
And tell me what thou notest about the field.—

[Pindarus goes up.]

This day I breathed first: time is come round,
And where I did begin, there shall I end;
My life is run his compass.—Sirrah, what news?

PINDARUS.
[Above.] O my lord!

CASSIUS.
What news?

PINDARUS.
[Above.] Titinius is enclosed round about
With horsemen, that make to him on the spur:
Yet he spurs on. Now they are almost on him.—
Now, Titinius!—Now some light. O, he lights too:
He's ta'en; *[Shout.]* and, hark! they shout for joy.

CASSIUS.
Come down; behold no more.—
O, coward that I am, to live so long,
To see my best friend ta'en before my face!

[Pindarus descends.]

Come hither, sirrah:
In Parthia did I take thee prisoner;
And then I swore thee, saving of thy life,
That whatsoever I did bid thee do,
Thou shouldst attempt it. Come now, keep thine oath;
Now be a freeman; and with this good sword,
That ran through Caesar's bowels, search this bosom.
Stand not to answer: here, take thou the hilts;
And when my face is cover'd, as 'tis now,
Guide thou the sword.—Caesar, thou art revenged,
Even with the sword that kill'd thee.

Classic Literature for Christian Homeschoolers

[Dies.]

PINDARUS.
So, I am free, yet would not so have been,
Durst I have done my will.—O Cassius!
Far from this country Pindarus shall run,
Where never Roman shall take note of him.

[Exit.]

[Re-enter Titinius with Messala.]

MESSALA.
It is but change, Titinius; for Octavius
Is overthrown by noble Brutus' power,
As Cassius' legions are by Antony.

TITINIUS.
These tidings would well comfort Cassius.

MESSALA.
Where did you leave him?

TITINIUS.
All disconsolate,
With Pindarus his bondman, on this hill.

MESSALA.
Is not that he that lies upon the ground?

TITINIUS.
He lies not like the living. O my heart!

MESSALA.
Is not that he?

TITINIUS.
No, this was he, Messala,
But Cassius is no more.—O setting Sun,
As in thy red rays thou dost sink to night,
So in his red blood Cassius' day is set,
The sun of Rome is set! Our day is gone;
Clouds, dews, and dangers come; our deeds are done!
Mistrust of my success hath done this deed.

MESSALA.
Mistrust of good success hath done this deed.
O hateful Error, Melancholy's child!
Why dost thou show to the apt thoughts of men
The things that are not? O Error, soon conceived,
Thou never comest unto a happy birth,
But kill'st the mother that engender'd thee!

TITINIUS.
What, Pindarus! where art thou, Pindarus?

MESSALA.
Seek him, Titinius, whilst I go to meet
The noble Brutus, thrusting this report
Into his ears: I may say, thrusting it;
For piercing steel and darts envenomed
Shall be as welcome to the ears of Brutus
As tidings of this sight.

TITINIUS.
Hie you, Messala,
And I will seek for Pindarus the while.—
[Exit Messala.]

Why didst thou send me forth, brave Cassius?
Did I not meet thy friends? And did not they
Put on my brows this wreath of victory,
And bid me give it thee? Didst thou not hear their shouts?
Alas, thou hast misconstrued every thing!
But, hold thee, take this garland on thy brow;
Thy Brutus bid me give it thee, and I
Will do his bidding.—Brutus, come apace,
And see how I regarded Caius Cassius.—
By your leave, gods: this is a Roman's part:
Come, Cassius' sword, and find Titinius' heart.

[Dies.]

[Alarum. Re-enter Messala, with Brutus, young Cato, Strato, Volumnius, and Lucilius.]

BRUTUS.
Where, where, Messala, doth his body lie?

MESSALA.
Lo, yonder, and Titinius mourning it.

BRUTUS.
Titinius' face is upward.

CATO.
He is slain.

BRUTUS.
O Julius Caesar, thou art mighty yet!
Thy spirit walks abroad, and turns our swords
In our own proper entrails.

[Low alarums.]

CATO.
Brave Titinius!
Look whether he have not crown'd dead Cassius!

BRUTUS.
Are yet two Romans living such as these?—
The last of all the Romans, fare thee well!
It is impossible that ever Rome
Should breed thy fellow.—Friends, I owe more tears
To this dead man than you shall see me pay.—
I shall find time, Cassius, I shall find time.—
Come therefore, and to Thassos send his body:
His funerals shall not be in our camp,
Lest it discomfort us.—Lucilius, come;—
And come, young Cato;—let us to the field.—
Labeo and Flavius, set our battles on:—
'Tis three o'clock; and Romans, yet ere night
We shall try fortune in a second fight.

[Exeunt.]

SCENE IV. ANOTHER PART OF THE FIELD.

[Alarum. Enter, fighting, Soldiers of both armies; then Brutus, young Cato, Lucilius, and Others.]

BRUTUS.
Yet, countrymen, O, yet hold up your heads!

CATO.
What [scoundrel] doth not? Who will go with me?
I will proclaim my name about the field:—
I am the son of Marcus Cato, ho!
A foe to tyrants, and my country's friend;
I am the son of Marcus Cato, ho!

[Charges the enemy.]

BRUTUS.
And I am Brutus, Marcus Brutus, I;
Brutus, my country's friend; know me for Brutus!

[Exit, charging the enemy. Cato is overpowered, and falls.]

LUCILIUS.
O young and noble Cato, art thou down?
Why, now thou diest as bravely as Titinius;
And mayst be honour'd, being Cato's son.

FIRST SOLDIER.
Yield, or thou diest.

LUCILIUS.
Only I yield to die:
There is so much that thou wilt kill me straight;

[Offering money.]

Kill Brutus, and be honour'd in his death.[132]

FIRST SOLDIER.
We must not. A noble prisoner!

SECOND SOLDIER.
Room, ho! Tell Antony, Brutus is ta'en.

FIRST SOLDIER.
I'll tell the news. Here comes the General.—

[Enter Antony.]

Brutus is ta'en, Brutus is ta'en, my lord.

---

[132] Here Lucilius pretends he's Brutus, and he offers the soldier money to kill him right then (and be "honoured in his death"), in an attempt to give the real Brutus more time to escape.

ANTONY.
Where is he?

LUCILIUS.
Safe, Antony; Brutus is safe enough:
I dare assure thee that no enemy
Shall ever take alive the noble Brutus:
The gods defend him from so great a shame!
When you do find him, or alive or dead,
He will be found like Brutus, like himself.

ANTONY.
This is not Brutus, friend; but, I assure you,
A prize no less in worth. Keep this man safe,
Give him all kindness; I had rather have
Such men my friends than enemies. Go on,
And see whether Brutus be alive or dead;
And bring us word unto Octavius' tent
How everything is chanced.

[Exeunt.]

SCENE V. ANOTHER PART OF THE FIELD.

[Enter Brutus, Dardanius, Clitus, Strato, and Volumnius.]

BRUTUS.
Come, poor remains of friends, rest on this rock.

CLITUS.
Statilius show'd the torch-light; but, my lord,
He came not back: he is or ta'en or slain.

BRUTUS.
Sit thee down, Clitus: slaying is the word;
It is a deed in fashion. Hark thee, Clitus.

[Whispering.]

CLITUS.
What, I, my lord? No, not for all the world.

BRUTUS.
Peace then! no words.

CLITUS.
I'll rather kill myself.

BRUTUS.
Hark thee, Dardanius.

[Whispers him.]

DARDANIUS.
Shall I do such a deed?

CLITUS.
O Dardanius!

DARDANIUS.
O Clitus!

CLITUS.
What ill request did Brutus make to thee?

DARDANIUS.
To kill him, Clitus. Look, he meditates.

CLITUS.
Now is that noble vessel full of grief,
That it runs over even at his eyes.

BRUTUS.
Come hither, good Volumnius; list a word.

VOLUMNIUS.
What says my lord?

BRUTUS.
Why, this, Volumnius:
The ghost of Caesar hath appear'd to me
Two several times by night; at Sardis once,
And this last night here in Philippi fields:
I know my hour is come.

VOLUMNIUS.
Not so, my lord.

BRUTUS.
Nay I am sure it is, Volumnius.

Thou seest the world, Volumnius, how it goes;
Our enemies have beat us to the pit:

[Low alarums.]

It is more worthy to leap in ourselves
Than tarry till they push us. Good Volumnius,
Thou know'st that we two went to school together;
Even for that our love of old, I pr'ythee,
Hold thou my sword-hilts, whilst I run on it.

VOLUMNIUS.
That's not an office for a friend, my lord.

[Alarums still.]

CLITUS.
Fly, fly, my lord! there is no tarrying here.

BRUTUS.
Farewell to you;—and you;—and you, Volumnius.—
Strato, thou hast been all this while asleep;
Farewell to thee too, Strato.—Countrymen,
My heart doth joy, that yet in all my life
I found no man but he was true to me.
I shall have glory by this losing day,
More than Octavius and Mark Antony
By this vile conquest shall attain unto.
So, fare you well at once; for Brutus' tongue
Hath almost ended his life's history:
Night hangs upon mine eyes; my bones would rest
That have but labour'd to attain this hour.

[Alarums. Cry within, "Fly, fly, fly!"]

CLITUS.
Fly, my lord, fly!

BRUTUS.
Hence! I will follow.—

[Exeunt Clitus, Dardanius, and Volumnius.]

I pr'ythee, Strato, stay thou by thy lord:
Thou art a fellow of a good respect;

Thy life hath had some smatch[133] of honor in it:
Hold, then, my sword, and turn away thy face,
While I do run upon it. Wilt thou, Strato?

STRATO.
Give me your hand first: fare you well, my lord.

BRUTUS.
Farewell, good Strato.—Caesar, now be still:
I kill'd not thee with half so good a will.

[He runs on his sword, and dies.]
[Alarum. Retreat. Enter Octavius, Antony, Messala, Lucilius, and Army.]

OCTAVIUS.
What man is that?

MESSALA.
My master's man.—Strato, where is thy master?

STRATO.
Free from the bondage you are in, Messala:
The conquerors can but make a fire of him;
For Brutus only overcame himself,
And no man else hath honour by his death.

LUCILIUS.
So Brutus should be found.—I thank thee, Brutus,
That thou hast proved Lucilius' saying true.

OCTAVIUS.
All that served Brutus, I will entertain them.—
Fellow, wilt thou bestow thy time with me?

STRATO.
Ay, if Messala will prefer me to you.

OCTAVIUS.
Do so, good Messala.

MESSALA.
How died my master, Strato?

---

[133] trace

STRATO.
I held the sword, and he did run on it.

MESSALA.
Octavius, then take him to follow thee,
That did the latest service to my master.

ANTONY.
This was the noblest Roman of them all:
All the conspirators, save only he,
Did that they did in envy of great Caesar;
He only, in a general-honest thought
And common good to all, made one of them.
His life was gentle; and the elements
So mix'd in him that Nature might stand up
And say to all the world, "This was a man!"

OCTAVIUS.
According to his virtue let us use him
With all respect and rites of burial.
Within my tent his bones to-night shall lie,
Most like a soldier, order'd honorably.—
So, call the field to rest; and let's away,
To part the glories of this happy day.

[Exeunt.]

THE END.

Questions for Review:

1. What happens to Cassius's army? What does he ask of Pindarus? What ironic news does Messala bring after this?

2. On what does Messala blame Cassius' death? What does Titinius mean by saying, "Alas, thou hast misconstrued every thing!"?

3. Why does Lucilius offer money to the soldiers? What does he "assure" Antony when he comes upon the scene?

4. What does Brutus ask of Clitus and Dardanius? Why?

5. Explain Brutus' words:: "Caesar, now be still: I kill'd not thee with half so good a will." What does Antony think of Brutus?

For Additional Thought:

1.   Brutus hoped that by killing Julius Caesar he would help to eliminate tyranny and provide peace and freedom for Rome. Why didn't this happen?

2.   What does *Julius Caesar* say about violence as a way of achieving peace and freedom? How does the Christian view violence against his fellow man or against rulers? (See 1 Samuel 24, Jonah 3, Luke 3:10-14, Proverbs 16:29, Romans 13, and 1 Timothy 2.)

3.   Explain how, in contrast with Julius Caesar, the death of one man was able to bring freedom, victory, and peace to the world. (See Romans 5:19, Romans 6:4, Romans 8:1-2, Hebrews 2:9, and Romans 5:1.)

Did you enjoy this book?

If so, I would be extremely grateful if you'd leave a brief review on Amazon.com!

It's fast and easy to leave a review! Here's how:

- Search for "Classic Literature for Christian Homeschoolers" at Amazon.com, and
- Hit "Ctrl+F" (for "Find") and type "Write a customer review."

Thank you so much!
Scott Clifton

P. S. – Don't forget to keep reading for your free offer!

Homeschool Humor

Do you like to laugh? (For example, "Ha, ha!")

Would you like to feel much better about your family's weird homeschooling experiences, since the ones in these books are even loonier?

Are you interested in soft, luxurious, and more manageable hair?

If you happened to answer "Yes" to any of those questions, *Homeschool Humor* books can help! (Except for the one about the soft, luxurious hair; maybe you should try egg whites or something.)

The two volumes of *Homeschool Humor* are packed with hilarious stories of the pitfalls and wackiness occurring in a somewhat-normal homeschool family, including chapters like...

- Let's Go Camping! Some Other Time!

- Naming Your Homeschooled Child

- Helping Your Children Build Strong Character by Smashing People Right in the Face

- Science and Other Mythical Creatures

- A Brief History of Homeschooling That Briefly Shows Homeschooling Throughout History, in a Brief Way That Is Also Historical

Also included: juicy lists of how to answer those complete strangers who ask, "Are those all your children?" or "What are those kids doing out of school?"

Homeschool Humor books are available here:

www.homeschoolpartners.net/books

7th—12th Grade Literature for Christian Homeschoolers:

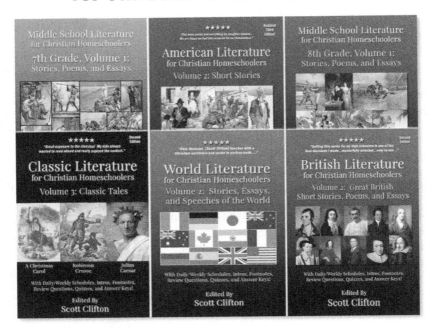

Here's what you get with the above sets of literature books for Christian middle school and high school homeschoolers:

- **Great Reads!** Many wonderful essays, short stories, speeches, poems, letters, and novels—in conveniently arranged sets for seventh grade, eighth grade, and four years of high school.

- **A 30-Week, Four-Days-Per-Week Reading Schedule.** No more asking, "What should we read this week?"

- **Introductions, Footnotes, Questions for Review.** These place writings into historical context, help students understand archaic terms, clear up potentially hazy passages, and help the student think about important ideas.

- **A Christian Worldview.** This worldview is reflected in the introductions, footnotes, and review questions.

- **Free Answer Keys to Tests and Review Questions.** Parents, you can discuss the review questions and administer tests—fully armed with answer keys!

www.homeschoolpartners.net/books

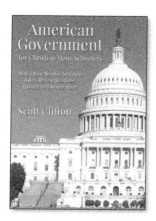

American Government for Christian Homeschoolers

• A helpful, 32-week, four-day reading schedule

• A good overview of American Government, in clear, short sections

• A Christian view of government and government types, the Constitution and how to interpret it, political parties, taxes, and more

• Review questions for each day's reading

• 10 tests (nine regular, one final)

• Free test and review question answer keys

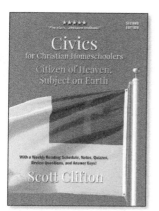

Civics for Christian Homeschoolers

• A helpful, 16-week, four-day reading schedule

• A good overview of Civics, in clear, short sections

• A Christian view of citizenship, types of law, types of government, the Declaration of Independence, a Christian's rights and responsibilities, juries, voting, and more

• Review questions for each day's reading

• Five tests (four regular, one final)

• Free test and review question answer keys

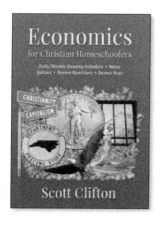

Economics for Christian Homeschoolers

• A helpful, 15-week, four-day reading schedule

• Clear, short sections

• A Christian view of economics, with a pro-free market viewpoint

• Explanations of the dangers of socialism, inflation, bureaucracies, taxes and business regulations, and other government meddling

• Review questions for each day's reading

• Five tests (four regular, one final)

• Free test and review question answer keys

www.homeschoolpartners.net/books

About Scott Clifton

North Carolina is where Scott Clifton makes his home, with his wife Julie and their children. Scott is a fervent homeschooling advocate, and just *seconds* after his first child was born, as he took his little baby boy and held him close to his chest, he looked down and immediately knew—right then in his heart—that he would never be able to wear that particular shirt again. (Also, that he and Julie would homeschool their children, which they have done since 1994.)

Scott earned his B.A. in Journalism from the University of Central Florida. He began his career writing and editing for a family newspaper and a state banking association. In 2002, the Lord led Scott into the field of home school education, and that year he began teaching once-a-week high school classes full time as the owner and operator of Home School Partners.

www.homeschoolpartners.net

Made in the USA
Monee, IL
24 June 2023

37185452R00243